In praise of Diane Duane's works

<u>On *Deep Wizardry*</u>

"Diane Duane is a skilled master of the genre."
—*The Philadelphia Enquirer*

". . . the author has remarkable and original imaginative powers."
—*Horn Book*

"Duane's ocean setting and her non-human characters are captivating, her human characters believable and likeable."
—*Science Fiction Chronicle*

<u>On *High Wizardry*</u>

"Duane is tops in the high adventure business . . ."
—*Publishers Weekly*

"Duane writes about people you can really care about, with lots of quirks and endearing traits that feel real in a way that most people don't manage."

—Tom Whitmore, *Locus*

D0249905

THE HARBINGER TRILOGY
DIANE DUANE

Volume One:
STARRISE AT CORRIVALE

Volume Two:
STORM AT ELDALA

Volume Three:
NIGHTFALL AT ALGEMRON
(2000)

STORM AT ELDALA

Volume Two of the HARBINGER TRILOGY

Diane Duane

For T.R. and Lee
. . . because Marines do more than drink coffee

STORM AT ELDALA

©1999 TSR, Inc.

All Rights Reserved.

Cover Art by rk post
First Printing: March 1999
Library of Congress Catalog Card Number: 98-85787
9 8 7 6 5 4 3 2 1
ISBN: 0-7869-1334-7
21334XXX1501

U.S., CANADA, ASIA,
PACIFIC, & LATIN AMERICA
Wizards of the Coast, Inc.
P.O. Box 707
Renton, WA 98057-0707
+1-800-324-6496

EUROPEAN HEADQUARTERS
Wizards of the Coast, Belgium
P.B. 2031
2600 Berchem
Belgium
Tel. +32.70233277

Visit our web-site at **www.tsr.com**

When Heaven is about to confer great office upon a man,
it first exercises his mind with suffering, and his sinews and
    bones with toil:
it exposes him to poverty and confounds all his undertakings.
Then it is seen if he is ready . . .

Meng-Tse, Sol, 6 B.C.

Chapter One

STRUGGLING INSIDE *Sunshine*'s fighting field, Gabriel Connor flung himself and their small ship through space while the plasma bolts of their pursuers arrowed past on either side of him, so close he could have sworn he could feel the heat straight through the hull. He stared frantically around him into the darkness, but there was nowhere to go. They were surrounded.

This time, for sure, this time we're going to die.

We cannot keep this up much longer, Enda's seemingly disembodied voice came to him from somewhere on the other side of the field. She was handling gunnery, having a talent for it, but the gift seemed not to be serving her well today.

There are too many of them left, she said, *and we are running low on power.*

Gabriel glanced at the power readouts inside the gunnery field. They were down to ten percent on both sets of weapons. His big gun, the rail cannon on top of *Sunshine*, was recharging, but not quickly enough. It wanted another thirty seconds, and whether it was going to get them was uncertain.

Gabriel tumbled the ship to make sure of the field of fire. One of the little ball bearing ships that had chased them out into the depths of the Corrivale system came plunging through his sights. He took aim with the plasma cannon and fired.

Clear miss.

He cursed, the sweat running down his back and tickling, but there was nothing he could do about it.

Slow down, Enda cried, *make them count!*

He saw her take aim and fire at another of the ships as it

plunged past them. She scored a hit, but not a killing one. The ship arced away, leaking atmosphere in a ghostly silvery veil, but its engines were untouched.

How many now?

The targeting software says sixteen, Enda said.

Gabriel cursed again and tumbled the ship once more, wishing that he did not have to handle piloting as well as firing. The attack unfolding around them was a standard englobement with ten small vessels at the vertices and six stitching in and out of the defined space. The enemy craft held *Sunshine* at the optimum locus of the englobement.

There were tactics for this kind of engagement, and Gabriel had tried all three kinds. He had used the "place holder," where you shoot from optimum locus because it's the best position. That had worked only as long as the gunnery power was at optimum power. He had then tried the pattern-breaker approach in which you killed enough of the englobers to make the number of ships at the vertices ineffective. Unfortunately, *Sunshine*'s weapons had begun to run low just as this approach began to work.

There were still sixteen of them and no realistic hope of reducing the numbers to the critical eight or below. There was nothing left but the rush-and-break, the set of moves enacted simply to escape. This Gabriel hated, first because he suspected these little ships could outrun them; second because he suspected they would chase *Sunshine* straight into the welcoming field of fire of the big ship that had dropped them out here in the distant dark of Corrivale's fringes.

Also, he hated to run. Marines didn't run. They fought.

But you're not a marine any more.

Surprising, still, the access of fury that simple statement could provide him. He was not one of those people in whom rage clouded the vision. For Gabriel, things became clear—entirely too clear.

Three of the ships holding the vertices closest to Gabriel moved closer together to stop the break, but he could see that one of them was slightly out of alignment. He twisted *Sunshine* off to the left, and the enemy ship followed.

Mistake, Gabriel thought, as he flipped without warning, coasting backward on his inertia and letting the nearest ship have it with the forward plasma cannon. Enda, warned by who-knew-what touch of fraal precognition, was already firing that way. She hit another of the little round ships as Gabriel hit a third. From all the targets, metal cracked and splintered outward; vapor spit out under pressure and sprayed away as snow. More sluggish materials slopped out, went rigid and tumbled away in frozen lumps and gobbets with the shattered remains of the vessels that had emitted them. It was Gabriel's first close look at the destruction of one of these ships, and it confirmed what he had thought earlier.

Undead. The pilots had been people once. Humans, fraal, sesheyans, weren . . . The important thing was that they weren't those people any more. This killing was a kindness.

Gabriel!

He barely reacted in time as the set-of-three came diving at them. The englobement had been reduced to thirteen and was less viable than it had been, but it was still all too effective. The ten vessels holding aloof were defining the interior again, this time on the vertices of paired pyramids.

There were more places for *Sunshine* to break out; the faces of the solid were wider now. Gabriel spun *Sunshine* on her longitudinal axis, raking all around with the plasma cannon. The set-of-three dived away but still in unison.

Got to break that up, Gabriel thought and glanced hurriedly at the indicator for the rail cannon. It was only up to sixty percent. It wouldn't even fire until eighty.

Enda was firing. Gabriel fired too, his plasma cannons down to twenty percent now. Bolts from their adversaries shot right past him, blinding and scorching him. Gabriel preferred to work with the ship's sensors acting like his own nerves—there were times when the effect could mean the difference between being alive and dead. We'll see if it's enough this time, he thought. Maybe, just maybe—

The rail cannon was up to sixty-five. Just a few minutes, he thought. Come on, *Sunshine*, just a few minutes more—

It all happened at once. The three ships broke formation, two to the right and above, one below and to the left. Enda concentrated on the two. Gabriel fired at the one but missed. He felt the scorch raking up *Sunshine*'s underbelly, and then he felt another bolt hit. He yelped, the ship lurched upwards, possibly saving them both from being killed right then, but another bolt lanced down from above, hitting the rail cannon.

It blew. Gone, the rails twisted all askew; it wouldn't fire anything now.

The englobement dissolved as the other little vessels registered the destruction of the one weapon that had been keeping them at a distance all this while. It was gone now; they could swarm in and take *Sunshine* at their pleasure.

Enda was firing nonstop. Gabriel was firing at anything he could see, and the fury was helping again. Along with the utter terror, he was burning with the knowledge that they were both about to be killed. It was amazing how life became not less intense at such a time, but more so, a fury of life, ready to burn itself out but not give up.

One hit, then another, blowing up so close to *Sunshine* that the entire ship shook, but it was not going to be enough. More plasma bolts came stitching in from behind, and Gabriel cried out in agony and rage as one of them hit the engine compartment.

Then came an intolerable glory of light off to one side, a burning pain all up and down Gabriel's side, as if someone had thrown burning fuel on him. He rolled *Sunshine* away from the pain. He had just enough power left in his emergency jets to do that. The first light had just been the "pilot" detonation. Now came the secondary one, and Gabriel squeezed his eyes closed tight.

The little ships were fleeing in all directions, but six of them were caught together as the squeezed nuke went off. The remainder knew they had no chance against *Sunshine* even damaged as she was. They kept running.

Space grew still and dark, and in it *Sunshine* drifted, tumbling gently and losing power. Gabriel sat there gasping in the darkness of the fighting field as the power ebbed away, the weapons losing what little charge they had left.

"Okay," said a gravelly voice from out in the darkness. "That went pretty well, I thought."

"Helm," Enda said sternly. "You were *not* supposed to do that."

"Aw, Enda, you're too rough on the two of you."

Gabriel knew what the words meant, but he found them hard to believe at the moment. It's the software, he told himself. But his brain insisted that he couldn't let down his guard, that something terrible might still happen. Those little ships were only fighters. They could not have come all this way by themselves. Somewhere around here was the fortress ship or dreadnought that would have dropped them. It could not be allowed to find Gabriel and Enda, not alive—not even dead and in one piece. The pilots of those little ships were reminders enough that there were some fates worse than death.

"All the same, we cannot be constantly relying on overarmed allies to come sweeping in out of the darkness to save us!"

"I thought that was what you kept me around for."

Even through the fear, Gabriel had to grin. "He's incorrigible," Gabriel said, still gasping for air. "You should know that by now."

"Maybe I should," Enda said with a sigh. "Meanwhile, let it go now, Gabriel. This has been enough exercise for one day. Shut it down."

Gabriel reached out in the fighting field to the glowing collection of virtual lights, indicators, and slider controls that appeared within his reach. One slider well off to his right was pushed right up to the top of its course. He reached out and pulled it down.

Reality ebbed out of everything. The blackness of space melted away to the virtual gridlines of the system's training mode . . . and it was all a dream. Gabriel's muscles unknotted themselves for the first time in about five minutes.

"Better?" Enda said.

"Much."

"Then come out of it, now. I do not see why you feel you must drive yourself so hard, just for an exercise."

"It's a human thing," he said, taking another breath for the appreciation of it not being his last. "You wouldn't understand."

He could sense Enda putting her eyebrows up. A couple of moments later Gabriel was alone in the field. He took his time about getting out, shutting down instruments, making gunnery safe, and checking the pieces that purported to have been made safe. It was not that he didn't trust Enda, but partners checked one another's work when weapons were involved. Besides, said that nasty hard-edged part of his mind, someday you might have to do all this yourself. Get used to the possibility now so that when it catches you by surprise, you will survive. She would want it that way.

He finished his checks, then made the small movement of mind that folded the fighting field away from him. A moment later he was sitting in the normal lighting of *Sunshine*'s narrow cockpit looking over at Enda.

"Helm," she said as she unbuckled her restraints, "do not change the subject."

"I got tired of fighting for their side," Helm said. "Besides, you were winning."

"You should have let the business take its course regardless," Enda said. "That is the purpose of these exercises, so I am told." She glanced over at Gabriel, who was wiping the sweat off his face.

"How did we do?" he said to the air.

"Twenty-six minutes," said Helm. "You should be pleased with yourself. It's precious few engagements that run much longer than fifteen these days, especially with numbers like that. You're getting a better tactical sense, that's certain."

"He is also running himself ragged," said Enda, watching Gabriel mop himself up with the cleaning cloth that he had started to keep by his seat for these exercises. "Are you all right?"

"I was nearly dead, I thought," Gabriel said, still finding it hard to talk without gasping for air. "*Boy,* is that real. It's worth it, even if I do hate it more than anything."

"Well, you were the one to discover how effective it is," Enda said, levering herself out of the left-hand seat and standing up to take a good long stretch. "It is not my fault if the 'deep limbic' implementation of the fighting software deprives you of any sense that this is a simulation. If you have a problem with that, take it up with the programmers at Insight."

"They'd probably just say that there's no difference between a simulation and the real thing if the simulation's real enough," said Helm. "Like to see some of them out here testing the software under conditions like this."

Gabriel made a face.

"It might be amusing," Enda said to Helm. "Anyway, I do not see that it makes the experience of fighting any less useful for Gabriel if, during the fight, he *feels* as if is real. Surely that should sharpen one's reactions. The more frequently that particular reaction is sharpened—the terror and coping with it—the easier it should get for you, or so it seems, from what I know of human habituation training. Am I wrong?"

"Not in the concrete sense," Gabriel muttered. "I just don't like to have to do the laundry after every session."

"You do the laundry after every session anyway," Enda said, wandering out of the pilot's cabin and back toward the little living area, "whether we work out in limbic mode or not. Sweat, you keep telling me, is something no marine can ever put up with."

"The problem's not the sweat," Gabriel said, more or less under his breath. Then he laughed and pried himself out of his seat.

Even though he had been using the fighting field every day for six months now, it still sometimes came as a shock to Gabriel how cramped the cockpit felt by comparison when he came out. The beauty of the Insight "JustWadeIn" weapons management system was to make you feel as if you *were* the ship—moving freely in space with your weapons available to you in the form you liked best.

At any rate, Gabriel was becoming more expert with *Sunshine*'s gunnery software all the time. He thought he would probably never master the cool grace-in-fire that Enda displayed. It constantly bemused him how someone so peaceful and serene could be so very good at gunnery.

"Guns are the soul of rationality," Enda had said to him late one night. "They have a certainty of purpose, and they fulfill it— when they don't jam—and like any other fine weapon, they pass on some of that certainty to their users, if the user is wise enough to hear what the gun has to say to him."

To hear this coming from a delicate ethereal-looking fraal who might mass forty-five kilos if she put on all the clothes she owned, turned Gabriel's brain right around in his head. What guns mostly said to him was, *Shoot me, shoot me! Yes, oh yes!*— with various appropriate sound effects. Nonetheless, Enda's communion with her gunnery was something to be envied, and Gabriel occasionally listened to see if the guns had anything further to say to him on the subject.

He walked down into the living area and found Enda already ensconced in one of the two fold-down chairs in the sitting room, talking to Helm again over comms and looking as fresh as if she had not been in battle for the better part of half an hour.

"How do you do it?" he asked her.

She looked at him with amusement. "I pull the chair down, like this—"

"Never mind," Gabriel said. "When did he say he was coming?"

"Twenty minutes. We can finish debriefing as soon as you're done playing with the new hardware."

"Good," Gabriel said, grinning, and walked on down to the little laundry room to get rid of his present shipsuit, which smelled as if it had seen better days.

Gabriel shoved his clothes down the chute, clamped the hatch closed and hit "Cycle." Straightening, he looked at the newly installed shower cubicle and dallied with the idea of a real water shower. *Might as well do it while we're close to someplace where water's cheap.* If it ever *really* was, when you were part owner in a spacecraft, when mass cost money to lift, and noncompressible mass twice as much.

Finally, he opted for a steam-and-scrape cycle, with ten seconds of water at the end. Gabriel punched the options in, let the machine get itself ready. To save time, he stood over the sink, wet his head, and took a squirt of shampoo out of the in-bulkhead dispenser.

Getting grayer, Gabriel thought, scrubbing for a few moments in front of the mirror. And why not? The last six months would probably be enough to gray anybody out a little bit. Still, his father hadn't gone gray this fast, and he couldn't remember his mother ever saying anything about early gray running in her family. Gabriel had never thought about this before, but now that he was interested, there was no way to ask—or maybe no one to ask. He hadn't heard from his father since before . . .

The shower chimed, letting him know it was ready for him. Gabriel got in, closed the door tight, and hit the control for the steam.

After a few minutes, through the ship's structure Gabriel could feel the very faint bump and rock, which meant someone was at the airlock. He's early, Gabriel thought, turning to catch the steam. Probably wants to chat with Enda without me in the way.

The steam stopped. Gabriel lathered up in a hurry from the scrub dispenser set in the wall and peered through the steamy glass at the mirror where he could see nothing. He knew what would be visible there. He was looking more lined than he ought to at twenty-six. The stress. We've been through a lot in the last half-year. When things even out, when we find work we like better, when the money settles down to a steadier income . . .

When I find out who framed me.

That was the underlying problem, the one not likely to be solved any time soon. That was what they were probably already settling in to discuss out in the sitting room, Enda over a tumbler of kalwine, and Helm over something stronger.

Gabriel shook his head, scattering water and lather. The water spat down from the shower head above, and he started counting so as not to be caught with soap all over him when it ran out. Every drop would be recycled, of course. It had not been like this on his old ship, which had water to spare. Whole bathtubs full of it, Gabriel thought. Hot. You could splash it around. There had been times over the past six months when, while hunted from one world to the next, shot at, driven into hiding, kidnapped and attacked with knives and guns and God knew what else, the thing that had *really* bothered Gabriel was that he couldn't have a real bath.

The shower warning chimed. Gabriel scrubbed frantically, turning to rinse himself. *Bang*! The water valve slammed itself shut, unforgiving. Gabriel stood there, steaming and wistful, trying to see over his shoulder whether he had gotten the last of the soap off his back.

He got out, pulled a towel out of the dispenser, dried himself, and put the towel down the chute as well. In the delivery-side hatch was his other shipsuit, rigorously clean and a little too stiff for his tastes. Gabriel shook it out, slipped into it, stroked the seam closed, and did a couple of deep knee-flexes to let the fabric remember where he bent. He paused before the mirror to make sure the nap of his hair was lying in the right direction before walking out.

The place smelled of hot food—something Helm had brought over from *Longshot* with him.

"I swear," Gabriel said as he came up the hall, pausing by one of the storage cabinets to get out a tumbler, "I don't know where you get that stuff from. It's not like you don't shop in the same places we do. Why does your food always smell so terrific?"

"It doesn't dare do otherwise," said the rough gravelly voice in the sitting room. There was Helm Ragnarsson, sitting immense in the foldout guest chair, which had extended itself valiantly to its full extent in both dimensions but was sagging under Helm's massive and muscular bulk, originally engineered for heavy-planet and high-pressure work. "Here you are finally," Helm said. "Still wet behind the ears."

"Yeah, thanks loads," Gabriel said. "I'm going to have to fix that thing again, you know that? We should make you bring your own chair." He turned to Enda, picked up the kalwine bottle sitting by the steaming covered casserole on the table, which was now folded down between the chairs. "Refill?"

"Yes, thank you, Gabriel," she said, and held out her glass.

Gabriel poured for them both, then lifted the lid of the casserole. "What is this?"

"Eshk in red brandy sauce," Helm said.

"Now you did *not* buy that at the package commissary at Iphus Collective," said Enda. "Helm, confess. You *cooked* it."

Helm grinned, and the look made Gabriel think that the top of his head might fall off. There was always something unexpected about this huge, near-rectangular brick of a man with his meter-wide shoulders and his iron-colored hair, suddenly producing one of these face-wide grins. It was the kind of smile you could imagine a carnivore producing at a social gathering of prey animals. "And if I did?" Helm said.

"Then I think we should eat it," Gabriel said. "Plates?"

Enda reached under the table. "I have them here. Helm, tongs or a fork?"

"Tongs, please."

Gabriel went and got the third freestanding folding chair from his bunk cubicle, came back, set it up, and fell to with the others. There was not a lot of discussion during this period, except about the sauce, which had even Helm breaking out in a sweat within a matter of minutes.

"I thought you said humans developed a resistance to this kind of spicery," Enda said, looking from one to the other of them.

"Eventually," Helm said.

Gabriel was unable to speak for the moment and resigned himself to suffering in silence and drinking more wine.

Finally the edge of their hunger was blunted enough to talk over the afternoon's simulation, its high points and low, and the ways in which Gabriel and Enda's reactions could improve to deal with the combat situations—particularly those little ball bearing ships that had been attacking them. Ships of the same kind had pressed Gabriel and Enda here in Corrivale and over in Thalaassa as well. All this side of the Verge was buzzing with rumors of them now, ships of a strange construction, appearing from nowhere, vanishing again. Nothing more had been seen of them around here, but this did not make Gabriel feel any better about the area or their prospects in it.

"You didn't call me in for this practice session so close to our last one without reason," Helm said, wiping his mouth with a paper cloth and folding it carefully.

"No," Gabriel said. "I think we should be thinking about leaving."

"I suppose it will come as something of a wrench for the locals," Enda said. "They have been coming to depend on our custom . . ."

"And on us paying their outrageous prices," Gabriel muttered. "Well, no more."

"You have decided, then."

"Since when is it 'I'?" Gabriel asked.

Enda leaned back and sighed, giving him a look that might have translated as affectionate exasperation. "Gabriel, I have been wandering around this part of the worlds for a long time. My opinion about where we take *Sunshine* is simple. I don't care. I am delighted to defer to you in this regard. Where shall we go?"

"Someplace with work," Helm said. "I mean, there's not much money in staying here. If work were the only problem, you'd have angled your jets and moved right after we got back from Thalaassa, since I don't think you want to work in this system any more. Well, about time, is all I can say."

"I'm surprised you haven't said anything about it before now," Gabriel said.

"Before you made up your mind?" Helm said as he put his feet up. "No point. You're still a typical shiphead—all strong-and-silent stuff until it's actually time to move. Then get up and do it with no warning. Which is smart. The best starfall is the unadvertised one."

"A masterly summation," Enda said. "Perhaps, Helm, you will tell us as well what Gabriel now has in mind, for this has been a matter of interest to me also."

Helm snickered. "I'd go into futures trading if I could do that." He leaned back and looked at Gabriel. "What's the word?"

Gabriel shook his head. "I haven't found out anything further here about the people responsible for getting me cashiered," he said, "and the money in this system isn't worth the trouble of staying. At the same time I hate getting too far away from the Grid, but it's also occurred to me that the need to be close to the data had obscured a possibility . . . and I thought we might look into doing some infotrading."

Enda bowed her head, a "thinking" gesture. Gabriel glanced at Helm.

"Big profit margins there," said Helm. "Big risks, too. You have a software or hardware crash while you're transiting with live stuff from a drivesat relay, or you run into some kind of transportation problem, miss a starfall, drop the data, and suddenly there are people suing you from here back to the First Worlds."

"Not somewhere I'd been planning to go at this point," said Gabriel.

"Not someplace you'd ever go again," Helm muttered, "if you lose a load of data. Lawyers . . ." He shivered. "But the profit margins . . ." He looked as thoughtful as Enda. "Twenty to fifty percent on a load, if you pick somewhere just opening up. 'Course places like that are dangerous too."

"I had thought," Gabriel said, "about hiring some armed backup."

Helm grinned from ear to ear. His ship was full from core to shell with weaponry of all kinds. But then Helm was a mutant, and unless you were a mutant who was also tired of life, armament out in these less than perfectly policed spaces was a good idea. Too many humans considered being a mutant some kind of treason against the human genotype to be punished in any way that wouldn't get you caught. Helm clearly did not intend to be caught assisting anyone in this kind of rough justice by lacking the kind of hardware that would dissuade them.

"Where were you thinking of going?" Helm said. "Got to consider fuel, victualling—"

"Terivine," said Gabriel.

Enda nodded sidewise. "It would make sense," she said. "Terivine has become a common enough waystation for ships doing the runs between Corrivale and Aegis, and Lucullus as well, but the place is not heavily populated . . ."

"That's not a huge problem," Gabriel said. "Besides the colonists, there's a considerable presence of scientists studying the riglia, those avian sentients they found. They need to move their data back and forth at something better than the crawl they'd get from using unscheduled infotraders. Tendril and Aegis both have to move administrative information pertaining to their colonies there. It looks like a good small market for a beginning infotrading business."

"You have obviously been doing your research," Enda said, "so you will know what kind of competition is there."

"Not much," Gabriel said. "Two firms work the system at present. One's native, a one-ship company called Alwhirn. Another is a licensee, Infotrade Interstellar Aegis."

Helm's eyebrows went up. "Isn't Infotrade Interstellar a subsidiary of VoidCorp?"

"These days, what isn't?" Gabriel said wearily.

"Us," said Enda. She pursed her lips in an expression that made her look unusually like a disapproving grandmother.

"You think they don't know it?" said Helm. "But here you sit in the system, bold as brass plate, as if they didn't dare touch you."

"They do not," Enda said, "for the moment. Not after we put so sharp a thorn in their side at Thalaassa and Corrivale, and Gabriel became the hammer to drive it in. They would be eager enough to repay him the trouble. The Concord would be quick to lay that at their doors if they tried that now. However, once we move elsewhere . . ."

That was always the problem. Since the vast expanse of the Verge began to reopen, the stellar nations had been moving in with various degrees of eagerness, acquisitiveness, or plain old-fashioned greed. Trade was opening out again, or for the first time. The wars that had cut off the Verge from the rest of humanity for so long had kept major trade routes and infrastructure from being established. Now what should have happened a quarter century earlier was beginning to happen again and in a rush. Every stellar nation or multistellar-national with the funds to spare was expanding into this area, hunting markets to master and resources to exploit. Systems that were backwaters ten years ago had become trading crossroads of considerable wealth and power. Through such systems, like Corrivale, Terivine, and Aegis, the huge cruisers of the stellar nations passed, both to trade and to find ways to extend their own influence. Mutual-assistance treaties, joint-use agreements for planets or whole systems, "understandings" and "gentlemen's agreements" could result in a world becoming the property of a stellar empire or company based thousands of light-years away. VoidCorp was probably the least principled of these. Once a software company, VoidCorp was now an interstellar power with many systems under its domination and many more becoming increasingly entangled in its web of interlocking corporate affiliations, treaties, and licensing agreements.

Gabriel sighed. "If we try to force ourselves into a position where we don't go *anywhere* that VoidCorp goes, we won't have a lot of choices. I don't like them any better than either of you do, especially considering that some part of VoidCorp Intelligence may have had something to do with setting me up. There are millions of VoidCorp Employees scattered across space who've never heard of us, won't have a clue who we are, and even if they're told, they may not care."

Enda frowned. "I would not be too sure. We only liberated about a thousand sesheyans that the Corporation is sure should be Employees. That the Concord declared them not to have been so is fortunate, but it will not count for much with VoidCorp."

"I.I. Aegis is just a licensee," Gabriel said, "local people running the business with VC equipment and contracts. It's a common enough arrangement, and licensees don't necessarily agree with the Company's overall policies."

Enda nodded. "It is too easy, I suppose, to become paranoid, and see Corpses hiding behind every asteroid, plotting our downfall. Have you done initial price-estimates as well? We would have to make alterations to the hold. The armoring we installed for mining work would need to be removed, and the new data storage facilities would not come cheap."

"Depends where you get them," Gabriel said and reached out to touch the part of the wall that hid the display for *Sunshine*'s Grid access. It came alive with imagery from the ship's internal Grid handling computers—a vast green plain rippling with some kind of long grass, a favorite image of Enda's.

"Data trading," Gabriel said, and the display flickered into an image of many rows of text and columns of figures.

"Oh, brother," Helm said, reaching down under his chair. "Half a moment while I get something to strengthen me."

"Why, Helm," Enda said, "surely so acute a businessman cannot look on a sight such as this unmoved."

"Yes I can," Helm said. "Wake me when we get to the weapons allocations."

Gabriel threw a sidewise glance at the bottle Helm now held. "How can you *drink* that stuff?" Gabriel asked, for the bottle was one of those squat square ones that Bols Luculliana came in.

Helm poured out two fingers of the thick clear stuff and shrugged. "It clears the mind. Want some?"

Gabriel shuddered at the thought and looked at the screen again. For a few minutes he went over the figures with Enda. She looked cautiously at the ones for the installation of the data tanks, which Gabriel suggested should be done by a small independent firm at Diamond Point on Grith.

"It is close by," Enda said, "and would be convenient for maintenance on return runs, but the firm has not been in business for long."

"It comes with good recommendations," Gabriel said. "Ondway told me about it."

Enda blinked at that and smiled. "Indeed. He would have some interest in seeing that our money is well spent, and in distributing business to the local community."

Gabriel nodded. They had met Ondway in Iphus Collective. The meeting had been an unusual one. In these spaces where VoidCorp's influence was strong, it was almost unheard-of to run into a sesheyan who did interplanetary work and was not an Employee. Ondway had put Gabriel and Enda in the way of some unusual business opportunities and also had given them hints about conditions on one of the supposedly uninhabited planets in the Thalaassa system—hints that had led Gabriel to investigate farther and get them into trouble. After the dust settled, Gabriel and Enda had been awarded a small public bounty from the Concord civil liberties fund. What had amused Gabriel immensely was the notion that, while one arm of the Concord government wanted him imprisoned, another was giving him grants for catching VoidCorp with its Corporate pants down. However, there had also been a less public award, not so much a bounty as a thank you from a sesheyan interest group of which Ondway was a prominent member—a group of native activists profoundly moved at Gabriel's single-handed rescue of more than a thousand of their kind from the Thalaassan world where VoidCorp was attempting to quietly exterminate them. Gabriel had insisted that there had been nothing single-handed about it. Enda had been in the thick of things with him, and he had merely been well positioned to intimidate some people whom he loathed. The sesheyans were not interested in his excuses, and they insisted on crediting *Sunshine*'s expense accounts with a considerable sum. Between these two awards, Gabriel and Enda were in a position to live less marginally than they had when they first went into business together.

Then had come the question of what to do with the money. Their first indulgence had been a shower for *Sunshine*, and there had been no argument about that, but such a small luxury had not made much of a dent in their new funds. Enda, conservative as a fraal in her second century might be expected to be, was all for investment of the rest. So was Gabriel, but there had been little agreement about the kind of investment to do. Now, though, Enda was looking interested.

"All right," she said. "I concede that installation may as well be done on Grith. But the general risk still gives me pause in comparison with, say, mining." She reached out to pour another glass of kalwine. "A cargo of ore does not go stale, nor does it have value until one delivers it to the processor. This kind of cargo is more sensitive and needs to be better protected."

Helm looked up at that. "The weapons allocations," he said.

"We need more guns," Gabriel said, "or upgrades on the old ones."

Helm grinned.

Gabriel brought up another page of price lists, and Helm commented at length on the virtues and vices of the weaponry available in this part of the Verge.

"I have my own preferences," he said, "and you don't have to go all the way to Austrin-Ontis for decent weapons any more. You should think about upgrading that rail cannon, at the very least. It would be even better to get rid of it. What I'd *really* like to see you get would be a mass cannon, but—"

Gabriel laughed. "Oh, sure, let's just stop the next passing Star Force cruiser and pull one off!"

"Some day," Helm said, "the cost of the things will drop so that people who aren't military can get their hands on one." His expression suggested that he intended to be the first. "Meanwhile, those upgrades. I have a friend who knows where you could get a discount."

"Delde Sota," Gabriel and Enda said in chorus. Enda chuckled. "Helm, is there *any* business in this system that mechalus does not have her braid or her brain plugged into?"

"You want good machinery," Helm said, "go to a mechalus. Who would know it better? The good doctor collects favors from everyone she fixes up. She put me onto somebody who's done fairly well by me. Any more figures?"

Gabriel looked over at Enda and said, "I don't think this is a decision I should make by myself, no matter how you insist that the things I did got us the awards that would make this possible."

Enda merely produced one of those demure little fraal smiles.

"You were a marine too long," Helm said to Gabriel. "You were good at taking orders, but now you have other problems—staying alive, mostly. That means making decisions, not taking orders."

"What made it hard," Gabriel said, "was the prospect of moving too far from where my trouble happened."

"You haven't had much luck with tracing the ones responsible, have you?" Helm said.

"Not much. The trail leading back to 'Jacob Ricel,' or whatever his name was before he boarded *Falada*, is cold. There's no way for me to go where it might still be warm without being arrested. The marines have never been happy with the outcome of my trial. They'd prefer to do it again their way." Gabriel shook his head. "Grid information's cold as well, or getting that way, and getting at it is expensive."

"Whereas if you were hauling data," Helm said, "you would have periodic access to the drivesat relays from which you were hauling . . . *and* hauler's discount on data access, while spending a lot of safe time away from the Conkers."

Gabriel nodded. He had no desire to spend time closer to Concord space than he had to. There were bounty hunters who would be willing to turn Gabriel in for the reward. Yet outside of Concord space there was no resolution of his problem. Sooner or later, Gabriel would have to go back with what evidence he was able to garner and take his chances with Concord justice.

"As regards 'riding shotgun' for us," Enda said, "would you be available?"

When Helm looked up from pouring another splash of Bols, there was an odd expression in his eyes. Gabriel thought it looked like gratitude, but it sealed over quickly into the old no-nonsense humor.

"Been waiting for you to make up your mind. My schedule's wide open. When do we leave?"

"About a week," Gabriel said. "Getting the data tanks installed will take most of the time."

"And arranging to see what kind of first load we can acquire," Enda said. "I will see to that."

"I'll talk to the doctor in the morning," Helm said. "Meanwhile, I could use a nap, and I have to clean up after myself. Cooking!" He stood, looming over Enda, huge and amused. "I did it with an autolaser. In a pot."

"You do most things with an autolaser," Enda said mildly. "The pot was doubtless added in a moment of inspiration."

Helm laughed, picked up his bottle and put it on the table for them, and went off down toward the airlock. "Call me in the morning," he said to Gabriel, "when you get your schedule sorted out."

"I will."

The airlock cycled shut behind Helm, and Gabriel got up to help Enda clean up after their meal. It was something they were both punctilious about—a ship in which some parties are tidy and some are sloppy soon turns into a little hell. Once the table was uncovered and folded away and the plates and utensils were washed and stowed, Gabriel folded a chair down and just sat there looking at the screen, which had defaulted to that view of the green field under some alien sun, the long grass rippling silkily as water in the wind that stroked it.

Down in her cubicle, Gabriel could hear Enda moving around, putting her bed in order for the night. A year ago he had known nothing of her, known no fraal at all and precious few aliens of any kind. Now he could hardly imagine a world without her—a world circumscribed by these scrubbed gray walls and floors— the fire of starrises and starfalls, some new primary burning golden or blue-white or green through the front viewports, the fierce sky-blue of Enda's huge eyes.

Once the world had been different, not gray-walled but white-walled, the color of marine country in a Star Force ship. Life had been simple, explicable, neatly circumscribed. You went where you were ordered—or were taken there. You fought who you were told to, and you cleaned up afterwards. *Ready to fight . . .* He had been, but the nature of the enemies had changed overnight, and the conflict had become difficult to understand. Too difficult for the marine he was then—and Gabriel had found himself cashiered, cast loose on a world he didn't know, alone and friendless.

Then Enda had turned up. There were aspects of their first meeting and their subsequent dealings that Gabriel still did not understand. But he was certain that it was a better world with her in it, and that he owed her most of what he had now. He was partner in a ship, half of a business, and had come through some difficult times getting used to it. He had survived, but there was always the question of how long he could keep on doing it.

"You are thinking harder than usual," Enda said.

Gabriel glanced up. "Does it show?"

"I heard you. You are still unsure . . ."

Gabriel chuckled. "Mindwalkers. I can't even brood without being overheard any more."

She pulled down the chair opposite him. "I have had much less training in the art than most. However, if you think loudly, I cannot help it. You also must not think I desire to pressure you in any direction. If I have been doing so, you must tell me so."

Gabriel shook his head. "You misheard me. You can be pretty forceful, but not that way. In fact, it's hard to get you to tell me what to do even about little things."

"Perhaps I refuse to be lured into a role that you would accept too easily," Enda said. "Gabriel, is your choice firm?"

"Yup. Let's get out of here."

Enda tilted her head to one side, one of the fraal versions of the human nod.

"We had not discussed how we will leave. Do we make starfall to Terivine by ourselves, or hitch a ride with some larger vessel?"

"Maybe not on the first leg," Gabriel said. "If you set out on your own, sometimes people assume you're going to keep going that way. If we picked up a hitch *after* we make our first starfall . . ." He shrugged.

"This deviousness," Enda said, "suits you well enough, you who were such an innocent only six months ago. Beware lest you lose track of who you are beneath all the twists and turns."

She smiled as she said it, but Enda's look was more than usually thoughtful. Gabriel had never had a living grandmother to look at him in this particular way. Now it occurred to him that this was how one might look if she were about a meter and a half tall and so slender that she looked like you could break her in half like a stick.

"There are times," Gabriel said, "when I've considered that."

Enda blinked at him. "What exactly?"

"Losing track, of who I am, or was. A little discreet cosmetic surgery, maybe . . . a change of look, a change of name. Let Gabriel Connor have an accident somewhere. Change the name appearing on *Sunshine's* registry. Become someone else . . ."

"It would be a logistical problem to change our registry," Enda said. "Not impossible, but expensive, and it *is* impossible to do such things without leaving an electron trail. Additionally, for those who are determined to know where you are, and who you are . . . I question whether the stratagem would work for long."

"More to the point," Gabriel said at last, "is whether I really want to hide. I don't want to throw away my name. I want to clear it."

"But you are finding that hard," Enda said, "and potentially harder as time goes on."

"Without the evidence I need to prove I didn't kill those people willingly, yes."

"The frustration," Enda said softly, "can wear a soul down, if allowed to do so."

"Even a stone wears down under water," Gabriel said. "Every time someone hears the name 'Gabriel Connor' and looks at me that way—'Oh, *that* Gabriel Connor, you were on the Gridnews, you murdered your best friend and got away with it, some legal loophole or other. Aren't you proud of yourself?' Every time I see that look, it's another drip on the stone. Is it so strange to wish it would just stop?"

He tried to look steadily at her. Even now, even with half a year of time between him and the deaths of his comrades in that shuttle explosion, it was hard to talk about it, even with someone as coolly compassionate as Enda.

"It is one of your people's sayings," Enda said, "long ago I heard it. 'When Heaven intends to confer great office upon a man, it sheds disaster upon him and brings all his plans to naught; reduces him in the sight of the world, and confounds all his undertakings. Then it is seen if he is ready.'"

Gabriel laughed. "That's all very reassuring if you know that you're intended for some 'great office.' Otherwise, it just seems delusional, a way to rationalize the act of the universe doing what it usually does—crapping on the ordinary guy."

"In this then," Enda said, "plainly there is universal justice. The great and the lowly are treated the same. Perhaps what makes the difference is in how they react to it."

Chapter Two

A STARFALL AWAY FOR a big ship, or five or six starfalls off for a small one, a Concord cruiser slipped massively through the outer fringes of the Lucullus system. If no one in the system was sure what its business was, that state of affairs well suited one of its passengers.

Lorand Kharls sat quietly in the room he had occupied since arriving aboard the cruiser. It was very bare, for he did not have time to go in for much decoration. His work required him to change residence often, and he disliked having to pack much more than a change of clothes and a box of reference works, books and solids and so forth. He had come far enough along in his job that this was more than enough to help him get his business done—that, and hours of talking and listening.

There was a soft knock at his door. "Yes?" he said, and his assistant, a tall young man wearing mufti and a complete lack of expression, slid the panel aside.

"She's here."

"Thank you, Rand. Ask her to come in."

The door slid wider, and a dark-haired young woman walked in. She wore a Star Force uniform with Intel pips at the collar, and an expression pleasanter than his assistant's, though as neutral. She would never have been able to manage anything like his assistant's fade-into-the-veneer quality. Her face had too much character—a stubborn forehead, strong chin, and those large brown eyes that somehow made the rest of her face seem insignificant.

"Aleen Delonghi, sir," she said, saluting him.

"You're welcome. Please sit down."

She did, in the one other chair that the room contained. There was nothing else in the place but a table with some data solids on it.

"The captain tells me that you've been asking your superior for a chance to speak to me regarding the mission that brought me here."

"Yes, sir."

"This suggests that you think you know what should be done about the situation."

"I think so, sir."

"After, of course, having gone through all the salient information that we have spent the last months collecting and collating."

"All of it that has been made available to me, sir, yes."

Kharls looked at her. She was experienced enough at what she had been doing over the past few years. The administrative department that had sent her to him along with several other Concord Intelligence operatives had spoken highly of her talents. Now he would see whether they were justified in doing so.

"Very well. You've seen the subject's statements on the matter, and you've seen Intel's recommendations regarding the situation so far. What is your opinion of them?"

She took a deep breath. "I think they look like a pack of misdirections and lies from beginning to end."

"Any ideas as to *whose* lies?" Kharls asked.

She said nothing.

He sat back in his chair. "You know," Kharls said slowly, "there was a time, a culture—a human culture, mind you—in which, if someone accused you of lying, they had the right to try to kill you. Right there. Isn't that fascinating?"

She paled, and her eyes slid to the tri-staff that leaned casually against the wall within Kharls's reach. "They called it 'giving someone the lie,' " Kharls said, "or 'the lie direct'. What a busy time it must have been, human nature being what it was and is."

"Administrator Kharls," Delonghi said, sounding much more cautious now, "maybe I should rephrase that."

"Maybe you should."

"Your behavior as regards this . . . asset, if that's the word I'm fumbling for—for he looks more like a liability every time I consider him—your behavior regarding him is undermining a genuine Intelligence priority. How is Concord Intel—or Star Force Intel for that matter, since that's my cover at the moment—supposed to find out anything useful when you allow other assets to contaminate him?"

" 'Allow?' " He looked at her with surprise. "That suggests that I know in advance what they're going to do."

"Of course you—" She stopped.

Kharls looked at her hard from under those bushy eyebrows. "Miss Delonghi," he said. "Forgive me if I do not take you entirely into my confidence at the moment. I have a very large remit, as you may know—"

"You are a Concord Administrator," she said, with the air of someone trying to cut straight to the heart of the matter, "and probably the most powerful being in these spaces."

He leaned back again, though not with any look of being flattered or mollified. "Would it shock you," Kharls began, "if you knew that my main purpose, as so powerful a being—let me for the moment adopt your language—was to create the conditions in which my job description, and my job, became unnecessary?"

Her eyes widened. Kharls did not smile at her, though the temptation briefly crossed his mind.

"You won't believe me when I say as much," Kharls said. "What sane being would? Who would want to put himself out of a job in which planetary governments take his lightest word as the equivalent of enacted primary legislation, in which he can exercise what used to be called 'high, low, and middle justice'— the powers of judge, jury, and executioner? Would you believe something like that? Of course not. So I can make such outrageous statements and get away with it. Not being believed is a tool of considerable utility when one exercises it with care." He waited to see if she would at least react to the irony. Not a flicker, he thought. It will be a while yet before this one has come along to where I want her. "At any rate, I have not sent this particular asset out into the night to remain uncontaminated."

"There are those who say he's contaminated enough as it is," said Delonghi, trying unsuccessfully to restrain an expression of scorn.

"So they have and will," Kharls replied. "That's all to the good, for the moment. If the situation changes, I will judge it accordingly . . . but not before."

"You're telling me that you've purposely sent this operative out to make contact with enemy intelligence organizations—"

" 'Enemy' is such a narrowing term," said Kharls. "Who knows in what relationship the Concord will stand within, say, twenty or thirty years to any of the stellar nations that presently are not part of it? Or how matters will stand in the Verge? And even inside the Concord, as you well know, there's considerable difference of opinion about what nations and issues are most important. Nearly *infinite* difference of opinion." He smiled grimly. "Fortunately, my job is not about reconciling opinion, which is just as well, since that would be impossible. My job is to make things out here in the Verge work as well as they can for the moment, and to figure out how to make them work better still for the people who'll come out here to live, and those who are here already. In particular, my remit charges me to look out toward the edges of things, the unpoliced and untravelled spaces all around the Verge where situations are not as clear-cut as they are in toward the First Worlds—much less structured and more chaotic. The textbooks don't do much good out here for even the best-intentioned agent, ambassador, or ship's commander. One learns to strike out into the dark and try techniques that might seem foolish elsewhere."

Kharls sat back again, looking at his folded hands. "I have no scruples about using agents who may seem tainted or chaotic to the textbook types. If that conceals such agents' true value, so much the better, for valuable assets, unfortunately, tend to be killed the most quickly. As regards the object of our discussion, however, you need to be clear that *I* have not sent him anywhere.

He is one of the very few genuinely free operatives I manage—if manage is even the word, since he completely rejects any idea that I have any such power over him."

"Then he's a fool," Delonghi said.

"Possibly, but he's also right."

Delonghi kept her face still. Kharls watched this exercise with interest. "See that," he said, "you *still* don't believe me. I wonder if the ancients had an offense called '*disbelief* direct'?"

He got up, stretched, and stepped around to the big viewport that was the room's only other indulgence. "If he draws the attention of other intelligence assets," Kharls said, looking out into the starry blackness, "that is all to the good. He is a lightning rod, Delonghi. He is being held out into the dark specifically to see what forces he attracts. But he is not to be seen as having no value simply because he is being used as a lightning rod. In the old days, the very best ones used to be made at least partially of precious metal."

Kharls turned away from the viewport. "Now, obviously you want to go out and have a personal look into this situation . . . and meddle." Her face did not move at the word. "Well, you were a talented meddler for some years, which is why you're here with me and my people at all. I suppose we can hardly blame you for wanting to revert to type."

He sat down again. "In short, I've decided to allow you to do so. I am instructing you to go and examine this situation personally." Her eyes narrowed. Badly concealed triumph, which for the moment he declined to notice. "With the following conditions. You are not to interfere in any way with the subject's free pursuit of his own objectives. You may try to determine what they are or what he *thinks* they are. I require you to report to me regularly on the details. You are to pay particular attention to the attempts of other intelligence organizations to interfere with him. You are not yourself to interfere with those attempts."

"Even if they kill him?"

"They may look like they want to," said Kharls softly, "but I assure you, they do not. They *will* not either, unless someone fumbles badly. They are eager to find out why *we* are so interested in him. As eager as *you* are, I dare say."

At *that,* she did have the grace to blush. Kharls did not react to this either. "You are to keep your own head down. Do not be noticed by them. For our own part, I want to know the sources of *their* interest—the motivations of whoever you find watching him or trying to affect him. No one spends so much time watching someone merely to discover what he knows that they don't. More often they watch to see what he knows that *they* know too . . . and what they fear for anyone else to find out."

She nodded.

"You will return on recall," Kharls said. "Consult with the colonel and the captain about your equipment and cover. Otherwise, go do your work."

"Thank you, sir," Delonghi said.

"I wouldn't," Kharls said, "until you come back with your job successfully completed."

She turned to go.

" 'Middle justice,' " Kharls said softly. "I always wondered about that one."

He glanced up again. Hurriedly, she saluted him and left. The door slid shut behind her, leaving Kharls alone in his office.

She had her own agenda. Well, he had no interest in agents who didn't. The truly agendaless ones were too dangerous to trust with anything. It was always a risk, sending an operative out on really difficult business—especially since it was difficult to tell exactly how he or she would react. As he had said, he did not scruple to use the tainted or skewed asset when the moment came right. His job required him to use his tools—the lightning rod or the gun—with equanimity, to use them as effectively as their structures allowed, and to destroy them if necessary . . . and not to count the cost until the job was done. For Lorand Kharls, as he felt his way toward the secrets of the deadly and dangerous things that were slowly beginning to reveal themselves at the edges of the Verge, that would most likely be many years. For the lightning rod . . .

. . . he would have to wait and see.

* * * * *

Gabriel was desperately busy for a week and a half. Arrangements had to be made with the data tank installers on Grith, and while that happened *Sunshine* had to be landed at Diamond Point and kept in bond, with all the nuisance that entailed—signing in and out every time you came aboard and executing a full "incoming" inventory. Then came provisioning and victualling, with all those supplies having to be delivered to a different part of the bond facility, every box opened, every piece of replacement equipment checked. Then for the weaponry installation, *Sunshine* had to be taken out of bond again and trucked over to one of the unsealed parts of the port. Gabriel had laughed at the description of the area as "low security." He didn't think he had ever seen as many discreetly disguised missile launchers and energy weapons arrayed around a shipchandler's yard as he saw here.

This part of the work was easiest for Gabriel, for Helm came into his own here—never leaving the shipchandlery while anyone was working on *Sunshine*, hanging over the mechanics' and engineers' shoulders, seeming to watch everything at once. They swore at him, but not too often. Everyone there knew that Helm was expert with weaponry, and though he did not seem to be "carrying," this impression could be a mistake.

"I never shot anybody for an honest mistake," he'd joke with them. The installers would laugh and keep a close eye on Helm while he checked the installation schematics against the circuit-solids that were going in.

The gunnery work—a very hush-hush removal of the old plasma cannon energy conduits and their replacement with new ones and new software to match—took three days. It might have taken four if Gabriel had allowed what Helm wanted, the removal of the rail cannon, but at the last moment he decided to keep it. Helm argued the point, but not hard, perhaps detecting that Gabriel had something on his mind. He did, but he couldn't explain it and refused to try. He was nervous enough about the work being done on the plasma cannons. They were not legal and were being carried "concealed" with flap ports typical of much more innocuous weapons covering them. The thought that some-one whose silence had not been paid for might drop a word about those guns into the wrong ears was one that recurred more fre-quently to Gabriel the longer they stayed.

On the morning of the fourth day, they took *Sunshine* over to the other side of Diamond Point to a little private pad. There they left her under the supervision of guards whom Helm had hired while the data tanks were installed. All their shopping was done, so Gabriel had a day or so free—indeed, Helm told him to get lost, and Enda was nowhere to be found, still busy with lining up their infotrading contracts. Gabriel therefore spent a happy day doing tourist things, finally climbing up to the observation plat-form on the hundred-meter-high bluffs, a spot he had once visit-ed as a marine and once again as a tourist a few months ago. Now he stood there in silence around sunset, watching as the huge reaches of Grith's tidal sea started to fill with the daily inrush. Despite all the activity in which he had been involved over the last few days, Gabriel's mind felt oddly empty, as if waiting for something to happen.

He reached idly into his pocket and began to turn his luckstone over in his fingers. In some ways, the little stone was the last remnant of the life he'd led before being held for murder. Every-thing else from that pre-life was gone now . . . his uniforms, the notebooks for his studies, the various bits and pieces that a young man on active service picks up over a tour of duty. Only this remained, a token given him as a "lightening exercise" by a buddy who was going home and happily giving away every pos-sible ounce of freight. Sometimes Gabriel thought he should get rid of this too, but the little thing was too evocative of the last of the good things about being a marine—the companionship, the sense that there were things worth fighting for and friends to fight beside. At first, he had not been able to think much about those friends. The screams of the ones he had killed echoed through his dreams for weeks. He still heard them, but not as often. Gabriel thought as he looked down at the ten-kilometer-long waves of the shallow tidal sea, when will I stop hearing them altogether?

Will that be a good thing if I *haven't* found out who killed them?

There would be time for that. He would not stop looking. In the meantime . . . better to try to get on with some other kind of life.

He made his way back to the ship that evening to sleep aboard. The next morning, the installation crew unceremoniously rousted Gabriel out, telling him not to come back until lunchtime. When he did, he heard a voice echoing down *Sunshine*'s middle corridor. Gabriel paused —then realized with a jolt of happy surprise whose voice that was.

"Delde Sota!" he called.

She turned toward him, smiling that cool wise smile of hers as Gabriel stepped out. "Greeting: looking well, Gabriel."

"So are you," Gabriel said.

It was true, for she was quite handsome, even when you reckoned her looks by strictly human standards. Easily two meters tall, Delde Sota had long dark silvershot hair pulled straight back from her high forehead. Around shoulder level her shaggy mane was braided, the silver sheen of the cyberneural fiber and custom-made prehensile fibrils weaving in patterns through the hair as the braid tapered and became more complex. Finally, there was only a slender silver tail at the end, which might lie still or part itself again and weave itself into many-fibrilled patterns while the doctor considered something. This was most of the time. Delde Sota was not one whose mind was long inactive, and she seemed to consider it part of her business to keep you thinking, too.

Enda was there as well, which surprised Gabriel. He had expected her to spend another day out in town, but here she was chatting with doctor, who was dressed for travel in the usual mechalus *rlin noch'i*, the simple utilitarian one-piece garment that covered the body from neck to feet—a soft gray-silver, in Delde Sota's case. Over this, she wore a long, wide-sleeved, floppy overcoat of some soft fluffy charcoal-colored material, a marked contrast to the slick gleam of the *rlin noch'i*. Gabriel was bemused by how pleased he was to see the doctor. It was not merely that she had been a great help to him and Enda—she had. There was a peculiarly cheerful quality to her that made the power and complexity of her personality pleasant to be around.

"Doctor, what brings you over this way?" Gabriel said. "I'd hoped we'd see you before we left, but I didn't think it would be here."

"Agenda: business," said the doctor. "Also have been in touch with Helm Ragnarsson about your plans. Suggestion from him: desired in-depth system check of your ship's software with an eye to—shall we say?—tampering. Have found none."

She paused as if to give Gabriel a chance to say something, but the silence was a comment. There were indeed some devices aboard *Sunshine* that enabled the ship to be monitored from outside. They were there at Gabriel's sufferance, for the time being, and he only thought about them when he chose to.

Gabriel simply blinked at Delde Sota, and the end of her braid wreathed about and tied itself into a brief knot before undoing itself again. "Thank you, Doctor," he said.

"Query: departure time?" Delde Sota said.

"Response: uncertain as yet."

Gabriel looked over at Enda. She gave him a smile that, for its intensity, was unusual.

"We have no more business to do here after our tanks are full," Enda said, "and full they will be. The response has been better than I had hoped—far better. We now are only delayed by the remaining time that the tank installation will take. When that is done, we may download from the planetary Grid and be away immediately."

"Reaction: congratulation," said Delde Sota. "Propitious start. Wish that your business may continue so." She gave Gabriel a look, suggesting that she was referring to other aspects of his business as well.

"If you'd like to check the tanks when the loading is finished," Gabriel said, "also with an eye to 'tampering,' I would appreciate it."

"Statement: would appreciate it myself," said Delde Sota, her eyes glinting with amusement. Data tanking was usually proprietary hardware—something into which a mechalus was always delighted to get her wires with an eye to simulating it for her own purposes. "Query: this will not violate any end-user agreements?"

Enda bowed her head "no" and said, "Obviously you may not examine the data itself, which lies within confidentiality seal and encryption, but as for the tanks—"

Delde Sota smiled. "Statement: know something about confidentiality myself," she said. "Ancillary statement—"

She broke off. Gabriel smiled, hearing a mechalus joke. Computer circuitry and software were part of the physical world through which Delde Sota moved, almost an element, like air or water, and part of her own being. As a skilled former Grid pilot, no level of encryption would long have kept Delde Sota out if she had her mind set on making her way through it, but she did not. Her ethics were as hard and dependable as the circuitry she had weaving through her.

"How long will you be with us, Doctor?" Enda said. "Will you have time for a meal before we leave?"

"Reply: numerous," Delde Sota said, turning away from her brief attention to the Grid access panel across the hall from them. "Information: I will be accompanying Helm Ragnarsson on *Longshot* to Terivine."

Gabriel's mouth fell open. "Wha— Delde Sota, that's wonderful! But what about your job on Iphus?"

"Clarification: have taken extended sabbatical," said the doctor. "Requirements for service at Iphus Collective, medical, medico-mechanical, have dropped off nearly thirty percent over past two months. Assistant physician complaining of boredom." She grinned, a briefly fierce look. "Conjecture: no more complaints for the immediate future."

"Why the drop-off, do you think?" Enda said.

Delde Sota gave Enda a thoughtful look. "Theory: pressure from VoidCorp against independent mining operations on Iphus Collective increasing. Theory: VoidCorp pressure also being exerted against Collective facility proper, with a view to forcing closure."

"They have wanted that for a long time," Enda said. "Do you think our recent activities might be responsible for this increased pressure?"

"Reply: uncertain," the doctor said. "Agreement: action has been in train for some time. Speculation: other influences may also be responsible."

She turned to look over at the Grid access panel. "Extenuating circumstances: any job grows wearying with too much time in a single place. Medicine may be practiced anywhere. Oaths pack small and light. Other equipment requires more time." She glanced sideways at Gabriel. "Phymech on Helm's ship has been upgraded to high standard. Query: has yours been serviced lately?"

"Not since you last looked at it."

"Have closeout deal on new upgrade pack," Delde Sota said. "Twenty percent off. Twenty-five for old and trusted customers."

Enda laughed and covered her eyes, a gesture indicating that the fraal who made it could not cope with present events and was considering taking up the contemplative life. "Another of your discounts! Gabriel, take her somewhere quiet and negotiate with her, or push her into the tank hold and lock her in, whichever you please."

"Twenty-*three* percent," Delde Sota said over her shoulder as Gabriel guided her away, "for insufficient show of enthusiasm."

They walked down *Sunshine*'s hall to look through the round port in the door that gave onto the main hold. Once the hold would have been a large empty space. Now it was filled with rack after rack of data storage facility, the "tank," a series of ceiling-to-floor frames filled with heavy-duty data storage solids and their holding and processing shells. Occasionally a fraal or human technician could be seen squeezing among the racks, always with arms full of more solids. Closer to the door, another technician was installing the high-speed upload and download channeling transmitters that would allow the carried data to be dumped to a system grid or planetary facility on arrival.

"Very impressive," Delde Sota said, peering through the heavy glass, and the end of her braid twitched.

"It'll be another couple of days before they assign us our system address and bring the automatic router online," Gabriel said. "They have to finish the local network testing first." He sighed. "A whole new set of software to learn and no room to maneuver if a mistake gets made."

"Opinion: software not all that complex," said Delde Sota, "and will be within call if you need assistance."

Gabriel leaned against the wall. "What brought this on?" he said.

"Statement: have dealt with that issue," said Delde Sota, but her neural braid was wreathing again, tying itself in a small tight knot. "Addendum . . ." She looked through the window. "Sense of things moving. Generalized shifts in political stances, of balance of power among stellar nations. Feeling . . . that there might be wisdom in relocation elsewhere while situation settles down."

Gabriel nodded. "I was going to ask if you'd be willing to act as a recipient for some data for me, but since you're coming with us . . . Do you have anyone remaining in Corrivale that you trust to receive sensitive material?"

"Response: Ondway, certainly. Query: type of data?"

"I have some Grid searches underway for old personnel information on the man who called himself 'Jacob Ricel,' " Gabriel said. "The search material is coming to our local Corrivale-based Grid address. But with *Sunshine* now designated for infotrading, she'll get a new address and routing codes, and the old ones can't be carried aboard her any more—the infotrade authorities won't permit multiple addressing for haulers. I was wondering if someone in the system could hold anything that came in for me till we pass this way again."

"Solution: pass keywords to Ondway," Delde Sota said. "Research materials safe with him. Query: manage for you?"

"I'd appreciate that," Gabriel said. "Come on through and you can take what you need out of the ship's Grid system."

She wandered back up the hallway with Gabriel and leaned against the bulkhead in the sitting room while her braid insinuated itself into the fold-down control panel that serviced the ship's Grid access. Gabriel leaned over the control panel and touched in his password.

Delde Sota raised her eyebrows. "Result," she said, "system configuration and keyword material found. Store?"

"Please."

She nodded and straightened up. "Secure. Intention: will pass this information to Ondway this evening. Satisfactory?"

"Absolutely. Thanks, Doctor."

"Mission statement: mental health requirements not to be ignored in favor of physical/infrastructure needs," said Delde Sota as Enda came back in, carrying the small plastic water bottle that she used to water her pet plant. "Body, mind, dichotomy illusory/false. Query: plant sprout yet?"

Enda gave her a look. "There is no point in hurrying something that is not ready," she said. "Some would say that owning a *Gyrofresia* is simply a disguised exercise in the art of patience."

"Opinion: too much patience bad for the bile ducts," said Delde Sota, and turned toward the lift. "Intention: completion of errands. Helm will contact me when departure imminent." Delde Sota waved a hand; she vanished into the lift, and her braid followed a moment later.

Gabriel sat down. "You said we were going out full?"

Enda nodded, putting the *Gyrofresia* bulb in its little ceramic pot onto one of the service ledges. "We have done unusually well for a first load," Enda said, pouring water carefully on the bulb.

"You mean we had a lot of help."

"From Ondway and his connections in Diamond Point . . . yes."

"Connections that would not otherwise have given their business to a first-time operation," Gabriel said.

Enda tilted her head to one side. "Goodwill, as they call it, is worth a great deal. We have a lot of it aboard, and we must do what we can to repay it. We must make this first run with all due speed. Some people will be watching carefully how we perform."

"And some to see how our performance can be interfered with."

Enda sighed. "Unquestionably. For the meantime, doing our job with care will be the best defense."

She went down the hall again, leaving Gabriel to sit and wonder whether it would be enough. *Still, with Helm along to help with defense and Delde Sota there for computer and medical problems, we're as well prepared as we can be.*

Gabriel sighed, got up, and headed off to the utility closet down the hall. If he was going to worry, he could at least scrub something while he did it.

Chapter Three

THREE DAYS LATER, *Sunshine* departed Grith.

The day before departure was the tensest because of a bureaucratic problem. The ship's infotrader routing address, the complex set of passwords, encryption routines, and system information that would identify it to planetary grids, had not come through from the nearest assigning authority on Aegis. That information itself was coming in on another infotrader, since Corrivale had no drivesat relay of its own. Without that address, there was no point in *Sunshine* leaving the system at all. Yet much of the data she was carrying was time-sensitive. The guarantees under which the data had been embarked in *Sunshine* specified that most of it had to be dumped at Terivine within fifty-five days. If the guarantees were broken, the fees for the data haulage had to be first discounted, then refunded if the delay was more than a hundred and twenty-one hours past the designated time of delivery.

Gabriel and Enda spent the day worrying in their respective styles. Gabriel paced up and down outside the ship, since he had already cleaned everything aboard that could be cleaned. Enda sat still, looking at her favorite vista of grass flowing in an alien wind on the Grid access display.

"At least," she said to Gabriel, "I will find out quickly enough when anything happens."

Two hours later, everything moved into high gear as the other infotrader made starrise in the system, cleared Grith landing control, and dumped its data to the planetary Grid. The access panel chimed, then lit up with all manner of bizarre error messages.

"Oh no, something else has gone wrong," Gabriel moaned and ran back to the hold.

"Gabriel," Enda called from the sitting room, "is the holding system set to 'active'?"

"How would I know? They didn't—" He stared at the control panel set against the near bulkhead wall on the inside of the hold. "Oh," Gabriel said, finding himself staring at a blinking telltale buried in the black plastic of the control panel, while out of the blackness next to it, the words *Go to Active?* came burning up.

He touched the words. *Active*, the panel said, and then immediately after that, *Storing waiting inload . . .*

The inload process took a half-hour or so, while the system loaded the waiting information, checked itself, checked that the storage was secure, and then encrypted everything. By then the hum of in-system drivers could be heard as *Longshot* came to rest on the pad beside them.

Gabriel was already in the left-hand pilot's seat, running *Sunshine* through her pre-starfall checks. "I thought you were meeting us at the spaceport," he said to Helm via audio comms.

That gravelly laugh came rumbling back. "You don't go nowhere unescorted," Helm said, "now that you're carrying. Let me know when you're secure and we'll make our last stop."

It took another ten minutes for the infotrading system to convince itself that the data destined for *Sunshine* had been safely loaded.

"Delde Sota was right," Enda said, looking over Gabriel's shoulder at the new sets of telltales flashing in the master 3D control display. "This software leaves little to chance."

"It would be nice if it would let us take off," Gabriel muttered. Finally the readouts said, *Secure. Clear. Ready for transport.*

Enda strapped herself in. They made the quick jump into the spaceport's bond area and admitted the usual port reps, an officious and very well spoken sesheyan named Se'tali accompanied by several assistants. They confirmed the supplies now going into *Sunshine*'s cargo hold. Their procedures required electronic signatures, spot-card payment for port services, and last of all, sign-off on the ship's registry documents. Gabriel provided all these as requested.

Se'tali said something polite and wedged himself into the lift. His assistants followed. Several of them winked at Gabriel, a gesture they had adopted from humans. Somehow, it looked more impressive than usual because of all the eyes that sesheyans had to work with. The last of them exited the lift, which retracted itself into *Sunshine*'s girth and locked up.

"You were mentioning good will," Gabriel said, checking all the indicators to make sure everything was closed tight for space. "We seem to have a lot."

"May it follow us," Enda said. "Helm?"

"Ready."

The port clearance control flashed permission-to-depart to their console. Helm lifted clear first, the scream of his engines dwindling upward and away. Gabriel touched the system drive into life and followed. The furious golden fire of Corrivale on Grith's green and violet surface dropped away beneath them, glinting blindingly but briefly on the girdling turquoise-violet tidal seas. Behind the curve of Grith, growing smaller now, the vast red-and-ochre striped bulk of Hydrocus loomed up over the thin bright band of atmosphere as it grew and dwarfed its jungle moon.

"Out of atmosphere," Enda said. "Ten minutes on system drive to the exit coordinates. Is the stardrive ready?"

Gabriel checked the readouts three times, making sure that the coordinates matched the hard copy in his personal data pad. "We're set."

"You ready over there?" Helm's voice came down comms.

"Yup. Check your info against ours?"

A pause.

"On the nose," Helm said. "Weapons ready."

Gabriel's were ready too, but he had not brought up the fighting field, not expecting to need to do any shooting at the moment.

It was at the other end of the transit that his concerns lay.

Enda too was looking at the gunnery readouts. "Are these latent energy readings supposed to be this high?" she said softly.

Helm chuckled. "The readings are fine. We'll play with the new toys when we get where we're going. Meanwhile, coming up on the tick—"

Gabriel had his eyes on the countdown. Ten seconds. He cut out the system drive and brought the stardrive to standby, watching the status indicators as the gravity induction coils and the mass reactor wound their waveforms into synch. Five seconds. The coordinates for the drop-out point at Terivine system converted into a third set of waveforms interwoven with the first two. Two seconds. One—

Blue fire sheeted up over *Sunshine* in tendrils and waves, obscuring the burning gold of Corrivale as *Longshot* dropped into drivespace with a flare of crimson off to one side. Like liquid flowing upward, blue light webbed over the front viewport and fell into the pilot's cabin as *Sunshine* dropped into starfall. It was dark again, the unrelieved blackness of drivespace clinging all around them.

Enda checked her instruments. "A new beginning for us, then," she said, "and well begun. Gabriel, when did you last eat?"

His stomach growled at him. "About a year ago," he said, "or at least it feels like it. Let's see what the new catering packs look like."

* * * * *

Some light-years away, down a Grid commline that was as secure as a large amount of money spent could make it, a conversation was taking place. One end of the conversation was on Iphus in the Corrivale system. The far end of the conversation was in a small secured cabin of a large and well-armed ship presently orbiting Grith.

The tall, thin man sitting in the thick-carpeted office on Iphus was leaning forward on his elbows at his big polished desk, looking down into the small tank that he preferred to the large flashy 3D displays of some others on this floor. The things leaked signal, for one thing. That was wasteful, no matter how secure you thought your comms were. The big displays were tasteless as well. He had no desire to imply that his communications were unimportant enough to let just *anyone* who walked in see them. That was not the way to get ahead in the Company. Perception, if not everything, was a substantial part of it.

". . . don't care what they think," said the woman at the other end. "There's been a lot of comm traffic from that end. I've dumped it to your location. They're getting ready to move."

"Where?" he said. "If they take themselves anywhere there's a significant Concord presence, there's no point in it."

"They won't," the woman said. Her expression was scornful. "They don't dare. He's wanted. There's a reward out now, thanks to us, enough to arouse interest. Sooner or later, somebody is bound to fit the face to the offer and pick up on him."

"Is it one of those 'dead or alive' things?"

She sniffed. "You're living in the wrong century. What point is there in just letting someone kill him? Due process has to be followed if you're going to make any kind of example that will stick in people's minds. It would be too obvious . . . not to mention creating problems at *this* end."

"Well, when it comes to problems," he said, hunching down lower, "we've got some at this end."

Her eyebrows went up at that. "What kind? After what that bunch of traitors and renegades did to you at Thalaassa, I'd have thought everyone would have agreed about what to do for a change."

He laughed. "You know how big this company is. Everyone with a letter higher than J in front of their ID thinks they're entitled to an opinion, and some of them *act* on them, the misguided idiots. Discipline has been going to hell around here lately. That shuffle up high three weeks ago—"

He stopped himself. Some topics it was unwise to discuss, no matter how carefully you thought you had secured your comms . . . always remembering that the people who had installed your lines in the first place were also Company and might have agendas of their own.

"Never mind." He sighed. "Our Intel people are apparently involved again."

She looked suspiciously at him. "Why?"

"They think they missed something the first time. Apparently Concord Intel is after him too, and they want to know why."

She swore. "They dumped him the first time as waste, and now they—" She broke off, shaking her head. "Do you seriously think they might be onto something?"

"I have no idea. If you think I can get anything significant out of our own Intel people about this, you're mistaken. They're all creeping around in hush-hush mode. The *only* thing that's certain is that somebody whose ID starts with X or Y has had his nose pushed right off his face by this hashmash at Thalaassa. Action has to be taken to calm his or her ruffled temper, and this probably means exposing the subject as Intel from the other side."

"He's not," she said fiercely. "We know that."

"As if that matters! If they have their way, they'll make him look as if he is, and then either side can chuck him away into whatever jail they like to waste the rest of his days away. The example will be taken by those who need it, believe me. Unless certain others get their way—"

She shook her head. "You lost me."

"There is a strong line of opinion in some offices up here," he said, "and not Intel—the *Enforcement* offices, I mean—that he should just have an accident. Safer, quicker, less trouble in the long run. What he did was a one-off, they think. Crazy guy, thrashing around for some kind of vengeance, took it against the nearest target—if he even knew that much of what he was doing."

She swore again. "There's got to be more to it than that."

He let out an annoyed breath. "I know. They're simplistic. *Yes*, the guy needs watching. We'll see if he really needs to be killed. He might find out something useful about the other side, and if he does . . . fine, then let the mouse run a little farther. We've got all the time in the world, and we have him outnumbered. The minute he's no longer useful . . ." The man's thin hand came down, clenched clawlike, on the shining desk. "For now, wait and see."

Then he chuckled. "Yes, why not make life as interesting for him as possible in the meantime? There are all kinds of possibilities."

"As long as none of them are pleasant for him," she said, "I can cope with that for the time being."

"I'll be in touch," the man said. He reached out to cut the connection. "Don't let them move without us knowing."

"It's handled."

He killed the comms circuit and sat back in his chair. When the mouse had run for the last time, she might have to be taken care of as well. It would be unfortunate if her knowledge about this line of action should become public.

Well, time enough to think about that. Meanwhile, he had other business. Within a few days, there would be more data to help him work out what to do. He slipped a long finger into the tank display, touching the dumped data into life. Columns and figures, rows of text scrolled by, and he smiled slightly.

Interesting times, he thought. Yes, those can be arranged. Intel can just deal with it the best they can.

*   *   *   *   *

Just over six weeks later, *Sunshine* and *Longshot* made starrise at Terivine.

Terivine A and B, the two main stars—a pair of G-class yellows—had been too close together at only ninety million kilometers to allow any exception to the no-planets tendency of binary systems. When the Verge started to open up again, transiting vessels had used a spot outside A and B's rotational locus as a target for starfall and rested there for recharge before moving on. No one bothered with the little cool orange dwarf, Terivine C, orbiting a hundred AUs out.

Ten years previously, the Alaundrin freighter *Desert Wind* had a navigational accident—the computer involved with calculating her path through drivespace dropped a decimal place in the coordinates due to a power fluctuation. When she made starrise,

Desert Wind was no more than two million kilometers out of the little star's atmosphere. They were lucky to have come out no closer. When the ship's crew got their composure back, they had reason to lose it again. There, orbiting the star no further out than forty-five million kilometers, was a Class 1 planet that no one had ever noticed.

As *Sunshine* made starrise in a down-sliding sleet of trickling white fire, Gabriel looked out on the little system and tried to imagine what that first crew's reactions must have been. No one looks for what they don't expect, and no one had ever expected a planet around a star so small and possibly so old. Argument was still raging as to whether the little world, eventually named Rivendale, was a capture or the remnant of a natural formation. In any case, the planet had suffered from tremendous tidal stresses and volcanism while it was forming. Its crust was unusually strong on the light elements and thoroughly faulted so that even the world's older mountain ranges were spectacularly shattered by time and tidal spasms. The younger ranges were labyrinths of splintered basalt needles and pinnacles, spearing upward over valleys torn deep between them, rearing above oxide-streaked canyons kilometers deep and cliffs kilometers high. All these features might have been expected of a low-gravity world, but in Rivendale's case, it was as if someone had attempted to produce a particularly extreme example of the class.

There were other oddities, again due to tidal effects. Terivine's unusually powerful braking effect on so light a planet had left Rivendale with a rotation period nearly seven days long. Fierce heat and numbing cold alternated on a weekly basis and grew worse with the turning of the seasons. The initial surveyors had looked down at this dramatic and intimidating landscape and had been sure that, whatever future settlers might talk about on a regular basis, one topic would always be the weather.

Nor did it take long before the settlers began to arrive. Rivendale's discovery attracted the inevitable attention from the nearest stellar nations. Alaundril, located in the Tendril system, and the Regency of Bluefall, based around Aegis, got in first and

settled their claims in 2492, splitting the colonization rights
70–30. It was only a few years after the first colonization parties
arrived that a completely unforeseen complication arose. Rivendale turned out to already be inhabited by intelligent life.

Gabriel had checked this aspect of the planet with some care.
His acquaintance with Enda had made him more curious about
alien life than he had been during his marine years, and he had
not been surprised to discover that it had been a fraal xenobiolo-
gist who stumbled on the truth. Riglia had been known since
Alaundril and Bluefall's Regency conducted the first joint pre-
colonization survey. Long, graceful, translucent creatures,
gossamer-thin, like ribbons of shimmering air, they excited some
brief interest. Though avian, they were very unlike other avian
species so far discovered. They spent their whole lives in the air,
subsisting on airborne algae and plankton native to the high mists
of the Rivendale mountain chains. The fraal, who with various
other scientists had come to study the unique Rivendale ecosystem, had looked up at a passing riglia, glinting and wreathing its
rainbowy way past in the warming sun of early noon, and had
thought, *Cousin, you are fair.* The fraal had not expected the
chilly and pragmatic response, tentative but clear. *You are no
cousin of mine, but you are right.*

The fraal, a mindwalker as well as a scientist, had gone to the
authorities and explained that they had a problem. The riglia were
fully aware that their planet was being colonized—or from their
point of view, invaded—and were furious. The Alaundril and
Regency authorities were annoyed but also sensible enough to be
cautious. There was no chance of reversing their own plans and
removing the colonies. That would have constituted an unaccept-
able loss of status for both nations, but they stopped further colonization, citing concern about the local ecology.

Gabriel, during his investigations, had reason to smile at that.
It was not the Rivendale ecology that was in danger. Humans and
fraal who lived on that world literally had to hang on by their
nails, suspended more or less between heaven and earth in a
realm where air pressures could range from near vacuum to

nearly three bars down in the deepest canyons.

The one city, Sunbreak, perched precariously on a nine-kilometer high col between two fourteen-kilometer high mountains. There, two thousand people lived—breathing deeply, Gabriel thought, and being very careful where they put their feet. Some intrepid homesteaders had struck out into the surrounding mountain range to make themselves small farms, terracing some of the less intractable, lower reaches and collecting water from the warmweek mists with condensers. It was a dangerous life. The riglia regarded any damage to their environment, no matter how minimal, as damage to them and were likely enough to attack solitary humans simply out of pique. There were other creatures, like spidermist, that would strip the flesh off you right down to the bones without pique being involved.

"Hey, *Sunshine!* Everything all right over there?" Helm's voice came over comms.

"No problems at all," Gabriel said. "You two have a quiet time?"

Helm chuckled. "When Delde Sota is around, you wouldn't ever describe anything as 'quiet.' She reprogrammed my entertainment system somehow—"

"Correction: did no such thing," came a sharp voice from the background. "Augmented gamma correction for imagery player. Long overdue."

"All the colors of everything are strange now," Helm muttered. "I liked my playback the way it was."

"You have brought this on yourself, Helm," Enda said, unstrapping herself from her seat beside Gabriel. "It is a mechalus's business to seek perfection in the machinery around her, as well as the machinery which *is* her, unless you desire the doctor to reshape her personal ethics while riding with you."

"Don't start with me," Helm said, though there was humor in his voice. "Got a hail from Terivine control down in Sunbreak. They've got a spot ready for us at the port."

"Good," Gabriel said and checked his coordinates. "Not a big place, that. Are they going to warehouse us somewhere else after we land? They can't have more than a few acres of active space down there."

"I know. It's like landing on a dinner plate. No matter. You just follow me down."

"Helm, have you been here before?" Enda said.

"No," said Helm, "but I'm here to ride shotgun, which means I go down first and impress everybody. Stay back a couple kilometers."

They rode their system drives in toward Terivine then let the planet's gravity well pull them in. This was one of the few parts of piloting that still made Gabriel nervous: waiting for the feel of the air to make a difference to *Sunshine*'s flight characteristics. It was not that she was a tricky or difficult ship to manage in atmosphere, but the speed with which atmospheric densities varied sometimes made for a rocky ride until Gabriel could work out which attitude the ship preferred on the way in. Terivine, with a "sea level" pressure much higher than most worlds', could produce problems during landing if the sequence wasn't carefully managed.

The problems did not materialize, and Gabriel followed Helm down through the banks of mist—almost too thin to be thought of as cloud—which layered the upper atmosphere. After a few minutes, they broke out of these and into an intermediate layer of clear air above the highest mountains. Gabriel shook his head at the broad, jagged, green and cream streaked landscape below them, all warm-tinged from Terivine's orange-yellow light. On the milky, misty horizon lay wave after wave of fiercely jagged mountains, like a frozen sea. Fog lay far down between them in most of the valleys, hiding greater depths. "Forbidding" was one word that immediately occurred to Gabriel at the sight of the place. Too much vertical and not enough horizontal!

It was a beautiful place as well. Gabriel liked mountains and mountainous worlds. He liked to stand and look up at a landscape that was far too big to be conquered, a kind of reminder that humans might be a great power among the worlds, but single beings still had to fight their own battles with the physical universe. And the physical universe sometimes had them completely outclassed.

From *Longshot*, Helm grunted and said, "Deep valleys down there. Full of those . . . what did they call them . . . Rigla?"

"Riglia," Gabriel replied. "Very annoyed people, if I got the right impression. I wouldn't waste my time trying to have a friendly chat with the natives."

"Wouldn't normally have been on my list anyway," Helm said. "All they've got are little cilia, if I remember what you told me before we left Grith. Can't pick things up, except with their minds . . . Don't think they'd go in big for arms sales."

Gabriel gave Enda a sideways look as they dropped deeper into the atmosphere. "Think you might make some sales down here?" he said.

Helm chuckled deep. "There are humans here," he said. "No matter where they live, these days, what human ever feels really secure?"

Gabriel had no quick answer to that one.

"There's our port," Helm said. "About ten degrees to starboard. Watch your approach as you come in. We've got to follow this valley, and it twists."

He dropped into a broad valley that wound between two huge mountain walls. Gabriel nosed *Sunshine* down after him. There was less striation among the mountains here and more volcanic rock. Here and there, you could pick out a peak that had clearly once been a volcano, now shattered or undermined by the pressures of other local formations against it. The colors were darker—browns and blacks, mostly, old basalt, faulted in massive square or hexagonal blocks, or shattered to pinnacles by millions of years' worth of lateral pressure.

Away ahead of them two great peaks soared up, high and narrow, angling away from each other like the horns of a bull. There was a pale patch on the yoke of stone that connected them.

"That's it?" Gabriel asked.

"That's the spot. Five degrees to the right at the back of the settlement—"

"I see it," Gabriel said. His 3D display crosshaired the spot for him. As spaceports went, Sunbreak's was nearly nonexistent—you could have dropped the whole of it into one of the service yards that surrounded the port at Diamond Point.

Helm led them down, the golden light of Terivine on *Longshot*'s hull going out like a snuffed flame as he dropped between the mountains and descended toward the spaceport. It was still warmweek, but not for long. There would be no direct sunlight on the city for another ten days, until coldweek was past and the new warmweek was coming.

If city is the word I'm looking for, Gabriel thought. The pale patch had resolved itself into a scatter of buildings, some large, some small, a jumble of locally quarried stone and caststone edifices. The place certainly could not house more than a couple thousand people.

In front of them, Gabriel saw Helm skirt around the high back of the yoke between the two mountains, coming at the port beacon from the back side. He came to a halt in midair, hanging on his system drivers, not even engaging his attitudinals as yet. Showoff, Gabriel thought, getting ready to cut in his own landing systems, but he had to admire the featherlike way Helm settled himself down on exactly the tiny scrap of light-bounded tarmac. He came down so slowly that there was no way that anyone could have missed the size, orientation or number of his gun ports.

Enda's smile was small and prim. "Art comes in strange forms," she said, looking down at *Longshot* half a kilometer beneath them. "Helm? Shall we follow?"

They saw a tiny figure exit and walk around *Longshot,* looking carefully at the surroundings. The shape was carrying something that looked like a twig at this altitude and was probably capable of making a hole in a Concord cruiser.

"Yeah," Helm said, "you might as well. The locals are all looking out the windows now."

Gabriel brought *Sunshine* in and down—perhaps not with the same expertise, but in the manner of someone unconcerned with the locals' opinions. He grounded her about three meters from

Longshot, where the smaller ship's main guns covered her, and powered the drives down.

"Sunbreak control, good afternoon," Gabriel said, reckoning that it would safely be afternoon for another day and a half yet. "We have an infotrade cargo for you. Can we conclude port formalities and get the material away?"

"Formalities have already been concluded, *Sunshine,*" said a man's voice down station comms. "We're not big enough to need much in the way of paperwork here: the detectors told us you were coming."

Did his voice sound uneasy? Gabriel glanced at Enda. She reached into the 3D display between them and touched the "privacy" light.

"It is to be expected," she said. "Any world so isolated would normally have the best starfall detection hardware it could afford. They would have known the time and location of our arrival nearly as soon as we departed."

She slipped her finger away from the control-light, which dulled. "Thanks, Sunbreak," Gabriel said. "Then we'd like to dump, if you would pass us your authentication protocols. The dump addresses we have already."

Enda shifted the infotrade control systems into the front display. It filled with lines of code, as the two Grid systems— Rivendale's planetary-level one and *Sunshine*'s local portable Grid—acknowledged one another's bona fides. The code display dissolved, leaving them with the message *Discharging cargo.*

They watched the words blink. This was the part of the process that Gabriel dreaded—when the machines were in control, and being built by mortal beings in a universe where entropy was in force, could conceivably fail. If that happened, no one would blame the machines. It would be Gabriel and Enda who would be responsible. They could sue the people who installed the machinery and might someday recoup some of the losses they would have had to pay out of their own pockets for the lost data.

The display went black. Gabriel swallowed.

Darkness followed, for several seconds. Then, *Discharge*

complete, said the display. *Receiving facility backup complete and confirmed. Cleaning cycle begins.*

Gabriel sat back in his seat and said, "Look at me. I'm wringing wet."

He had never been clear about whether fraal sweated. Enda breathed out one long breath, and said, "It *is* nice when things work. Shall we go out and see about a meal?"

"Not until I shower," Gabriel said, unstrapped himself and went down the hall.

* * * * *

Some while later, Helm was coming up in the lift, and Gabriel was stretched out in one of the chairs in the sitting room in a clean singlesuit, while Enda looked over the local Grid access channels. They were spare—a few music channels, some solid or 3D entertainment, most of it stale.

"You could make some money," Gabriel said, "just bringing entertainment material in here."

"If we had cargo space to spare," Enda said, distracted by the list of local amenities, which was also brief. The lift door opened. "Look, there is a fraal restaurant here."

"Feeling the need for home cooking?" Helm said.

"Sweet heaven," Gabriel said. Helm was in a costume that could only be described as full battle armor—tunic and breeches and boots and armlets and greaves of dull refractory materials, shiny in places but mostly scarred with use, and huge pistols on both hips. "Helm, you look like a tank, but better armed."

"I always wear the armor on my first night out on a new planet," said Helm, grinning that innocent grin. "Saves me having to wear it later."

Enda laughed. "As for home cooking, I eat that every day; *Sunshine* is my home. I would simply be interested in seeing exactly *how* 'fraal' the cooking here is. Such a tiny settlement is not the kind of place you would expect to find cosmopolitan ingredients. For real fraal cooking, you would need such.

We never saw a cuisine we did not borrow from."

She and Gabriel got up. "What is it like out, Helm?" Enda said. She too had chosen to wear a singlesuit, a plasma-blue number in which Gabriel had first seen her long ago, and which picked up the vivid blue of her eyes startlingly well.

"About nineteen. A little breeze."

"No need to bother with a wrap, then. Let's lock up . . ."

They met Doctor Delde Sota on the blacktop at the bottom of the lift. She was standing and looking around her at the spectacular ebony or cream and ebony striped mountain vista, all gilded in the orange light that surrounded them.

"Opinion: gravity level enjoyable," she said.

It *was* lighter than usual: about six tenths of a gee, and there was a slight tendency to bounce until one got used to how to put one's feet down. "I wouldn't overeat in this climate," Helm said, as they walked toward the port buildings and the road into town. "Don't think it would stay down long."

Laughing and talking, they made their way into the heart of the settlement past the port buildings. Those were stone, but the business and leisure heart of the settlement was a mixture of stone and prefab. The little blocky apartment houses and shopping clusters were set amid carefully maintained but minimal landscaping, on ground which was little more than bare stone. They did not see many people—a few humans and some fraal, walking in small groups or heading home with bags or parcels of shopping from the local stores. Everything seemed quiet and peaceful, but also lonely—the influence of the terrible jagged peaks looking down from all sides, even in the subdued, prolonged afternoon light, was somber.

It couldn't much affect Gabriel's mood, though. He was too relieved. "It was easy," Gabriel said as they slowed down, hunting for Enda's fraal restaurant, which was supposed to be on the Main Thoroughfare. "The software really did handle it all."

"That was just one run," Enda said. "I would not be inclined to class this work as 'easy' just yet. We may have come out full, but will we go back that way? If we do not, the fine fat-looking profit we have made on this run will be undermined. If the message traffic we have brought with us from Grith does not generate some in the opposite direction, there will be no point in continuing this particular run. We will have to look elsewhere."

Gabriel nodded. "I know, but it's too soon to think about that. We just got here! Let's see what tomorrow brings."

The fraal restaurant turned out to be attached to one side of a kind of community center for the local inhabitants, a long low stonebuilt edifice, quarried from black basalt blocks and boasting a wide shallow-peaked roof of some other dark stone split in thin layers. Inside, there was light and talk; large round lights hung down over a great number of trestle tables spread over a wide expanse of stone floor. People, humans and fraal and a mechalus or two, glanced up with interest and bemusement from their meals or drinks as Gabriel, Enda, Helm, and Delde Sota came in and looked around.

From off to their right came the smell of something aromatic frying. Gabriel thought it smelled like ginger. Dining tables were gathered there around a circular counter, and Enda sniffed the air with delight. "I swear, that *is* delya," she said, heading off in that direction. "What wonders the worlds hold!"

The others followed her and found a table. The fraal-gentleman who was doing the cooking came out to greet them, and he and Enda began a long conversation in their own language, with much bowing and waving of hands. After a moment the chef went off, and Enda looked at them all, slightly abashed.

"He will be happy to bring you menus if you want," she said, "but I think we are onto something excellent here. Will you let me order for you?"

"Everything but the booze," Helm said amiably.

"That I leave to you with joy," Enda said.

Shortly thereafter, they had bottles of kalwine, and small metal dishes began arriving, full of portions of cooked vegetables. At least that was what Gabriel thought they were. It became plain that the dinner was going to be one of those at which you eat a great number of unidentifiable but delicious things and are never afterwards clear about exactly what you had or how to get it again.

The laughter and the talking at their table got ever more cheerful and seemed to spread as the evening drew on (though the light outside didn't change) and the community center around them filled with people eating, drinking, talking, and laughing. Gabriel found himself enjoying the good cheer, though he wondered if there wasn't a slightly nervous cast to it—as if practically the whole community of Sunbreak was gathered in this large room, making a brave noise against the vast silence of the world outside, a world beautiful but essentially inimical, a world very much alone.

The second time the thought came up, Gabriel shook his head and poured himself another glass of the kalwine, turning his attention to Delde Sota, who was in the middle of some mechalus joke that she was telling Helm for the second time. "—couldn't find his head. Result: the captain says, 'Screw its eyes out and see if they work better.' "

"I still don't get it."

"Semantic problem," Delde Sota said, lifting her glass with her braid, while propping her chin up on both fists, her elbows on the table. " 'Head' is—"

"Excuse me," said a voice off to the left. They all looked up.

Standing by the table was a small man, dressed in the kind of long tunic and baggy breeches that some people from Bluefall favored. He was plump and round faced, with little eyes looking at them dubiously. "You the people who landed those two ships up the port this afternoon?"

"Yes," Gabriel answered.

"Infotrading?" the man said.

"That's right," Helm said.

"Well, I run the infotrading company here. Alwhirn Company. I'm Rae Alwhirn."

"Yes, we've heard of you," Gabriel said and got up to extend a hand to the man. "Pleased to meet you. Gabriel Connor—"

"The pleasure's not mutual," Alwhirn said, and looked at Gabriel's hand as if it were dirty. Then he darted a glance at Helm, and quickly away again. "Not at all. We don't want your kind here."

"What exactly would 'my kind' be?" Gabriel said.

"Speculation: competition?" said Delde Sota.

The man glared at her, then at Gabriel. "You think we don't read the news we carry? We know what you were up to in the Thalaassa system. First murder—then union-busting—"

Gabriel stared, and laughed. "*Excuse* me?"

"Those sesheyans you were hauling all over space were Employees," Alwhirn said. "You were in the middle of that big Concord PR exercise to make them look like 'free' sesheyans, poor oppressed people who got the wrong end of the stick somehow." He sneered. "The same way you did, huh? I suppose you're going to try to tell us someone set you up to make it look like you killed all those marines, your own buddies, that someone framed you—"

Gabriel was silent for a moment. "Were you there?"

"What? I read the—"

"Were you there?"

"Of course I wasn't there, I have a job to do, unlike some people who try to come in out of nowhere and take my business away. If you think—"

"What we've brought into the system is new business," Gabriel said, "from Grith and Iphus. Business you never went out of your way to find. You've been bringing in data from Aegis and Tendril and not much else. Now if I wanted to—"

"See that," Alwhirn growled. "You come to spy on us and—"

"Your business here is a matter of public record," Gabriel said wearily. "If you—"

"So is yours," Alwhirn said. *"Murder.* Get out of here before you regret having come in the first place."

Gabriel took a breath. "If I *was* a murderer, you'd be asking for trouble. A good thing that there are witnesses to the statement."

Alwhirn glanced around the table then turned away. As he went, he muttered something. They stared after him, but he was out the front door a few seconds later. Other people turned to watch him go, then looked at Gabriel and the others. Not all the looks were friendly.

Gabriel sat down again, and looked at the glass of kalwine in front of him, just refilled. All of a sudden it had lost a great deal of its savor.

"*That* was strange," he said.

"Granted," Enda said. "What do you make of it?"

Delde Sota shook her head. Helm, for the moment, was looking toward the door and windows. "Bad news travels fast," he said under his breath.

"It's Infotrade Interstellar that I would have expected this kind of thing from," Gabriel said. "Not the local independents!" He pulled his glass close again. "What's the matter with these people, anyway? It's not as if we're taking food out of their mouths."

"I have seen much human behavior in my time," Enda said, "but I do not consider myself a specialist. Though the likeliest answer would seem to be that, for some reason, they feel threatened. As for I.I., they sent us a very pleasant message."

"*What?*"

"It's in *Sunshine*'s Grid mail center—it came in while you were showering. It is nothing fulsome. They acknowledge our presence here and wish us luck."

That piece of news made Gabriel shake his head. "As for the rest of that, the idea that VoidCorp's Employees have a *union*—"

"Very likely they do," Enda said. "Probably it seems, superficially, to have the same kind of rules that other labor unions do, though membership is probably mandatory . . . .as Employee status remains mandatory."

Helm was still looking around, watching the people who were watching them. "No great interest," he said after a moment. "I think we're safe for the moment."

"Query: later?" Delde Sota said softly.

"There is no way to tell," Enda said, sounding rueful. "With the active opposition of some of these people, our business may not be pleasant."

Gabriel frowned. "We'll see, but as for Alwhirn—does he think he owns this system? I don't want trouble with him, but if he wants to start it, he's going to get some back, possibly more than he bargained for."

A silence fell at that. Then Delde Sota said, forcefully, "Dessert."

They had dessert, a flambéed concoction that drew applause from some of the tables around them. They paid their bill, said "good evening" to the people around them, congratulated the fraal chef, and then walked back to the ships, making little of the uncomfortable incident during dinner. Gabriel did his best to sound untroubled as they went. He was tired and that helped him. One issue kept rearing up at the back of his mind to be dealt with.

Terivine had no drivesat relay. All its data came to it via info-traders. No information could have come to Rivendale about Gabriel's arrival before today.

How did this guy know so quickly that I was here and who I am?

Helm and Delde Sota went off to *Longshot.* Enda and Gabriel headed back to *Sunshine,* secured her, and turned in. As Gabriel lay down and spoke his light out, the thought hung in the darkness there with him for a long time, all too clear.

So much for my new beginning . . .

Chapter Four

THE NEXT MORNING was still the same afternoon, although the orange light of the sun came in at a lower angle. Light slid in long golden rays between the peaks and tangled in the mists that were starting to rise to higher levels now, filling the invisible valleys below like water. Warmweek was fading, that leisurely afternoon tarnishing down to a brassy orange pre-sunset hue, a light with color but progressively less warmth.

Gabriel stood on the cracked gray tarmac outside *Sunshine* and looked across at the fanglike peaks serrating the horizon on all sides. The landscape well suited how he felt at the moment—hemmed in and unable to escape the atmosphere of silent, low-level threat, no matter how far he went. And not so low-level, he thought, thinking of Alwhirn's angry, frightened face last night.

How did they find me?

It was a good guess that someone at Diamond Point had been spying on *Sunshine* and her crew, watching to see where they were going. That information would have been no secret for a day and a half before their departure when they filed their starfall/starrise plan. Someone gets into a ship, Gabriel thought, and hurries here with the news that we're coming and what we're coming for. He recalled again the edgy sound in the port controller's voice when they had come in. "The detectors told us you were coming."

Yes, Gabriel thought, and who else?

Who would have the funds and inclination to send someone all the way over here in a ship when a holomessage could have done as well? We could have been carrying a message like that ourselves, Gabriel thought, and we'd never have known it. It would certainly have been cheaper.

But there had been a couple of hours between their arrival and Alwhirn's appearance at their table. *Am I just being paranoid?* Gabriel thought. *Did he receive a message about us in the same load we brought in, or did he just hear gossip about us from the port people?* In a place this small, a new infotrader suddenly turning up in the system would be discussed.

Gabriel sat down on one of *Sunshine*'s landing skids and gazed out at the morning-cum-late afternoon. He hadn't slept well. It had been another of *those* dreams last night, a repetitive conflict of light and shadow. Flares of brilliance lashed out against some inward-pressing darkness, all of it haunted by unexplained feelings of fear and excitement. Gabriel took these dreams for some kind of obscure message from his subconscious, though he had no idea what the message might mean.

Something to do with starrise and starfall, he thought. He was not yet sufficiently inured to them that the excitement of a jump failed to move him. While living in a Concord Cruiser that carried the marine complement of which he was part, Gabriel had gone through starrises and starfalls without comment. They were pilots' business, an insignificant artifact of getting where you were going. Now that Gabriel flew himself, suddenly drivespace was a serious part of the day, and he listened to whatever Helm or Enda might say about the fables and rumors of starfalls—what caused the differing color, which ones were supposed to be lucky . . . Gabriel shivered.

The sound of the lift coming down distracted him. Amazing how noises that would have been completely lost in the rumble at Diamond Point now seemed louder among the peaks and rolling mists. All sound fell into that moist quiet as if into a sack where they were dampened and lost. That silence seemed to say, *There are very few of you. We can wait. Some day you will be gone.*

"What a beautiful morning," Enda said. She walked out to join him, looking around at the swirling, churning mists and hugging herself against the cool dampness of the morning.

"Nnnh," Gabriel said. He disliked pouring cold water on her pleasures, but in his present mood he had trouble seeing the beauty.

"Did you sleep well?"

"Not really."

"That dream again?"

Gabriel shrugged. "I think so, but I may be getting used to it now." *Not that it was any easier to bear while he was inside it. At least it doesn't make me wake up yelling any more.*

Enda nodded. "I am still thinking about our gentleman at table last night," she said.

"Not much of a gentleman."

"Well, his manners were not the best. His reasons for being angry with us did not ring particularly true, either." She sat down on the skid next to Gabriel. "I cannot help feeling that he was more frightened than angry, but of what or whom?"

Gabriel shook his head. "Don't ask me until after I've had my chai," he said. "Come to think of it, don't bother asking then, either. I'm still wondering how we're going to pick up any business with this guy out poisoning people's minds against us, and whether it's realistic to think we're going to get any business at *all* when the place is this small."

"I would definitely wait until you have had your chai," Enda replied. "You should also walk around and talk to people. Our business is to see exactly what the other firms have been doing here, then examine which parts of the local market they may have missed."

Gabriel gave her a cockeyed look. "You sound like some kind of sales representative."

She chuckled. "Well, so I was, once long ago."

Gabriel sat back against the upright of the landing skid and laughed at that. "I thought you were in suit maintenance."

"Oh, I did that too," Enda said. "Gabriel, when you live in a great spacegoing city, conscientious marketing is something you cannot ignore, especially when you tend to keep your contacts with other species to a minimum. You will not succeed if you go barging into established business relations between planets or between a planet and another free trading facility that serves it. Trade wars only make life harder for everyone . . . and eventually people die of them. One must rather work to become part of a network, a cooperative structure." She looked out across the mountains. "Life among the stars is too hard as it is—resources all stretched too thin over the terrible distances, and communication much too difficult and expensive to waste on attempting to destroy infrastructure that others have built. To compete without an eye to your competitors' continued success as well as yours is to court disaster."

Gabriel had to shake his head at that. "Enda, are all fraal as *nice* as you?"

Enda looked at him in some shock, then she began to laugh softly. "Many are far nicer. I have had my failures, which is one of the reasons I do not travel with my own kind any more. I thank you, Gabriel." She looked out into the mist, then turned to him again. "Meanwhile, you have driven out of my mind what I came out to tell you. There is more mail for you in the ship's system."

"For me? Where from?"

Enda had pulled her hair down out of its long tail and began braiding it. To Gabriel, it looked like the braid Delde Sota used, which reflected the Sealed Knot of her particular medical profession—a four-strand braid with a strange sort of "hiccup" in its pattern.

"Some of the data we dumped came back to us through the local sorting facility," Enda said, weaving the long silver-gilt strands over and under one another, "at least, if I read the log files correctly. A good question whether I do. The software manuals are not exactly lucid, but certainly there is a packet of mail for you."

"Probably hate mail from our friend from last night."

Enda raised her eyebrows. "I hardly see why he would waste the money when he can deliver his hatred in person. But no. This was data we brought in with us."

"Huh," Gabriel said as he gazed over toward *Longshot*.

"No sign of them yet?"

Gabriel shook his head.

Enda shrugged. "After last night, I think that Helm did not care to sleep right away. He told me before we left Grith that he needed to do more work on his external security and surveillance fields. I doubt he would have felt comfortable about dropping off while his work was still incomplete."

Gabriel shook his head. "I'm still not sure I understand why he's doing this. Coming over here for no particular reason, watching out for us this way. . . ."

Enda looked over toward *Longshot* as she finished her braid. "I would not care to hazard detailed guesses," she said. "But this time I doubt he is repaying Delde Sota any favors."

"Think not?"

Enda turned away from *Longshot,* looking toward the eastern sky, which was gradually beginning to deepen toward something that would be dusk in another day and a half or so. "It must be a bitter life at times," she said softly, "being a mutant—having to hold your own worth like a shield in front of you, never knowing for certain what a 'normal' human might think. Friendship, even casual friendship that does not much touch the depths, could be a precious thing to someone in such circumstances." She gave Gabriel a look. "I would not say our dealings with Helm are all one-sided, or that we do not offer him something he much needs, though it might seem a light and easy gift to us."

Gabriel nodded. It was not a subject he would normally have discussed with Helm. He had a feeling that one of the reasons their friendship worked was precisely because he didn't think about Helm being a mutant. "You may have something there. As for Delde Sota . . . who knows why she does what she does? Though she *is* curious about most things."

"There was not much for her at Iphus, perhaps," Enda said, "even when it was busiest. Mechalus, too, have their problems with the world outside Aleer and the Rigunmor sphere of influence, people who feel that it's wrong to meddle with biological life. The Hatire are only the most outspoken of many." She shrugged. "Perhaps Delde Sota sees it as a worthwhile challenge to be out among those who live another kind of life. Perhaps something else is on her mind. Certainly she will have a chance to explore other modes of existence besides the strictly virtual or mechanical. There is not much to keep a former Grid pilot busy here." She looked out at the mists, which had begun to billow up almost to the level of the yoke between the two mountains.

"Look," Gabriel said, gazing westward.

Enda followed his glance. Away off in the distance, in the high airs above the mist, they could see a few thin, twisting ribbons of translucence, writhing and weaving their way through the lengthening afternoon, catching the light of Terivine high above the mountains in brief gleams of tarnished gold.

"Riglia," Enda said, and shivered.

"They won't bother us," Gabriel said. "They avoid this place, supposedly. Too many well-armed humans and others."

"I would wonder," Enda said, standing up again. "I think I will have some chai myself."

"Wait for me," Gabriel said. "I want a shower, and then I'll have a look at that mail."

* * * * *

As it happened, the mail came first, and the shower was forgotten as Gabriel sat down at the Grid panel and touched the controls that brought up the mail. He keyed in his passwords and then took a quick breath as the package of mail de-encrypted.

"Altai!" he said. "It's from the research service."

Enda came to look over his shoulder, handed him a mug of chai, black as he preferred it, and stood sipping her own while Gabriel scrolled through the great blocks of text that suddenly began to spill out into the display.

"What is it?" she said. "They have used one of those hard-to-read typestyles again."

"Ricel," Gabriel said. "They've finally turned up something on him."

"Ricel" was not the man's real name or his only name. He had served on board the Star Force cruiser *Falada*, to which Gabriel had last been posted. Ricel's position was ostensibly in engineering. Early on in Gabriel's assignment to *Falada*, he had been instructed by Concord Intelligence—to which he had been "seconded"—that Jacob Ricel was his shipboard contact, someone who might get in touch with him and have him investigate one matter or another. It had only happened once or twice. The problem was that the last intervention Ricel asked Gabriel to perform was the passing of a small data chip to someone aboard ship. The person in question was the assistant to the Ambassador Plenipotentiary dealing with the crisis in the Thalaassa system to which *Falada* had been sent to intervene. The data chip was not a message coded in solid form, as Gabriel had thought, but the trigger for a detonator in a shuttle transporting the ambassador and her party. Everyone aboard died. One of Gabriel's best friends, acting as marine security escort aboard that shuttle, had died.

The deaths had happened in atmosphere, so the government of the planet Phorcys demanded the right to conduct the trial, much to the annoyance of the Concord Marines. To their even greater annoyance, the trial body refused to convict Gabriel of the murders—though he had not been exonerated either. Gabriel's insistence that Ricel had given him the data chip and that Ricel was his Intel contact aboard the ship had been rejected by the marine prosecutors. Elinke Darayev, *Falada*'s captain, had insisted that Ricel had *not* been Intel, and she should have known. This left Gabriel with the question: who *was* "Ricel"? Apparently he was now dead, due to a space suit accident, but Gabriel could not let matters rest there. He needed whatever information he could find on the man if he was to clear himself.

Gabriel shook his head in combined annoyance and satisfaction. "I can't believe it. We spent six weeks with this stuff in our hold, and I never knew it. We have *got* to have a word with our sorting software."

"I am not sure the software was at fault," Enda said. "We left in a rush, and there was no time to de-encrypt or sort the material.

Next time we will leave in a more leisurely manner and do our sorting first."

"You bet," Gabriel muttered. The display flickered, and several images, each tagged below with more text, came up.

Gabriel took a deep breath. "Look at these," he said.

Three images rotated there. They were all the same if you looked past superficial differences. One of the images was clear, the other two grainy, but this had not bothered the AI software that Altai had been using to hunt through public records in the systems it had scanned. Gabriel had paid extra for the image-search facility. Now he saw that the extra investment was beginning to pay off.

"There were at least three of him at one time or another," Gabriel said quietly. "How many lives has this guy *had?*"

"Discovering that may take some time," Enda said, looking over his shoulder. "Does it not say there that 'Ricel' has died?"

"Yeah, well, I'm becoming suspicious about such claims when they're made about anyone attached to this face." Gabriel shook his head. "Why doesn't he change it?"

"What?"

"His face. You'd think he would, if he really wanted to stay secret. Look at this one: a mustache, but that doesn't hide anything. And this one, the tattoos are a distraction, but take them off and it's still the same face. Why doesn't he have his nose done, or his hair color or skin color changed, or the hairline inhibited from 'life' to 'life'?"

Enda tilted her head to one side. "I have no answer for you, but it does seem to be the same man."

Gabriel studied the four precis. "These span ten years," he said. "What was he doing in between? Where else was he that hasn't shown up yet?" He sighed. "These results aren't bad, but Enda, the price!"

"You must not count the price," she said, "not while you are still hunting answers, not unless you value your peace of mind so cheaply. We are not without resources, and we made a healthy profit on this run."

"Will we make another, though?" Gabriel said, sitting back. "Any offers on the return-leg screen this morning?"

She tilted her head sideways again, this time more slowly. "Nothing yet, but there is no need for buyers at this end to be sudden, especially not with Mr. Alwhirn in his present mood. If anyone wants to ship data with us, well enough; but they would have shipped with Alwhirn or I.I. before now. No one in so small a place is going to rush off to give their business to someone they have never seen before. Time will be taken to study us. Therefore we should be out and about today. We should see about resupplying."

"With what? We're full up after Diamond Point—"

"You know that, and I know that, but the storekeepers here will not. Besides," Enda said with an amused look, "I want to find out where Oraan, our chef of last evening, is getting his vegetables. Canned they may be, but they are of high quality. If he is growing them, then we will be back here, infotrading or not."

Gabriel got up and stretched, thinking about his shower. Enda gave the screen one last look, then went down the hall. After a moment, she stuck her head out of her cabin door and looked at him. "I wonder about these dreams you have been having. They seem to be making you circumstantial."

"Maybe they have," Gabriel said, uncertain what she meant.

She came down the hall with the plant pot. "Good. Meanwhile, a little natural sunlight can do this no harm."

"You know what I think?" Gabriel said. "I think that thing's made of some kind of plastic. It's a joke on a poor human who doesn't know any better."

Enda smiled. "When I play a joke on you, it will be a better one than that. When you are ready, let us go into town and see about those vegetables and anything else we can discover."

* * * * *

They went out an hour or so later. By the time they finished their stops at the various shops and businesses in Sunbreak, lunch was starting when they finally got to the community center.

Enda sat down with a glass of the bubbling water and started making notes on the morning's discussions. Gabriel had chai while he gazed out the windows at the extraordinary view, row after row of serried peaks in the now-fading afternoon light.

Rather to his pleasure, they didn't stay alone for long. A couple of people came along to sit and chat with them. "Just curious," said the lady, an Alaundrin, who sat down with a tall mug of some pungent kind of hotdraft that Gabriel couldn't identify.

"Nosey," said the man who sat down across from her, a short broad man with a big nose and merry little eyes.

The lady was Merielle Esephanne. Her husband was still in the office taking care of some paperwork in his job as a secretary to the Regency Expansion Bureau, the department that oversaw infrastructure matters in Sunbreak. The man introduced himself as Rov Melek, cousin to a homesteader growing beef lichen and broadleaf maleaster on a small terraced farm just across the valley from Sunbreak on Black Mountain.

"But they're all black around here," said Gabriel.

Rov winked at him as he turned around his own glass of chai, waiting for it to cool. "Makes it easier to name them."

Enda looked up from her notes. "*You* are responsible for the vegetables. Let me finish this, then I want to talk to you about those."

Rov grinned. "We're becoming a gourmet's paradise," he said to Gabriel. "People come, oh, tens of light-years for our food, but it would be nice if more of them came back more than once. We get so many of these one-time charlies."

Gabriel chatted with the two Sunbreakers while Enda finished her notes. As he had suspected, it turned out that most people in the settlement worked for either Alaundril or the Regency of Bluefall. There was not a lot else to do here. However, the settlers seemed to consider one administration about as good (or bad) as the other, and Gabriel heard Merielle or Rov refer to "the government" and mean both sides of the colonial divide.

Maybe, Gabriel thought, it's because this place is so small and isolated. Making a big deal over one side or the other wouldn't get you far. They're all stuck here together, a long way from anywhere else.

They were eager enough to hear what news Gabriel had to pass on from Grith. Everyone in town knew about Rae Alwhirn's outburst of the previous evening, but no one knew what it was about or had connected recent events at Corrivale with them. Merielle and Rov listened without much comment to Gabriel's much-edited story of his visit to Rhynchus in company with Enda and Helm.

"That guy," Rov said in reference to Helm, "looks like he might own a gun or so."

Gabriel agreed. When he finished telling about their arrival at Grith and the standoff between a VoidCorp dreadnought, *Falada,* and a group of Concord cruisers, Merielle whistled softly. "There's why Rae got so upset. He's sure that VoidCorp's trying to shut him down."

Gabriel blinked. "But they were trying to shut *us* down. I'm not sure why he was angry at us for being on the wrong side of them . . ."

"Rae's got more conspiracy theories than a riglia's got cilia," Rov said. "He's always been on a hair trigger, seeing something hiding behind every rock. He's had a lot of trouble in his business. Bad luck, mostly. A power failure a while back cost him a lot in insurance; there were lawsuits. . . . Now Rae thinks everything that happens around here is aimed at him." Rov scratched his head. "Have to admit, I haven't seen him pop like that before. He must think you're out to get him in particular because you're info-traders."

"Did he treat the I.I. people the same way?" Gabriel asked.

"Frikes, no, they were here six years before he started. They've been trading in and out of this system, to Aegis and Tendril all that while, but you see the problem." Rov gestured around him. "We're so small here, and so quiet. Our Grid's so small you could spit across it. A lot of people don't like the idea of them," he jerked a desultory thumb over his shoulder, "the riglia."

Enda pushed her notepad aside. "Do you not like the idea of them either?"

"Don't see that they care about my opinion one way or the other," Rov said, "but they were here first. We didn't know when we came that they were more than dumb animals. A lot of us came a long way to settle here, got ourselves set up, and then what do we find?" He pulled his head down between his shoulders as if seeking protection from something. "Government shoulda checked things out more carefully before they let anyone settle here, before those fraal scientists came in and told everybody 'Guess what, you've got company.' " He sighed. "Sorry, lady. I know it wasn't your fault. Anyway, there are people leaving all the time. The feeling that you're being watched . . . it gets to you after a while."

"I've felt that," Gabriel said. "An uneasy kind of feeling."

"That's right," Merielle said. "Well, it's the riglia, I suppose. They're mindwalkers, so they can do that. There are a lot more of them than there are of us." She sighed. "Some day maybe there'll be nobody but them here again, but meantime a lot of us have spent everything we had to come here. We can't just go. There's nothing to go *with*."

Gabriel nodded and took a drink of his chai.

"This isn't a busy part of space, anyway," said Rov. "No other well-settled systems are nearby. There are some useless ones—stars but no planets, or planets that're just rocks, no point even in mining 'em. You hear stories, rumors about one world or another that got missed when they did the surveys, but you can't take things like that too seriously."

"They missed Rivendale that same way," said Enda, "when they first came through the system. No one thought so small a dwarf star would have a planet."

"Well, true enough, lady," Rov said. "It's rare, isn't it? Hasn't happened since, though you keep hearing stories and rumors. People go out looking for those places and don't come back." He dropped his voice lower. "And there are ships out there, too, that nobody knows where they come from—out in the empty spaces, the 'back of the Verge,' the Barrens. Nobody sensible goes out that way. Crazy explorers, *they* go, but you don't see them again. We had a couple through here," he said as he reached for the wine bottle, "had themselves an exploration contract from the CSS and everything. They were on their way to someplace out past Coulomb."

Gabriel looked at Enda. "What's past Coulomb?"

"Nothing that I know of."

"That's just my point," Rov said, "but they were going that way anyhow. Something called Elder? Caldera? Something . . . No, Eldala, it was."

Enda shook her head. "I have never heard of it."

"You're not alone. But off they went, she and her friend, and we haven't seen hide or hair of them since. Hair enough her friend had, too." Rov chuckled.

"Maybe," Gabriel said, wondering what Rov's last comment might have meant but deciding not to press it. "Were they just more of the one-time visitors you mentioned?"

"I wouldn't have thought so," said Rov, drinking the last of his drink and eyeing the glass absently. "The one lady, the human, she was real taken with this place. She said it reminded her of home. Wouldn't want to think what her home looked like, but she said she was definitely coming back." He shrugged. "Infinity only knows where she is now. And there've been others. A few went missing in transit to somewhere else—Aegis, Richards, Anna-hoy—and didn't turn up at the other end. They found one or two ships, but no sign of the pilots or passengers. *That* was weird."

"Where were the ships found?" Enda said.

"Just floating near their outward transit points. One of those was strange. The detectors said the ship had gone into drivespace, all right, but it didn't transit. No starfall."

"Bad coordinates," Gabriel said, "but nothing happens when you do that. You just pop out in the same place a few seconds later. You feel stupid—"

"This wasn't like that. The one ship, *Wauksha* its name was, should have come out at a halfway point on its way to Aegis. It didn't, though the detector showed it on its way. It turned up just out of system, over by Terivine A. They were lucky to have found it. The star would have pulled it in, in a few more weeks. The other ship was by its departure point, but it never left. They just found it, empty. . . ."

"That is very odd," Enda said.

Marielle shook her head. "Not half as odd as some things you hear," she said softly. "Remember the ghost ships, Rov?"

Rov nodded. Marielle looked over at Enda and said, "A few people have seen this, over—what—two, three years or so? They made starfall, were coming in on system drive, and saw something on the way in. Like a big ship that just came up out of drive-space, then went away again. Can't be a ship. A ship would have to recharge. But this thing, this big dark ghost, just comes bobbing up out of drivespace like a sat relay and sinks right back again."

Gabriel did not look at Enda, though he very much wanted to. "What was it?"

"No one knows," Marielle said, "but it gives me the jillies. I may not be on kissing terms with the laws of physics, but I don't like hearing about things that can just throw them out the door like that, either."

Rov nodded. "One guy—didn't hear this myself, a friend of a friend heard it—one guy who saw this said, 'I thought it was alive. It looked at me before it went off again.' "

"Ghost stories," Gabriel said.

"Oh, I know," said Rov. "Every place has them. Some of them are just that. People like to scare themselves, but this is different. You won't hear people talking about these a lot. Maybe some folks here are a little superstitious. They think that these things might creep closer if you mention them."

It was a warning, however gently phrased. Gabriel nodded. "You're right, of course, but you were telling us about Rae Alwhirn."

The conversation veered off into good-natured gossip after that, though Gabriel had trouble concentrating on the chat after what he had just heard. He and Enda had seen just such a huge vessel come looming up out of drivespace at them before sinking away into the darkness again. A deep uncomfortable green color it had been . . . very like the little green ball bearing ships that had come after them way out in the Thalaassa system, the ones with the pilots who had once been alive but were not any more. Gabriel reminded himself once more that he needed to talk to Delde Sota about what had come of the autopsy she had done for them at Iphus Station on the body of one of those vessels' pilots.

He stretched, turned to yawn, then froze as he caught a glimpse of someone off to one side of the room. Slowly Gabriel turned back forward again and leaned on the table.

". . . but it's been busy anyway," Rov was saying. "Unusual number of visitors for this time of year."

Enda looked at him, then briefly past him, with mild interest. "You mean you have a tourist season?"

"Not as such," said Rov. "Government pretty strictly controls the number of people who come in here. They're concerned about the riglia taking it wrong. You wouldn't have been affected. Info-traders aren't regulated, but a few ships came in over the past week. One was a tourist—another was a trader, bringing in entertainment solids."

"Oh really," Gabriel said, crossing another business possibility off an ever-decreasing mental list.

"Gabriel," Enda said then, "something occurs to me. I want to talk to Helm about plans for this afternoon. Do you want to come back to the ship with me? It won't take long."

"Sure," Gabriel said. "Marielle, Rov . . . see you later?"

"This evening, maybe," Marielle said. "Here's my husband coming. Rov, talk to you later."

Gabriel and Enda went out. "Gabriel," Enda said quietly to him as they made their way up the street toward the port entrance, "did you see where I was looking?"

He shook his head. "It was behind me. I didn't want to stare. I thought you were looking at what I'd been looking at."

"Perhaps. There was a woman sitting away at the back of the

room, having chai or some such. I have seen her before."

He gave her a look. "Where?"

"In the port offices at Diamond Point. She was going in as I was coming out."

"Interesting," Gabriel said, "because I saw someone here whom *I* saw back on Grith. Not at the back of the room. Over on the left side."

"What a small universe it's becoming," Enda said. "Listen, Gabriel, we have more important business. After that talk with the owner of the provisioner's this morning, I would definitely bring in a load of foodstuffs when we come again. They have little here except pre-packs and staples of the most elementary kind. You would get very tired of starch noodles if you lived here long. I think we would get good results if we brought in some of the simpler dried and preserved fish and fungus packs, vegetable dumplings and so forth—"

Gabriel went along with this, and they were well into the virtues of a major dried soup brand native to Aegis, and discussing where in the ship they would stow it by the time they got up into *Sunshine*'s lift. When they finally got inside, Gabriel laughed.

"You are incredible!"

"In what regard?"

"Your ability to talk about anything but what's on your mind."

Enda gave him a dry look. "I assure you, I am thinking about the soup as well. Wait a moment." She stepped over to the Grid access panel and touched it for local network access. "Helm?"

"Wondered when you were going to call."

"I did not want to wake you untimely. Would you and Delde Sota come over? There are some things I want to check in our mutual inventory before lunch."

"Lunch," said Helm, immediately interested. "Be right over."

Enda turned away. "We may want an excuse to come back that does not involve data, if we are unable to pick up an outward data load or another Terivine-bound load from Grith. I am more interested in your sighting. Whom exactly did you see?"

"Like you, someone from Diamond Point," Gabriel said. "She was parked over in bond a couple of slots down from *Longshot*. Little brunette woman, maybe about fifty kilos, short, with pale eyes."

"Not dark ones?" Enda said.

"No. The eyes got my attention first. She was dressed as if she was from Austrin-Ontis—you know, those layered rigs with pockets all over them—not that that proves anything one way or the other. She was exchanging docs with a port official—I'm not sure whether she was coming or going at the time. She had a little all-purpose ship, a Westhame or something similar. Light haulage, possibly converted from a live-in ship." He closed his eyes for a moment, trying to see the vessel in memory. "Fairly new. I remember thinking a fair bit of money would have been tied up in that."

"Indeed. Now both of these people are here. What would you say the odds are of this being an accident, Gabriel?"

"Hard to say. 'What a small universe it's becoming.' "

Enda reached up and thumped Gabriel on top of his head. "I will take the imitation as flattery, poor though it be. Now we face another question: which of these is the spy you have been expecting?"

"Both of them?" Gabriel said.

Enda gave him a thoughtful look. "Well, why not? We know that the Concord has evinced interest in your movements . . . if only through your friend Lorand Kharls." Gabriel snorted at the word "friend."

"Yes," Enda continued, "well, we know he has some interest in using you as a—'stalking horse,' your phrase was? Though from what you told me of your conversation with him, he was not forthcoming about what he was stalking." Enda pulled down one of the chairs and sat in it. "He could not come into this part of space without attracting considerable attention. So he has sent someone to keep an eye on you."

"Seems likely. The question is, who's the other one?"

They looked at each other.

"VoidCorp," Gabriel said.

"You would not have many friends in that camp," Enda said. "Nor would I. Nor Helm, not after Thalaassa. Even Delde Sota might have crossed paths with them. She was cautious enough about the possibility that they were monitoring her medical facility back on Iphus." She sighed. "Now all we must do is discover which of these people is working for which side."

"And do what then?" Gabriel could imagine what Helm would suggest. "Besides feed them disinformation."

"All we can," Enda said, "keeping the information as mutually contradictory as possible. Indeed, it might be wise to find some way to split away from Helm and Delde Sota, so we can see which operative follows who where." She smiled, a wicked look.

"I don't know if Helm's going to be wild about letting us go off on our own," Gabriel said.

"If we have no load to take back to Grith, that might change," said Enda. "Meanwhile we must let Helm and Delde Sota know about this. We should go into town again, seeing and being seen. If we see our spies, we should make common cause with them as fellow visitors. Buy them a drink and hear their lies so that we may more carefully shape our own."

The lift chimed. Enda moved to the lift column and touched the "allow" panel.

"What would you know about lies?" Gabriel said. "A nice respectable fraal like you."

"Only that, in life as in marketing, they have their place," Enda said. "Though you must be willing to pay the price afterwards."

* * * * *

The four of them went to lunch at the community center but didn't see the two people they wanted to see. Instead, they had to console themselves with another meal of astonishing quality. Gabriel was amazed, for in his marine days he had eaten on much richer and well-visited planets, but rarely as well as he was doing here.

"It's not just the vegetables," he said to Delde Sota as they fought over the last few spoonfuls of something brown but ineluctably delicious. "Oraan is a genius."

Gabriel managed to come up with a second spoon to get the last of whatever was in the bowl, but Delde Sota's braid came up and took it neatly out of his hand and held it out of reach. The braid had brushed Gabriel's hand in passing.

Now, amid Enda and Helm's laughter, Delde Sota said quietly, "Query: adjusted electrolyte balance recently?"

Gabriel, confused, looked at her. She ate the last spoonful of sauce and put the spoon down.

"Analysis: body electrolytes are out of kilter," she said.

"Just stress . . ."

Delde Sota shook her head. "Negation: not the kind of shifts that are stress-related. Diet changes?"

"Not until we got here. I've rarely eaten so many things that I didn't know what they were. Not even on a marine transport."

Delde Sota looked wry as she said, "Intention: to run full enzyme/endocrine series on you. Premature gray in family history?"

That brought Gabriel up short. "No. You think they're connected?"

"Etiology: impossible to judge except on case-by-case basis. Insufficient data at the moment. Require more concrete information and analysis."

"You were a Grid pilot once," Gabriel said, thinking with some distaste about what that "concrete information" was probably going to involve—blood and tissue samples and the like. Gabriel had always been able to cope with the sight of his own blood in battle, but in a clean quiet office full of ominous-looking medical instruments, blood became a completely different matter. "Can't you just sneak into my old marine records?"

"Do not have to sneak," Delde Sota said with an amused glint in her eye. As usual when dealing with medical issues, her language started to contain less of the mechalus dialect and become more common. "Copies included in your vehicle registry seals aboard *Sunshine* and in your present personal data and credit chip. However, that data is antiquated. New data is required."

Gabriel groaned. "Do I have to be conscious for this?"

"Preferable," said Delde Sota, "especially for extraction of brain tissue. Hard to know whether one is in the right spot, otherwise. You are unlikely to miss it, in any case."

Wide-eyed, Gabriel pushed back his chair. The end of Delde Sota's neurobraid came up and patted him on the wrist. She smiled at him and said, "Stress may actually be a factor. Unable to recognize joke when presented with one. Examination can wait, but not too long. Some concern about physical status."

"Uh," Gabriel said. "Uh, all right." He was having trouble with the concept of the removal of his brain tissue. He liked it where it was.

Helm was glancing around and drinking kalwine as if it was much later in the day. "No sign of them," he said. "Must have flown the coop."

"Must have. Helm, what's a 'coop'?" Gabriel asked.

"It's a small hangar," Helm replied. "Haven't seen our cranky guy here, either. What's his name, Alwhere?"

"Alwhirn," Enda said. "No, he too is conspicuous by his absence."

"Statement: no surprise, since departing plus minus twelve hours with data load," said Delde Sota.

Helm gave her a bemused look. "You been in their system?"

Delde Sota looked innocent. "Value judgment: hard to avoid," she said quietly, "since port scheduling system security similar to air in opacity and impermeability. Ship *Quatsch* in pre-loading cycle, purging tanks, overwriting data solids, usual security routines running."

Gabriel knew that some mechalus Grid pilots did not even have to physically touch a computer to infiltrate it, but knowing that in the abstract and being presented with it as an accomplished fact were two different things.

"You could get in trouble for that!"

"Requirement: have to be caught first," said Delde Sota. She lifted her glass and drank.

"Well, one less thing to worry about," Helm said. "What about us?"

"I have been up one side of the main street and down the other," said Enda, "and have found no one willing to ship data with us. Now we know why. Indeed I can hardly blame them when there is a scheduled departure imminent, and the local hauler is probably offering them better than usual rates to keep us from taking his business."

"If you'd moved a little faster," Helm growled as he downed another drink, "we might not be sitting here with empty holds our only option."

Enda looked annoyed. "Helm," she said, "it was not *I* who slept in this morning."

"It wasn't *my* business to be up early. *I* was up late taking care of you-know-what. If you had been a little sharper off the pad, we wouldn't have to—"

"Wait a minute, you can't talk to her like that," Gabriel said.

"Who says I can't, you runty little—"

It got loud and relatively content-free after that, but that was how they had planned it. Lunch was over, and the community center was beginning to empty out, but that process stopped as the inhabitants paused to watch a fraal, a mechalus, a human, and some kind of mutant all shouting at one another. Even Oraan the chef stopped in the middle of scouring a pan to watch the argument scale up. Enda caught Gabriel around the arm and dragged him away from Helm. Delde Sota, in turn, grabbed Helm and hauled him out of range of the other two. People seemed generally impressed by how strong Enda was, to be able to control such a big young man. She pushed him out the front door and marched him down the street, yelling at him like an annoyed grandmother. Behind her, at a distance, came the doctor with Helm roped up in her braid while the mutant blared threats and imprecations.

The two parties went into their separate ships and did not stir for the rest of the afternoon. Later that evening, Gabriel and Enda came out to go to dinner. They sat by themselves, looking sour and pained. The locals noticed this and commented quietly to themselves. A couple of others noticed this as well. One was a small, dark-haired woman with striking pale eyes. Another woman, dark-haired as well, but with brown eyes, was petite and dressed like someone from one of the Aegis worlds. They sat on opposite sides of the room and took no notice of one another. All their attention was on Gabriel and Enda, eating their dinner stiffly and in haste, like people anxious to get something over with and leave. Finally, they left without a backward glance. Shortly thereafter—though not so soon as to arouse any particular notice—one of the women, then another, went out as well.

*   *   *   *   *

"And?" Enda said down the comms to Helm a while later.

There was a slight pause, due to an extra layer of encryption that Delde Sota had laid into the ship-to-ship network channels.

"Nothing new," Helm replied. "Both of them are at their ships at the moment. They haven't filed any plans with Joel at the port's systems. We'd know right away if they had."

"Well," Enda said and turned to Gabriel. "Now we must make our choices. We will not be getting any Rivendale-originating data to take with us on this run. Nor do I see much point in waiting here until our competition has left."

"Not when the I.I. ship is due to arrive in another two days," Gabriel said. He was sitting in one of the sitting room chairs with his feet up and his arms folded. "I don't see why we should linger with not one, but two, of someone's covert agents sitting out there and waiting to see what we do. We ought to hop and make *them* do something, if only to annoy them."

Helm laughed at that. "All right. Hop where?"

"I'd be tempted to say back to Grith," Gabriel said, "but that seems too predictable. Also, I've seen enough of Corrivale for a while."

"You could do Aegis in three starfalls," said Helm. "It'd make sense, anyway. Once there you could see if there's any data for Corrivale or Terivine and haul it back out."

"It is not a bad idea," said Enda. "Unscheduled courier runs pay ten or fifteen percent better than the scheduled ones."

Gabriel was thinking more along the lines of how busy a system Aegis was, and how much easier it would be to lose a stalker or two there than here. "All right," he said. "Aegis in three starfalls, twenty light-years and some small change. Is there an established 'tween-jump recharge point?"

"There are a couple spots that people use," said Helm, "just out by themselves in empty space. Star called Mikoa on your second-to-last jump."

"Fine," Gabriel said and headed forward to talk to the piloting computers.

After checking the coordinates and the timings, he came back to the sitting room and said, "Helm, how soon would you feel like leaving?"

"Any time." He paused. "Delde Sota says nothing would keep her here except the food, but she's had enough beef lichen to last her a month or so."

"Well, then," Gabriel said, looking over at Enda, "anything else that needs to be done before we leave? Did you get enough canned vegetables?"

Enda sighed and said, "The ones I was interested in were not canned, and like Delde Sota, I think I have had enough of them for the moment. When we come back this way again under less pressing circumstances, I shall see about bringing some away with us. Meantime, let us go."

"Right," Helm said. "Four hours from now? Most everyone'll be in bed. No comms activity within an hour of the takeoff time. We'll do a fast heat-up to give them least warning. You'll want to program the preheat sequence for your system drive into the computer. Want a time tick?"

"Hold on and you can give it to me in the cockpit," Gabriel said, getting up to go forward again. "Wait. If we want our two ladies to follow us, shouldn't we give them plenty of warning?"

"We shouldn't give them too much of a warning," said Helm. "If they're any good, they'll catch up. In fact, how fast they catch up will indicate how good they are. If they're inept, I'd sooner find out this way."

Gabriel laughed and went up to the cockpit again. A few minutes later, *Sunshine*'s departure time was set. They would warm engines for exactly three minutes, then take off and make starfall about twenty minutes later.

"This way you've got time for a few last errands," Helm said.

"I'm not leaving the ship," Gabriel said. "I've had enough of Rivendale for now."

He glanced over at Enda. She shook her head. "Let's get out of here."

Chapter Five

F OUR HOURS LATER, Gabriel and Enda were in the pilots' seats, strapped in and waiting for *Sunshine's* preheat cycle to start. Rivendale's long afternoon was finally shading toward evening. The sun was well down below the jagged peaks, and the eastern sky was slowly purpling.

Gabriel stretched in the straps and looked out the windows. "It's a pretty place," he said, "but it's trying. So much day gets to be a nuisance, and I wouldn't even want to think about a week's worth of night. How can anyone live here and stay sane?"

"Obviously they manage," said Enda, "though I think I prefer shorter days myself."

The ship went *hhup* around them, a soft awakening hum, and half the system indicators that had been dormant or gray in the 3D display now began to show power readings as they slowly escalated. Gabriel glanced over at *Longshot*. With the sunset glancing off her windshield, it was hard to see inside; but he thought he caught a flash of motion—probably Helm giving him a thumbs-up. He returned the gesture and looked around outside the ship.

At the port building, a male figure came out the front door, looked at them curiously. After a few seconds, another human, shorter and rounder than the first, came out and looked as well. The two looked at the ships. One of them pointed; the other gestured.

"Two minutes," Gabriel said.

One of the two humans went back inside. A few moments later, *Sunshine's* comms chirped. Someone was hailing them.

"Oops," Gabriel said, reaching out to kill the local network connection. "Another systems failure. We really ought to have that looked at when we make port again."

"Somewhere else," Enda said, smiling.

Another half minute ticked by, and another. The man who had gone in now came out, and he and his companion stood watching the ships. They made no move to come any closer.

"Thirty seconds," Enda said, reaching into the 3D display to touch one of the driver displays into "query" mode. The telltale folded itself into a wider display of ship's power levels, all showing 100% or better. "Everything is as it should be."

"Good," Gabriel said.

He was looking around the field for any sign of activity, and also watching the street that led up to Sunbreak town proper. There was no sign of anyone. Am I spoiling someone's sleep over there? he thought. Wouldn't that be a terrible thing?

"Ten seconds," Enda said. "Do you want to take her up, or shall I?"

"You have control," Gabriel said. "I'm going to get into the fighting field."

Enda put her eyebrows up as Gabriel reached into that part of the display. "No harm in that," she said. "Five seconds."

The final countdown bled away, Enda said, "Now," and *Sunshine* lifted straight up, gracefully but with rapidly increasing speed. That was very much Enda's piloting style as Gabriel had observed it. Smooth acceleration, but plenty of it. Up they went, through layers of mist, over the rapidly widening terrain of jagged peaks, and up into Terivine's orange light again. With Helm pacing them off to starboard, they cleared the peaks and slanted low over the beautiful but hostile landscape. Gabriel perceived all this briefly as visual input while the fighting field was still settling over him. When it took as a schematic, bright lines and curves stitched against diagrammatic darkness with lines of galactic latitude and longitude.

"Out of atmosphere," Enda said.

Gabriel shifted his body in the seat to get the feeling of where his weapons were. The rail gun was reporting almost ready, and the plasma cannons were hot.

"That didn't take long," he commented.

"With their gravity, I would be surprised if it did," Enda said as she spun *Sunshine* on her axis to point away from Terivine and Rivendale, out toward the point where they had agreed with Helm they would make starfall. "Anything of interest behind us?"

Gabriel looked back at Rivendale in the fighting schematic and said, "Nothing coming, at least not at the moment."

He jumped then as the alarms howled. Something was coming, but not from the direction in which Gabriel was looking. The virtual display whipped around to show him the direction from which the threat now approached. Gabriel had instructed the display to disallow *Longshot* but to alert him of anything of unknown mass over a ton. Here came something, a small tight knot of light in the display with a "comet's tail" spread out behind it to illustrate course and speed.

"Another ship, all right," Gabriel said, and felt around him for the paired joysticks that were his preferred method for handling the plasma cannons.

The other ship was diving straight at him. "Helm," Gabriel said, "Company—"

"I see him. It's our friend *Quatsch*," Helm replied.

"You mean *Alwhirn?*" Gabriel said. "He wasn't supposed to be leaving for another twelve hours!"

"Damn," came Helm's voice, sounding more gravelly and annoyed than usual. " 'Plus minus twelve hours.' Sonofabitch must have sneaked right out past us while we were in the community center!"

"Even schedules can lie," said Enda. Her face set grim as she broke off to starboard. *Quatsch* came after them.

"He's not eager to try conclusions with *me*, that's plain," Helm said with some amusement as he curved around to match course with *Sunshine* again. "Let's see if I can—"

The first plasma bolts lanced by *Sunshine* much too closely for Gabriel's tastes.

"What's the matter with him?" he muttered.

"*Quatsch!*" he shouted over an open channel. "What are you doing? *Quatsch!* Alwhirn!"

No answer.

"He's not in a mood to negotiate, I would say," said Enda. "Helm, one of us is going to have to do something about this poor creature, at least enough to make him break this off. I dislike the idea of harming him, and it would do our return business on Rivendale no good, but it is preferable to—"

She threw *Sunshine* to port as *Quatsch* dived at them again, firing. The bolts went wide.

"I'm not sure that his craziness isn't some kind of act he uses when it's going to get him somewhere with his friends," Gabriel muttered, getting his own plasma cannon ready. "Helm, if your sharpshooting's better than mine, you'd better do something about this boy, because I'm in no mood for him."

"Targeting," Helm said and fired. At the last moment, *Quatsch* tumbled aside, diving away from both *Longshot* and *Sunshine*.

"Let's not bother with this," Enda said. "Helm, is your stardrive ready?"

"Three minutes for prep," said Helm, "and we'll be—Uh-oh."

Gabriel's insides twisted as he saw what Helm saw. Another ship was accelerating toward them from Rivendale.

"Small," Helm said. "Not much bigger than *Sunshine*."

"Thanks loads," Gabriel said. "It's that Westhame. That's Miss Blue Eyes."

"She doesn't have much," said Helm. "One plasma cannon. One rail gun. No help; she's alone aboard."

"Doesn't make that much difference," Gabriel muttered. It was perfectly possible to fly and fight a small ship with the computer to help you. "Enda, get us ready for starfall."

"Here comes the rest of the party," said Helm. "Third trace. Must be your brown-eyed number, I think. My good gods in a bucket of ale, what *has* she got fastened onto that thing?"

Gabriel did not much care to hear this kind of language from Helm. "What *has* she got?" he asked, eyeing their stardrive energy level indicators. They were nowhere near ready.

"Too much. I want to know where she bought it," Helm said. Gabriel could hear more than a hint of gleeful awe creeping into Helm's voice. "Hell, I wish I'd sold it to her, what a commission I'd have—"

"*Helm!*" Enda said. "Details would be useful!"

"She's got that mass cannon we were discussing," said Helm. "Don't let her get within a kilometer of you. The results could be unfortunate—"

"Damn it!" Gabriel said as *Quatsch* dived at them again, firing. "*Quatsch*, stop it! We don't want to hurt you, but if you—"

Gabriel fired in frustration, intending to miss. *Quatsch* veered past as Enda threw *Sunshine* out of the way. "I'll shoot him next time," Gabriel muttered, "I swear I will." He punched the comms open again. "*Quatsch*, that was the last piece of slack I'm going to cut you. Next time I'm going to put one right through your hold, and there goes your business. Get out of our way!"

"Go on and try," came a shrill response. "I don't care! You and your kind have tried before! You're just one more of them! Won't let a man make a decent living, you and the big companies, you're all the same—"

Gabriel could hear Enda breathe out. "He is unstable," she said, "but he might damage us. Maybe one through the rear hull would be the kindest thing—"

"Trouble," Helm broke in.

He flipped *Longshot* end for end and came streaking past Gabriel at great speed. He was firing hard and fast. Gabriel swung in the fighting field to follow where Helm was going and saw the third trace. The third ship, more massive than any of the others, swung from side to side in quick graceful curves, skillfully avoiding Helm's fire and firing something that Gabriel didn't recognize. There were no bright bolts of power or clouds of projectile vapor, just a pale streak of cloudy fire that shot out, enveloped *Quatsch* and tore it to shreds. Not an explosion—though that followed, as all the air inside the craft flew out through a hundred suddenly formed gaps. *Quatsch* became a thousand twisted fragments, spinning away in all directions while continuing briefly along the same general course.

Gabriel stared. "She killed him," he whispered. *"Why would she have killed him?"*

Enda was as shocked as Gabriel but had her mind on other problems. "Helm, where is that third ship?"

"The smaller one? Away up in 'zenith' direction now. No action. Watching."

And listening, Gabriel thought. On whose behalf?

"Possibility," Delde Sota's came over comms. "Open communications with hostile vessel."

"What for?"

"Stall," said Delde Sota. "Pump for information. Have other business to attend to."

"Right," Gabriel said. He swallowed, for all this was his fault. It was not Helm or Delde Sota that these people wanted. He opened a clear channel and said, "Pursuing vessels, this is *Sunshine*. State your intentions or be prepared to face the consequences."

"There's no point in running," said a very cool, very calm female voice. "I can outrun you. If you make starfall, that won't matter either. I'll know where you're going sooner or later and find you there. Give it up now and resign yourself to being boarded."

"You can forget that," Gabriel said, furious. "Why did you kill him? No one needed to do that!"

"You were about to," said the cool voice, "not that it matters. Everyone's going to think you did, anyway."

A terrible shock of fear ran down Gabriel's spine like ice water. *She's right. I'm the one who murdered a bunch of my best friends. Why wouldn't I kill a crazy man who gave me an excuse?*

"You can just come along with me," said the calm female voice, "or suffer the consequences."

" 'Come along with you.' For what purpose?"

"You know very well. There's interest in you that you've been avoiding with varying amounts of success, but the gameplay has to stop now. We're past that."

"Oh, are we?" Gabriel said. *Delde Sota, whatever you're up to, get on with it.*

"Don't try my patience. If you cooperate, things will be made a lot easier for you. If you don't . . ."

He felt a long tremor go through *Sunshine*, and all her displays and readouts wavered as if they had lost power for a fraction of a second. Gabriel shot a glance at Enda. She shook her head and threw *Sunshine* away in the opposite direction.

"I'm willing to disable you if I have to," said the cool voice. "You won't be dead, but you'll have a lot of repairs to make—and this poor little place isn't set up for them. When the rescue parties come up from Rivendale—if they manage to organize anything—and they discover what's happened to poor Alwhirn—"

Enda kept running. *Helm* followed, not firing, possibly to avoid interfering with whatever Delde Sota had in mind. Gabriel slipped deeper into the fighting field, getting into synch with the rail cannon. If he could get off one well-aimed shot, even from a few kilometers away, she'd have a nasty surprise.

"Stop running," Gabriel told Enda.

"What?"

"Stop running. Let her catch us."

He felt her looking at him.

"Are you sure?"

"Just do it!"

"Gabriel—" came Helm's voice.

"*No,* Helm," Gabriel said, as forcefully as he could—trying to have him get the message that he was not to interfere, without saying so openly. "I'm not going to run. I'm through running."

"I wouldn't try anything at this point if I were you," said the cool voice.

"You idiot," Gabriel shouted, "you're not as delicate with that damned thing as you think you are! I can hear atmosphere leaking, half my weapons are off line, and my rail gun's been pulled right out of track. It wouldn't fire now if I got out there and hit it with a hammer! After I spent *how* many thousand dollars having it replaced! You—"

He swore as creatively as he could under the circumstances. The woman laughed at him. Gabriel's anger made everything extremely clear for a moment as he reached for the large joystick that managed the rail cannon. For just a moment he had an image of how nice it would be to throttle that pretty little neck and watch those lustrous brown eyes goggle out. His fist tightened on the virtual control.

Slowly she came drifting in. He watched carefully, waiting. The ship was coming quite close now, less than half a kilometer away. Well out past it, *Longshot* was coasting away, watching. Closer and closer the other ship drifted. Gabriel saw the change. There had been cockpit lights. Abruptly, they went out.

Power loss. Delde Sota got into her system over carrier—

Gabriel fired the rail cannon. He had not been lying; it had indeed been pulled out of alignment by that first ripple of force from the mass cannon . . . but not *that* much. The meter-wide ball of heavy metal hit the back of her ship and took it right off, but there was not the huge bloom of silvery air that he had been expecting.

"Gabriel—" Helm said.

"Don't bother, Helm!" he yelled. "We're all right! Just *go!*"

"Going," Helm said. Liquid fire streaked up around *Longshot,* veiling her in a ferocious electric blue; then she was gone.

Ship's comms suddenly filled with the sound of more cursing, from two different sources this time. Enda tilted her head in an evaluatory way as she activated the stardrive.

"Colorful language," Enda commented.

All around *Sunshine,* blue-black fire trickled and ran, obliterating the view of the space around Terivine. Good luck, Gabriel thought distractedly. The best starfall there is, supposedly.

They vanished into the empty blackness of drivespace.

* * * * *

The next five days were as quiet as Gabriel had expected them to be, almost so much that he had trouble dealing with it.

He found himself wishing that he had more to keep him busy.

He could not rid himself of the image of *Quatsch* blooming into a thousand cracks with air pouring out of them, freezing as it came. Though he had not pushed the button, he was feeling increasingly responsible.

Whoever these people are, Gabriel thought, I don't mind them coming after me, but when they start taking out people who just happen to be in the neighborhood . . . that's another matter. If this is anything to do with Lorand Kharls, I'm going to rip his head off when I see him next.

On consideration, he didn't think Kharls was involved. The man might be manipulative, obscure, and underhanded, but Gabriel felt certain he would not have countenanced cold-blooded murder. Nor, Gabriel thought, would he have sent out anyone likely to behave that way.

Now what? he wondered. What happens when we turn up at Aegis and someone says, "Hear you killed somebody else out by Terivine." I can tell them all I like that it isn't true, but I know what they're going to think, and whoever she is, she knew too.

Who *is* she?

Who was that other one—Miss Blue Eyes, who just sat there and watched it all?

Gabriel sat in the pilot's seat a long time that first day after they jumped, trying to work out what could possibly be going on in the larger world around him. Finally, he turned to find Enda leaning over his shoulder and gazing into the blackness.

"What's on *your* mind?" he said.

She sighed. "Food. Perhaps I was not as tired of the beef lichen as I thought I was."

Gabriel gave her a look.

"Well, more than that, of course," Enda said as she sat down beside him. "Poor Alwhirn. As for Rivendale, who knows whether we will ever go back there now? What value the place might have had for us will now be lost, no matter what the investigation into Alwhirn's death may reveal. The presence there of two different agents spying on us makes it plain that seeking out 'small quiet' markets in which to work is not going to work."

Gabriel shook his head and said, "Alwhirn might have been crazy, but there was no reason to just *kill* him like that. Whoever that woman is—I don't like her. We're going to have words if we ever meet again."

"I suspect it would be more than words," said Enda. She paused for a moment, then continued, "I wonder if she killed him because it looked like *he* might actually have been about to kill *us?*"

Gabriel stared at her.

"Well," she said, "granted, there are people out there who would prefer to see you dead. Elinke Darayev, the captain who was your shuttle pilot's lover strikes me as one of these. Doubtless there are others. Are there not, at the moment, also those for whom you are more useful alive than dead?"

Gabriel brooded over that for a few moments. "Some, but if this is typical of their protection, I don't think much of their methods."

"Insofar as they leave such people with another possible hold over you," said Enda, "I would agree." She frowned. "It is too easy a tactic, now, and one which you will have to guard against in the future."

"It's likely enough to be pretty effective right now," Gabriel said. "Is it even going to be safe for me to show my face in the Aegis system?"

"Well. First of all, we are riding the crest of that news, so to speak. No one will come to Aegis with it any sooner than we will, unless a much larger, faster ship than ours becomes involved."

"Not beyond possibility," Gabriel said.

Enda bowed her head in acknowledgment. "I would suggest, though," she said, "that under the circumstances, we should go straight to the authorities when we arrive there and file a report. First of all, that would not be the act of a guilty person. Second, it may put the people who were trailing us on the defensive— however briefly. If someone comes hot-jets behind us to accuse you of murder, you will have left them in a much weaker position."

The authorities. Gabriel thought about that. All his life, the authorities had been nothing that he feared, and in the marines, he had considered himself part of "the authorities." Now he routinely found it difficult dealing with the pang of discomfort that went through him when he heard the phrase. He knew that until he cleared his name—maybe for a long time thereafter—he was on the wrong side of that invisible line and had to consider whether it was safe to speak to the people on the "right" side.

"That would probably mean one or another of the embassies on Bluefall," Gabriel said, "the Alaundrin or the Regency, since they both have a foothold in Rivendale."

"And more to the point," Enda said, "the Concord one."

Gabriel threw her a quick glance.

"Naturally you would not have to file those reports in person," she added.

"*Especially* not the Concord one," Gabriel muttered. "The Regency may be running the planet as functionally neutral, but if I walked into the Concord offices there, extraterritoriality would function. They'd arrest me as soon as look at me."

"Indeed. Well, you need not." She gave him a more thoughtful look. "Would you want to stop on Bluefall at all? That was home for you once. . . ."

Gabriel took a long breath and let it out. It had been years since he had been home—just after his mother died, in fact. As far as he knew, his father was still there, but lacking any answer to recent holomessages, Gabriel didn't know for sure and was becoming nervous of finding out. Do I want to walk up to him and have him reject me as a murderer? Gabriel thought.

"I don't know," Gabriel answered. "We don't need to, I guess, but also we don't need to decide right now. The first thing we need to find out is what data we can pick up at Aegis and where we'll go after that."

He stretched, leaned back in the seat again, and said, "It's just so unfair. I would never have killed him."

"Forensics will prove that you did not," Enda said. "We have no weaponry of the kind that destroyed Alwhirn's ship. The people who did our installations at Diamond Point will be able to verify that. There was certainly nowhere to get such equipment at Sunbreak—even if we could have afforded it."

Gabriel sighed. "I know that, and you know that, but will the people at Diamond Point testify? Who knows who might be getting at them even as we speak? Besides, considering some of the weaponry we had installed, their testimony might be more damning than helpful."

Enda got up. "I refuse to speculate in that direction," she said. "There is no point in imagining complications that may never arise. Besides, right now I am wondering how Delde Sota managed to interfere with that other ship's power."

"So am I," Gabriel muttered. "It's more like magic than anything else."

"I daresay she had a connection to comms through Helm's computers," Enda said. "Past that point, it certainly looks like magic to me as well—if by that you mean something outside natural experience. Let us just be grateful that it is being exercised on our side."

She went away and left Gabriel to his thoughts. If she was able to get into that ship's system, he thought, what else might she have been able to find out? That information was going to have to wait until they came out of drivespace.

* * * * *

The next morning, and again the morning after that, Gabriel sat down with the information about Jacob Ricel. He had time to try to work out what to do with it, but he found himself wondering whether it was really worthwhile trying to follow any of this. The information was all between five and ten years old . . . all stale. If he went back and questioned the people who had known this man, what would he find? Eroded memories, more stale data leading . . . where?

He gazed at the three faces with the three different names and wondered what other lives Ricel might have changed the way he had changed Gabriel's? How many other lives had the man

destroyed or altered out of recognition . . . and then just changed
his name and passed on into other circumstances? What kind of
person do you have to be to do things like that to people? And in
the name of what, exactly? Intelligence . . . planetary or stellar-
national security?

"Thoughts are free, they say," said Enda quietly from behind
him, "but I would pay a small fortune for yours."

Gabriel shut off the Grid access array and let it relapse to
Enda's green field again. "I sometimes wonder if this is ever
going to be worth my while."

"What? Clearing your name?"

He nodded. "I think it would be nice to forget about it, to just
go off and explore strange places where no one would know me
or care where I'd been."

"Exploration contracts . . ." Enda said, sitting down across
from him. "They are not lightly awarded. Nor are they cheap."

"Oh, I know. It's just something to think about." Gabriel
stretched. "I remember—what was his name, Rov?—talking
about that system—or was it a planet?—out past Coulomb. . . ."

"Eldala," Enda said after a moment. "Not a name I know, and
I know quite a few."

Gabriel shook his head and said, "I don't know much about
the details of survey methods. I know no one thought to look for
Rivendale because Terivine C seemed such an unlikely primary.
Could they still make a mistake like that? Miss an entire planet
on survey?"

"Or misclassify it?" Enda shrugged. "In a hurry, one may
make all kinds of mistakes. I suppose you would have to look at
the survey information."

"Well, you know, I got curious earlier," Gabriel said, and
pulled out the Grid access keypad again. He touched it in a few
places, and the waving grass vanished to be replaced by a long,
dry-looking page of figures and names.

Enda blinked at that. "Surely we do not routinely carry planetary exploration information in our own computers."

"In the raw form, yes we do," Gabriel said. "The compiled

CSS listings are there under 'Standard Reference, Gazetteer.' There's nothing more involved than that. No graphics or descriptive detail. Look, there's the name. Eldala."

"A system name," Enda said, leaning closer. "Goodness. That *is* a long way out." She squinted at the display. "Planets indeterminate. Distances indeterminate." She tilted her head to one side. "What kind of survey information is that?"

"All the listing says is 'Incomplete,' " Gabriel said. "They didn't finish. They left early for some reason. When we get at a drivesat relay, we can send off for the information and wait for it to come back."

"Morbid curiosity," said Enda.

"Well, admit it. Wouldn't *you* like to know what happened?"

Enda looked doubtful. "My guess is that it is some kind of bureaucratic hitch. A civil servant made a mistake compiling the information. It would not surprise me if someone misfiled a whole planet."

The thought of the necessary size of the filing closet made Gabriel grin. "All the same . . . we could go find out, after we've done some more infotrading, enough to get ourselves supplied."

Enda leaned on the bulkhead, musing. "You might be able to convince me," she said, "but I would want to make sure we are well equipped with emergency stores and the like, and the phymech would have to be checked again."

"Of course. The idea of a whole planet falling between the cracks . . ."

Enda shook her head. "It is interesting. Nevertheless, there is Aegis to think about first, and what may be picked up there. We will not have any difficulty finding information to haul. There are never enough infotraders to service all the deaf Grids and minor systems out this way, but we will have to consider where we might go besides Terivine."

Gabriel sat back and folded his arms. "Not much choice in the Verge," he said, "unless you want to go right back into the Stellar Ring. A long way . . ."

"I don't think so," Enda said. "Nor, I think, would you desire to get too far away from your own researches into Mr. Ricel." She stretched, so that the blue crewsuit she wore shimmered, then steadied down into matte blue again. "Aegis, Tendril, and Hammer's Star are our opportunities. Aegis is most central. Tendril—"

"No, they're not," Gabriel said.

Enda looked at him, confused. "Have I missed something? In the Verge, there are only the three drivesats."

"There's a fourth," Gabriel said. "The *Lighthouse*."

Her eyes widened.

"At the time," Gabriel said, "I didn't think much of it. I had my mind on those three pictures of Ricel yesterday, but Altai routinely sends along a news package to its subscribers. I skimmed it and forgot about it. One of the stories says that the *Lighthouse* is passing through this part of the Verge. It's going to be stopping at Aegis on its way further out."

Enda shook her head. "Now, I feel foolish, for I have not thought about the *Lighthouse* in some time. It jumps about so . . ."

Gabriel chuckled softly, for Enda was understating again. Originally that massive construction, a kilometer and a half long, had been an Orlamu Theocracy space station called the *Lighthouse of Faith*. Now it journeyed through the Verge accompanied by several Star Force cruisers and various smaller vessels, bringing trade, news, and a semblance of armed security to the scattered worlds of the Verge. It housed the headquarters of the Concord Survey Services, which supervised and assisted independent exploration contractors through the Verge and beyond. It also carried large diplomatic and trading complements, a city's worth of permanent inhabitants, and numerous docking ports, repair stations, and cargo bays. It had a larger population than some planets, was better armed than many, and had the additional advantage of a massive stardrive that could take it fifty light-years in a single starfall.

There was one aspect of the *Lighthouse* that bore some consideration. It had a drivespace comms relay. Infotraders flocked to it to transfer data when it came into or near their systems.

"Certainly we can drop our data at either the *Lighthouse* or

Aegis," Enda said slowly, "but after that . . . Gabriel, why stop there?"

Gabriel looked at her dubiously. "You're suggesting that we might hitch a ride wherever she's going?"

"The thought crossed my mind."

Gabriel considered that. The *Lighthouse*'s provenance—originally it had belonged to the Orlamu Theocracy—meant that its status in Concord terms had become peculiar. The Orlamu had no problems with the Concord refurbishing their "great experiment" after it had almost been completely destroyed by a Solar raid into their space in 2461, but they had insisted—and so had others suddenly faced with the prospect of this behemoth turning up in their systems—that it should be considered strictly a neutral facility. The negotiations had gone on for a good while, but at last the station's neutrality had been accepted by all parties involved.

"Well . . ." Gabriel said. For his own part, neutrality was all very well, but he was uncertain how it would hold if a party wanted by the Concord was suddenly to turn up inside the place. "If we wanted to pick up or drop data there, I don't think there'd be any trouble with that. Actually piggybacking *Sunshine* onto the thing concerns me. I wouldn't like to test the facility's neutrality too rigorously."

"And have it fail, you mean," Enda said. "You also mean that there are marines there, a permanent contingent."

She said nothing more, only wandered back toward crew quarters. A few moments later she came out again with the squeeze bottle she used for her plant.

Gabriel watched her water the small brown bulb, of which maybe a couple of centimeters stuck up from the surrounding gravel. "Is there something that plant needs that it might be missing?" he asked after a moment.

Enda glanced up. "As regards its nourishment or its normal growth cycle? Not at all. It is behaving perfectly normally."

"How long is it supposed to stay like that?"

"As long as it likes," said Enda. "Rather like you."

Gabriel put his eyebrows up in a way that was meant to look ironic.

Enda turned to go down to her quarters with the bottle again. "I understand that you might find it uncomfortable to be within range," she said from down the hall. "You would have to decide whether the discomfort would be so unbearable as to put aside a useful business opportunity. As for dropping data at *Lighthouse,* the 'physical ingress' rules would matter only if we had no right of egress to begin with. As infotraders, we have such a right."

She came back up the hall again and folded down her seat by the Grid access panel. "As for hitching a ride, that depends on whether we pass the usual security check when we apply for space. It also depends on where *Lighthouse* would be going after we visited her. Her schedule varies without warning and is much affected by local conditions and the political requirements of the moment. Myself, I would not disdain a fifty light-year hitch in a useful direction, but we would need more recent information on where she is headed next."

Gabriel nodded. There was no question but that the *Lighthouse* could be useful. One long starfall instead of many small ones . . .

"If you were serious about exploratory work," Enda said, "the Concord Survey Services are located aboard *Lighthouse.*"

Gabriel shook his head. "Again, I'm not sure I want to just walk in there."

Enda shrugged. "It is not a decision that needs to be made now. We should deal with Aegis first." She glanced up the hallway into the cockpit. "We now have only a little over a day until we make starrise and recharge our drives for Mikoa. While doing that, we will want to discuss this with Helm and Doctor Sota, but first things first. When did you last eat anything?"

"Uh," Gabriel said.

"Precisely 'uh,' " Enda said, getting up. "It is a good thing the starfall/starrise interval is no longer than it is. You become philosophical and would waste away unless you were reminded to take nourishment every now and then."

"You're just trying to get rid of those prepacks you got on Rivendale," Gabriel said, "the ones you've decided you don't like after all." Nonetheless, he got up and followed her down to the galley.

The *Lighthouse*, he thought.

Why not?

Chapter Six

TWO DAYS LATER, *Sunshine* made starrise in the endless black between Terivine and Mikoa. This jump made Gabriel nervous, for he still hated jumping to a location that didn't have a planet or a star associated with it. Such approximate destinations, defined by agreement rather than by some physical feature, struck him as a perfect place to be ambushed.

"Paranoia," Enda said to him cheerfully after he had expressed this to her.

Nonetheless, when they were ready to come out of drivespace again, Gabriel had the fighting field down over him.

"Thirty seconds," Enda said. "Are you set?"

"As set as I'm going to be," Gabriel said, muffled in his darkness with the controls for the plasma cannons in his hands.

They waited.

"Five seconds now," Enda said.

Gabriel nodded.

"Starrise," Enda said.

Gabriel saw it rendered in the field. Light washed into the cockpit, a pale gold, trickling away to one side.

"Right," he said, tumbling the ship slowly and looking around him for another starrise, but there was none. "Where's Helm?"

"I do not know," Enda said. "The detectors do not see him anywhere."

"What happened? We dropped into drivespace at the same time. The last time we went into starfall together, we came out together, tight as you please."

"The last time we went into starfall together," said Enda,

"Delde Sota had not been doing something unspecified to another ship down *Longshot*'s comm circuits."

She reached into the 3D display, touched one of the indicators, and the whole thing wavered and jumped as if there had been a power surge. Gabriel swallowed, starting to feel twitchy in his gut. It reminded him too clearly of what had happened when the mass cannon had hit them. She couldn't be here, he thought. I shot her butt off. Impossible—

Then his nerves steadied down, though his stomach was still burning him, a surprising discomfort low down on his left side. Gas pain? Cramp?

Who needs this right now? Gabriel thought, squirming.

The display jumped again.

"We have lost the mass detectors," Enda said. "Gabriel, how could that *happen?*" She started touching other controls inside the display, one after another, and Gabriel watched them go ash-pale and nonfunctional.

Ow. That hurts. The pain was becoming unbearable. After this I'm not going to eat within six hours of a starrise, I don't care how hungry I am.

"I have no idea," Gabriel said, "but how could anything Delde Sota did to that woman's ship have possibly affected Helm's stardrive?"

"I don't know," Enda said. "I would prefer to wait until Delde Sota turns up and ask her myself."

No one was there. Gabriel watched his in-field version of the main display flicker, waver, and then pale to nothing. *Everything*—ship's environmental energy levels, her fuel, all her stardrive readouts—faded and were gone.

Gabriel's stomach was churning. Without instrumentation, the ship not only couldn't fight, she could barely move. That burning was now like a coal, fierce and concentrated. That's not gas. Gas doesn't burn on the outside! What the—

Gabriel hurriedly unfastened his straps and jumped up. The pain slipped down his leg.

Not the stomach. My pocket—

He started to reach into it, then hurriedly changed his mind and grabbed the fabric of the pocket so that he could dump the contents on the floor.

The luckstone fell out. It was fiery hot and blazing with light. It bounced to the floor, lay still, and began sizzling itself a little hole into the supposedly indestructible plastic decking. The smooth oval stone, normally dead black, now shone with a greenish-golden-white light. The fierce little glow slowly pulsed bright to pale to bright again.

Enda stole a glance downward, and her eyes widened as Gabriel hurriedly sat back into his chair and began refastening his straps.

"It has never done anything like that before, has it?" Enda asked.

"What, try to burn a hole in me and then succeed in doing the same to my deck?" Gabriel said. "Now that you mention it, no!" He threw the luckstone a very annoyed glance. "What if it keeps on doing this? It's going to burn straight down into the personal cargo hold!"

"It may if it pleases," Enda said, reaching into the display again. "I have other problems. Oh!"

The display lit up again with a sudden flash. Enda scowled as if she didn't trust it. Gabriel busied himself with getting back into the fighting field, which still seemed functional for the moment.

"Everything is back again," Enda said, "and the mass detectors are up and running once more. What a relief."

"I'd be a lot more relieved if we knew where Helm was."

"Somewhere else, plainly."

Gabriel gave Enda a look. "Have I mentioned to you that the fraal sense of humor can be a little strange?"

"Several times," Enda said. "Similar claims can be made about the human one. That joke about the wire brush, now—"

One of the warning lights, the one that said EMERGENCY, grew to an alarming size in the 3D display and began flashing on and off.

Gabriel looked frantically at all the other indicators, but nothing seemed to be wrong with *Sunshine*.

"Enda?"

"It is not our emergency," she said, reaching out to the indicator. "Someone else's."

"Helm?"

"No. He is not here, but someone else is."

The display filled with data—not just text, for once, but a schematic.

"Small," he said as he studied the data. "A cargo ship?"

"Possibly. We have not seen this one before?"

"You mean, is this the other little ship that was at Rivendale? No."

"That," Enda sighed, "is a relief."

The emergency message now began to play in several different sets of characters, several different sets of colors, and one sound. "This is free ship *Lalique,* out of Richards, en route from Mantebron to Aegis. We have suffered stardrive failure and are near the Mikoa-Aegis transit point. Transiting vessels, please render assistance, or if passing through on emergency transit, please convey emergency message to nearest drivesat relay. This is free ship *Lalique*—"

"It's recorded," Gabriel said. "Still, I'm surprised we're the first ones on the scene."

"Assuming we are," Enda said, "and that they have not merely forgotten to turn off the broadcast." She studied the display. "Well, let us go see what we can do for them. This is a bad place to have a stardrive failure."

Gabriel nodded. They might have to take the passengers aboard and leave the ship here, then go for help. Aegis would be the logical place to take them, so Gabriel and Enda's own plans would not suffer much, but he didn't much like the thought of having strangers aboard *Sunshine*. He looked down at the luckstone, which was still glowing in the little socket it had melted for itself in the floor, though it no longer seemed to be working its way any further in.

"Have you got a fix on them?" he asked.

"Yes, no problem. They're no more than forty or fifty thousand kilometers away. They were probably using the same arbitrary starfall figures for the system that we were."

Gabriel nodded. *Sunshine*'s system drive kicked in, and the two of them sat there looking outside for any sign of the ship and stealing glances at the floor between them.

"It seems to be quieting down," Enda said. "Are you all right, Gabriel?"

He touched the seam of the top of his shipsuit open and stared down inside, then frowned. "I got scorched. It burned right through the pocket material."

Enda blinked at that. "The material is supposed to be fire-proof, I thought."

"Then that wasn't fire," Gabriel said. "I thought the decking was indestructible, too. Can we claim for repairs on the guarantee?"

"You would probably have to explain to them how you did it," Enda said, "and then they might ask you to reproduce the effect. First you will have to work out just why the stone behaved that way."

Gabriel shook his head. "Never mind. I'll just use some hull patching on the hole. It's just a shame. That's the first real scratch or damage that *Sunshine* has had. She was perfect until now."

"Ah. You mean, except for when the hold came apart and nearly fell off when you landed on Grith that time."

"Oh, *that*," Gabriel said with a smile.

Enda laughed softly. "Take a look in the field and tell me if that is the ship we're looking for."

Gabriel could see the gravity "dimple" of the vessel, drifting intact. At least the stardrive hadn't caused any structural damage to the vessel.

"*Lalique, Lalique,* this is free ship *Sunshine*," Enda said. "We are within two hundred fifty kilometers and closing. Can we render you assistance? How many are you, and are there any medical problems to deal with before the mechanical ones?"

There was a long pause. "*Sunshine?*" said a woman's voice after a moment. "Oh, what a relief! Thank you so much! There are just two of us. No medical problems, thanks. Can you manage airlock-to-airlock?"

"We have a collapsible tube, yes," Enda said. "I will squirt the tube specs and coordinates to your computer when you're ready."

"Ready now."

They closed in slowly and caught their first glimpse of the ship just a kilometer away. *Lalique* was obviously an old family-style ship. She was big, nearly twice *Sunshine*'s length, and broad in the beam. Two pair of short wings, a little bigger than canards, just out from the cigar-shaped main hull. Four big cargo pods slung high, two and two, sat snug against the hull near the back.

"Nice," Gabriel said as they closed in. "Plenty of room in there."

Enda maneuvered *Sunshine* in close to *Lalique* until the two vessels were drifting at the same speed and in the same direction. The computer confirmed the match. Enda then triggered the flexible airlock tube so that its counterpart program on the other ship could lock the ships together.

This took several minutes. Gabriel stayed in the fighting field, looking everywhere for Helm. "Where the frikes *is* he?" Gabriel muttered.

Enda sighed and said, "He has probably popped out further out in the system where the mass detector cannot see him. Let us wait and see what happens."

There came a soft chime from the display. "This is working, at least," Enda said. "*Lalique,* our computer is showing the mating as complete and secure. Are you showing the same?"

"Yes, we are. Please come aboard," said the woman's voice.

"Five minutes," said Enda and cut the channel. "Gabriel, I think you can safely come out of that for the moment."

He nodded and collapsed the field, blinking in the normal ship's light. "I'll leave it on automatic announce, though," Gabriel said, unstrapping himself and heading down the hall to the arms and equipment locker. "I want to know when Helm turns up."

Enda nodded as they both paused by the locker to pick up hand comms and a sidearm each. "It's not like I don't trust them," Gabriel said, "but—"

"You don't trust them," said Enda approvingly. "Why should you? At any rate, this far out from anywhere, no one is going to be offended by anyone carrying defensive weaponry."

"Right," he said as he checked the charge and the safety of his pistol. He holstered it at his hip, and then reached down into the bottom of the locker for his roll of general access tools, the ones used to get into panels and under deckplates. The other ship probably had tools of its own that were suited to the fastenings its own hardware used, but Gabriel liked to have his tools with him.

I just hope I don't have to try to do anything really technical, he thought as they made their way through the hold to the airlock. If *Lalique*'s stardrive was anything like *Sunshine*'s, it was covered with alarming labels saying things like *No user-serviceable parts inside* and *Opening casing invalidates warranty*. Sometimes such warnings were just clever ways of making sure that the drive manufacturer and its licensees were not cheated out of the price of service calls, but sometimes they were genuine indicators that anything you did to the drive might cause you, it, and everything around you to suddenly become collapsed matter. The trouble lay in telling which was which.

They paused by the airlock port, and Enda touched the opening combination into the locking pad. The door hissed open, and the two of them slipped into the tube and pulled themselves along the cables down the orange-walled corridor.

Another hiss of air heralded the opening of the door at the far end. "Come in," said that female voice, sounding more cheery this time.

Gabriel was concentrating on keeping his stomach under control. He had never liked going rapidly back and forth from gravity to non-gravity areas, though it was something every marine learned to handle, if not enjoy. Mostly it involved keeping your cardiac sphincter shut by muscle pressure, and this meant single-minded concentration until you got back to gravity again.

Shortly he saw floor in front of him, or what would be floor in a moment. He braced himself against the cables and put his feet through.

A moment later he was upright and looking around at a kind of entrance hall with several doors and a corridor leading out of it. A hand seized his upper arm, steadying him.

"Welcome aboard," said the hand's owner, "I'm Angela Valiz."

Gabriel looked up and replied, "Gabriel Connor."

He looked at her closely as he said it, watching for any reaction, but there was no flicker of recognition in her face. She was a tall, strongly-built young woman, maybe Gabriel's age. Her fair hair tailed down the back of her neck rather the way Enda did her own. She was dressed in the baggy trousers, tunic, and soft boots popular for casual wear in most places of the Aegis system.

She looked at him curiously and asked, "Bluefall?"

"Uh, yes."

She nodded and said, "I recognized the accent." She turned to Enda, who had come in behind Gabriel. "Respected, welcome."

"Thank you indeed. Enda, they call me." She made a graceful gesture with her left hand, a variant on the human handshake. Most fraal were left-handed, and this gesture showed that the hand was empty of weapons.

"You're very welcome, Enda."

Gabriel looked around him. What he could see of *Lalique* was handsome-looking. The ship's walls and ceiling panels were soft pastel beiges and blues. High ceilings and broad doorways gave the interior an unusually open and airy look.

"Nice place you've got here," Gabriel said.

"Thanks. It's been in the family for the last fifty years, but right now I just want to get it home safe." She looked down the hallway with a concerned expression.

"What happened, exactly?" Gabriel said.

"Come on down to the control room," Angela said. "You can look at the drive controls there. We made starrise here five days ago, recharged, and got ready to drop into starfall again, but the drive wouldn't engage. Everything else seems fine. The drive diagnostics report it ready to go, but when you hit the go button . . . nothing."

They came into the control room. It was genuinely a room, not

just a large cockpit as in *Sunshine*. Several people could crew the
bridge at five stations arranged around a small circular array of
panels. The viewport ran three-quarters of the way around the
circle above the panel array.

"Over here," Angela said and indicated one panel.

Gabriel sat down and studied the control configuration of the
keypad for a moment. Fortunately it was one of the configurable
control pads that the major manufacturers had been using for the
last couple of decades, having finally realized that no one had to
relearn the system every time it needed to be checked out.

"Right," Gabriel said, and started working his way down
through the diagnostics tree to where the stardrive's inboard routines could be accessed.

The drive itself was a RoanTech, one of the ten or fifteen main
manufacturers. Stardrive manufacturers too had begun to produce
drives along broadly similar lines, partly so they could start dealing in replacement parts for one another's drives, and partly
because it made sense—there were only so many ways you could
put a gravity induction engine and a mass reactor together. Their
diagnostic routines tended to look much the same these days for
the same reasons as the control pads did.

Enda leaned over Gabriel's shoulder, watching him examine
the drive's controlling software, and then looked at Angela.

"By the way," Enda asked, "have you been suffering any irreg-
ularities in the way your instrumentation works?"

"Yes we have," Angela said. "Right after we got here, all our
displays and readouts started to act up. I was wondering if it had
something to do with the stardrive. When *that* went, the instrumentation kept misbehaving, but don't ask me why."

"Well, at least it wasn't just us," Gabriel said, "but I can't think
what might be causing it."

There was a noise from down the hallway through which
they'd just come. Angela glanced in that direction. "Oh, here's
my partner."

Down the central hallway was a door belonging to a lift that
apparently serviced the lower level of the ship. The lift door

opened, and he could hear footsteps in the hall. There was something odd about the rhythm. A second later, through the control room door, came the largest weren that Gabriel had ever seen in his life.

"Grawl, these are the people who answered our distress call," Angela said. "Gabriel, Enda, this is Grawl."

Weren could be twice the height of a small human, and this one was. They also could be twice the breadth, and this one was. She was absolutely massive, with fur much more silver than was usual for weren. It had light striping that made Gabriel think of a pale gray tabby that one of his family's neighbors on Bluefall had owned. The neighbor's tabby, fierce as it had been on occasion, did not have ten-centimeter claws, three-centimeter tusks, or a very large gun slung on a baldric over its shoulder. This weren had all of these, and she looked at Gabriel and Enda with an expression of which Gabriel could make absolutely nothing.

Gabriel did not have much experience with the species. The marine contingent he had served with had not spent much time in the worlds where the weren had much of a presence. He knew enough about them to understand that politeness was much valued in their culture and likely to keep one's own head from being torn off in an excitable moment.

"I greet you," he said, "and hope that we are not intruding."

The dark eyes looked at him. "Welcome enough you are," the weren said in a soft rumbling voice, "here where any visitor is likely enough to be welcome, were he half your size."

Gabriel nodded noncommittally. He wasn't sure if she had complimented or insulted him.

"Cousin," said Enda, "well met on the journey."

The weren swept an arm low before her body. "Respected, starlight shine on your road as well."

Enda smiled. "A long road—nearly as long as yours. Kurg is far away indeed."

"Distance," said the weren, "is an artifact of the mind."

Angela chuckled and said, "Grawl and I ran into each other in

Alaundril about a year ago. We've been together since. She was traveling . . ."

"I was outcast," Grawl corrected.

Gabriel looked at her with surprise. "I can't imagine who would have had the nerve to throw you out of *anywhere.*"

She gave him a look that he hoped was a smile. "I was the daughter of warriors, the granddaughter of warriors," Grawl rumbled, "but I was a disgrace among my family."

"In what manner?" Enda said.

Gabriel looked at Enda in shock, but Grawl lowered her head to Enda's level—a good way down—and said, softly, "I was the smallest of my kindred, the weakest, the poorest fighter, last-born, last in regard, but there was worse than that to come."

Gabriel looked up at her, easily two hundred kilograms of muscle and claws, and could do little but shake his head. She saw the movement and turned toward him. Hot breath blew about him with a peculiar cinnamony scent, ruffling his hair.

"I am a poetess," Grawl whispered.

"Poetry is hardly an art scorned among the weren," Enda said. "What was your clan's objection with this?"

"There have been no artists of any note in my family for some generations," Grawl said. "My clan-sire felt that mine was an unsuitable calling for the daughter and granddaughter of warriors, and though the rest of the clan did not agree with him, he *is* our sire. When he said I had gotten the best of my brothers by skill and stealth and craft when I could not do so by force and fight, the other clan members dared not argue with him."

Then a sound came out of her the likes of which Gabriel had never heard. Weren laughter, the sound of a pot boiling, but a pot full of lava. "Get the best of them I did. None of them can wind words as I do. None of them could stand before me when I made satires upon them! I caused my eldest brother to go den-living from embarrassment, and my eldest sister to snatch her mate half bald, all by merely telling the truth about them in public, in meter, in the meeting-place of our people. Furious my family was, and they raged and shrieked in housemoot! They sought to tear me with their claws, but the claws of my words were sharper. They sought to blast me with their flintlocks, but the bullets of my scorn flew truer. Finally they gathered together outlawed me, and paid my way off planet." She smiled. The expression, even with those tusks, was surprisingly benign from such a massive creature. "Having received what I desired from them, I went out into the Old Night with a good heart and sought my hire in ships, doing security work. So we met, Angela and I, and we have done well together."

Gabriel glanced over at Angela during this. She had the expression of someone hearing a very familiar story.

"The meter is reminiscent of the sesheyan double-stave," Enda said, "though not as telegraphic."

Grawl's eyes went wide. "You too are an artist!" she cried. "Always and far and wide the fraal are known for their sensitivity and craft."

And flattery, Gabriel thought, keeping his face straight. "About your stardrive . . ." he said.

Angela looked at him. "Don't tell me you know what's the matter with it already!"

Gabriel laughed. "I wish. Does the drive have its own display panel?"

"Yes," Angela said, "though I would think that it would display everything necessary up here."

"So would I," Gabriel said, "but it doesn't. Can we go down and have a look at it?"

"Certainly," Angela said. "Come on."

She led him down the hall and to the lift again, while behind them Enda and Grawl began to discuss poetry. "How long have you been out with this ship?" Gabriel asked Angela as the lift door slid open.

"About a year and a half now," she replied. "I have a five year lease from the family. After that, if I can demonstrate a profit when I get back, I get another five years. Otherwise my little brother gets a turn."

They stood in the lift, and it sank toward the hold level. "Have you been back home since?" Gabriel said.

Angela shook her head. "Not a chance. I wanted to get the family out of my hair for a while . . . find out what life without constant commitments hanging over your head looks like." She sighed as the lift door opened. "It's been refreshing. A little hectic, sometimes, but I wouldn't give it up. One way or the other I'm going to make the best of these five years, not get tied down, and roam around a good ways."

Gabriel raised his eyebrows at that as she led him down a hallway that was twin to the one above them. "So how was Eldala?" he asked.

She stopped and stared at Gabriel in complete disbelief.

"Eldala," Gabriel said. "Did you get there, eventually?"

"Where did you hear about that?" she asked, more surprised than suspicious.

"We were in the Terivine system the other day. On Rivendale."

She looked at Gabriel uncomprehendingly. "So?"

"So were you, apparently. One of the locals mentioned you and where you were going."

"Well, yes, we were there, but—" Angela shook her head, started walking down the hall again. "I don't remember telling anyone about Eldala."

"Little guy named Rov something," Gabriel said. "He remembered that moderately well, and he remembered *you* well enough to wonder where you were. They're worried about you."

Now, as Angela paused by a sliding door and touched a combination onto the face of it, she looked completely confused. "Why would they be worried?"

The door opened, and they went in.

"You're kidding, right?" Gabriel said, pausing to look around the room. "It's just a small town, that settlement. They gossip about everything there. You told someone you were coming back through, and then you never came back. They think you're lying dead in a ditch somewhere."

The room was small, square and empty. The sealed main drive array took up the entire back wall, and a black metal panel with

Qualified Service Personnel Only sealed the main access panel. Faired into the black metal was a big square panel of glass with a keypad at the top of it. Gabriel reached up, typed in the access command, and the entire diagnostic and drive system management directory rosette fanned out across the glass panel.

Angela leaned against the nearby wall. "It's so strange. I don't remember mentioning where I was going to anybody on Rivendale, although," she added, "we *were* partying a lot while we were there. . . ."

"Ah," Gabriel said as he studied the directory rosette. They got blitzed, told everybody where they were going, what they were going to do . . .

Gabriel was beginning to form some opinions about this girl, and they were not flattering. Rich, probably. Careless. Mouth like a ramscoop.

"Aha," he said, finding the spot he wanted on the rosette. Gabriel touched that petal, and it became the core of another "flower" of options, one of which was log play. He selected that one. His old friend Hal had been an e-suit engineer on *Falada,* and Hal's second rule—after the one about reading the dumb-ass documentation—was to read the dumber-ass logs as well. "If nothing else," Hal had said, "it makes you look like you know what you're doing, however spurious this impression may be."

Gabriel began working his way through the stardrive's logs. It had a diagnostic program to help him with this. The program looked at the logs, then at what they should look like, and then it finally showed any major differences it found.

Gabriel quickly scanned through the last several starfalls and starrises, and then started to read them with more care while the program was doing the same for the entire log. To Angela he said, "When they told me about this place you were going, I got curious. I'd never heard of it before. What caused your interest in it?"

"Well, it was a blank in the gazetteer," Angela said. "There had been some kind of accident when the original survey came through. Said they were having mechanical trouble. Anyway, they reported the planet as too cold and went on to their next stop."

"Too cold?"

"Bad ambient temperature," said Angela. "Eight C below zero, apparently."

Gabriel nodded. That would have been reason enough to pass on when there were hopes of finding something better in the next system along. Eight was a very low ambient, if he remembered the planetary climatic information he'd been taught as a marine. It suggested that even summer highs might not be much better than twelve C, which was bad for crops, even those that had been genetically tailored for chilly conditions. There was little point in settling a planet that was both far away and where food could not be successfully grown. You wound up having to bring everything in, and if there was no other resource there to make the trip worthwhile, no stellar nation or company would bother investigating settlement any further.

He paused, looking at something the diagnostic program had flagged. "Let me look at that," he told the computer.

"So you gave up on it?" Gabriel asked Angela.

She shrugged and said, "It wasn't what we had in mind. We got tired of being far away from everything . . . starfall after starfall, never seeing anyone, watching the same old entertainment over and over on the ship's channels . . ."

"You have Grawl to make poetry for you," Gabriel said with an absolutely straight face.

Angela punched him in the shoulder, more fiercely than Gabriel had braced himself to withstand. He rocked and barely kept from falling over sideways. "Don't mock her," Angela said. "She's had a hard time."

"She looks like she's survived it," Gabriel said, touching the panel again to focus the diagnostic's attention on what he thought he had found.

Angela folded her arms and stared down at the toes of her boots. "Survival isn't joy," she said.

Gabriel paused, glancing at her. "I wouldn't know a lot about what constitutes joy for a weren."

Angela gave him a resigned look. "How clear can any of us be about what goes on in an alien's mind? Any more than any of them can be clear about what *we're* thinking? I just worry about her, that's all. I think she'd really rather be home on Kurg, getting involved in tribal politics and ripping out the occasional suitor's throat, but she's made the best she can out of her life." She scratched at a worn place on the decking. "It must have been awful," Angela said softly, "always being beaten up and sat on, having the food stolen out from under your nose and everything else worthwhile being taken away from you by the stronger ones, the faster ones. Grawl found another way."

Angela looked up again and said, "But is she happy?"

A touch of familiarity there? Gabriel thought. "And you," he said, "you got beaten up and sat on as well?"

She gave him a look both indignant and amused. "Ah, an amateur thought-wrangler," she said. "For your information, I was one of two and bigger than my brother. As a matter of fact *I* beat *him* up whenever he needed it, which was most of the time. Brothers are always getting out of hand. If you don't show them the error of their ways early on, they run around making messes forever after."

Gabriel smiled at that. "I'll take your word for it. Meanwhile, look at this." He pointed at the log display in the glass and at the diagnostic program's suggestion of what should be present there. "I'm no expert, but this might be the trouble. I know our drive has routines to keep this from happening. Yours is enough like ours to suggest this is the problem. I think the synch between the two atomic clocks that handle the drive has been failing. See." He pointed. "The logs show them having gotten progressively more out of synch over the past few weeks. This one in particular, the gravity induction apparatus, looks like its clock has been speeding up. Not by huge amounts, but enough for it to start interfering now. Has this started acting strangely over the last couple of starfalls?"

Angela nodded. "Just after we left Mantebron."

Gabriel stared at the diagnostics showing in the panel. "All right. I'm going to try to reset it. You willing to have me do that?"

"Yes. I don't see that it can do that much harm."

I hope you're right, Gabriel thought. He backed up through the diagnostic program again and went down the tree to where the clock routines were. Touching a spot labeled *Synchrony,* he was rewarded by a message that asked, *Reset clocks to match?*

"Aha," he said. "That they have this particular routine makes it sound like this problem might come up more than infrequently." Gabriel looked sideways at her. "Have you missed a scheduled service, by any chance?"

"Uh . . ." She looked embarrassed. "Possibly."

"This may be one of the things they do on those routine services," Gabriel said, and touched the fork of the choice-tree that said YES.

DONE, it said a second later.

"All right," he said. "When we're off the ship, punch it and see what happens. We won't leave until we see you safely away. If you can't get out, you and Grawl come aboard *Sunshine* with us, and we'll get you to Aegis so you can arrange a return-and-tow with somebody there."

"Seems fair enough," Angela said as she went out. Gabriel closed down the panel routines and went after her.

As they were walking back to the lift, Angela looked at him curiously. "Something leak in your pocket?"

"Huh? Oh." Gabriel glanced down at the pocket where the luckstone had been. "No, just a burn. I got careless with some equipment."

"Must have been some equipment. I thought those things were burn-proof."

"So did I," Gabriel said, thinking morosely of that spot on the decking. "Another of life's little surprises."

In the lift, Angela leaned against its wall, looking thoughtful. She glanced up at him then, and Gabriel thought, Oh, please, don't invite me to dinner; I just want to get out of here and get on with what we were doing.

"Eldala," Angela said. "Are you interested in it?"

Gabriel blinked. "Uh . . . why?"

"You mentioned it first. Plainly it must have stuck in your mind when you heard about it."

"Well," Gabriel said, "yes." He shrugged. "It hardly matters, though. You've got the exploration contract."

"I'll sell it to you," Angela said.

Gabriel stared at her as the lift door opened.

"Why?"

"It's no good to me now," said Angela. "If you're right about the drive clocks, I'll be glad, but I'm not going anywhere again without having this drive serviced. That may take me a while. By then . . ." She shrugged.

By then you may have found something more interesting to do with your money, Gabriel thought. Hmf.

She looked at him as they walked back into the control room. "Are you interested?"

Gabriel looked over at Enda, who was seated next to Grawl. Enda, looking from him to Angela to him again, gave Gabriel a look that said, Should I ask?

"Angela's interested in selling the exploration contract for Eldala," Gabriel said.

At this, Grawl screwed her face down into what looked like a frown. Enda looked more than usually thoughtful. "The price?"

"Is negotiable, believe me," Angela said. "I just don't feel prepared to carry on with that contract at this point."

"You were there, I take it?" said Enda.

Angela nodded and Enda continued, "Not for long, though. Is the world habitable for humans?"

"Not without a lot of support, I think," Angela said.

"Low ambient, supposedly," said Gabriel.

"We landed, looked around the place, picked up some mineral samples and things like that," Angela said. "Rocks, mostly. We ran assay on some soil samples for ore artifact but didn't find anything terribly useful."

"There was much snow," said Grawl. "Great white peaks that towered to the blue heavens. Snow bannered from them in the sun, and the winds blew the snow about—"

"Wait a minute," Gabriel said. "How glaciated was this planet?"

"A mighty polar cap straddled the world's nadir," Grawl said, "and a lesser one the pole which pointed toward the sun. Seasonal, we reckoned the difference, for the ambient temperature—"

"It was cold," Angela cut her off.

Gabriel looked at Enda.

"Well, cold is not sufficient to disallow colonization, as we have seen elsewhere," Enda suggested. "Distance is likely to be more of a preventative factor. Still . . ."

The back of Gabriel's mind was caught in a noisy argument. One part of it was claiming that this rich girl was just trying to cut her losses and make some money off a wasted investment . . . possibly adding to this the amusement of selling someone something worthless. Another part of his mind was sure that she had missed something and that this might be a good idea . . . a very good idea.

"By the way," Enda said, "I did not have a chance to mention that Helm is in the system. He just got within detection range."

"What kept him?"

Enda shrugged. " 'Standard error,' he said. You know as well as I that there can be a considerable difference in arrival distance between vessels departing at the same time and from the same area."

"He's just got me spoiled," Gabriel said. "He's such a hot pilot. That's a relief, though."

He looked back at Angela, then. "How much money are we discussing here?"

"I'll give you a flat price for the whole thing," Angela said. "Half what we paid: contracts, exploration pack, the support software, all that."

" 'Support software'?" Enda asked.

Angela laughed and said, "It's just a big reference library on survival in hostile environments, a translator, and some other stuff. I never even configured some parts of it. The manuals are terrible, and when we got there and realized the environment wasn't anything we couldn't handle with overcoats and common sense, and there wasn't anything to use the translator on . . ." She shrugged.

"And you paid . . . ?" Gabriel asked.

"Seven thousand Concord."

Gabriel thought about that. "Refund guarantee? If we go to these coordinates and don't find a planet—"

Rather suddenly, Grawl loomed over him. "There *is*," she growled, "a planet."

"Grawl, I think he was making a joke," Enda said hurriedly. "It can be a strange thing, the human sense of humor. There is this story about a wire brush—"

"Contract becomes effective immediately on sale?" Gabriel said, refusing to move, no matter how Grawl tried to intimidate him.

Angela nodded. "The only thing that would affect the contract would be transmission time to a Concord Survey facility."

"Well," Gabriel said, "we're infotraders. We can carry the contract transfer ourselves, if you're comfortable with that."

"It's going encrypted, so it's fine with me," Angela said with a shrug.

"A deal, then," Gabriel said. They struck hands on it.

The remainder of the deal took little time. Gabriel had to go back over to *Sunshine* for his accounting chip. He brought it back aboard *Lalique,* and they recorded the sale in both ship's computers at the same time, passing the software and other files into *Sunshine*'s databanks. Gabriel took possession of the "hard" documentation and software copies on solids, and then looked around one last time.

"Well, a pleasure doing business with you," he said. "I hope all this works out well for you."

"So do I," Angela said, "because otherwise we're going to need a ride to Aegis."

"Well," Gabriel said, hoping this wouldn't happen, "let's see what happens first. We'll break the ships' connection and stand away the usual safe distance—"

"Right," Angela said. Suddenly she looked anxious to be gone, as well. "Come on, Grawl, let's get her hot."

At least she walked them down to the airlock first. "Listen, Gabriel, Enda," she said, "if this does work out all right, our comms info is in the solids and the contracts. Get in touch when you make Aegis. We can get together."

"Certainly," Enda said. They slipped into the tube again, and the door closed behind them.

When they were on their side again, Enda asked Gabriel, "Is that what humans call 'impulse buying'?"

"Probably," Gabriel said. He looked down at the solids in his hands. "It was kind of a hunch."

"I think it was stress," Enda said. "Having things burn holes in your pocket seems to make money do the same."

Gabriel smiled, though weakly, and they made their way back up to the pilot's cabin. Gabriel paused by the door and reached down to gingerly touch the stone. It was as cool as it had ever been. "Weird."

"You do not seem terribly eager to put it in your pocket at the moment," Enda said as Gabriel stowed the manual and contract solids.

"No, and you won't see me acting eager until we're out of this system. Let it just sit there until I'm sure it wants to behave." Gabriel sat down in the right-hand chair and opened a comms channel. "Helm?"

"Hey, you're back. How bad was her drive busted?"

"Maybe not at all. We'll find out." He changed channels. *"Lalique?"*

"Here," said Angela's voice. "We'll be ready to test in thirty seconds. Hey, Gabriel, I meant it about dinner."

"Uh, thanks," Gabriel said. "Half a moment while we move out of range."

He backed *Sunshine* well away, then gave the system drive a two-second pulse, pushing them some kilometers away from *Lalique*.

"Good luck," Gabriel said.

"Thanks."

The seconds ticked by as they watched out the viewport.

"Please," Gabriel muttered, "please let it work."

Enda threw him an amused glance.

"Here we go," said Angela. "Five, four, three—"

She broke off. Gabriel swallowed, hoping desperately that their drive had not failed again.

Starfall light sheeted in brilliant gold all over *Lalique*'s shape, and she vanished.

Gabriel breathed out.

From *Longshot,* Helm said, "Are they gone now? Can we talk?"

"There's plenty of time for that," Gabriel said. "A few days to recharge, then we'll get out of here. Come on over and we'll have dinner."

"Bring the autolaser," Enda said.

Chapter Seven

"WERE YOU ABLE to find out anything interesting from our . . . *friend's* . . . ship while you were making her power fluctuate?" Gabriel asked Doctor Sota in the middle of ingesting another of Helm's pot-and-autolaser entrees.

Delde Sota shook her head and replied, "Result: much ship registry information. Of academic interest, but such information can be forged—and was, I think. Ship claimed to come from Tendril, private-use vessel; no guarantee of accuracy of claim. Analysis: had been, in her computer, records of previous comms back to her base, wherever that might have been. All purged, data solids overwritten." Her braid fidgeted in the air, tied itself in a knot, and untied itself again, fretful. "Can do little about genuinely erased data. Apologies."

"How *did* you do that?" Enda said.

Delde Sota raised her eyebrows. "Methodology: any transmission carrier is an open door, even for less talented beings/systems. Addendum: encryption never really that complete in 'realtime' applications like live comms. Second addendum: systems often inadequately shielded. Signal leakage can be exploited, even mechanical/physical problems like bad grounding . . ." She shrugged. "Method: simple to convince secondary/tertiary power source of bad phasing, poor fusing, or short in system. Too-eager 'safety feature' cuts in, fails system out." She shook her head regretfully. "Problem appears to have had some other cause entirely when diagnostics are run." And then she smiled, just a little.

"You *enjoy* that kind of thing," Gabriel said.

"Analysis incomplete and simplistic," said Delde Sota, and her smile grew.

"So we have one person chasing us whose ship says it's from Tendril and is probably lying," Gabriel said. "Anything on the other ship? Miss Blue Eyes?"

"Result: negative," Delde Sota said. "Insufficient time."

"Well," Gabriel said, "I'd like to get out of here before she comes along, anyway. Though we didn't file a plan, it strikes me as likely that she'll work out we were heading for Aegis and that we'd have stopped somewhere in this vicinity."

There was general agreement on this point, and then the conversation slipped into more mundane topics. Gabriel paid little attention, musing upon his own thoughts instead.

"*Something* in this space," Gabriel said after dinner, "is weird."

"Well," Helm replied, "it's not weird now."

The dishes and dinner things were put away, and they were all squeezed together around the table in the sitting room. Gabriel's luckstone sat on the table by itself. If a piece of smooth, dark stone could look innocent, it did.

"*This* thing," Gabriel said, "I thought it was going to burn a hole in my stomach."

"Good thing it was just loose in your pocket," Helm said, "instead of on a chain or something."

Delde Sota had been examining with the luckstone with her braid. Now she pulled it close and touched it with one finger. "Nothing," she said. "Former opinion: lightrock. Source: beaches on numerous planets; silicate natural chip or solid, conducts bio-electricity. Now—"

"Are you saying that's *not* what it is?"

Delde Sota shook her head. "*New* opinion: old opinion incorrect/incomplete. New one not formed. Structure *appears* to be silicate quartz. Energy states of atoms not normal."

" 'Energy states'? It's not radioactive or anything, is it?"

Delde Sota shook her head and said, "Occasional jitters in shell structure of atoms. Like superconductor 'jitter' in supercooled gold; quick change of energy states, as if to jump to higher ones or relapse to lower, but not cyclic." She poked the little stone again with her braid.

"It did this when exactly?" Helm asked.

"When we dropped into the system. Our instruments were acting up around then, so I didn't notice it for a few moments."

"Can't have been very hot to begin with."

Gabriel gingerly picked up the stone again. It glowed slightly at his touch, but that was all.

"Well," Helm said. "I had a look at your instrumentation, and I can't find anything wrong. So you might have had some kind of power surge and *that*"—he pointed with his chin at the stone— "reacted to it."

Gabriel shook his head. "It didn't persist after that first moment."

"At least you fixed *that* problem." He paused, and the barest hint of a mischievous grin played across his features. "Now, back to this . . . *Angela*. Did you find any proof that the desynchrony was what made her drive fail?"

"No," Gabriel said, eyeing Helm cautiously, "and I probably couldn't have if the damned machine had written me a note, because I didn't know what I was looking for. What was I supposed to *do*, Helm? You can't just sit there and do nothing in a situation like that, even if you don't know what to do."

Helm gave him a wicked look. "Good-looking woman like that, I suppose not."

"Helm," Gabriel said, annoyed, "don't go looking for it, because it's not there."

The grin only broadened, almost splitting Helm's face in half. He downed the last of his drink and was about to say something else when Delde Sota cut him off.

"Opinion: shame I did not have a chance to look at her drive."

"Yeah," Gabriel said, glad to be off the subject of Angela Valiz. "Well, they're gone, and now we can be on our way." He glanced up from the stone. "Preferably before this decides to do something odd again."

"It looks so unthreatening now," Enda said, "but I would not argue the point. Should some pursuit catch up with us, I would sooner it did so at Aegis. After that . . . ?"

They all looked at Gabriel.

"Well . . ." he said. "Give me a few minutes, would you? I have a few things to sort out in my head."

"Go ahead," Enda said.

Delde Sota added, "Opportunity: sit and digest."

Gabriel got up and ambled up to the pilot's compartment, sat down in the left-hand seat and looked out into the darkness. Behind him, Enda and Delde Sota were softly discussing the luckstone. *Maybe the thing to do is let the pursuit catch up while we're there,* he thought. *Find out just who these people are who are after me, but, as Enda says, somewhere with plenty of witnesses.*

Helm came up into the pilots' cabin and glanced around him. He squeezed past Gabriel into the right hand seat and looked out at the stars.

"You thinking what I think you're thinking?" Helm said.

"I wouldn't know how to be sure," Gabriel said.

Helm laughed under his breath and said, "The *Lighthouse?*"

"You noticed that it's coming in, too."

"I keep an eye on its whereabouts. Sometimes people jump into Corrivale from it when it passes by one of the other systems, and some of them like an armed escort if they're carrying dangerous cargoes, or time-sensitive ones."

"So you wouldn't have trouble picking up work there?"

"No," Helm said, "and neither would you. But it's your call. I don't know that I like the idea of getting too cozy with that thing, myself."

Gabriel's eyes widened slightly. "You don't think the Concord would be coming after *you,* after Rivendale?"

"Huh? Of course not," Helm said. "The residues in the area will give a clear indication of what happened." He waved a massive hand. "On the other hand . . ." He sighed. "Gabe, as a general rule it's too busy for me in a given area when *that* thing shows

up. Oh, I know it's a good sign. Civilization coming back to the
Verge and all that. Good business for the people who live here,
but it smacks of . . . I don't know . . . *bureaucracy,*" Helm scowled
as if he had taken a bite of something sour, "the kind of thing you
got caught up in. Too many people living too close together, arguing and scrabbling over rights to exploit this, defend that, and colonize the other. Big money changing hands, and people's lives
getting ruined by it all, just being rolled over without a second
glance, by the big weight and momentum of big companies, big
forces . . ."

He paused and looked out into the darkness. Almost in a whisper, he continued, "The Concord's just another big force. I know
it means well. Maybe it'll be big and powerful enough some day
to do well, but right now there are too many other forces arguing
the point. Where it goes, they go too, and you're likely to get run
over in the traffic without anyone noticing. Me, I prefer the wide
open spaces."

"Even without the security?" Gabriel asked.

Helm laughed softly. "It always comes back to that, doesn't it?
There isn't any, Gabe, no security anywhere. Oh, people think
there was once. They tell stories about the Good Ol' Days when
our parents were young . . ." He shook his head. "It wasn't any
better for them or their parents, not even when humans lived on
just one planet, before the fraal turned up to keep them company.
It was *never* secure. People either didn't have enough money or
food or time—or if they did, they didn't know how long it would
last them. Their lives might work for a while, but sooner or later
luck would change, times would change . . . and death came to
them all." He did not sound terribly somber about it, more matter-
of-fact. "Security's just so much nebula-glimmer. See it far off
and it looks real and shining. Try to get into the middle of it, and
there's nothing there but dust and the glow's all gone."

Gabriel smiled. "So speaks Helm the Philosopher."

Helm looked amused. "Well, maybe I won't be famous for it,
but you must look out into the dark while you're in drivespace
and have long thoughts. It's an occupational hazard. If that idea

hasn't occurred to you by now, it will eventually. Meantime, I don't hunt security. I just get on with business."

"Business isn't going to take you as far as Mantebron?"

"I don't think so," Helm said. "Now, if you're thinking of going that way and hitching a ride with the *Lighthouse,* it'll certainly save you time. Four, maybe five starfalls?"

"Five. The better part of forty days."

"Definitely an advantage if you want to go take a look at this new contract property of yours and see what's worth exploiting."

Gabriel shifted in his seat and said, "I don't know that I'm going to *exploit* anything."

Helm gave him a bemused look. "This is what people buy exploration contracts *for.* If you just wanted to hide, you could do that in drivespace. If you wanted to go work somewhere quiet, there are a lot of places more comfortable. Sounds like your intentions are a little mixed, Gabe."

"I can't argue with that," Gabriel said after a moment, "but it's what I want to do."

Helm's eyebrows climbed his forehead in surprise, and he said, "Unusually good sense from you today. Well, no matter. Doubtless you'll relapse shortly."

Gabriel punched Helm in the arm as hard as possible. Helm hardly noticed.

"So you'll go then?" Helm asked. "You'll send word of where you are, though, and how things go?"

"Naturally. We'll go back to infotrading after we finish this run. It's a long way, and we'll need more funds."

"We'll rendezvous with you quick as we can," Helm said. "Delde Sota has some things she wants to look into over the next month, so she says. Didn't go into too much detail, but she made it sound like it was private business. I don't want to pry."

"Probably smart," Gabriel said, "when dealing with a woman who can crash a ship's systems down its *comms.*"

"No argument there. Speaking of which"—he looked over his shoulder—"Doctor?"

After a few moments Delde Sota came lounging up the

hallway to peer past them into the starscape. "Speculation: enjoying view?"

"And the exercise of philosophy," Helm said, "but less important stuff too, one thing in particular. These two are going to hitch on the *Lighthouse* after all."

Delde Sota looked thoughtful. "Diagnosis: possible psychiatric disorder? *Sunshine* carries proscribed weaponry, and one crew member wanted by Concord, however erroneously. Security and background checks mandatory for all hitching vessels. Results: likely to be unfortunate."

"That's what I was going to say," Helm said, "but if someone had a word with *Sunshine*'s computers and made them look and act like the 'proscribed weaponry' wasn't there . . . Silly laws about those anyway. They deserve to be broken. How are you supposed to take care of yourself when every crook and pirate has stuff like this?"

"Helm," Enda said from behind Delde Sota, peering around her, "into what are you tempting this virtuous mechalus *now?*"

"Opinion: interesting problem," Delde Sota said, getting a more than usually wicked gleam in her eye. "Weapons 'redescription' insufficient to job at hand. Proper intervention also requires at least one altered set of personal ID, negative for any possible background checks. Transit log with altered timestamps also necessary. Fooling proprietary infotrading and messaging systems into accepting altered ship registry without affecting other performance . . . *Hmm.*"

The hair stood up all over Gabriel. He had never heard Delde Sota say "hmm" before, and in its present tone, the word acquired an unexpectedly dangerous quality. "It's going to be possible to put everything back the way it was afterwards, won't it?"

Delde Sota's braid waved airily. "Fact: removal of intervention insignificant problem. Emplacement of 'disguise' requires programming of some elegance and skill." She raised her eyebrows, a pleased look. "Opinion: nothing like a challenge."

"This won't violate any of your oaths or anything, will it?" Gabriel said.

Delde Sota blinked at him, bemused. "Medical oaths? Hardly."

"I mean, any others. Do Grid pilots have oaths?"

She smiled a very slow smile. "Spectrum of response: from 'What you do rebounds on you threefold' to 'If it harms none, do as you will.' Value judgment: suggested course of action comes under latter." The end of her braid began weaving itself into ever more complex and subtle patterns. "Intention: ought to get started. Enjoyable challenge and profitable use of remaining recharge time."

"Beats knitting," said Helm.

"Believe I said that," said Delde Sota, and went off down toward the rear cargo hold.

Helm grinned and said, "You'll be all set shortly. Let's go back down in the sitting room where it's comfortable and sort out the post-starrise logistics." He got up, squeezed past Gabriel and then Enda, and headed off down the hall. "Where's that bottle of Luculliana gone?"

Gabriel glanced up at Enda.

She gave him a resigned shrug, and the two of them went after Helm.

*   *   *   *   *

They spent another three and a half days waiting for their stardrives to recharge. Gabriel passed the time by mulling over the information on Jacob Ricel but could glean nothing new from it. Delde Sota spent every waking moment tinkering, manipulating, and restructuring all of *Sunshine*'s registry data and Gabriel's personal ID, while Helm and Enda entertained themselves on the Grid and kept up with the ships' maintenance and cleaning.

After a brief stopover to recharge their drives in the Mikoa system, *Sunshine* and *Longshot* finally arrived in Aegis. They made starrise a hundred-and-fifty-million kilometers from the star itself. There, in the plane of the system's ecliptic, hung the Aegis drivesat, its various relays dipping in and out of drivespace with flashes of multicolored light. Starrise followed starfall in pulsing regularity, the visible manifestation of millions of conversations, messages, images, and data flowing out to the rest of civilization and back again.

The drivesat was a lifeline, and the factor that combined with the system's favorable location to make Aegis the center of the Verge. It was hardly central from the point of view of the older parts of the settled universe. The worlds of the Stellar Ring were a thousand light-years away, six months' journey even for a fortress ship capable of fifty light-year jumps. For smaller vessels, that journey would have taken a year or more.

Such distances were too vast for almost all freight except the most precious things that could not be made locally. Trade within the Verge had thus become one of the most important things to re-establish after the Long Silence. Aegis, no more than four starfalls from its surrounding systems for most vessels, became the *de facto* hub of the Verge's gradual reconstruction. Some would argue that the location itself, even more than the presence of the planet Bluefall in the system, would have been reason enough for the construction of the drivesat relay there.

Others might suggest that the readiness of the Regency government on Bluefall to deal with almost every major stellar nation from the Concord to VoidCorp had more to do with it. The planet's still-unrevoked open immigration policy had brought sentient beings there from all over settled space. Many brought their business with them, happy to be based on one of the most beautiful planets in known space. In any case, the Aegis drivesat relay had turned the system into *the* major crossroads of the Verge, where fortunes were made and sometimes lost, and the great powers of the 25th century rubbed elbows, sometimes jabbing one another as they sought advantage.

Hundreds of ships transited Aegis every day, so Gabriel was not surprised when the only acknowledgement from system control was a harried-sounding automated message asking *Sunshine* to declare a destination and move to a less crowded part of space.

"Well," Enda said, as the display between them filled with transit information, "where shall we go?"

Gabriel watched the data scroll by. There were only three planets in the system: Bluefall, the gas giant Redcrown, and little Jetsam. "I've seen enough giants for a while."

"And Bluefall?" Enda said.

Gabriel shook his head. "Not this trip. When is the *Lighthouse* due in?"

"Within several hours. We have timed it nicely. Look, the data transfer system is waking up . . ."

No one at Rivendale had given them anything to carry, but *Sunshine*'s infotrading systems seemed unconcerned by this. Any time they detected a drivesat's carrier-signature, they automatically contacted it in case there was traffic waiting for the ship or other general information to be picked up. The display in the pilot's cabin showed the usual Grid contact heralds, a splash screen for the Aegis Grid, and the special heralds for contact with a drivesat. Then in rapid succession, the system announced *No outgoing cargo. No new out-system cargo. Standard inward in-system cargo. Cargo embarked. Cleaning cycle begins.*

"No sign of any trouble from Delde Sota's 'tinkering,' " Gabriel said, much relieved. "But what was that? We weren't due to pick anything up yet."

Enda peered at the display. "It seems to be a general information and system bulletin package . . . a 'newspaper.' "

"I would have thought that would come in from the in-system mass transceiver."

"Maybe this is for infotraders serving the relay?"

"Hm." Gabriel nodded noncommittally and said, "No sign of Helm yet."

"The ship will call us when he turns up, or Helm will," Enda said as she got up and went back to the sitting room to have a more leisurely look at the material.

Gabriel told the autopilot to take the ship well out of the "incoming traffic" area. When he got back to the sitting room, Enda was already working her way through data from the drivesat's news package—an hourly summary of planetary, system, and stellar nation news with a live "bulletin board" listing ships passing through the system, data available for outward transit, and so forth.

"Heh," Gabriel said after a moment, having spotted *Lalique* on the list. "She made it back safely."

"So it seems." Enda gave him a look. "Did I detect correctly that you were not overwhelmed by the idea of dinner with her?"

"You detected correctly."

"We will avoid that, then. Why, though?"

Gabriel shook his head. "A few things, but mostly . . . she didn't seem to think things through, somehow. At the moment, that's a problem I don't much like."

"Because you have that problem yourself?"

"The weren was interesting, though," Gabriel said, not answering that last comment. "Now I understand Rov's crack about Angela's friend's hair—or fur, in this case."

Enda nodded. "Yes. Well, we have other things to do." She turned her attention back to the listings, working her way down the long scroll of entries offering credit for ships that would trade info back into specific systems. "A lot of interest in data going to Exile and Cambria . . . a lot going to Coulomb. Very little traffic for Mantebron or Walin, but that would make sense since the *Lighthouse* is on its way. No point in hauling data to a system that is about to have a drivesat in the neighborhood."

"Most of these are short run contracts," Gabriel said. "They want delivery within one or two starfalls . . . fourteen to twenty days of pickup." He leaned against the wall, shaking his head. "Those aren't much good to us. It's going to take us the better part of a month to get back to Aegis from Mantebron, let alone Corrivale."

"Look a little further down the list," Enda said and went down to her quarters.

Gabriel did. By the time she came back, carrying the squeeze bottle for her plant, he was well down into listings for data not so time-sensitive. "Slow runs," he said. "There's a fair number of cargoes here that have no due dates on them at all. Just 'expedited delivery.' "

"That usually means 'Please just get it there within the next few months,'" Enda said. "A fair amount of data travels that way, archival material mostly. No one would call it 'nonessential,' but there is no point for it to hurry."

"No point for anyone to go out of their way carrying it, either," Gabriel said. "It doesn't carry much of a premium. Costs plus five percent."

"Why would it?" Enda said. "It is not dangerous cargo or time-sensitive. Easy work for low pay. This is the kind of info-trading just suited for people who might be carrying other cargoes on the side." She watered her bulb. "Is there anything slow destined for Coulomb? That would not be far out of our way and can be quickly dropped before our run to Eldala."

"Or after," Gabriel said. "We might not be there long. If there's no urgency on the shipment at the contract end, why hurry?"

"I don't know," Enda said. "I would sooner take care of it beforehand."

Gabriel looked at the list. "There you are. Coulomb. Assorted entertainment material, administrative matters . . . About half our capacity, I'd say."

"Do you want to file the application?"

"Let me see if anything else is available to go out the same direction," Gabriel said. "No point in going out half empty if we don't have to." He spent a little more time with the list and finally said, "That seems to be it for Coulomb. There's material for Armstrong, but that's too far out of the way."

"I agree. Let us file for that Coulomb load before someone beats us to it."

Gabriel called up the information tanks' support programs, brought the new scheduling list to their attention, and instructed the programs to speak to the drivesat, laying claim to the waiting loads. After the interrogate/answer cycle completed, the display lit up with the Concord Communications Commission template contract and the Aegis drivesat's loading parameters. The drivesat would load the material to *Sunshine* in pulses each time it surfaced from drivespace.

"That suit you?" Gabriel said, as Enda read the terms of the contract.

"Next page?" she said. Gabriel scrolled down. "Yes, that seems fine to me. Identical to our Terivine contract except for the time limitations, or lack of them." She went off down the hall. "If you approve, Gabriel, so do I."

"On its way." Gabriel touched the controls on the keypad that completed the contract and sent it out.

No sooner had he done so than Gabriel began feeling nervous. The previous contact with the drivesat had been automatic. If anyone had any reason to want to stop *Sunshine* from picking up another load—like wanting to ask questions about a fatality at Terivine, or if Delde Sota's tampering with their system ID had failed—it would happen now.

What am I supposed to do, sit here and hide forever? I didn't murder anyone. I'm innocent, and I'll bloody well act like it.

Those long hours in the cell back on Phorcys still came back to Gabriel in dreams sometimes. In the dreams, he would be there forever; he was found guilty even though he knew he was innocent. He would never get out . . .

The screen flickered, breaking his reverie and churning his insides. Gabriel swore under his breath.

Message encrypted and packed. Cargo scheduled.

A second later the screen said, *Cargo dispatched. Drivesat relay confirms backup. Original saved. Cleaning cycle begins . . .*

Gabriel got up and stretched. "Done," he said, as Enda came back.

"Now we wait," said Enda. She yawned and added, "I might sleep. We have been very busy for a while."

"You do that," Gabriel said. "I'll wait for Helm."

Gabriel sat there for a few more minutes, wondering if the display would suddenly fill with some message from the Concord Communications Commission saying that *Sunshine*'s infotrading license had been revoked because of the incident at Rivendale, or that it was revoked because it had been given in error to a ship part-owned by a wanted murderer, or they had

…nshine's tampered ID codes.

…of these things happened, and he relaxed enough to start am…g himself with the local Grid. It had been a long while since Gabriel had been in his home Grid, and he found it not much changed, especially not the fifty channels belonging to Mask and Bauble Studios, "the oldest continuously running studio in the Verge," with its numerous space operas, soap operas, and other holoserials. Other things also had not changed—particularly the long waiting times, broken transmissions, and other annoyances inherent to the Aegis Grid. It was really very much behind the times, despite the presence of a busy system government, huge amounts of traffic, and entertainment firms like M&B pumping it full of content.

A little leisurely paging through the local news revealed that the Regent was still in negotiations with both VoidCorp and Insight over the contracts for installation of new Grid software and hardware. *Neither of them is going to let the other win,* Gabriel thought. *They hate each other too much. All the Regent has to do is let them keep outbidding each other. Hale's not stupid. He needn't do anything concrete, and when someone finally puts their seal on the bottom of the deal, he'll have enough Concord dollars to build another island out of—*

Up in the pilots' cabin, *Sunshine's* comms channel chirped. Gabriel touched the keypad in front of him to route it to the sitting room. In the display, *Longshot's* ID flashed.

"Hey, Helm," Gabriel said.

"Seem to be running a little off-course," Helm said. "Maybe I should look at the stardrive."

"Hey, it got you here. Don't fix what isn't broken."

Helm chuckled. "You have any problems?"

"Not a thing."

"Everything else OK?"

"No problems," Gabriel said, knowing what Helm meant.

"Your stone behaving itself now?"

Gabriel looked over at it, on the shelf next to Enda's bulb. "Not a squeak out of it."

"Anything more about your Ricel guy catch up with you?"

"Not a word as yet. Meantime, we're waiting for clearance on a load of non-time-sensitive stuff."

"Mantebron?"

"Coulomb."

"A little out of our way, that. Delde Sota'n me are going to recharge the drive and head back to Corrivale. Delde Sota's getting concerned about those errands she has to run."

"Got time for one last dinner?" Gabriel said, suddenly feeling a little wistful.

"Before recharge? At least. After that, she's kind of urgent. We may need to meet you back here."

"Or somewhere else on our way back from Eldala, yeah . . . a few weeks along. You sure you feel comfortable leaving us by ourselves with all this highly valuable data we're going to be carrying?"

Helm laughed softly and said, "You're good enough with the guns—I'm less worried about you than I was. Word about Terivine may get around in good ways as well as bad."

"I hope you're right," Gabriel said. "See you soon."

"Right," Helm said, and cut the channel.

If the *Lighthouse* was about to turn up, and they were leaving on it, there was one more thing Gabriel needed to do, and he did not care to be rushed doing it. Quietly, taking his time so as not to sound nervous, Gabriel dictated his report to the authorities of what had happened on Rivendale and in space above it. In the middle of the process, his insides jumped again as comms went off once more. The ID in the display said CCC BLUEFALL.

Gabriel swallowed. "This is *Sunshine*," he said.

"This is CCC Bluefall," a bored-sounding voice said. "We wish to apologize for the delay in handling your contract application." Gabriel swallowed again. "Your approved contract is in the system and will be forwarded to you at the earliest opportunity consonant with decreased traffic in the drivesat or in-system relays. Thank you for your patience. Repeating, this is CCC Bluefall—"

Gabriel let it repeat. They approved it. No problems!

He briefly entertained the idea of waking up Enda to tell her.
No, let her sleep. She was right; we're fine.

The subject of the events at Terivine had come up several
times in their passage to Aegis. Now, here he sat with the report
all but completed and additional "exhibits" appended—copies of
Sunshine's logs, and her flight recordings. Like most ships, she
was programmed to make such recordings when her weapons
were cast loose. Gabriel was nervous enough about this aspect of
the report, even though Delde Sota's delicate "adjustments" to
Sunshine's logs had apparently concealed the presence of her
plasma cannon. If they detected the forgery, he would be in more
than enough trouble, but that trouble wouldn't start right away.
Gabriel was now down to his last piece of business—which
bureau to send the report to. The CCC had to see a copy. Info-
traders, after all, were required to keep an eye out for each other.
The more obvious destinations for the report were the Regency
and Alaundril embassies on Bluefall. Gabriel tagged one copy for
each embassy's colonial attaché, then sat looking for a few
moments at the files. Logs, 3D recordings, weapons records,
everything was ready, waiting to be sent. In a moment of grim
humor, he added one more destination, to Lorand Kharls, wherever he was at the moment.

If he doesn't know all about this already . . .

Though this time, even Kharls would have trouble knowing
anything so soon. No harm then in surprising him, if anything
truly could surprise that nasty, devious little man.

Gabriel looked down at the keypad and the SEND key, but
paused. *Do I really have to send this? And if I do, who knows
what'll happen to my life as a result?*

He couldn't get rid of the idea that however good his intentions, this was going to misfire. Another thought went through
Gabriel's head. With all the confusion, why bother putting your
head in the noose? They might never notice, or not for a long
time.

A phrase from somewhere went through his head. *The guilty
flee when no man pursueth.* Gabriel's face went grim again.

I am not guilty!

He reached out; his hand hovered over the key.

He touched it.

The messages encrypted and filed themselves away among the data transfer routines in *Sunshine*'s insides.

Messages encrypted and packed, the display said. *Cargo scheduled.*

A few seconds past, then a new message flashed onscreen. *Cargo dispatched. Drivesat relay confirms backups. Originals saved. Cleaning cycle begins . . .*

That was that. If anything was going to happen, Gabriel doubted he would wait have to wait long for it to happen. The Alaundrin and Regency embassies would have the reports now.

When Enda appeared again from her quarters nearly an hour later, it was almost a shock to see her looking so untroubled and normal.

"Any news about that application?" she said.

"Yes," Gabriel replied. "No problems. Helm called. He and Delde Sota are going back to Corrivale after they recharge. That unfinished business she mentioned . . ."

"I thought they might," Enda said, rubbing her face a little wearily. "Well, they have been good to come so far with us. Now we will go out alone and see what new things the worlds hold in store for us."

New cycle, the display said suddenly. *Delayed embarkation. Confirming reception facility clean. Embarking data . . .*

The comms circuits chirped again. Off to one side of the Aegis heralds in the display, *Longshot*'s little ID came up.

Gabriel touched the keypad. This time, 3D and sound came up together: and there was Helm and Delde Sota.

"Dinner this evening?" Helm said. "Seems smart, since you'll be leaving before we've finished recharging."

"It's a good idea. After that, when will we see you again?"

"When you're back from the back of beyond. We'll meet you here, if you like. The doctor wouldn't mind checking out some of the local options."

"It's a pretty world, Bluefall," Gabriel said, "and they'd be glad to have someone with your talents. Any one of a hundred companies would hire you, if you feel like settling in."

"Possibility: might consider it," said Delde Sota. "Have a few loose ends to tie up back on Iphus."

Enda nodded. "Well, we should move ourselves to the coordinates where traffic for the *Lighthouse* is meant to wait. Meet us there?"

"No problem," Helm said.

Comms went dark.

Chapter Eight

AFTER DINNER, HELM and the doctor left and Gabriel tried to rest but did not sleep well. The dreams came again, light and darkness, and fear, but stronger than usual. Excitement. A sense of something happening, and something *about* to happen. Something profound and profoundly moving, so that in the midst of the darkness and the flaring fire, Gabriel trembled. *Is* it fear, he found himself thinking in the middle of the dream, or something else? He hardly knew what to call it. Neither did what watched him. Something—

He sat up in the bed, panting, sweating.

Again, Gabriel thought, but this time there had been more. And this time, he had not been alone in the dream.

Across his cabin, the luckstone, glowing a very faint gold under the matte-dark outer shell, lay benignly on a shelf next to a couple of solids and old books.

It has something to do with *that,* he thought.

He had no proof, but he had not had such dreams until . . .

Until after I was thrown out of the marines. It *could* have something to do with that. The stress, the displacement . . .

Reasonable as that seemed, Gabriel was sure the dreams had nothing to do with his trial or cashiering. Just looking at the stone after one of these dreams caused a peculiar feeling of resonance, as if the stone had something to do with what he had seen. It was no part of the action in the dreams—if action was the right word for it—but it was involved.

There was someone there . . .

He put his face down in his hands for a moment, closing his eyes again as he chased the memory.

Useless. Gone.

Gabriel looked at the stone.

I wish I knew how to find out more about this, but I don't have a clue. It's going to have to wait.

He sighed and went to shower, thinking he would step up to the pilots' cabin afterwards and have one more look at the Aegis drivesat before he and Enda had to start their linkage to *Lighthouse*.

The drivespace relay had always fascinated him, not least because he had been science-mad as a boy. The drivesat and its kindred had thrown a wrench into the particle-wave theories of slower-than-light communication. Since messages sent through drivespace did their "jump" in only eleven hours, as opposed to the hundred-and-twenty-one hours required for matter, then the basic units of that energy could not be particles, waves, or anything to do with matter at all. There were noisy arguments among the more "exotic" physicists as to whether this theory impugned the formally "equal" status of matter and energy. Every now and then, someone came wandering along the news channels suggesting that the physical world didn't really exist and drivespace relays proved it.

In his teens, Gabriel had been less concerned about whether he and the physical world existed. His father had bought him a telescope when he was very young, and Gabriel had spent many happy nights looking out into space, especially at Redcrown and its eccentric rings. The drivesat relay had been entirely another kind of thrill, starfall and starrise every second, distant but tempting. Some day, he had thought, someday I'll do that. I'll see that fire outside my ship, and a few days later, I'll look at a new world no one's ever seen. . . .

Gabriel found himself looking at the system with new eyes. When they first arrived, he had felt little interest in the drivesat, but now, sitting in the pilots' cabin, he looked longingly out the viewshield for a glimpse of something else. The fierce sapphire gleam of Bluefall, like nothing else in this part of space—vast oceans reflecting the yellow light of Aegis, the pure blue-white glimmer of the disk, the home to which he could not go.

Next time, perhaps . . .

He was not even sure in which direction he should be looking. Aegis he could see, though not in its full splendor with the viewshield dimmed to keep him from suffering eye damage.

Gabriel reached into the 3D display and triggered the controls for the system drive, just enough to tumble *Sunshine* in place. She pitched forward, and reflected light began pouring in through the viewshield. There, with craft small and large clustered around it, was the *Lighthouse*.

Gabriel, looking down the length of the huge structure, touched the control to stop *Sunshine*'s tumble. People might talk casually about craft kilometers long, but when it came your turn to snuggle up to one in a ship measuring only sixty meters long, you came to appreciate the size. At one end of the long spindle-like central structure was a broad, conical engineering section. At the other end was the "city section," a tall dome-like structure crowned with spires and towers, and below that the docking section lay nestled like a broad, flat drum. Staggered between the docking area and the engineering section were four huge sets of docking spars meant for smaller vessels to grapple onto. The spars were already loaded with numerous spacecraft of all kinds: cargo ships, private vessels, a few larger freighters, but there were plenty of empty spaces. The entire structure rotated gently in Aegis's light, glittering with artificial illumination where shadow fell. Looking at it gave Gabriel the same kind of feeling he got from mountains, a pleasant sense of physical insignificance, except that this was due to something manmade, and the feeling therefore had a slight and peculiar quality of pride associated with it as well.

"It is impressive," Enda said as she came up to lean on the back of his seat and gaze past him. "Have you reviewed her schedule?"

"Not yet."

"She made starrise about an hour ago and sent out a news package. It is in *Sunshine*'s mail system. It confirms what we had heard. The stop in Aegis system will be brief—forty-eight hours only, just enough time to recharge."

"Any changes in its transit schedule?"

"A small one," Enda said, "a change of order in destinations. Mantebron first, and then Walin rather than the other way around."

"Do they say why?"

"Domestic concerns."

"Walin's or Mantebron's? Or local ones aboard *Lighthouse?*"

"They do not say," Enda said, "but I suppose I can see why they would not. This vessel's movements are carefully watched. Sudden changes in its schedule can have political implications or would be assumed to have them."

They looked out at the vast rotating shape beneath them.

"This is your last chance to change your mind," Enda said. "We will be going a long way from help."

"It's also a long way from the people who're chasing us," Gabriel said. "Maybe it'll make them think twice about following. If they have a large ship, there's nothing we can do to stop them, but if they're just single-shipping it, then they'll be far behind us."

Enda tilted her head in agreement. "We should contact the *Lighthouse* then and book ourselves a spar location. They do not look too full. I doubt there will be a problem."

In fact, it turned out to be surprisingly easy. Five minutes spent on the *Lighthouse*'s Grid gave them a clearance for spar six, spaces nineteen through twenty, and a courteous request to make fast to the spar as quickly as possible so that later-arriving vessels could be accommodated without difficulty.

The docking itself took less than half an hour, most of which was spent piloting *Sunshine* into position near the docking spar and equalizing her motion to that of the *Lighthouse.* For this, too, there was specialized assistance, the spar having its own docking computer that spoke directly to *Sunshine*'s system drive. Docking clamps mated to *Sunshine*'s landing skids, pulling her close to the spar and fastening her down. A tube then extended from the spar and offered itself up to *Sunshine*, leaving her airlock mated to the rapid transit system inside the spar. With no more than several loud thumps and bumps, it was all over.

Stuck, Gabriel thought. Until *Lighthouse* made starrise at Mantebron, there was no escape. Not that he would have considered pushing off a vessel while in drivespace, especially when the larger vessel owned the drive. *Sunshine* would never be seen again.

"Well," Enda said, "I shall go aboard and have a look around. There is no need to wait until after starfall."

"I might wait," Gabriel said.

She looked at him and sighed. "You are still afraid that someone is going to take umbrage at your presence. You must try to relax about this."

"Having stood in court in Phorcys and seen the looks on the faces of the Concord prosecutors when they were told they couldn't have me," Gabriel said, "relaxation isn't as easy as you might think, no matter how good I know Delde Sota is."

. "Well," Enda said, "I will go out and possibly find something interesting for lunch. I doubt they will have any fraal restaurants here as good as the one we found in Sunbreak, but there may be something worth bringing back."

Enda vanished into her quarters for a few moments and came back dressed as Gabriel had rarely seen her: in fraal high fashion. She wasn't wearing one of the singlesuits she normally favored, but a sleeveless vest and mid-calf kilt, all made from silken fabric with a subdued sheen of blue over a deep green. Beneath the kilt, she wore dark buskins laced up high.

"Very chic," Gabriel commented.

"First impressions are important," Enda said, and headed down the hall to *Sunshine*'s airlock. "Can I bring you anything?"

Gabriel shook his head. "Enjoy."

* * * * *

Gabriel spent a good while catching up with news from around the stellar nations, partly out of a feeling of duty, and partly out of habit. While posted on *Falada,* assisting the ambassador who had been working with the Phorcyn and Inoan governments, Gabriel had made it a personal requirement to be as well informed as anyone about interstellar relations. Now, after an hour reading the news, Gabriel found himself feeling that the worlds were going to hell and that Mantebron was not far enough away from the mess.

Realizing that this was not a healthy state of mind, Gabriel turned his attention to the entertainment channels. He found more of the M&B serials, all desperately alike and all written by the same small coterie of names. Gabriel began to think there was a prison island somewhere on Bluefall where, far from the glitz and glamor of the Watertower District, writers were kept chained to the gently waving trees and forced to write for their bread.

Other channels were better supplied. One showed nothing but features about the fauna and flora of various worlds, and Gabriel got entirely too fascinated by one documentary about the sex life of the scraaghek. Another channel showed nothing but the output of various people aboard *Lighthouse* playing virtual combat games. Gabriel watched with increasing amusement, as only a small percentage of the space combat games paid attention to details like gravity, acceleration, or the speed of light. He was relieved when Enda came back with a large bag full of parcels and began to unload them on the table in front of him.

"What in the worlds . . . ?" Gabriel said, as she came up with a box, opened it, and produced an odd sort of keypad. The keys were very wide, all black plastic without any sort of signage on them.

"It goes with the translation software that Angela sold us along with the exploration contract. She never completed registering the software or sending off for the extra parts." Gabriel didn't comment. This sounded all too like Angela. "The company that makes them has a distributor here," Enda continued, "and I had the registration information with me, so I picked these up."

Gabriel poked at the keypad. "Is the whole thing configurable?"

"So it seems, and here are some language modules for it.

'Formal Middle Fraal,' " she said with approval and handed that
data solid to Gabriel. "You can use this. Your accent is terrible."

"What accent?"

"Exactly," Enda said. "The one time you said hello to me . . ."
She smiled. "Let us just say I made allowances."

"Why? What did I say?"

"You meant to say 'Greeting and honor to you as well,' but I
am afraid it came out, 'You greet the sickness with my shoes,' or,
'You are sick on my—' "

Gabriel spluttered. "Oh, *Enda!*"

"The marine language course may have been recorded by
someone with a vile regional accent," Enda said, "or by one of
our people who had been away traveling so long that the form of
the language he spoke drifted considerably from the norm." She
sighed. "It is a danger, of course, but when a people fragment   "

Enda stopped. Gabriel turned to look at her. "Is something
wrong?"

Enda was gazing at the keypad on the table. "No, not as such,
but one does find oneself having the occasional argument with
someone who is no longer there. Another accident of much travel.
In any case, if you do that Fraal course, check with me. We have
a very slippery preterite, and I may be able to keep you from
being sick on someone else's shoes."

Enda rooted around in the box and came up with a couple
more solids. "Sheyan. Another good choice. Your accent at that
was fair—better than mine. And another manual. I do not know if
this is the same one we have already. You will want to check."

Enda went and changed back into her shipboard clothes and
then began cooking. Gabriel was distracted from the good smells
when the ship's mail system chimed for attention—something
either from Aegis or *Lighthouse*. Swallowing, Gabriel reached
out and touched the keypad, bringing the display to life again.

The infotrading system displayed the usual heralds as it
unpacked the message and decrypted it. Suddenly Gabriel found
himself staring at the CCC logo. The display cleared and began
to fill with text.

Gabriel began reading, aware of Enda looking over his shoulder with a pan in one hand. *This is to confirm your data trading contract for the following dates . . .*

"So, then," Enda said and went back to the galley.

Gabriel let out a long breath and scrolled on down. No notes, no addenda, no nothing, and no reference to his report.

"When do we eat?" asked Gabriel, now that he suddenly had an appetite again.

They had their lunch or dinner. Gabriel had no idea what it was, but it tasted wonderful. Afterwards, Enda went off to her cabin to rest. Gabriel, still feeling cautious, sat waiting for any further messages. None came. Finally he pulled down the chair on the far side of the table, put his feet up, and let the Grid display babble stellar nations' news at him until it lulled him to sleep.

How long he dozed there he was not sure, but the chime of ship's comms woke him up. Gabriel reached out to the control keypad, touched it, and found himself looking at Helm and Delde Sota.

"You're about to jump," Helm said. "Thought we'd make sure you were comfortable."

Gabriel smiled. "As much so as possible, under the circumstances."

Enda came in, looking past him at the display. Delde Sota's braid could be seen knotting itself several times, partly behind her back, as if in secret. "Intention/wish: go safely, you two. Phymech is in order; checked. Command: do not need it."

"We're in agreement there, Doctor," Gabriel said. "You take care too. Helm—"

"Don't say it," Helm said. "You're welcome. Take care and send word."

Their images blanked out.

Data Embarkation Complete, the herald said a moment later. Enda looked at Gabriel.

"He is a gentle creature," she said, "and hates long farewells."

"I don't know about the 'gentle' part," Gabriel said, "but I'll miss him too." A slight vibration went through *Sunshine*'s frame,

and a sudden sheen of green-blue light came down the hall from
the pilots' cabin.

Gabriel leaned around the sitting room wall to look down the
hall. Through the open door to the cabin he saw sheets of blue
light, like water that glowed, come streaking up over *Sunshine*'s
viewshield. Quietly, without fuss, it happened—fifty light-years'
worth of starfall. *Lighthouse* slipped into drivespace, the darkness
falling around them like a curtain that would rise again, five days
later at Mantebron.

*   *   *   *   *

For the first couple of days, Gabriel was increasingly obsessed
with trying to get the translation software to work. This proved to
be a maddening business. The manuals appeared to have been
compiled by people for whom the kind of Standard spoken on
Bluefall and other Verge worlds was a second language, and
Gabriel became so infuriated with the infernal machine that he
just couldn't let it alone.

The basic idea was simple enough. The translation software
operated in two modes, one for known languages and one for new
ones. The keypad operated either as a whole screen or in con-
junction with one, "listening" to spoken words in one language
while showing and speaking the words in the other. When you
had both language modules complete and present, the order could
be reversed. The "learning" mode was simpler. The keypad displayed simple images—sun, tree, water—and learned the spoken
words for them, building them into the beginnings of a grammar.

Gabriel would have enjoyed playing with that part of the program, but the operating instructions were inconsistent. What one
chapter of the manual said about running, say, a verb placement
module, another later chapter might contradict.

The more frustrated Gabriel got, the more time he spent with
the hardware, determined either to make it work or to take a
hammer to it. *Chalice, the All Purpose Translation Tool,* the program called itself. He remembered his old marine friend Hal

saying, "Anything claiming to be 'All Purpose' is probably good for nothing. Useful software and hardware are designed to specific purposes. Nothing is good at everything, even people."

Eventually Gabriel put the program aside and took more time to regale himself with the delights of the *Lighthouse* Grid. It was far beyond impressive. During this period, Enda came and went without comment, though Gabriel noticed that she was getting more sleep than usual.

She was sleeping again now, and Gabriel was immured in the sitting room, paging through the Grid. He looked over at the translation module, laying mulish and mute over on one of the shelves, and could not bear the thought of dealing with it any further. There was only one thing left for him to do.

I've been putting it off long enough. If something is going to happen, let it happen.

Gabriel went to get something from his quarters that he had laughed at when Delde Sota had given it to him: a package of hair-shift and a set of eye-change lenses. The latter produced a perfect fake retinal pattern for scanners that used such technologies. Gabriel had been too unnerved to ask where or how Delde Sota had come by them—it occurred to him that there might be things it was better for him not to know.

He retired into the refresher and came out blond and blue-eyed, though Delde Sota had warned him that the blondness would last for only a few hours, and after that would tarnish.

Gabriel dressed quickly in his best clothes, put his credit chip in his pocket, and picked up one last thing: his luckstone.

He locked *Sunshine*'s airlock from the outside and pulled himself down the tube to its far end, clenching his stomach harder than usual since he did not know what the gravity situation was going to be at the far end. To Gabriel's surprise, there was gravity even in the spar. The other end gave onto a cylindrical metal-paneled hallway about ten meters wide. Down the middle of it, faired into the floor, was a stator track for transport. Walkways lay along both sides of the track, which ran about a quarter kilometer in either direction.

Gabriel walked toward the central core. After a few minutes, a little bullet-shaped transport pulled up next to him and dilated a doorway.

Gabriel got in and sat on one of the two benches that ran down each side of the transport. The door constricted and the transport took off smoothly, pausing again after about a minute to pick up a dark-skinned lady in the voluminous gown and hood of an Orlamu. After another minute's travel, the transport stopped.

"Main core," said a feminine computer-voice. "Engineering transport to the right, city transport to the left. *Whtala vheirna, daikash leil'hairhe . . .*"

Gabriel exited and headed to the left, wondering if his fraal would ever sound that mellifluous. Probably not without a lot of work, but one thing's for sure: I'm not going to be sick on anyone's shoes again.

Once he entered the core, the gravity disappeared, and Gabriel pulled himself along by convenient handholds to the first open door he found, a large elevator with a sign above its doors labeled *Express. Deck 197, Deck 198.* Humans in every kind of clothes were hanging onto the handholds, though there were a few mechalus, a number of weren—their relationship with the Orlamu had always been close—as well as assorted human and fraal Star Force personnel, and a couple of Orlamu priests. The lift closed and took off for the long run up to 197.

Gabriel looked out into a broad plaza as the door hissed opened and several occupants began to empty out. The interiors here looked nothing like those of the usual space station. Walls, columns, and buildings here were faced in wood and stone as well as plastic. The feeling of sheer openness and space surprised Gabriel as the elevator took off and stopped in a second plaza, even bigger than the first and centered on an upward-gushing fountain.

It's not just the materials, he thought as he hauled himself out and took a moment to get used to gravity again, it's the basic architecture. The Orlamu had originally constructed the *Lighthouse of Faith* as a religious facility, and like many other religious organizations, they had used a sense of space and height to attempt to draw the mind upward and outward. Where their architecture had not been overlaid or replaced by newer building—as it had all over Deck 198—the effect worked extremely well.

This area was hardly Orlamist at all, having over the years become the social center of the *Lighthouse*. Numerous pathways led across the central plaza. Scattered across the broad expanse of pale, gleaming stone floor were sales kiosks, food and news booths, lounging areas, hotels, restaurants, bars, and a cluster of specialty purchasing facilities that constituted a shopping area astonishingly well supplied by anyone's definition.

Gabriel spent the better part of an hour there, spotting the gourmet shop where Enda had picked up their lunch two days before. Next to it was an entertainment kiosk with preprogrammed solids, and Gabriel was much amused to see a large stack of solids labeled as *The Complete Verge Hunter*. It could hardly be the complete run, since that turgid and inadvertently funny space opera was still in production. Elinke Dareyev had been terribly fond of it. Hearing the captain of a seriously armed vessel shouting with terrifying enthusiasm at the end of a boozy officer's mess night, "Not for myself, but *For The Force!*" had sometimes made Gabriel very glad that someone else's finger was on the firing buttons until next morning.

Where is she now, I wonder? Gabriel thought. There was something else lost to him, one more reason to get on with clearing his name. He had no idea whether he would ever be able to regain Elinke's friendship, but at least he wanted her to understand that he was not guilty of her lover or anyone else's murder.

Gabriel went on among the kiosks, admiring the clothes and the jewelry laid out there, the books and frozen images, the gifts and knickknacks from many worlds. *I could afford a few things if I felt like it,* Gabriel thought. As he turned toward one shop with some semiformal clothes in its forward display area, he caught a glimpse of midnight blue and silver coming toward him.

He froze. Marines, five of them: two men, three women. They glanced at him, glanced at the window, and glanced away. Gabriel stiffened, holding his breath.

The soldiers just kept going, not even sparing Gabriel a second glance.

They don't even know me. Why should they? Gabriel thought, turning back toward the window. It's not like I have *TRAITOR* branded on my forehead. Even if they had recognized me, how do I know they'd necessarily have shared the 'official' opinion that I'm guilty? It's not like the marines are some vast many-bodied, one-headed beast with no brain.

Gabriel looked over the clothes, decided they didn't suit him, and wandered farther across the plaza. He became extremely interested in an Insight software distributor's kiosk. The JustWadeIn fighting hardware in *Sunshine* was Insight-made, but there was no new version available yet. After that, he spent a good while looking at a long case full of delicacies, sweets and tiny savories of a kind he had seen Enda gorge herself on more than once.

He would have been hard-pressed to say exactly when he realized he was being followed. Gabriel had been taught to have an instinct about this kind of thing, since having one could keep you from being killed. For some time now, since after the marines had passed him, he had been aware of something constantly near him . . . a patch of the same color, a sound of footsteps that repeated and didn't change pitch. Not too close, but close enough.

He "lost interest" in the sweets and went wandering more purposefully, trying to see how closely his shadow was willing to follow. At no point would Gabriel actually allow himself to look in that direction. That would spoil the game and possibly alert his quarry. He stopped by an open eating area and paused to lift the menu pad from an empty table. The shape following him—a woman, not very tall, dressed somberly in what might have been a jumpsuit—put herself behind a news kiosk where he couldn't see. Gabriel put the pad down and strolled away to another of the shopping areas, where he tucked himself behind another clothing sales outlet.

A few flickers of motion wavered off among the kiosks about a hundred yards away. Whoever was following him was better at

it than Gabriel knew how to be. He was torn between appreciation of a genuine talent and wondering whether that talent was
shortly going to place a knife in his back. While weapons were
not to be carried here, there were some weapons too small to
detect and others, like knives, that could be easily concealed.

Gabriel knew a fair amount about stalking an adversary himself, but it felt odd to slink and skulk without being armed. Additionally, it was hard to skulk profitably in a place this wide open.
His own training, at least the part which involved board-and-
sneak work on ships and space stations, was better suited to
narrow corridors with low ceilings and corners to hide behind.
This was like hiding in a cathedral, with the additional hint that
more than the temporal powers might be watching you.

He made his way casually around the lower walls of the dome
to one of the lifts that lead to the higher levels. One chimed and
opened for him. He slipped in, waited for it to close, and then
punched for the level marked *Deck 200*.

Let them play with that, he thought while the lift waited for
any additional passengers. There were guards up there, Gabriel
knew, but he was willing to have a brief brush with them if it
would discomfit the person following him. It was possible that
the "shadow" would have trouble with them too.

As the lift door began to close, he saw her come out from behind
a kiosk, briefly looking in another direction—a slim little woman
with dark hair. She was turning her head away from Gabriel just as
he got that glimpse, but not before he saw the blue eyes.

Now let her wonder, Gabriel thought. She would have to stand
there watching the lift indicator until it revealed his destination,
then she would have to follow him up, and he would have time to
hide himself or find a position where getting at him would get her
in trouble.

The lift proceeded upwards at a good speed and finally let
Gabriel out into a bare round area. A few bored guards stood off
to one side. A bank of chip-access entryways intended for the
wealthy residents of the city lined the opposite wall. Gabriel
walked toward them unconcernedly, getting out his chip as if he

were just one more guest of some wealthy resident of the city.

Gabriel slipped his chip into the machine and was astonished to see the door snap back silently. The guards on the other side didn't even bother looking at him as he walked through, trying not to gawk.

He was in a large common access area, with numerous corridors leading off toward the bases of various towers. One lift stood by itself. An Orlamu guard, looking as bored as his colleagues out by the main access, stood at the base of it. Gabriel headed that way, and the guard looked at him with an expression suggesting he was going to tell Gabriel to go back the way he had come.

Gabriel wondered if the guard would let him up there if he claimed to be a "seeker," someone in the early stages of the Orlamist faith.

Behind him, a bizarre strangled hooting noise went up. Gabriel swallowed, turned to look behind him, and saw the access-area guards converging on one of the doorways. One of the uniformed guards was kicking the thing in a desultory way, but there was no apparent result, and the noise did not stop.

Gabriel stopped to watch this too. Behind him, the Orlamu guard was also watching with a suddenly amused expression, like someone who has seen this happen before. He turned to touch the lift column behind him, apparently touching in some combination, and then went down toward the access gates, giving Gabriel a glance as he went.

The guard joined his fellows working over the turnstile. Gabriel, watching this, turned away and went over to the lift column, curious. It had no summons controls that he could see, only a chip slot. Out of sheer curiosity, Gabriel stuck his ID in.

Around the side of the column, the lift opened.

Outside, the strangled hooting of the alarms was still going on, and the Orlamu guard was trying to help the others with the malfunctioning turnstile. Gabriel shook his head and slipped into the lift. The door closed.

The panel inside was labeled *1-22* and *Temple*. Gabriel hit the control for *Temple* and then spent the brief ride upward staring at his ID card. What did Delde Sota do to this thing? What else could I get into on this station?

The lift stopped and opened into a dimly lit corridor that ended in what looked like another lift access. Gabriel walked along the hallway as if he belonged there, although he was sweating slightly—he was not going to be able to keep this act up for long. At the end of the hall he paused and looked around, trying not to look lost. A lift door lined the wall on the right, but on his left were very different doors, tall and arched and black. As he stepped toward one, it opened silently outward. He slipped in, and it closed behind him.

Darkness. Gabriel paused to let his eyes become marginally used to the dimness, and then stepped forward. His eyes quickly accustomed themselves to the light, just a dim gleam from further inside and higher up. Gabriel smiled in the dark. If Miss Blue Eyes was still with him, which now seemed very unlikely, she would have trouble sneaking up on him in here. There was no cover, nowhere to hide. The room was sixty meters across, round and empty, with only the one entrance and a simple round podium in the middle.

He moved out into it silently, toward the center of the great expanse, listening carefully as he went for the sound of any door or portal opening. The floor of the place was all black unpolished stone. The ceiling was not a ceiling as such, but another dome, tall, narrow, and pointed, with only a few telltale gleams to betray its structure. In that vast, graceful space of darkness, suspended high above Gabriel, burned a single point of light.

The sharp-pointed dome itself was at least a hundred meters high from the pediment, to the point where the great inward-curving triangles of reinforced ceiling drew together. How splendid this room and the vista beyond it would look when the *Lighthouse* was in normal space, Gabriel could imagine. But here, surrounded by the velvet blackness of drivespace, its aspect was possibly even more affecting. Up high, the single light burned, white, invisibly suspended in the darkness, not too remote, yet not too close—an eye that watched, or the symbol for life burning in defiance of darkness always held at bay.

A simple enough symbol, Gabriel thought. One could read just about anything into it. A focus for meditation, an image of good versus evil, a simple contrast between extremes . . .

Gabriel stood quiet in the darkness for some moments, listening, though not only for footsteps. He thought of Lorand Kharls saying to him, *The Concord may have the power to kick you out of the Service, but it has no power to absolve you of the oaths you swore. Only the Power to which you swore them has that authority. Heard anything from that quarter lately?*

The question had no better answer now than then, though it made Gabriel less angry than it had when he had first heard it. He was still trying to work out exactly what Kharls had been getting at.

My oath. To that at least Gabriel had held firm, not only because he had been surrounded by other people who took them equally seriously, but because they were right.

To protect the Concord and the peace of her peoples against all threats overt and covert, public and private—

Someone had to stand up and make worlds safe for people to lead peaceful lives. It was hard, in a universe where forces as diverse as pirates and big business moved at will, taking whatever they thought they could get away with. Other forces also were moving that Gabriel understood less, but which troubled him more. He thought of those little ball bearing ships with pilots in them who might have been human once, but were now dead and horribly changed. They hinted that something out there was coming, something with unknown motivations . . . motivations Gabriel doubted intended much good for anyone.

Undeath. Bondage. Pain.

He remembered the faces of the man and the sesheyan he had seen, one after the delicate autopsy that Doctor Sota had performed, one after the rather rough dissection he'd done himself on Grith. Both faces had been twisted into shapes of anguish or rage at what had been done to them. Whatever dark things were causing this fate to fall upon innocent creatures, Gabriel thought they needed to be stopped.

As for oaths—

The Marine Oath allowed you to supply your own authority, as long as it was the one you considered Supreme, the Force to which you would answer for things well done or ill done, promises made or broken. Gabriel, like others of his intake group, had simply invoked the Creator, though by no specific name. He was still not sure in what, exactly, he believed. His father and mother had raised him in the Humanity Reformation tradition, but from early on Gabriel had rejected that, hearing doctrine in it that simply made no sense to him, even when he was eleven. Gabriel had gone without protest to the small local Reformation services with his parents until he was adult enough not to have to go any more if he chose not to, then he went into the marines and was relieved to find that no one cared what religion he was.

It had always astonished Gabriel that there were people who seriously believed, that Helm would suffer terrible tortures in some afterlife simply because he had the misfortune of being born with tailored genes.

As if that was his fault! If anyone should have done any burning, it should have been his parents. Many of the more radical Hatire even believed that mechalus like Doctor Sota would be punished for the cybernetic parts of her makeup. The idea of such a punitive afterlife made no sense to Gabriel.

Gabriel listened, heard nothing around him, and walked forward to one side of the dome, looking around at this simple and elegant place that the Orlamu had made. For them, this darkness of drivespace was the Divine Unconscious in which all potential dwelt unseen, the endless expanse over which the mind of God moved before the beginning of things. Their founding Prophet said he had felt a Presence out there in the darkness, listening attentively to the thoughts and fears of the first human being to be subjected to starfall. He had, however, brought back no message from that listening Presence.

Gabriel's breath caught in his throat. There, off in the darkness under the edge of the dome, a shadow paused, then retreated into shadow.

Two can play at that game.

Gabriel melted back into the shadow under the overhanging pediment as quickly as he could. His night vision had had a good while to adjust. He could see the shape slipping sideways, toward him.

Gabriel grinned and silently slid back toward the wall, hiding from the slight illumination of the single light up in the dome. He waited.

Very softly, he heard the footsteps coming. He listened to them even more attentively, for they were not the same footsteps that had been following him before. Those had been lighter. This was a heavier person, walking with a different rhythm.

Gabriel pressed against the wall and waited, watching the darkness come. It was not a woman, but a man, nearly as tall as Gabriel. The man held something slightly in front of his body in one hand. A gun? A knife?

Always hope for a gun, his weapons instructor had said to him. *Guns are easier than knives to take away, and they make their users careless and overconfident. If it's a knife, here's what to do—*

Cautiously, the shadow came toward him.

Gabriel did not move until the man was three steps away, then he took two of those steps, reached out for the thing in the man's hand, and clamped the hand tight around it. A sabot pistol!

Gabriel bent the man's wrist inward and applied the pressure in the spot he'd been taught. A strangled grunt came out of the man, and the gun fell. Gabriel kicked it away, not wanting to kill this person or be killed himself.

The man grappled with him, flailed at Gabriel's throat, catching it with his free hand. Gabriel wound his other arm through the man's, over and under, breaking the hold, then gripped the other arm, pulled the man close, swung him around so that the light from that solitary white beacon high above shone, however feebly, in his face.

Gabriel's insides jumped as the other struggled.

It was Jacob Ricel.

But he's dead!

Or supposed *to be dead—*

Suddenly everything reversed. It had been Ricel grappling Gabriel, and Gabriel working to free himself. Now Ricel was pushing him desperately away, and Gabriel was trying to hold him but couldn't get a firm grip. He did a leg sweep instead, catching Ricel behind one knee. Ricel went down, and Gabriel threw himself down hard on top of him—or onto where he should have been. Ricel rolled, scrambled to his feet, and ran.

Gabriel, stunned by his impact against the stone floor, levered himself up and went after Ricel as fast as he could. Light shone blinding in his eyes as Ricel threw himself out the door.

No, Gabriel thought, gasping as he ran after Ricel. No, *no!*

He plunged through the door into the antechamber. Empty. Gabriel glared at the lift, which the light above its door indicated was heading back down toward Level 200. Having no other option, Gabriel ran back to the lift he had come up in and slipped his ID chip into the slot. The door opened.

He slipped in and rode it down, trying to get his breath back and to make himself look less like he had just been in a fight. When the door opened again, he slipped out of the lift in the direction away from the turnstiles—

—right into the Orlamu guard.

"Uh, sorry," Gabriel said, "wrong floor . . ."

The guard took Gabriel firmly, if gently, by the arm and escorted him back to the turnstiles, putting him through one of the "outbound" ones and watching while Gabriel made his way back to the public access lift. All the guards were staring at him now. He wasn't sure he cared. Certainly no one would attack him at the moment.

There was no way to tell where Ricel had gone. Gabriel took the lift back down to Deck 198, his mind full of questions. Regardless of what Miss Blue Eyes had been up to, Ricel had to have been following him for a good while as well. The man had to have some kind of high-level clearance to have caught up with Gabriel where he did, but there would be no finding him now.

Gabriel came out of the lift and looked out across the huge deck. There was nothing but the buzzing, murmuring crowd going about its business—no Jacob Ricel and no petite blue-eyed woman, either.

Helplessly, Gabriel began to laugh. Gone, both of them, lost in this huge place and probably going to ground right this minute, God only knew where. It was too ironic that it had been the darkness that revealed Gabriel's enemy to him, and the light that had snatched him away.

He's here, and it has something to do with me. Now all I have to do is find out what.

Chapter Nine

THE *LIGHTHOUSE* MADE starrise with as little fuss as the starfall. A brief tremor pulsed through her huge fabric, and a sheet of crimson light blanketed her bulk like a lowering dawn. Gabriel watched it all on the *Lighthouse* Grid—saw the Concord cruisers that were the station's escort go arcing away, quartering her immediate area to see who was in the neighborhood. The sight reassured him, but he also wondered whether Ricel was hiding on one of them under some other name. He had gone out after his first encounter in faint hope of catching a glimpse of one of his shadows, but there had been no sign of either of them.

For the time being there was nothing to do but make *Sunshine* ready for her castoff. The *Lighthouse* had asked the ships riding with her not to depart simultaneously because of the increased possibility of an accident. Not that many ships appeared to be preparing to leave the *Lighthouse* here, and Gabriel could understand why.

They had come out of drivespace no more than fifty million kilometers from Mantebron's single inhabited planet, High Mojave. It was a cold, dry, desert world, isolated and nearly forgotten during the years of the Long Silence. Even the corsairs who ranged all through this distant part of space had passed High Mojave by, feeling that there was nothing there worth stealing—and probably they would have been right. With no air to breathe, barely enough water to condense, it was a world like old Mars in the Solar Union. Unlike Mars, it was not likely to survive more than another thirty or forty thousand years. Mantebron was near the end of its life, and most of the experts gave it thirty millennia at best before it would begin to expand into a red giant.

The settlers, mostly Orions and their descendants, didn't care. When all of human history spanned not that much more than six thousand years, thirty thousand seemed like enough time for their own purposes. Even so, reminders of the deaths of other cultures were scattered here and there across the planet.

Crumbling, ancient remains could be found in the heights or half buried in the silt of rivers that had been dry beds for fifty millennia. The Glassmakers, those old builders were called. No one knew if they had been a species or group of species. Their remnants were too old. Other Precursor species had been discovered here and there throughout explored space, but of all the Precursors, the Glassmakers were thought to be the oldest. As a result, almost nothing was known of them but a few ancient buildings, spires and minarets of great beauty and age, crystalline or milky, spearing up from promontories by seas now dry. Among the spires and the stones alike, the red-brown dust drifted and blew. It blew everywhere on High Mojave, over empty cracked lakebeds and fields occupied by tough, scrubby crops engineered not to mind little air and almost no water. Little domed communities dotted the desert where tiny groups of families held onto their independence and ignored the rest of the world as best they could.

"No place I'd want to linger," Gabriel said. He had seen little more than the *Lighthouse*'s current orientation information about the world, and that looked no more attractive than the general information he had picked up while doing his diplomatic work in the marines.

"No," said Enda. "The *Lighthouse* will stay for a couple of weeks, for it rarely comes out quite this far, so close to the edge of Open Space, but this area is no longer the backwater that it was. Since the Precursor ruins were found here, suddenly the stellar nations are showing interest, claiming that they want to bring the planet into the twenty-fifth century, improve conditions—"

"They just want to dig," Gabriel growled. "I bet VoidCorp is at the head of the line."

"Not just they," said Enda. "The Solar Union is interested, too, and the Hatire—partly, they say, for religious reasons. Though as always, power and wealth will have a great part in all of their reasoning."

Their turn to undock came. Gabriel retracted *Sunshine*'s tube and checked all the seals. The spar's clamps let go of *Sunshine*, and Gabriel lifted her carefully away, getting well clear before tumbling to look back. The warning for everyone not to depart *Lighthouse* at once turned out to have an ironic edge, for Gabriel saw only two other vessels leaving, both nondescript bulk freighters. One made its way straight down toward the planet— apparently a scheduled delivery of supplies. The other took itself a safe distance from the *Lighthouse* and went immediately into starfall in a blaze of yellow-white light.

"Not that anyone would be so foolish as to come after us while we are still obviously watching for them, I am sure," Enda said.

"Well," Gabriel said, "let's take ourselves a quarter million kilometers out to starfall. There's this, at least: anyone who bothers checking with the records on *Lighthouse* will see that we had a load of data for Coulomb. They may go there instead."

"Assuming they do not have starrise detection equipment," said Enda, "which will make our destination all too obvious."

Gabriel shrugged. If they did, there was nothing he could do about it.

They headed out past High Mojave above the plane of the ecliptic, and Gabriel went over his figures for their next jump. The starrise and starfall didn't particularly concern him, but coming into a system that had been explored only once or twice—and never completely—produced unique problems.

There was the matter of the planet's actual location. Settled planets all had at least one satellite that acted as a beacon for incoming ships. Such satellites indicated the planet's distance from its primary, its present position in its orbit, and a set of equations and baseline figures used to calculate the world's future positions around the primary for the next year or so. This information updated itself automatically and was uploaded to whatever infotrader passed. The infotrader's ship's systems would then pass the information into local planetary or system Grids and to whatever drivesat it passed. The information would also automatically disseminate itself to ships using those Grids, the coordinate info storing itself in ship's navigational computers until needed.

A newly explored planet did not acquire such a satellite unless the party responsible for the exploration was a stellar nation, a large company, or the Concord itself. Exploration contracts did not necessarily include such a satellite, since explorers typically were unwilling to pay for the equipment unless it was plain that the expenditure would be recouped. A planet explored in January would not be anywhere near that location in June. Unless the intrepid explorer felt like spending another five days in drivespace and another starfall and starrise's worth of fuel and energy, he would have to calculate where the planet would be at the time of his next starrise.

Gabriel had spent hours over Eldala's calculations because he did not trust Angela Valiz's figures. He knew he might be mistaken to judge someone by less than an hour's conversation, but he was none too sure of any observations she might have made about the new world, including its distance from its sun. That was another thing—

"Do the ephemerides we have say whether the planet has another name?" Gabriel said to Enda.

Sitting in the pilot's cabin, Enda shook her head. "No. The original survey called the star Eldala, so we may well call both star and planet that for the moment. We will be in no danger of confusing them when we get there."

Gabriel sighed. "Well, I can't do any more with these calculations. I've adjusted for the possibility that Angela may have misplaced the system's ecliptic, which is typically hard to nail down over a short period, but I don't dare adjust too much . . . and as for the rest of it, either she was right, or we'll just have to do another jump."

Enda reached into the 3D display between the pilots' seats and touched the controls for the stardrive. It was fully charged and began to cycle toward starfall on a two minute countdown.

"Last chance to fiddle with your figures," Enda said.

Gabriel shook his head. His attention was directed back the way they had come, toward *Lighthouse*. At this distance, it was impossible to see except as a faint spark reflecting Mantebron's light. He thought briefly of the darkness of the Temple of the Divine Unconscious, in which that single, seemingly distant light burned. Faint as it was, it had shown him something he had desperately wanted to see.

I'll be back soon, Gabriel thought.

Yellow-orange light, like fire, washed over *Sunshine* as she slipped into drivespace. If any other vessel followed them, her crew was in no position see it.

* * * * *

The five days went by quickly. Gabriel spent more time with the translator, working on his Formal Middle Fraal and avoiding anything to do with the language-analysis side of the machine. He had reason for keeping busy. After their first night in starfall, Gabriel was intent on staying awake as long as possible. That way, when he had to sleep, he might not dream.

The dream that first night had been like all the others: darkness, light in the darkness, and the two opposed to one another . . . fighting. Anger was added to the old fear, and a peculiar sense of both apprehension and desire. Something was trying to happen.

Again Gabriel was accompanied, but he could not tell by what. He didn't think it was a person. There was a sense of movement, but not through place. Everything came in abstracts, or at least everything that Gabriel could remember after the fact. It was maddening to wake up terrified, excited, exalted, and not know by *what*.

Enda let him alone to deal with it and did what she usually did—cooked, read, studied the stored Grid records they were carrying, and listened to music. As so often with her, it was choral music, ranging from vast choirs to ensembles of just four or five voices. For Gabriel, as he sat in his quarters with the translation module, the music evoked one of the more basic characteristics of fraal life, its essentially communal nature. He wondered more and more often what had led Enda to shift to so relatively isolated a lifestyle.

Gabriel knew that some hundreds of years back there had been a great division among fraal concerning the way they lived. Some of them became the Builders, who chose to live among other species, especially humans. Others, the Wanderers, took ever more exclusively to life in the great space-going fraal cities, drawing away from the other species, even shunning contact with them. Enda had been a Wanderer for a while, he knew, but she had given it up. She had hinted once or twice that she might have been "asked to leave," though sometimes Gabriel wasn't sure whether she was joking with him.

Gabriel refused to press her. He spent his time dealing with the Fraal preterite, which was as slippery and unpredictable as Enda had warned him. The language also presented him with other interesting difficulties, such as the fact that the Fraal language had two different sets of cardinal and ordinal numbers, one for counting objects and one for counting people.

He got up at one point and wandered into the sitting room to stretch his legs and back, which were betraying a tendency lately to cramp after these long sessions.

"Enda?"

"*Shei?*" she said, turning away from the Grid display. It was showing a news precis from one of the Solar Union channels, and the display was full of a great crowd of people gathered together in some broad public plaza under a vividly blue sky. As she turned away, the display froze and went silent, waiting for her to turn back to it.

He sat down across from her and looked idly at the crowd. "When you're counting and you're not sure whether the objects are sentient or not, what do you do?"

"Use the numbers for sentients," Enda said. "That way if you later find that those whom you have been counting are intelligent, no one has any reason to take offense; and if you find that they are inanimate objects after all, they will not have suffered from the extra courtesy."

Gabriel nodded. Enda said, "This sudden access of academic fervor is not entirely unmotivated, I think."

He widened his eyes slightly. Enda simply looked at his pocket.

"Uh," Gabriel said and reached into it with a resigned look.

He dropped the luckstone onto the table. Though cool, it was glowing softly. It had been glowing this morning when he awakened from that dream—a subdued light, one which somehow had given him the irrational idea that the stone was looking at him.

"This is where the dreams are coming from," Gabriel said. "I'm sure of it."

"How?"

"I don't know . . . but it's true." He turned the stone over on the table, and over again.

"What will you do?" Enda asked.

"I may have to get rid of this," Gabriel said, "but not before I understand why it does what it does. First, though, I think I might try putting it down in the hold at night to see what that does."

"I am sorry for your trouble with it," Enda said.

Gabriel snorted. "It's hardly your fault, but I hate it when it makes me cranky. Sleeping, and the way I feel afterwards, isn't much of an improvement on not sleeping."

"We have some somnifacients in the medical kit. You might try one of those."

Gabriel nodded. "Well, it's only a few more days till we starrise again. Then I should have more than enough to wear me out."

Enda tilted her head "yes" and waved at the Grid display. It went back to her wind-rippled green field. "I will have something to keep me busy besides the news. Always too depressing . . . and the farther we go out, the more depressing becomes the image of what everyone is doing to the worlds." She lifted a hand and let it fall. "The worlds we have, we have done ill by, for the most part. Yet still we go seeking new ones . . . with what reassurance that matters will be any better in the future?"

Gabriel got up and put the stone in his pocket. "You're always telling me about my blood sugar. I think yours could use some attention."

"Blood starch," Enda said, "more likely."

"I'll leave the etiology to Delde Sota," Gabriel said. "I'll make something for us to eat, and then I want you to check my Eldala figures once more."

Chapter Ten

I T TURNED OUT that his concerns had been unnecessary. They came
out without incident three days later through a starrise of unusually deep violet. Bright shadowing on the edges of the viewshield
told him immediately that they were fairly close to the primary. It
was off to the left and "above," a bright star, but hard to tell of
what size.

"Have you got a range on that?" Gabriel asked Enda, who sat
at the navigation and sensor array.

She was studying the readouts in the center display as they
settled themselves after the usual energy fluctuations of starrise.
"About a hundred-fifty-million kilometers. Wait a few minutes
and we will be able to get a rough estimate of the ecliptic from
the sunspot motion."

"Not much to work with there," Gabriel said, looking at the
enlarged image of Eldala in the 3D display. "It's fairly quiet."

"That leaves one less thing to worry about," Enda said. "Let us
see what we can find. Grawl said the planet had a lot of snow.
That suggests something with a largish albedo."

"Depends on the structure of the continents," Gabriel said,
"and the albedo might be low if it's far out the star."

He reached into the display and tickled down the controls for
the visible-light imagers, unpairing the imagers for the moment
from the IRs. While in drivespace, Gabriel had instructed the computer to look along the subset of coordinates that Angela's figures
had suggested. If those figures were accurate, fine. If they were
not, it meant at least a day of hanging in space and taking pictures
in all directions, then another day of doing the same, after which

the computer would compare the two sets of images for any light that seemed to be moving too fast. That would be the planet they were looking for, or some other planet in the system that escaped notice earlier, or an asteroid, or a comet wandering through, or—

"Now *that* is no star," Enda said.

"What?" said Gabriel, looking up from the display.

"Look at that," Enda said, and pointed with four fingers together, in the fraal fashion.

Gabriel looked off to *Sunshine*'s right. Near the lower corner of the viewshield he caught a gleam of blue-white, plainly a disk, though too far away to make out any phase.

"You're right," Gabriel said. He waved away the imager controls for the moment and brought up the system drive to tumble *Sunshine* forward and to the right.

"That's a planet's worth of gravity out there," Gabriel said, "no question. Final measurements will have to wait, but it looks like—maybe point eight five gee?"

"So it seems, about a hundred-fifty million kilometers out from Eldala. That is nearly a perfect G0, by the way," Enda said, looking at the computer's analysis of the star's spectrography, "but not a dwarf. The planet should be somewhat warmer than the primary-size-to-distance ratio would indicate, if Angela's figures, or the previous survey's, were correct."

"Let's go see." Gabriel brought up the system drive up to full.

It took them about an hour and a half to get there. They could have done it more quickly, but Gabriel wanted more imaging to see whether there were any other planets that both the original survey and Angela's quick exploration had missed. Nothing turned up.

The planet began to swell before them, and they saw that blinding blue-white gleam resolve itself into discrete patches of blue and white.

"They did not exaggerate about the south polar cap," Enda said as they settled into what would resolve itself into their survey orbit. For the moment, they orbited pole to pole at a hundred thousand kilometers, looking the planet over.

It was a handsome place, though Gabriel could see why Angela had called it "just cold." It looked it. The four or five major landmasses scattered around the planet were striped and streaked with mountainous terrain, most of it glinting white in Eldala's light. There was no telling how many oceans lay under that southern polar cap, which easily covered a quarter of the hemisphere. The northern one was in its summer, but the polar cap there was of a good size, and all around it was a great barren area with none of the green of the equatorial band—brown country, tundra perhaps, or permafrost with the top layers of snow thawed off it. Any high ground there had snow on it. Only in the equatorial areas did the snow really vanish, though here and there, some lone high peak stood out in the green as a single star of whiteness, stubborn against the summer.

"Well," Enda said, "Grawl was right. There certainly is a planet. Now we will find out more about what kind of planet it is."

"And increase the value of our investment," Gabriel said. If they were going to sell the contract on, this part of the work could double or triple its value. "Fortunately we can let the ship do most of it."

This part of the business of exploration was not anything like what one saw on *Verge Hunter*, in which the crew of the *Hunter* stumbled over unknown planets in a way that suggested that God had tripped and dropped a large box of them all over the floor of heaven. Planets were scattered around, yes, but like grains of sand on a very large, very bare floor . . . and very, very few grains. The majority of stars within the confines of explored space were barren. Most of the worlds that *had* been found around those stars were either completely barren or uninhabitable by humans. Indeed, there were some human religious essayists who had used this frustrating distribution as proof that a Creator did indeed exist, and that He was in a bad mood this aeon. Over the handful of readily human-habitable worlds that *did* exist, every stellar nation within a couple of hundred light-years scrabbled and fought. Every other marginally useful planet was either littered with domes or being terraformed, and there was too little comfortable room into which humanity and sentient alien life could expand.

Gabriel and Enda had discussed their tactics for this earliest part of their survey while still in drivespace.

"The usual ball-of-string orbit," Gabriel said, "starting polar and then precessing. We'll let the computer and the belly imagers get the visible spectrum imagery first—that'll take us a few hours for the whole planet. We don't need fine detail. Then duplicate the first set of orbits, and let the IR imager save those pictures for comparison."

"If we find nothing useful?" Enda said. "No minerals, no Glassmaker cities?"

Gabriel snickered and said, "Then straight out of here and off to Coulomb with our mail. With just the survey pictures, we'll still make at least twenty percent on the deal, then we'll go back to *Lighthouse* and do some shopping."

"And look for Ricel again," Enda said.

"If he's still there," said Gabriel. "But this lead, at least, is hot . . . not like those five year old pictures. If he's gone, we'll find out where. If he's not . . ."

It was something to think about. Meanwhile, here they were, and there was other business almost as interesting . . .

His own troubles pained him, but this was both figuratively and literally far bigger than Gabriel—a new world, a place where humans had stopped only briefly. As for other species, who knew who might have been here, and when?

"Let's start winding our ball of string," Gabriel said, and reached into the center display again to check the search parameters one more time.

Enda watched the central display come alive with the graphic showing the planet and their plotted course. The first line tracing itself around the world began to change color from untouched green to newly plotted and imaged red.

"I think I am going to get something to eat," she said, "and you should too . . . because I think, within a few hours, we will be down there." She got up and headed for the galley.

Gabriel suddenly realized how hungry he was and went after her.

* * * * *

The computer finished its first set of orbits more quickly than they had expected, and its soft chime called Gabriel and Enda from the galley into the sitting room. There the main display was already projecting a rough map of the planet.

Gabriel was surprised that there was much less water on the planet than he had thought. The cloud cover was considerable, but it had shifted while the first imaging run was happening, and the computer had had time to do some extrapolation on what surface was not presently showing. The IR confirmed that the sphere rotating in the air before them had no such world-girdling ocean as Bluefall had, nothing even as big as Earth's. What seas appeared were more like large interconnected inland oceans, with a few mini-seas or huge lakes scattered among the main continents. What might have been plate-sliding on the planet's crust had allowed at least one of these inland seas to extend a pair of winding straits northward and southward of itself, some thousands of kilometers each, so that it seemed to split the continent through which it ran in two.

"Probably going to get pretty good tides up and down those," Gabriel said, reaching into the holographic projection to stop its rotation for a moment and increase the size of the image.

"More to the point," Enda said, "look at that spot there—" She indicated a point where the northward-reaching strait narrowed down particularly tightly. "It will take another pass before the computer overlays detailed contours on the image, but if I read the terrain there correctly, that is a *downhill* plunge—the sea from which the strait runs is higher than the straits. Tides there may be farther down, but at that spot there should be a waterfall like nothing anyone has ever seen! A kilometer high, it might be: perhaps more. I want to take a closer look."

"You do love your landcapes," Gabriel said and smiled.

"Why would I not," Enda said, giving him a look, "after so many years spent between the worlds and so rarely on them? Permit me this slight foible after two centuries."

"I wasn't arguing. Let's take her in closer and do our next imaging run."

That took rather longer, several hours. By the end of that run, the spherical image that presented itself to Gabriel and Enda in the sitting room display had much more detail. The inside edges of the inland seas were massively crevassed with fjords, producing spectacular cliffs where mountain ranges ran straight into the seas. Elsewhere, in the center of the main continent, new mountain ranges fought with old ones for dominance. There seemed to be a lot of tectonic activity in the middle of the continent, the business of mountain-building going on actively.

"It is a young planet, I would guess," Enda said, "and a good-sized one. Just a shade smaller than Bluefall. Not too long a day, just over twenty-eight hours. The gravity is lighter."

"Not so even, though," Gabriel said. "I've been feeling the ship wiggle every now and then. A gravitational anomaly or two?"

"Many planets have such, but Gabriel, I think we should run the temperature assay again. Our results look nothing like those from the first survey."

Gabriel agreed. "The average does look more like five C, doesn't it? While a lot of the winter hemisphere is snow-covered right now, it's not glaciated. That early survey's IR array must have been malfunctioning with a vengeance."

Enda stopped the display and indicated the narrowing strait that she had pointed out earlier. Here, with preliminary contours laid over the imaging by the computer, it became clear how very high indeed was that drop from the "inland sea" level to the northern strait.

"I underestimated. I did not believe it could be as much as three kilometers, but there it is! We must go there. That is certainly one of the great wonders of the worlds."

"Take your imager," Gabriel said, "but keep the pictures to yourself. You don't want this system filling up with tourists."

Enda laughed and headed toward her cabin. "At this distance from the Stellar Ring? It seems unlikely." There was the sound of opening drawers as Enda looked for something. "The Verge is changing. Who knows who might be here in twenty years? Especially if we are right about the temperatures . . ."

Gabriel poked the hologram into a slow spin again and considered that. People were building domes all over real estate much less promising than this. If the temperature had been misassessed last time, and it *did* get warm enough here for crops to grow, then there would be stellar nations arguing over this world in very short order. The nations that were more of a power in the Verge, such as the Regency, would do what they could to stymie the outsiders. In any quarrel involving both Verge powers and the nations that had been on the far side of the Long Silence, the Vergers routinely banded together.

How long will it last? Will anyone who lives in this part of space get a chance to live here and make some use of whatever the planet has to offer, whatever that might be?

For a world of this size, its gravity was light enough to suggest that it might be low on metallic elements, and the temperature issue was still bothering Gabriel.

From down the hallway, Enda said, "Did you look at the atmospheric analysis?"

Gabriel reached into the hologram and touched the telltale hovering above the globe. It dropped down a list of constituents.

"We will have to check that when we're actually in atmosphere, of course," Enda said, "but it looks extremely welcoming."

Gabriel nodded. Seventy percent nitrogen, nearly two percent CO_2, eighteen percent oxygen, a little richer than humans liked it, but much to a fraal's liking.

"At least there's likely to be less trouble with altitude sickness," Gabriel said, "for me, anyway."

"Angela did not drop dead of breathing it, nor did she mention any other problems."

The notes that Angela had sold them along with the rest of the exploration contract package were less than illuminating in many places. "Cold" was the remark that summed up one entire afternoon. The next day was not much better: "Gathered mineral

samples. Unremarkable." Gabriel found it remarkable that someone could visit a planet where humans had been only once before,
if that, and find nothing to say but "unremarkable."

"I heard that," Enda said as she came into the sitting room
again. She was wearing one of her coveralls now, the one with the
adaptive insulation, and she had braided her long ponytail and
coiled it around her head, so as not to interfere with the coverall's
hood.

"Heard what?"

"You thinking with the silencer off," Enda said. She gave him
a partly humorous look. "Sometimes you are very loud. You
should make a few allowances for her, Gabriel. She admitted
readily enough that exploration was not what she had imagined,
and she got out of it as quickly as she could."

"Well, I suppose . . ." Gabriel said. "Do you want to take us
down? I'll go change."

"Do that. I will wait for you, though. If the ride becomes
bumpy for some reason, you would not want to be walking
around."

Chapter Eleven

GABRIEL WENT OFF to his cabin and changed into a coverall more like Enda's. He slipped a few useful items into the pockets: a knife with both steel and one molecule blades, a small sidearm that he holstered at his right hip, and a little canister that held a digital mensurator. Finally, he looked over at the shelf near his bed. There was the luckstone.

Why not? he thought, and put it in his pocket. So far, I've come back every time I've been carrying it. So what if it burns the occasional hole in the deck? We all have our bad days.

When he got up into the pilots' cabin and strapped himself in, Enda had the contoured globe rotating in the central display. Their course down to the planet was marked.

"I am not going to hurry, since we will be able to use the time for more imaging, and there are a few other features that I would like to look at more closely later."

"You're the pilot," Gabriel said. "I'm just going to sit here and admire the view."

Enda brought up the system drive and used it to give them their initial nudge of acceleration, but Gabriel could see that she was mostly letting the planet's own gravity do the work. He had teased her about this style of piloting once or twice in the past, asking why she didn't just use the drivers.

"Ah," she had said, "there speaks someone who has had a large military organization paying for his fuel. When you live a Wanderer's life as long as I have, Gabriel, you find ways to conserve. When the universe offers you energy for free, take it! Where is energy more free than in a planet's lovely gravity well beneath you? You will want the fuel for getting up out of it afterwards, believe me."

Gabriel watched Enda drop them gracefully toward the ever-growing blue curve of the planet. There was the usual brief sizzle and crackle of ionization as *Sunshine*'s hull bit into the outermost layers of atmosphere; a brief flicker of blue light danced over the viewshield. After that, the ship began to shudder a little as she dropped toward the highest-altitude clouds.

"The high altitude winds are more active than I would have expected," Enda commented.

The ship bounced and rattled, and in the one of the cabins, Gabriel heard something crash to the floor. "*Uh*-oh," he said.

"No, I think that was in my cabin," Enda said. "It sounded like my flowerpot."

"Oh, no! After all that watering . . ."

"I would not worry too much about it," Enda said. "An Ondothwait plant is fairly tough even after it leafs out, and this one has a while to go yet."

Sunshine steadied as she fell through another deep bank of cloud and came out. Beneath them on all sides spread a widening view of blue air and white mountains with the green of the equatorial belt presently off to their left as they descended.

"Our landing spot is about halfway around the planet now," Enda said. "I want to see if the temperature fluctuates much as we come in closer."

Gabriel watched the indicator linked to the IR imagers. "Still looks pretty close to five as an average. Some hot spots over by the equator. Do you want to stay with those?"

"No, I am angling north. I want another look at the brown areas near the north pole. We will come down in the equatorial band, though."

"Your waterfall?"

"It is on the fringes, but the area looked free of snow. It's just as well. Except for those huge polar tundras, this place is nearly as mountainous as Rivendale."

The curvature of the planet was lost now, and they arrowed

across a vista of mountains covered with more and more snow as they angled northward.

Gabriel peered down at one deep lake nestled among some of those mountains, and said, "There's something down there in the middle of that one, might be a little island."

"It would not surprise me if those lakes are simply drowned valleys," Enda said. "I wonder about the rainfall patterns, though, since the water is running out of the inland sea to other lakes." She tilted *Sunshine*'s nose down a little more sharply. "Either there are downpours here in the wet season that are something to see, or there is a great deal of snowfall in the winter with astonishing amounts of melt in the summer."

"Either way, the temperature assay from that earlier survey is looking wronger all the time . . ."

"Wronger?" Enda threw him an amused look. "Gabriel, you are speaking strangely of late."

"*Hesaite* as opposed to *hesai*," said Gabriel. The *-te* suffix was the commonest of the three fraal intensifiers and was hung off the end of words and then repeated as often as necessary to suggest how much more intense the word in question was becoming.

"Oh." She chuckled. "You are at that magic early time when the two languages begin to get confused with one another. I must speak more Fraal to you and see how confused we can get you."

"Thanks so much," Gabriel muttered.

Sunshine shuddered again as they dove closer to the planet, over the vast waste of northern tundra. This terrain was hugely crevassed as well, and as they passed one side of the polar cap at about thirty thousand meters, they could see the long fingers of glaciers running down into the brown land on all sides, like twisted, ever-narrowing white ribbons.

"Unusual structures," Enda said. "Have you ever seen anything like that?"

"Not recently."

The polar cap filled the entire landscape to the right of *Sunshine* as they descended. All the surface of the polar cap was tortuously wrinkled and cracked. Some of the cracks were huge enough to drop a Concord cruiser into.

"This is not a quiet planet," Gabriel said as *Sunshine* slipped around toward sunset and into night. "A lot of action down there."

"Yes. I wonder if some of the error in that first survey's readings might have been because there is more geothermic input to the local ecosystem than there was before?" She made a couple of adjustments to the controls.

Gabriel shrugged as they came around the side of the polar cap. Still dropping altitude, they headed southward again, making their way once more toward day. Being summer in this hemisphere, night did not extend very far across it.

"When we take these figures back to the CSS, we'll see what they have to say. Look at *that!*"

They were angling back toward the equatorial region. Even at this height, twenty thousand meters and dropping, Gabriel could see a single peak that stood above all the others in its range. Astonishingly pre-eminent, the mountain glinted with snow for about three-quarters of its height.

"That has to be ten thousand meters high."

Enda peered at the contour map, which had now flattened itself out in their display to match their course. "I would suspect more like twelve. Yes, it is extraordinary. We must be careful with our imaging. This place will become a haven for climbers if we are not careful."

"Are you happy with your landing spot?" Gabriel asked as they dropped lower still. The snow underneath them was giving way to greenery, except on the highest peaks, but he could see very little flat terrain anywhere.

"We will do well enough," Enda said. "I will put us down not too from that waterfall. See. You can make it out now on the horizon."

It came up faster than Gabriel expected, even though Enda was decelerating fairly hard. In the swiftly brightening twilight, a small ring of peaks, all low enough not to have any snow, were visible ahead. Just past them was a pair or a pair and a half of peaks—two large ones, one small, mostly covered with greenery—and from between them, half veiled in mist, a great rush and pour of greenish-white water was streaming down. It was so huge that it did not seem to move at all, but Gabriel only had to look at it to imagine the thunder of it. The bottom of the fall was one great cloud, and everything near it was invisible.

"Off in the smaller mountain-circle to the right of that," Enda said, "is a plateau. It showed as fairly flat in the second set of images. I would say it must be at least five kilometers wide."

Within a few minutes, they were over it. The imagery had been correct in showing it as "fairly flat" from a hundred thousand meters. Here it revealed itself as a foothill area for the mountains. Many small hills jostled together like an uneven heap of cobblestones that had been thinly sown with earth and planted over.

"Let us see now," said Enda, bringing up the system drive and slowing *Sunshine* nearly to a hover, so that they cruised forward at no more than a few meters per second.

The ground was covered with low scrub and some kind of blue-greenish creeping plant, but there were a few barren patches scattered about. Enda made her way toward one of them that was about twice *Sunshine's* length and lay near the edge of the plateau fairly close to the waterfall. The barren patch itself was surrounded by several low hills, and Enda slipped very carefully between the two highest of them and set *Sunshine* down on the bare ground.

Enda put the system drive on standby, and the ship went quiet. For a moment they both sat there and looked out the viewshield, where the deep dark blue of early morning was slowly beginning to lift.

"What would you say the latitude is here?" Gabriel asked.

Enda studied the chart showing in the display between them. "Around thirty degrees north—"

"We don't have a lot of morning twilight left. Do you want to wait?"

"Oh, you can stay if you like," Enda said, already undoing her straps. Gabriel grinned at her and followed suit. "I will leave the computer running so that it can do a more detailed analysis on the last round of images. Once we get back, we can decide what to investigate next."

Shortly they were both armed and in the lift. Gabriel, having noted from the main display that it was only five degrees C out there, paused a moment to add a neutralizer coat over his coverall.

At the bottom of its run, the lift door slipped silently aside and they looked out. The overall impression was of the kind of deep blue-green associated with being underwater, partly due to the color of the sky and the rising light, partly due to the color of a lot of the local flora. The ground was pale, scattered with small nondescript pebbles.

Gabriel felt slightly unsteady, but tremendously excited. He put his head back and drew a very deep breath. "Smell how clean that is."

"It is certainly not like ship's air," Enda said. "Our scrubbers do well enough, but this freshness reminds you of how air is *supposed* to smell." She looked around. "The contract is yours. Do you want to step out first?"

"You just want whatever's hiding in the bushes to bite me before it bites you." He drew his pistol, checked that it was ready, and stepped out past Enda to look around.

The silence was complete except for one thing: the continuous roar of the waterfall, which lay not far off to *Sunshine*'s left past the little hills that hemmed them in. Through the ground Gabriel could feel a slight tremor, the physical equivalent of white noise, the source of that "unsteady" feeling. Carefully Gabriel looked around for any sign of motion, listening as best he could for any other sound. There was none.

"Come on," he said. Gabriel led the way around the front of *Sunshine* and paused for a moment to check the other side. He saw nothing, and they began walking in the direction of the falls.

As they got off the barren spot, the feel of the ground became surprisingly springy. The ground cover was some kind of creeping succulent, blue-green like much else here, giving off a slight spicy fragrance when they stepped on it. Footsteps went silent on this natural carpeting, and the effect made Gabriel listen harder, but the sound of the falls drowned everything out. He paused for a moment, looking over his shoulder to make sure Enda was all right. She was just behind him, ghost-pale in this light, her eyes oddly colorless in this landscape where nearly everything seemed to match them. Gabriel turned toward the sound again and made his way up between the two nearest hills.

As he and Enda came up into the pass between the hills, the full force of the sound hit them, and they were face to face with the waterfall.

Gabriel looked up, and up, and up, and finally staggered backwards and had to brace himself so that he could continue looking up. It was one thing to stand on a ledge and look into deep valleys and across high cliffs a kilometer or more high. It was another to stand by such a cliff, even halfway up it, and see that there was still another kilometer or two to go.

There was no seeing the top of the waterfall. Mist veiled everything there. Vast sheets and drifts of water came down from high above like the rippling curtains of some pallid aurora. They tattered, shifted, and dissolved into a strange silvery fog—a fog with weight, pouring down the side of the mountain past them until it boiled and bubbled up again, slow as cloud. The thunder and roar of the fall filled land as tons and tons of water hammered onto the half-invisible stones. Gabriel could not hear himself breathing, could not hear his own heartbeat. He could hear himself think, but the sound of his mind running in its usual narrow channels suddenly seemed small and petty when set against this vast, unconcerned, glorious roar.

Enda brushed past him to a point where the ground sloped downward before falling away completely. The mist curled up beyond it. If anything, the view of the waterfall was even more spectacular from here, despite the uncertainty of twilight. Its waters plunged down into the valley and roared away northward among more cliffs and mountains. One of them, the tall one that they had seen earlier, shone in the east like a star. It was the ten thousand meter peak, which caught the rising sun and burned with its light as brightly as a planet against the indigo sky.

Gabriel felt minuscule, insignificant, ephemeral, yet he smiled. If anything should last, he thought as he turned his face up to the wet air and felt the infinitesimal touch of the fog upon it, let them be things like this. What does it matter if I exist, if I live or die, as long as things like this can be?

He stood like that for a few moments more, then turned and walked out of the mist to find Enda standing not far away and looking at him a little strangely.

"Did I have the silencer off again?" he said, more loudly than he usually would have.

She smiled. "Not as such, though under the circumstance, no one could misunderstand. If anything, you were rather more quiet than usual."

Gabriel looked up at the falls again. "Can you blame me?"

She bowed her head "no," looking around her again. "I think I might go back and have something to eat. What about you?"

He looked over his shoulder at the waterfall. "I don't suppose it'll go anywhere. Why not?"

Together they walked back to *Sunshine*. Very reassuring she looked, sitting there on the bare ground, embraced by the hills, a little light showing through her viewshield, warm against the lifting twilight. They did a walk-around to make sure that she had come through the landing unhurt then went back up in the lift.

"Unquestionably this is a beautiful place," Enda said, "but mere physical attractiveness is going to make little difference if it is too cold to colonize. Despite preliminary indications, we must still carefully check that. We can take some time over the IR analysis with the computer to see what we can deduce."

Gabriel nodded and went off to his cabin to dump his jacket. "What's beeping?" he asked Enda as he went. The sitting room display was making a plaintive noise that he couldn't remember having heard before.

Enda said something that Gabriel couldn't make out.

"What?" Gabriel said, making his way back up toward the sitting room.

"I said, *'Newhaihe ye'soithalensh,'* " Enda said. She looked pale, even for a fraal.

Gabriel started taking the phrase apart. " 'In the name of—' "

As he came into the sitting room he saw the display showing its spherical map of the planet, with a number of small bright points highlighted on it, and the single word, quite large, at the bottom of the image.

Positive result.

He froze. "Positive for what?"

"Heat above background at short range," said Enda, reading from the small print in the display, "and in particular, heat in diffusion with concentrations typical of inhabited buildings."

"What?"

Gabriel found that he was actually shaking as he stood there, looking around the corner of the sitting room. He had to take hold of the doorsill to brace himself. Enda reached into the display to bring up the visual and IR images, one after another, starting with the beginning of their final descent into atmosphere and continuing at five second intervals. For a good while the ship was too high for the IR data to be trusted, and much later there came a different point of diminishing returns, where IR readings became increasingly less reliable because exothermic heat from the ship's hull interfered with them. The overlaid images from an altitude of a thousand meters down to a hundred meters were quite clear. In a number of them they could see little regular splotches, glowing significantly warmer than background with stored heat. They were buildings.

"Houses," Gabriel said. "Oh, my God." He went into the sitting room and threw himself into a chair.

There are people here. A new alien species . . . I think. Oh, my God—

Enda adjusted the display to its largest size and recycled the images to look through them again. Starting with the shots taken from ten thousand meters, the IR scanner showed a couple of hot spots that were associated with high mountain peaks.

"Volcanic," Enda said, "or formerly volcanic. That one with

the flattish top, that might be a plug, but these . . ." She indicated
other spots on the planet that became more obvious over the long
curve of their descent. Various small points of heat had become
extremely bright to the IR scanners. Just before landing, six kilometers away under their approach path, were six or eight of these
close association.

Gabriel could only sit there and shake his head. "How could
Angela have *missed* this?"

"By being in the wrong place? They did not conduct an imaging survey, nor did they have IR scanners, and they did not come
to this place." She bowed her head in the fraal gesture of negation,
twice, like a human shaking his head in disbelief. When she
looked up again, she was close to laughter.

"Gabriel, there have been stranger accidents than this. Do you
know how close the first human surveyors of Mars came to finding our base there, a hundred years before we were prepared to
reveal ourselves? Do you know how near a thing it was that the
OSS *Brightfall* actually *found* the weren homeworld, and by what
complete mere accident it happened?" She covered her face with
her hands for a moment. "If the universe will play such jokes on
us, we should at least be grateful that it has a sense of humor."

"If you say so," Gabriel said, "but *now* what do we do?"

Enda too sat down, looking at the display, which she had left
frozen on one image, that circle of little houses some kilometers
away.

"I wonder," she said, "if perhaps we should leave."

Gabriel looked at her.

"We are not well equipped for this kind of problem," Enda
said, "and our chances of doing something that could make a
great deal of trouble for those who come after us are considerable."

"Just like that?" Gabriel said. "You just want to run off?"

"Not run precisely," Enda said, "but there are aspects—"

"Enda," Gabriel said, "you're *fraal.* Your people were the first
ones to seek humans out and explain yourselves to us. We've had
a good long time together, your people and mine. A lot of history

wouldn't have happened if we hadn't begun exploring the galaxy together. Stardrive wouldn't have—"

"Some history," Enda said, "would be *worth* avoiding, if you ask me. Both our species have made our share of mistakes."

"There's another problem," said Gabriel. "Remember Rov telling us how some people went into this part of space and didn't come back?"

"Angela had no problems," Enda said.

"Angela wasn't here very long," Gabriel said. "I wonder if someone came out this way and 'didn't come back' because of something they found here? Is that why we don't have any later reports about this planet?"

Now it was Enda's turn to look thoughtful. "I doubt we are likely to find anything that would shed much light on that."

Gabriel could see the look on her face slowly shifting. "I think we should sit still, at least until we have a chance to do some more analysis on these," he said. "We can go after breakfast, if you want, but if you think we should sell the contract at this point, there's no question that we would make back everything we spent on it and a lot more. *Somebody* lives here."

"I confess I would be curious to see who," Enda said.

Gabriel kept quiet while Enda turned to look at the little warm shapes glowing in the image.

"Very well," she said. "Let us have breakfast, by all means, and spend some more time with these pictures. Then . . ." She let out a long breath. "Let us just hope that our drive was no louder than the background noise from the waterfall. I would hate to have frightened the neighbors in the middle of the night. The results could be unfortunate."

She got up and headed back to the galley. Gabriel, for his own part, got up to make sure that the lower access was sealed and secured, and that the lift was up and locked. He turned to the display that showed that little half-circle of houses nestled in yet another small group of hills . . . and he swallowed hard.

* * * * *

Breakfast did not last long. They were too concerned about the images and spent a lot of time going over what they had.

The first thing they agreed on was that they needed another low-level survey, perhaps from about a thousand meters, and cover the whole equatorial zone. That was the best height for the IR and visual-light imagers to cover the maximum area at a resolution that would accurately pick up low-level heat emissions. Much higher than that, there was a good chance of missing something important. For his own part, Gabriel was becoming a little less annoyed than he had been at Angela Valiz, for as he studied their own initial approach, he appreciated Enda's point about the amount of sheer luck involved in finding those buildings.

There was no way that a survey even from low planetary orbit would have picked up any of this. For a civilization's works to be visible from space required either a species that possessed a high level of technology, huge built-up city areas, and a desire to turn the lights on at night, or a species that routinely built buildings bigger than twenty kilometers on a side. There were a good number of the first, but none of the second. Everything else was likely to go unnoticed.

Even a low survey might miss very obvious signs, Gabriel thought as he reached into the display and looked one more time at that nearest, clearest image, the little half-circle of houses. He backed up to examine several images before it. Buildings those might be, but there were no walls, no fences, no cultivated fields, no roads or visible paths. Houses could be mistaken for many other things that, in a landscape with no straight lines, could have looked like rocks.

Who knows how many houses Angela passed over on her own initial landing? Gabriel frowned, for again, Angela's notes gave no sense of exactly where she had been.

Enda was busy with the display's keypad, which she had briefly subdivided and was now programming with the path for their secondary survey.

"I hope Angela didn't come anywhere near here," Gabriel

said, glancing over at her work. "Otherwise, who knows how the locals might react to us?"

"Assuming they noticed," Enda said as she examined the planet's surface via a magnified holographic image. It was now girdled with a graceful braid of glowing sine curves, the course for the secondary survey. "Well, we must take our chances. How does this look to you?"

Gabriel leaned over to have a better look at it. "Seems optimum."

"Gabriel, there are other structures about which I have some doubts." She showed him an earlier image, taken from greater altitude, of a site further into the mountains.

Gabriel peered at it. It was triangular and there were odd extrusions in the middle. "How high were we when that was taken?"

"Five thousand meters."

Gabriel shook his head. "That's pretty big, then. It doesn't look like anything else we've seen."

"It looks rather like this," said Enda, and shifted images again. This time it was one taken from a lower altitude, and the size was proportionately bigger, though the shape was skewed.

"The angle," Gabriel said.

"Maybe, but the heat profile is different—much cooler than the other smaller buildings we've seen, whatever purpose they have been made for. These triangular structures are all at high altitudes, compared with everything else we have seen so far . . . and in spots which would be very difficult for even very motivated construction engineers to manage."

"You're thinking . . . what? That these might be artifacts from some other culture?"

"An older one possibly," Enda said. "We do not have nearly enough data for a judgment."

"Well," Gabriel said, "let's get up there and see what we can get." He turned down toward his cabin. "One thing first—the sun's going to be coming up shortly, and I want at least one picture of that waterfall to take with me."

Enda gave him an amused look as he came back down the hall with his pocket imager.

"What a tourist."

"Excuse me, but I've spent most of my career being carted around the galaxy fighting and shooting and never being allowed to do tourist things," Gabriel said with a smile. He shrugged into his neutralizer coat. It was still cool enough out there for him to want a little extra protection. He touched the lift controls and said, "Permit me this slight foible in my two-and-a-halfth decade."

"Two-and-a-halfth," Enda said admiringly. "Fraal ordinals will ruin you yet, Gabriel."

"Maybe they will. I'll be back in a few minutes."

"Oh, wait for me," Enda said, saving her work at the sitting room display and sending it on to the ship's computers. "I would not mind one more look myself."

The lift came, and they went down in it together, Enda having taken a moment to fetch her jacket. "It is not so much the cold," she said, "as the damp. That mist drifts about so."

Dawn was coming up as they came to the crest between the two hills.

"Oh, look at that," Gabriel said and lifted the imager, studying the guide screen for the best image. Light from the sun, now peering past the mountains in the distance, was rainbowing golden through the mist and falling water. "Let's go back down where we were standing before . . . the contrast's better down there."

They went down to nearly the edge of the precipice, and Gabriel stood and took several images, waiting for another breeze to come and push the water aside a little, hoping for the glint of golden sunlight on those rocks, but the breeze did not cooperate.

"It's amazing," he said. "I just worry that the imager won't catch the way this really is. It's so huge."

Enda tilted her head to one side. "I doubt it will do it justice, but images like these serve best as reminders. We will be out in space somewhere, and you will pull out the image and remember not how this looked, but how it felt."

"You're probably right," Gabriel said, smiling to himself as he turned the imager over and saw that he had nearly filled its short-term memory. "Come on. Let's get back to the ship."

They turned and started to walk up . . . and Gabriel froze.

Up at the top of the hill, silhouetted against the sky, standing and watching them carefully, was a short person with a gun.

Chapter Twelve

GABRIEL'S FIRST GLANCE gave him the idea that the person was wearing a dark red hooded coverall with some kind of pale mask. The second glance told him that this was a bipedal person about a meter and a half tall, covered with fur. The person was wearing a longish embroidered vest, but Gabriel found it hard to concentrate on that at the moment. The half-meter-long, fluffy, red and white striped tail was an attention-getter, and so was the rifle.

"Why do those guns look familiar?" Enda said.

"They resemble the black powder guns the weren use," Gabriel said. "They fire slugs, or something more accurate. In any case, I'd try to avoid being part of a test."

Although his neutralizer coat offered protection against energy weapons, he was unsure of its efficacy against bullets. There was a token composite layer that was supposed to stop a knife, but the velocities of bullets and knives were somewhat different.

The furred person slowly came down the hill, never taking its eyes off them. The "pale mask" turned out to be a cream-furred face with a short muzzle, the nose at the end of it dark red. Small, round ears pointed toward them as he paused, studying them carefully.

The creature barked at them. Though Gabriel did not doubt that it was language, it sounded like the barking sounds he had heard some kinds of small mammals make.

Gabriel, watching the expert and assured way in which this creature was handling his weapon, found himself wondering whether this creature might have its mind on food.

Are we game? Are we about to be asked to dinner in a way we won't like?

"Now what?" Enda said softly.

"I don't know about you," Gabriel said, "but I think a smart thing to do would be to sit down and be small." He did just that, sitting down on the springy ground and ducking his head while still keeping an eye on the alien watching them.

Enda stood looking at it for a moment, then sat down next to Gabriel and closely copied his pose.

The furred person watched them for about five minutes. Gabriel sat still. He hoped the alien did not see how convenient the seated position had made Gabriel's hands to his pistol, or how well it would hide a motion toward it if he felt he needed to make one. All in all, this situation had its embarrassing side for a former marine. *Ready To Fight* was the old motto. Certainly Gabriel always *had* been ready, in that far-off world where enemies were clearly defined. Now, when he was not sure whether there was any reason to fight, he was still ready, but it was much lonelier work.

The creature stood watching them, his gun ready, then suddenly he turned.

"Is he about to leave?" Gabriel said.

The creature lifted one of its hands and waved.

"Do you hear that?" Enda whispered.

Gabriel lifted his head a little. Footsteps: a lot of them, soft but audible even on the succulent ground cover. The sound was coming up the other side of the hill.

Suddenly there were about thirty of the red-furred people up there, and every one of them had guns. They looked down at Gabriel and Enda, and a soft chorus of barking went up on the morning air.

Gabriel did not move as the furred people started to come down the hill toward them. He was shaking, and there was no use in trying to control it, but he was ready.

"I don't want to hurt them," he said softly to Enda, "and we don't know that they want to hurt us either."

"I agree completely," she said, "but I also do not believe I am
scheduled to die today." He could see her, very carefully, thumb-
ing off the safety on her own pistol.

He had already clicked the safety off his own weapon. Now
they sat there and waited. The trembling passed, but Gabriel
found himself experiencing the unnatural awareness that he had
felt in battlefield situations before, the sudden shocking clarity of
his surroundings, the sharp taste of breath at the back of the nose,
and the oddly abstract moments during which he studied the
approaching enemy entirely with an eye to choosing targets.

It took barely a second for he and Enda to be surrounded by a
wall of russet-red fur, variously colored and patterned fabric,
tooled leather, and guns, many guns. Gabriel found himself
admiring one of the weapons for the beauty of the carving on its
stock, a pattern of leaves and what he assumed were flowers. He
also noticed that the reddish fur ran down on the backs of the
creatures' hands, but not to the fingers or palms. They were
seven-fingered hands with two thumbs each, very delicate and
obviously well suited for skilled work.

Slowly Gabriel lifted his head to look up into the eyes of the
creature who had first stood at the crest of the hill. The face was
an intelligent one, the eyes lively—but with what emotion, if any,
there was no way to tell.

"Good morning," Gabriel said.

There was silence around them. The scout leaned down to
Gabriel and spoke, a brief string of soft barks and growls.

"I really wish I could understand you," Gabriel said, "but I
don't have the slightest idea what you're saying."

He glanced around at some of the other faces. There was a lot
of variation among them—the basic pattern seemed to be short,
white fur that blended into a longer, slightly shaggier red pelt on
the head. However, some of the faces peering at them had orange
or white stripes on the muzzles where eyebrows would have been
on a human, or down on either side of the small round ears. The
mobility of the faces seemed limited, though here and there a lip
wrinkled up, showing extremely sharp white teeth.

The moment stretched out. Finally, the scout made an upward gesture with one hand, looked at Gabriel, and repeated it.

"I think we're supposed to go with them," Gabriel said.

"I am more than willing," said Enda. "This ground is rather wet."

Carefully they both stood up. The creatures watched them intently as they did this, and Gabriel noticed that most of the attention seemed to be on their hands as they rose.

"They're watching to see if we make a move toward the weapons," Gabriel said.

"I have no desire to use mine at the moment," Enda said. "Do you see the need?"

"No."

"Let us go with them, then."

A few of the furred people started up the hill. The scout gestured after them, and Gabriel followed, Enda walking beside him and a little behind. As they came to the top of the hill, Gabriel looked down and saw that *Sunshine* was surrounded by ten more of the aliens, some facing inward toward the ship, some outward.

"You do not think they have damaged her?" Enda asked.

"I can't see any evidence of it. She's locked, anyway. They can't get in."

Their escort walked them past *Sunshine*, and Gabriel glanced over but made no attempt to stop. The scout watched Gabriel's face as they went past. Gabriel looked down at him, then turned away and focused his attention on the way they were going. He and Enda might need to come back this way in a hurry, without help from their escort . . . or while trying to evade it.

The aliens led them northeast to the next line of hills and over. As Gabriel and Enda had seen on the way in, this whole area was hilly, and they wound between those hills for the most part, avoiding the highest crests. He watched all around him for landmarks. There were few, besides the occasional outcropping of stone or patch of scrub-bushes.

"You know what the worst thing is about this?" Gabriel asked Enda.

"Besides the language barrier," she replied, "and an unnerving number of weapons very close to us, and not having any idea what is happening?"

"Yeah."

"What?"

"I'm getting hungry again."

Enda laughed. "I *told* you you should have eaten more breakfast."

"Next time I'll listen."

The walk went on for another hour, and Gabriel became hungrier still. As they reached the top of a hill, he was breathing hard and had to rest. This last hill had been steep, but its ridge was broad and the leaders of the party seemed disinclined to head to the left or right where other hills joined this one. At the top of the hill, Gabriel paused for a moment, looking down, and Enda stopped beside him. Below them, at the foot of the hill, was that little half-circle of houses gathered together in a valley, under the shadow of a taller hill on the far side. From the fieldstone chimney of the biggest of these houses, thin smoke rose lazily on the slight morning breeze.

Gabriel shook his head. "Well," he said, "I think we can assume they noticed us coming over in the middle of the night."

"Yes. I would not be surprised if they were annoyed with us."

The scout made a gesture that Gabriel thought meant he and Enda should follow him. Everyone headed down the hill toward the small settlement. Gabriel and Enda followed.

All the houses were handsomely made from what looked like cemented fieldstone. Most of them seemed to be in a three-lobed construction, except for the middle building, which had three long "rooms," each with its own roof. The roofs, all wide and low-peaked, met in the middle of the structure. The roofs themselves were of some kind of brushwood, thin dark blue-green twigs of it bound tightly together in bundles and laid down in rows. At the edges where the roofs overhung their supporting walls, stones weighed the roofing down.

"It is an interesting shape," Enda said as they came down the hill. "I would guess the roofs are pitched to deal with large snow-falls."

Gabriel nodded; he had seen architecture like this elsewhere. From the open doorways of the other buildings, more of the furred people were peering at them as they came down. There were some very small ones peeking out from behind the taller aliens.

Children? he thought. There was no way to tell.

They walked down into the common area in front of the houses. Some of the escort party who had come with them were no longer carrying their guns at the ready; they had shouldered them, and a few were unloading. Gabriel looked with interest at the alien nearest them who did this, and then sucked in an alarmed breath at the size of the slug he saw being removed from the chamber.

"Don't be shot escaping," Gabriel said quietly to Enda as the scout gestured them toward the doors of the central house, the longest and largest of them.

"I always try to avoid such. Why?"

"Had to have been a hundred grams of lead in that pellet," Gabriel said. "Depending on the charge behind it, it could take the head right off you and leave you very unhappy afterwards."

"I will make a note of that."

The doors of the central longhouse were hinged sections of an oval, well made of some substance that looked metallic, but had been deeply carved, as ornately as the rifle stock Gabriel had seen earlier.

"Whatever else you can say about these people," Gabriel said, pausing by one of the doors and cautiously raising a hand to touch the carving, "they're artists. Look at these animals! They might be imaginary, but whether they are or not, they're beautiful." He looked at his hand in slight surprise and rubbed the fingers together. "This stuff is warm," he said. "I would swear it was something like aged bronze."

Enda came up beside him, reached up a hand, and touched the stuff. "Perhaps some kind of wood? I could not say . . . materials technology is not my strong point."

They were ushered through, Gabriel stooping a little as he went through the door, which was no more than a meter and a half high. He paused several paces inside the doorway to let his eyes get used to the reduced light. There were very small windows, positioned high up in the walls, in the single-room building.

The place was not as dark as he had expected. The fieldstone walls had been plastered white inside. Long, slim floor-based sconces ran down both sides of the room. Atop each stand, large illuminated globes gave off a gentle, warm light. There was not much in the way of furniture, but various benches and low chairs were set along the walls. Scattered over the stone-flagged floor were numerous shaggy dark skins and what looked like woven rugs in geometrical patterns. Many pillows or cushions were scattered on top of those. Here and there, a few of the aliens were sitting gathered together on the floor, bent toward one another in conversation. Those conversations stopped as Gabriel and Enda passed by, and dark eyes looked up at them in astonishment.

In company with their escort, Enda and Gabriel moved up the length of the big room where a fire was burning. The broad hearth, built deep into the building's back wall, was a handsome thing. There were short benches under the wide overhang of the hearth's "smoke hood," so that one could sit inside and be very close to the fire. An impressive array of fire-blackened metalwork— swinging arms and chains, and some kind of machinery with toothed gears—were bolted to the stone slabs that made up the back of the fireplace. The hearth itself was one seamless slab of smooth black stone. At the back of it, a small fire burned, but Gabriel could not make out what the fuel was. It was some dark substance that did not look like wood. The whole place was full of a spicy scent that Gabriel thought perhaps came from the fuel, but it was not a smoky smell.

Enda looked around her with wonder. "The fire is not for heat. That is coming from somewhere else."

"Those flat dark plates along the walls?"

"Possibly," said Enda. "I am more interested in the lights, myself."

The scout, who had walked up through the long room with them, now gestured at the pile of cushions nearest to the fire. Enda folded down gracefully into a crosslegged position on the flattest of the cushions. Gabriel looked at her rather ruefully. "I wish I could do that," he said. "You make it look like going down in a lift." He sat down, crossing his legs rather less gracefully.

The scout walked away, leaving them to sit and look around them. There was a little more furniture at this end of the room, some standing cupboards and a couple of long tables. On a smaller table off to one side of the fire there stood a beautiful small cabinet of carved wood and some other substance, something white, possibly bone. The scout went to it and turned a knob on the front.

The sound of music—strange percussive and woodwind sounds in an odd rhythm—startled them both. It was coming from the carved cabinet.

Gabriel blinked at that. After a moment the music stopped and was replaced by the sound of soft barking and growling.

"Powered transmission of some kind," Enda said, as the scout gave them a glance and went over to confer with several others of his people standing nearby. "Perhaps even wireless transmission."

Gabriel shook his head. "Radio! I wish more of ours looked this beautiful."

"Form following function, I suppose," Enda said. "If one does not have microminiaturization, one must evolve handsome furniture to contain the works." She looked around. "Gabriel, what is the source of the power? We did not see any exterior wiring or power conduits outside when we came."

Gabriel shook his head and said, "Wireless power transmission? Microwave, maybe?"

Enda tilted her head "no" and replied, "We would have picked that up from space."

"Even if it was a low-level transmission?" Gabriel asked. "Were we scanning for it?"

Enda let out a long breath. "No," she said, "but we were not expecting it, were we?"

The scout now came back with a couple more of his people, one of whom was carrying a rough brown jug and several cups. They sat down among the cushions across from Gabriel and Enda, and one, still holding his gun, stood guard behind. The scout poured out what looked like water into the cups, and very slowly handed one to Gabriel.

Gabriel lifted it and sniffed it, trying not to look too obvious. "Water, I think."

The scout poured out another cup and handed it to Enda. Gabriel, watching this, found himself wondering what was going on . . . for their host was gazing at Enda intently, and he looked ready to snatch his hand back.

He looks like he thinks she's going to bite him. Why? Why would she be a threat and I not, when I'm nearly twice her size?

Whether Enda noticed this or not, she took the cup carefully. She, Gabriel, and the scout all looked at one another uneasily.

"Does he go first," Gabriel asked softly, "or do we?"

He was all too aware how fraught a point drinking or not drinking with one's host could be in some cultures, but they had no guidelines to which they could refer.

The scout was looking at Gabriel's cup, and then at Gabriel, with what really looked like nervousness.

Oh, hell, Gabriel thought, *if they wanted to kill us, they could have shot us any number of times. Why drag us all the way here to poison us?* He lifted his cup to his host, said—"Up the marines, cousin!"—and drank the contents down.

Just water, with a slightly acid taste to it, and very refreshing. Enda followed his lead, and said, "It is rather like lemon or ver-juice."

"Yes," Gabriel said, watching their host.

The scout was still watching Enda out of the corner of his eye as he drank from his own cup. The other two were looking either at Enda or at the scout.

Once they had drunk, there was nothing Gabriel and Enda could think of to do but to try to communicate somehow. They sat there and tried words in every language they knew, which was not that many. He had no more than a few phrases in Fraal at this point, and he was unwilling to speak the language while Enda was available. In any case, he saw no reason to ask their hosts to be sick on his shoes. He also tried a few words of Weren, which he had picked up from the language software over the last starfall.

Gabriel at last shook his head and said, "You give it a try."

"Well enough," she said, "but our people have never been out this way." She spoke brief sentences in a number of human languages that Gabriel had not heard before. She tried Sheyan, Aleerin, and even a few words of T'sa, but there was no response. Finally she sighed and spoke a sentence in Fraal.

The furred people all looked at her, and something went *click*. Gabriel looked up to see the guard standing there with his weapon cocked and braced, ready to fire at Enda.

Enda was astonished. Gabriel saw that her hand was on her pistol, but she had not drawn.

"What's this all about?" he said softly. "What's their problem?"

"I cannot say," said Enda, "but I refuse to panic. I mean them no harm, no matter who else has troubled them that I may resemble."

She finally looked away from the person with the gun, and looked at their host again. Enda lifted her empty cup and held it out to him.

He looked at her for a long, long moment, then lifted the pitcher and poured for her again. As if unconcerned, Enda drank.

Gabriel held out his own cup, since he found his mouth extremely dry. The scout poured for him as well, and when he put the pitcher down again, Gabriel lifted the cup and toasted him, then drank the contents.

Their hosts looked at them and then glanced at each other.

"Look," Gabriel said to Enda. "We're at kind of an impasse here. I think I should head back to the ship and get that translator. It might be useful."

"It certainly cannot make matters any worse," Enda said.

Gabriel looked around them. "I don't know if I like leaving you here by yourself, though."

She laughed at him. "Gabriel, I have been in much worse places than this and come away from them unscathed."

"Oh? I want to hear all about this. You've been holding out on me."

"This is hardly the time," Enda said, but she had begun to smile again.

Gabriel kept his own expression under control for the moment, but hers had heartened him a little. He knew from experience the useful shift that a fierce look, purposefully assumed, could make in one's emotional state when about to lead a charge, and he was not above using the technique on those around him when it suited him.

"All right," he said, "but listen—"

"I am armed," Enda said, "very well armed. As I said, I do not believe that today is my death day. I will prevent any attempt to rush to conclusions in this regard . . . and I think I could do much more damage to them than they could possibly do to me in an equivalent time."

"What if they get your pistol away from you?"

"Not all my weapons are visible," Enda said, "but then again, not all yours are, as well." She gave him a knowing look.

"Right," he said. I have this awful feeling she's talking about my wits, he thought. I wish she wouldn't do that, because their charge pack is feeling a little low at the moment.

Gabriel stood up and turned to the nearest of their hosts, the alien he had been thinking of as the scout. To this gentleman Gabriel made what he hoped was a graceful and unthreatening gesture indicating that he wanted to go outside.

That alien and the others seated or standing about looked at him with narrowed eyes.

What does *that* mean around here? Gabriel thought. He looked at creatures and spread his hands. "Well?"

They watched him. He sighed and pointed at the door. They all looked at his hand. Gabriel hurriedly dropped the hand, wondering what pointing might mean in this culture.

This is ridiculous, he thought. I'm afraid even to move.

Very gently, he started to move toward the door. They watched him, but did nothing. Good, Gabriel thought.

"Enda," he said, "is there anything else you need?"

"Reassurance is in short supply at the moment," she said softly.

"Believe me, I'd trade all the data we're carrying for a load of that right now," Gabriel said. "I'll be back in a while."

He went out of the longhall and stood looking around for a moment. From the doorways of the other houses and lodges, other red-furred faces gazed at him, unreadable. A sound beside him made him turn. He found himself looking down into the face of the scout who had followed him out.

The look was as unreadable as before, but it was more intimate. Thoughtful? There was no telling exactly what those thoughts *were*.

"Buddy," Gabriel said, "translators aside, I wish we could talk right this minute."

The scout looked at him and tilted his head a little to one side. The ears moved, the eyes flickered. He spoke—just soft growling noises, unlike the imperative barking Gabriel had heard earlier.

Gabriel looked at the scout, looked toward the hills in the direction from which he and Enda had come, and made another slow sweeping gesture up that way.

The scout looked at him. Gabriel took a few steps in that direction, then looked back.

His host tilted his head again, that thoughtful look . . . then turned his back on Gabriel and went back into the building.

That was a dismissal . . . I think.

Gabriel hesitated. Was there any chance that their hosts would think he was abandoning Enda? She's capable of taking care of herself . . . she says.

Finally, he headed out of the half-circle of houses, quickly falling into the dogtrot that a marine used to cover ground in a hurry.

He quickened his pace. He and Enda had stumbled on a species that was moderately advanced, completely unknown until now, and seemed very hostile to the fraal. That alone Gabriel found bizarre. Here was a new species, presently impossible to talk to and probably angry about something, sitting on a planet hardly anyone knew existed . . . and here Gabriel and Enda were, by themselves in the middle of it all.

He ran faster.

Chapter Thirteen

GABRIEL CAME TO the last hill and paused at the top of it to look down. There was *Sunshine*, intact and seemingly unguarded. That surprised him, and made him suspicious. Who might be tucked away around here that I can't see? Gabriel thought, eyeing the hillsides. There was no cover here for anything bigger than a rat . . . just acres of the blue-green turf.

He trotted down the hillside to the bare patch where *Sunshine* was parked. The lift column showed no signs of tampering. Gabriel did a slow walk-round. The people here struck him as quick and smart, and it might have occurred to some of them that this strange vehicle might have removable, valuable parts, but nothing was missing. As far as Gabriel could tell from his minimal training in tracking, no one had been near *Sunshine* at all.

He touched the lift code into the column. The door unlocked itself and let him in. When it opened again, Gabriel hurried down toward the weapons locker and picked up a couple of items. These he slipped into the "secret" pockets in his coverall, ones that even a talented human investigator would not routinely find in a pat-down.

After that, Gabriel rooted around in the sitting room cupboards for the translator keypad and software solids. He picked up the "blank" ones for new species, both of which could record and had a book encoded into it, something called *Dodgson's Guide to First Contacts*. At first Gabriel had tossed this aside, not thinking it important. Now, though—

He found a carry bag to stow everything in and also picked up drypack lunches from the galley, bottles of water, and a few of the

high-protein-and-carbohydrate emergency ration bars that Enda
routinely referred to as "the inedibles."

Gabriel paused with the food in his hands. Suppose these creatures had some taboo against eating in public? No matter what
their taboos are, he thought, we're going to need to eat something
eventually.

He slung the bag over his shoulder, went down in the lift, and
locked *Sunshine* behind him. He started the dogtrot back to the
circle of houses and fell gratefully into the rhythm, hoping the
physical exertion would distract him from his own nervousness.

It didn't. There was simply nothing about this situation that
could be relied upon, nothing predictable.

Slowly, behind Gabriel, the thunder of the waterfall died away as
he put a kilometer between him and *Sunshine*, then another. Along
the way, he mused upon the strangeness of the place, not at all a
proper site for these people to be living. They had seen other settlements in the imaging, but this area was so remote from the others.

Is this some kind of vacation camp? Gabriel wondered. Where
is their technology coming from, the radios, the guns? Not to mention the energy to run these things. There were no big cities . . .
Have they got them hidden? Or are their large settlements in some
other form? What about those big buildings we saw, the triangular shapes?

Gabriel stopped atop a hillcrest, looked around him, then
headed down the far side. He panted his way down that hill and
up the next, the long-ridged hill before the furred people's settlement. Gabriel doubted that he and Enda were going to get
answers to any questions soon. Even if the translator program
worked, there was always the possibility that these people would
have no desire to discuss business with strangers. Certainly they
had already shown caution in their dealings with Gabriel and
Enda, which brought to Gabriel's mind, again, the image of the
one alien who had held his gun on Enda with real intent.

He paused on the last ridge, looking down at the settlement.
Everything seemed very much as he had left it. Gabriel headed
down the hillside and went to the central longhouse.

As Gabriel ducked through the oval doorway, there was a soft chorus of growls down at the end of the room, and he saw lifted weapons. He said, for all the world as if he were someplace familiar, "It's just me, folks, don't panic."

Gabriel came down to where Enda still lounged with some of the other furred people around her, looking at her with curiosity. "Is everything all right?" she asked.

"No problems. I brought you some lunch, and for our hosts . . . this."

He produced the translator keypad, putting it down on the furred rug that covered the floor among the cushions.

The furred people gathered there looked at the keypad with some bemusement. Gabriel held up one hand in what he desperately hoped would be taken as a "watch this" gesture, then activated the keypad.

All its keys flashed briefly with light, then darkened again. Gabriel looked at the alien whom he had been thinking of as the scout. That one showed no great amount of surprise at the keypad's actions, but he did reach out to lift the keypad by one corner and look at its underside. He glanced quizzically at Gabriel.

Enda said, "I think perhaps he wonders that it seems to have no power source. Everything else here seems to have some kind of power conduit cords attached. Look at the radio and the bottoms of those lamps."

Gabriel saw that she was right, though in the shadows at the bottoms of the walls, it was hard to tell where the cords went. "I wonder . . ." Gabriel said. "If they have electric power, why do they need fires?"

Enda shrugged. "Pleasure?" she said. "Some humans have them for such reasons, I've heard."

Gabriel nodded and turned his attention back to the translator keypad. He touched one of its keys, which lit up with the stylized stick figure for "man." The scout looked at this. Gabriel indicated the key, then indicated himself.

The scout regarded Gabriel with widened eyes.

Gabriel glanced over at the nearby bare stone flagging of the
hearth, where there were a few sticks of kindling. One had been
burnt at one end. Gabriel hitched himself closer to the hearth,
picked up the burnt stick, and started drawing. The contrast of
charcoal on the darkish stone of the flagging was not very great,
but he drew a round head, indicating his own. Next he drew a
stick body and thumped his own chest. Last of all, he sketched
one arm—

The aliens nearest him hissed.

The sound was alarming. Gabriel looked around. Some of the
aliens were still hissing, and all but a couple of them stared at
him. One got up and left. Another was poking the one that sat
next to him, and both were hissing hard. The scout, presently
closest to Gabriel, reached out and patted the hearth next to
Gabriel's drawing, and hissed again, his mouth open wide and the
fangs showing.

"I wonder," Enda said, "if he means that he considers your
style of artwork rather primitive."

"I wish I could tell him I agreed with him," Gabriel said, looking ruefully at the stick figure.

One of the smaller aliens came along with a roll of some pale
material. The little alien looked at Gabriel with big eyes and
would not come close. That look he knew, even across species: a
child's shyness.

"Come on," Gabriel said reassuringly, "don't be afraid."

The little one held out the roll. The scout took it, unrolled it,
and showed the roll to Gabriel.

Gabriel reached out carefully to take it. The roll itself was not,
as he had first thought, any kind of paper or composite, but some
very smooth slick material with tiny, tiny holes in it.

"This could be some kind of inner bark of a tree or plant,"
Gabriel said. "Remember back on Grith, we saw some of the
sesheyan longbooks made out of the inner membrane of galya
vine? They looked like this. But, oh, Enda . . ." He turned the roll
so that she could see the inside of it.

The drawing on the inside of the roll appeared to have been

done in the kind of charcoal Gabriel had been using to draw on the hearth, but it was many times more complex, a delicately shaded portrait of one of the warriors who sat in the circle with them—Gabriel recognized the elaborately embroidered overvest with its spiral patterns. The artist had very perfectly caught the faintly wise, grizzled look of the seated alien's face, the scarred muzzle, the ears, one of them nocked. The fraying of the vest in front of the one shoulder, in the place where the gunstock would normally rest, was faithfully reproduced. The curly pelt was there, and the tail, more hinted at than seen, just peeked out from under the overvest. The eyes looked into the distance, as if the hunter saw game atop the nearby hill, or perhaps looked into memory at yesterday's hunt, last year's kill, his own youth . . .

"Edanwe," said the alien who had given the drawing to Gabriel. He gestured at all of them. "Edanweir."

"That was a species name, I think," Gabriel said, handing the drawing to Enda. He leaned over the keypad, touched a key. "Edanwe," he said to it. The key went black, then flashed with a neutral symbol, and the keypad said, "Edanwe."

Gabriel poked his stick figure again, and said, "Human." He drew a few more beside it, hastily, and said, "Humans." Then he drew a shorter, thinner one with longer arms and legs next to the "human" stick figure, and said, "Fraal."

A rustle went through the watching edanweir. They looked at each other, then at Gabriel, with expressions that somehow seemed distressed.

"This is a lovely thing," Enda said softly. "Gabriel, the keypad can acquire drawings from outside sources. I was not sure how useful a feature that would be, but I begin to see the point. If you will lift the pad close to the drawing and touch the 'acquire key,' that small one with the up arrow . . ."

Gabriel did this, slowly, conscious of edanweir eyes on him. Nothing visible happened to either the drawing or the back of the keypad, but when Gabriel put the pad down again, he saw that the neutral symbol on the "edanwe" key had replaced itself with a miniature of the portrait.

The "scout" edanwe leaned in close to look at it. He looked over his shoulder and spoke to one of the others. Then he touched the key with Gabriel's stick figure. "Human," said the keyboard.

"Yrrrmh'n," said the scout, obviously straining his mouth out of its normal shape.

Gabriel nodded: then stopped himself. Don't bother with gestures, he told himself. Who knows what nodding might mean here?

"Human," Gabriel said.

"Yuuhm'n," said the scout.

"Yes!" Gabriel said, delighted, and touched the button with the sketch shown on it in small. "Edanwe."

"Edanwe," said the scout. *"Ntai!"*

The edanweir looked at each other. "Well," Gabriel said, "that's one word out of a thousand we need before we can have a decent conversation, not to mention the verbs."

"It is a start, Gabriel," Enda said. "Do not disparage it. At least we have this much in common with our hosts, that they understand the symbology of drawings. There are cultures which do not, or did not, even among humans."

"Well, I'm glad they can understand mine. Even if their drawing is much better."

*　*　*　*　*

The next four or five hours went by fairly quickly as the edanwe started working with the keypad. Several times, what seemed to be arguments broke out, though about what, Gabriel couldn't tell. Early on, he and Enda moved themselves away from those working with the keypad. They ate some of the rations that Gabriel had brought, and concentrated on looking through the documentation for the translator module.

It had been difficult enough to understand when there was no pressure on them. Now it seemed positively obscure.

"You'd swear this had never actually been *used* with a new alien species," Gabriel muttered as he scrolled through the logic solid, reading the back of it where words appeared when not connected by Grid software to a larger display.

"That is an interesting point. *Has* it?"

"If it has, I don't remember anything about it in the docs."

He looked over at the edanweir, one of whom was pushing key after key on the keypad with what might have been a frustrated look. The others working with him, including the scout, leaned over his shoulder, pointing and growling. Things seemed to be going all right at the moment, but what if the software couldn't cope? Language is so complex, Gabriel thought.

Gabriel blanked the data solid he was holding and looked at its title side. "This *Dodgson's* thing," he said, "you think it has anything to do with the translator itself? It did come bundled with it."

"Let us look through it and see."

Dodgson's Guide to First Contacts, it said when you activated it. There was a large table of contents, full of headings like "Initial Overtures" and "The First Worlds." Gabriel skimmed down through these to the first section, "Known Species."

"Fraal," he said. "Here." He started reading down through it. " 'A wandering species, much known for their aloof and mysterious behavior . . .' Enda, did you know that you're aloof and mysterious?"

"You forgot 'ethereal' and 'delicate,' " Enda muttered.

Gabriel shot her an amused look. For his own part, he had seen Enda, while suited, wrestle massive meteor fragments around with great skill and strength in zero-g, and "delicate" was not normally a word he would have chosen.

"Wandering," Enda said. "What about all the thousands and millions of us who have been Builders, who have settled among humans for hundreds of years? Certainly some of us do wander, but not all of us. This person seems not to have heard the news." Her lips were pursed in the annoyed-grandmother expression that she assumed every now and then when faced with extreme stupidity.

He grinned and went back to his own reading, going on to the weren section. " 'Massive and ferocious creatures of limited intelligence . . .' *What?*" It was possibly the commonest of the stereotypes about the weren, not stamped out by any means, but known to be untrue. The weren might originally have been the product of a nomadic tribal culture on Kurg, but they had proven themselves a subtle and clever people, both on planet and off, producing as many philosophers, poets, and mathematicians as any other species.

"Enda," Gabriel said, "is it possible that this book is a joke?"

"It *is* a joke," she said, scrolling further down the solid she was holding, "whether it is trying to be one or not. If you mean, 'is it an intentional work of humor', I have no answer for you. Have you looked at the real 'first contact' material yet?"

"Getting to it." Gabriel scrolled past the species-specific information and went to the chapter entitled "Initial Overtures."

The screen flickered and said, *In your travels, if you are extremely fortunate, you may come across species that are presently unknown to our science. While it is dangerous to generalize, any aliens may conceal a considerable intelligence, possibly even comparable to our own—*

Gabriel opened his mouth, closed it again. "When was this *written?*" Gabriel explained, scrolling back to look at the colophon.

Enda laughed, and the edanweir looked at her. After a few seconds she stifled her laughter, and Gabriel began scanning down to see what had caused it. The trouble was that there were so many possibilities. Gabriel stopped at one in particular: *Avoid loud noises or shouting. While it is dangerous to generalize, many species take this as an indication of hostility.*

"Oh, good," Gabriel said, "I'm so glad they told me that." He chucked the book off to one side, onto the nearest rug.

It squealed.

The edanweir turned shocked expressions on him. Gabriel picked the solid up again and saw large letters now spreading across the reading surface. *WARNING! Abuse of this solid may cause damage to the reader circuitry or loss of data. Please do not drop or shake.*

"This thing is pushing its luck," Gabriel muttered. To the edanweir, he held up the data solid, shrugged, made what he hoped they would understand as a conciliatory gesture. "Malfunction," he said.

They regarded him with totally unreadable expressions and turned their attention back to the keypad.

Gabriel flipped the data solid back to the "manual side" and spent another hour reading. He looked up from this largely unrewarding business to realize that the artificial lighting inside the longhouse had been turned up. Dusk was falling outside.

He stretched and looked around. The edanweir were still working over the keypad, though now there were only the scout and two others. Gabriel glanced at Enda, who was sitting with half-closed eyes against several cushions. As he looked at her, she opened her eyes.

"How are they doing?" he asked.

"I have not inquired," she said. "Gabriel, for whatever reason, they do not seem to like me to come too close to them. I thought it wiser not to press the point."

Gabriel glanced at the high windows under the eaves. "Getting to be our dinnertime. More to the point, I'd sooner be back in *Sunshine* before it gets completely dark. Not that I don't trust these nice people: but the local wildlife might be less hospitable." He looked around at the furs on the floor. They were large, the biggest of them nearly three meters by three.

"Yes," Enda said, and stood up.

There was an immediate response from the edanweir, a look almost of alarm. Enda did not look at them, but at Gabriel. Behind her, the edanweir calmed down.

"Right." Gabriel started tidying up after himself, putting the used packaging from their lunch into his carrybag. The last thing he picked up was the software manual with *Dodgson's Guide*. "I don't think we should leave this here. They might figure out how to read it, and *then* where would we be?"

"I would be tempted to leave it," Enda said, "on the off chance that they might be more successful at deciphering the translation manual than I have been, but perhaps you are right."

Gabriel chuckled and pocketed the solid. He looked toward

the scout-edanwe and made the same graceful gesture toward the doors that he had used earlier, but this time he included Enda as well.

The scout looked at them both. He got up from the keypad, leaving his companions still working with it, and copied Gabriel's gesture.

Together the three of them walked to the door. Gabriel paused just inside the doorway, and looked down at the scout. He was gazing up at them, eyeing first Gabriel, then Enda, and it was on Enda that his glance lingered longest.

"Goodbye for now," Gabriel said. The edanwe looked up at him and growled softly.

Enda and Gabriel walked away from the longhouse through the falling dusk, making their way up the long-ridged hill. Gabriel turned, just at the crest of that ridge, and looked back to see the smoke rising gently from that fieldstone chimney. His instincts began to itch him. Standing on a hilltop silhouetted against the sunset was asking to be made a target.

He headed down the other side, Enda following him. All the way down, and all the way back to *Sunshine*, Gabriel's back itched as if someone was taking aim at it. He was a target for something, he knew it—even here, practically at the edge of the explored universe. Something was coming toward him, coming after him, and he couldn't stop it. The darkness would not hide him for much longer.

Gabriel shivered, standing there by the lift column in twilight nearly gone to dark, and punched in the security code with unnecessary force.

* * * * *

Once they were safe inside and had a meal, Gabriel was able to relax. Enda took herself straight to bed afterwards, looking worn out. Gabriel was as weary as she. Though nothing bad had happened to either of them, the daylong stress of being in the presence of aliens with weapons—aliens that neither of them could understand—did wear on you after a while. Gabriel was glad to turn in early himself and retired to his room after cleaning up the remains of their dinner.

Yawning, he lay down on his bed, not even bothering to undress. He reached to shut off the light, first touching the alarm built into the shelf to set it for dawn. The cabin light faded. . . .

* * * * *

Darkness.

This part of the dream he was all too used to at the moment. The fear started to build, but Gabriel was getting used to that. In the dreams, he had begun to advance toward the experience of the fear, partly to get it over with, but also partly remembering a voice saying, *If a pain recurs, don't be afraid to get used to it. Once you've learned to accept it, you can move past it, to what it means . . .*

All the same, there was now something more vivid about the fear, a sense of it being closer, more real, more physical . . . though that was an odd word to use for a dream. Equally strong was the knowledge that this *was* a dream. Odd that this realization did not make the experience more bearable, but less.

The other presence was here in the dark with him, but somehow more familiar. The darkness broke ever so briefly as he saw something. A shape silhouetted on a hilltop—*a target*—strange thought that. Where did *that* come from? Warm darkness all around them, darkness that breathed. Gabriel braced himself, knowing what was coming next.

Fire, the brilliance in the darkness—*and the darkness comprehendeth it not*—strange thought. Where did *that* come from? No matter. The brilliance lashed out at the shapes that hid and skulked in the dark, illuminating them briefly in glimpses and flashes. This was always the hardest part of the dream to deal with, when you saw detail, always more than you wanted, and wished you could scream. The darkness choked the screams in your throat and left you gasping and helpless.

Not alone this time, though. *Not alone.* Gabriel exulted briefly in that fact. There was someone else with him, fighting the same fight. Together they took great spears of fire and threw it into the darkness at the menacing shadows. The shadows screamed and stretched tearing taloned limbs toward them, but Gabriel and the companion he could not see in the darkness or fire grasped the light and rained it on their enemies, fired it at them as if from weapons, hurled it on them like stones from a height. The screams out of the darkness scaled up, wailing, furious, and faded away. They were not beaten. They would be back.

They might well win, next time, Gabriel could hear that other presence thinking. Maybe they would both die next time, but for the moment, they had won. It was all they could do. When darkness next fell, they would fight again.

It could not be helped. It was their job.

Not mine! Gabriel cried into the dark. *I didn't sign up for this!*

You did. You swore the oath. That other job may be gone, but the duty remains. . . .

* * * * *

. . . and the alarm went off. It was just before dawn.

Gabriel lay staring at the ceiling in the dim light that the alarm had turned on. He swore. If there was anything he hated in the world, it was falling asleep and then waking up to the feeling that he had not really slept at all.

At the same time, Gabriel felt a peculiar sense of . . . what? *Satisfaction?* Just the feeling that, even in a dream, he was not completely helpless, that he was beginning to be able to affect what was happening to him . . .

Better than nothing, Gabriel thought. He got up and went off to shower before Enda awoke and wanted hers.

Chapter Fourteen

SOME HOURS AFTER dawn, he and Enda made their way back to the edanweir settlement. They paused at the open doors of the longhouse, looking in and waiting to see whether there would be some response to their return.

Various edanweir sat among the cushions by the fire. They looked up as Gabriel and Enda walked toward them. One of them, an edanwe Gabriel did not immediately recognize, had the keypad. He sported one of the handsome woven vests some of them wore, a short one with bright leaf-patterns woven into it in green and a dark green-blue like that of the ground cover.

As Gabriel and Enda got closer, there were a few more uncomfortable looks directed at Enda. "I wish I knew what that was about," Gabriel said to her. "You sit down over there and make yourself comfortable, and I'll check out what's happening."

He walked over to the blue-vested edanwe and knelt down beside it. The edanwe glanced at Gabriel and growled.

"Yeah, good morning to you too," Gabriel said and peered at the keypad, looking to see what kind of images had been programmed into the pad so far. There were very few. The preprogrammed ones, with stick-images of leaves, falling water, and so on, produced no Standard words when he touched them, only edanweir.

"No wonder you look so pissed off," Gabriel said softly. "You've been sitting here doing this with no result . . . or at least none that does *you* any good."

He looked over the keys one more time. "Did I misconfigure this thing, maybe?" Gabriel said, reaching for the keypad. The edanwe moved his hands to let Gabriel take it.

Gabriel turned the keypad over and brought up the flat display on the back that held the configuration profiles. The edanwe looked over his shoulder and made soft grunting and growling sounds. Gabriel shook his head.

"I don't know. I *thought* I had this set up right."

He got up and brought the keypad over to Enda, showing her the back of it. She too looked at it and could only tilt her head to one side in negation. "I thought you had it set up correctly, but it would seem our friends are making little headway. Certainly we saw many arguments yesterday over what the images meant."

"Yeah. I can't shake the idea that they just don't like this machine . . . that either they don't understand what's needed, or they don't like the methodology."

"You might be right." Enda turned the keypad over to study the keys. "They cannot have entered more than twenty concepts."

Gabriel sat down beside her. "This is going to take all year. I really wish some other survey had been here before us."

"If one had, I think this world would very likely have been embargoed to keep its culture from being contaminated."

"Depends on whose survey would have found them," Gabriel said. "If it was the Concord, well and good, but if VoidCorp turned up here and tried to sell the edanweir the same deal as they sold the sesheyans . . ." He shook his head. "I wouldn't like that much."

"Neither would they," said Enda as she looked across at the edanweir.

"As it is," Gabriel said, "for the moment, they've lucked out. One survey passes through and has its equipment break down, so nothing comes of it. Another one is too brief and half-hearted to make any difference, then we come along and can't understand a thing that's going on." He laughed. "Are these people religious, I wonder? Something sure seems to be protecting them."

He was also wondering if other travelers might once have come this way without giving anyone prior warning and then had simply gone missing—some of Rov's "went out and never came back" types. Some disagreement with the locals? Or something less local, perhaps? There was no evidence of that.

Gabriel took the keypad back to the blue-vested cdanwe, and together they sat for nearly two hours and took turns hammering on the thing. Besides trying to program in simple words like hand, finger, wrist, which they did have in common, Gabriel tried again and again to get the machine to speak in Standard. Again and again it refused to say anything but "human." Gabriel started to wonder whether the thing was simply broken. He spent nearly another hour reading the manual, while the edanweir came and went around him, looking at him curiously.

A shadow fell over him around lunchtime. Gabriel looked up to see the scout, in a different vest today, but Gabriel knew him by his face markings and the slant of his eyes, slightly more tilted than those of the other edanweir. He was carrying the pitcher and cups again.

"Hyuman," said the edanwe.

"Edanwe," said Gabriel. It would do for a greeting.

"Hyuman," said the edanwe, pointing at the keypad and wrinkling his muzzle so that a lot of his teeth showed. *"Hyuman hyuman hyuman hyuman hyuman."*

"Yeah," Gabriel said, "I'm sick and tired of hearing it say that myself." He reached over to Blue Vest and tapped the corner of the keypad with one finger. The edanwe looked up and handed it to him.

Gabriel started pressing the keys that had been programmed, speaking the edanwe words, and the scout lifted his long tail over his shoulder, so that the tip of it twitched where Gabriel could see it. Was that a nod? Gabriel thought perhaps it was, since it repeated each time Gabriel pronounced a word correctly. He touched each key and said the Standard words for them . . . and the keyboard refused to say anything but "human." Gabriel picked the keypad up and shook it, grimacing.

The scout hissed. Laughter, Gabriel thought. At least he has a sense of humor about this. I wish I had more of one.

Gabriel gave the keypad back to the blue-vested edanwe and looked up at the scout again. The scout handed him a cup of water and Gabriel toasted him with it. "Edanwe . . ." he said.

The other lifted his cup too. "Hyuman!"

They drank together, and after a while the scout went off, leaving Gabriel looking over the blue-vested edanwe's shoulder and trying to help. It did no good. Something was wrong with the keypad's programming that Gabriel couldn't understand, no matter how many times he went back to the manual. After a while Gabriel stopped interrupting Blue Vest and turned to Enda. "Could it be broken?"

She bowed her head. "All its diagnostics keep coming up clean. I suppose the diagnostic problem itself could be faulty, but the manual has no information about how to troubleshoot that."

Gabriel stretched. The day was well gone. Dusk was falling, and the edanweir were going around to their artificial lights, turning them up. Another one had turned on the radio, and more soft clunky edanwen music was coming from it.

"This is so frustrating," Gabriel said. "I want to ask them where they got this technology from. I want to ask them where they shot *that!*" He gestured with his chin at the biggest fur rug in the middle of the floor. "But I can't."

Enda tilted her head to one side. "I do not know what we can do about it."

Gabriel sat there considering. "You know," he said at last, "maybe there's something."

"I listen attentively," Enda said, and yawned.

"Thanks lots. You said the other day that you heard me 'without my silencer on.' You do hear thoughts sometimes."

"Not usually at will," Enda said, and frowned.

"I know, but would you be willing to try?"

She looked alarmed. "With *them?*"

"Why not? Would listening hurt?"

"It might," she said. "They might become angry."

"You can't tell until you try."

Enda was looking very thoughtful. "Gabriel, even among beings who know what is about to happen, trying to overhear thought can be considered offensive. To those who do *not* know what is happening . . ."

"I don't mean anything like trying to read their minds," Gabriel said. "I know it doesn't work like that. If you can just pick up a few words, enough to explain to them that we're from another world, that we don't mean them any harm . . . that kind of thing."

Enda considered that. "Well, is your friend here? He seems to be most likely to help us. We do not know the others here so well."

Gabriel looked around. "There, he just came in again. Let's try."

Gabriel went over to the doors, where the scout was talking to another edanwe and unloading his rifle. Gabriel waited until he finished, unwilling to bother someone who was making his weapon safe. When the scout had placed the last of the bullets into his belt pouch, Gabriel gestured to him and then Enda.

The scout twitched his tail over his shoulder and went with him. Gabriel sat down by Enda again, wondering how he was going to get this next point across. Finally, all he could think of to do was to touch Enda's head, and then to touch his own, and hers again.

Enda looked rather wry as this was going on. "Do these people even believe that the process of thought resides in any organ associated with the head?" she said to Gabriel, folding her hands together. "He may not understand what this is about at all."

"Well," Gabriel said, "give it a try."

Enda sighed and closed her eyes, holding very still.

The scout peered at her curiously. He looked at Gabriel, as if in question, then his eyes went wide.

The high-pitched howl that followed was terrible. Gabriel scrambled to his feet. So did every edanwe around. The scout staggered back, cried something in a series of sharp furious barks, and began loading his gun frantically.

Gabriel and Enda were suddenly surrounded in a frenzied, barking crowd of edanweir, all clutching and tearing at their clothes and equipment. Gabriel's pistol was pulled off him and passed out of reach before he could react, as was Enda's. She struggled to sit up, but about five edanwe were pinning her, and one of them, snarling, had lifted a hand as if to strike her.

Gabriel caught that hand and stopped it with some difficulty, only to find the furious face of the hand's owner staring up into his, the lips skinned back away from the teeth in a growl that looked nearly insane with anger. *Or fear?* The hair stood up all over Gabriel as the edanwe hauled Enda to her feet.

There was some pushing and shoving as the group tried to go in a couple of different directions amid a chorus of growls. Then the scout barked again, and the crowd reacted, pushing Enda roughly away toward the back of the longroom, off to the right of the fireplace. The scout had not laid hands on Enda, but he clutched his gun and stared at Gabriel with such perfect rage that Gabriel stepped back a pace, then looked after Enda. She was not struggling as they dragged her off—probably a wise decision.

The scout stared at Gabriel. Rage, yes, but there was something else too. Betrayal?

He hurried after the crowd taking Enda away. At the far end of the hall was a small door that led to a narrow passage. Down the passage were smaller rooms with doors made of planks, perhaps intended for storage.

"Enda, are you all right?" Gabriel shouted after her.

"For the moment." Half hidden by the crowd pushing her down the hallway in an angry chorus of yowls and barks, she was trying to catch her breath. "But I would say—he understood—what I was trying!"

Down at the end of the hallway was a last room with a thick plank door, and one little window that seemed to be covered in some kind of mesh. The door was closed with a heavy bar. Several edanwe hurriedly lifted this, pushed Enda in, then pulled the door closed and barred it.

For his own part, Gabriel was trying not to overreact to so many guns being pointed at his face. "Is there anybody in there with you?" Gabriel called.

"No," Enda said, still gasping. "It is quite empty . . ." She paused. "Except for some meat."

"Meat?"

Gabriel held his hands up in a gesture intended to suggest that he was not going to do anything sudden, and moved toward the door. There was a chorus of barks and yelps, and hammers were cocked before him and behind him, but he did not stop. Very gently he pushed through the crowd of edanweir, and went up to the door.

Gabriel peered in through the grille-window, which was covered with a very delicately made metal mesh. The room in which Enda was now standing had straw on the floor, and plastered fieldstone walls. Around the walls ran a well-made iron railing, and more such railings crisscrossed the ceiling.

"I think this is their larder," Enda said. Sure enough, hooks hung from the railings, and on some of them were suspended carcasses of some animal. These had been very expertly butchered, Gabriel thought, and he did not care for the symbolism. He also wondered if these huge haunches of meat were from the same animals as the large furry pelts on the floor of the common room. If they were, his estimation of their hosts' skill as hunters went up somewhat, for they had seen no indication that these creatures were being farmed.

He turned away from the door to find all the edanweir glaring at him, guns raised. "Enda," he said very softly, "I'm not going to let them keep you in here."

"Gabriel, calm yourself. They have done nothing to me as yet," Enda said. "If it looks like they might . . . *that* would be the time to do something."

"I just hate waiting until the situation gets worse. It tends to make the required response more extreme."

He didn't move. The edanweir fidgeted, but they didn't move either.

"Harming or killing these people will not help us," Enda said. "If they believe I meant them harm to begin with, it will only confirm them in that opinion, and make things worse!"

Gabriel wasn't so sure, but he had always disliked being the one to start the shooting—it tended to create misunderstandings later about who had been responsible. The edanweir looked at him, and didn't move.

"By the way," Gabriel said, "they missed my holdouts."

"I suppose that is reassuring," Enda said. "Gabriel, please . . . think three times before you harm any of these people. I have brought this on myself. There would be no point in punishing them for their reaction."

Gabriel leaned against the door, looking at their captors. A few of the edanweir in the hall sat down, with weapons at the ready. Various others, the scout among them, looked suspiciously at Gabriel and then slipped back toward the main hall.

"Well," Gabriel said. "What do we do now?"

"That is a good question," Enda said. "I am short of answers, unfortunately, and I have an uncomfortable feeling that this eventuality is not covered in *Dodgson's*."

Gabriel laughed a little hollowly. "Did you get anything?"

"From your friend?" He could hear Enda gulp. "No. The moment he felt the touch and knew it for what it was . . . then there came the fear, Gabriel, awful fear and loathing."

"Why?"

"I wish I knew for sure," Enda said, producing a rustling noise as she sat down in the straw on the floor of the larder. "There are species that are against any mind touch. This may simply be another. Gabriel, this situation does not look promising, and we still have a load of data to deliver to Coulomb. Perhaps it might be wise if you left."

Gabriel laughed. "This is no time to bring that up. The data isn't even remotely time-sensitive!"

"It must get where it is going, or our contract—"

"If you don't get out of here safely," Gabriel said, *"I'm* not getting out either. If that particular line of thought continues to its logical conclusion, the reason we won't be leaving is that we'll be dead. The CCC can sue our estates if it likes."

Gabriel looked around at the watching edanweir and said to Enda, "I'm not going anywhere, since you're not. The data's not a big problem, compared to what's sitting in front of us." More softly, he added, "Besides, this is my fault. I talked you into it. I'm not going to leave you here to suffer the consequences."

Enda was silent. Finally, she said, "I understand the sentiment, but there are no other marines here to back you up."

"For a situation as small as this," Gabriel said, "one marine should be enough."

Enda was silent, leaving Gabriel to hope very much that this would be true.

* * * * *

He sat outside the cell a long time. Night had long since fallen, leaving him in near-total darkness. For a while this had not bothered Gabriel. Now that Enda's breathing had changed, and he knew that she was asleep in the larder, Gabriel started feeling very alone. The edanwe guard sitting down the hall from him with his gun in his hands made this feeling slightly worse. The edanwe could plainly see well enough in the dark to be able to shoot.

Gabriel fished around in his pocket and came out with the luckstone. He put it down on the ground beside him. It flickered, a very faint pale gleam, then lost its light again. Gabriel had seen it do this before. Sometimes, if you were going to get it to make any light, you had to hold it for a while. He picked the luckstone up, held it in his fist, leaned back against the wall, and closed his eyes, trying hard to relax.

It was hard, for the loneliness seemed palpable tonight, the darkness closing in around Gabriel, shutting everything away. Here he sat, outside a prison cell on a world that no one knew . . . far from civilization, far from life as Gabriel knew it, light-years away from help or any friendly voice. This little local darkness suddenly seemed more like the darkness of drivespace—silent, featureless, utterly isolated.

Gabriel sighed, looked down at the luckstone in his hands. It was beginning to shine through his fingers. He put it down beside him on the ground, where it sat glowing quietly, like a coal burnt down low.

Even with this slight light, the guard was hardly more than a
dark shape looking at him, and the faint glint of eyes catching the
luckstone's light. Gabriel folded his arms and leaned against the
door, trying to think of a way out of this problem. He could find
none, and he was tired. Hungry, too . . . but he had no real
appetite, and wasn't willing to eat any of the small supply of
ration bars he was carrying. Enda might need them.

Nothing more's going to happen tonight, Gabriel thought. I
should try to rest if I can. If anyone comes near me, I'll hear it,
but for the meantime . . . .

*   *   *   *   *

. . . darkness. It was hardly even surprising any more. He stood
waiting for the fire, for that made the darkness bearable. Additionally, Gabriel was beginning to wait for that other presence.
Fighting together was better than being alone in the dark, even if
you had no idea who the other was. *Well?* he shouted. *Is it going
to be the same again this time? Let's begin!*

No answer came, but he heard something through the darkness
that he had heard before and disliked: a low, soft hiss at the edge
of hearing. It always suggested that it might start to get louder,
and the more one listened to it, the more the fear grew. It was
louder than usual, and in the darkness Gabriel turned, trying to
work out from which direction it came.

It was hard to tell. Abruptly, though, that other who could not
be seen in the darkness was with him. Together they turned to
face the sound.

It has always been there, said the other. *Even with the fire, we
may not be able to burn it away. If we try—*

Something in that darkness touched Gabriel. He knew it to be
his companion and did not fear. Fire burst out and burnt him, the
fire that had been their shared weapon. In the darkness, Gabriel
screamed—

—started awake, and looked around him. He still sat in darkness, but it was the normal kind. A faint gleam of light off to one

side was the luckstone. He breathed out. Also near the stone, looking down at him, were his guard and the scout.

The scout crouched down beside him, looked at the stone, then up at Gabriel. He held out his hand to the stone, then to Gabriel, almost touching his chest, but not quite.

"Yes," Gabriel said. "Yes, it's mine." He picked the stone up.

The scout looked at it, eyes wide. Fear? Awe? Surprise?

"Here," Gabriel said. "It's nothing to be afraid of."

He held out the hand with the stone in it. The scout shrank back a little . . . then reached out his own hand, palm up, tentative. Gabriel put the stone into the two-thumbed hand. Just for a fraction of a second, they were both touching it at once . . . and Gabriel found out how long a fraction of a second could be.

* * * * *

He was born out of darkness into light.

A world of blurred images and warmth surrounded him. He grew into language and understanding of the imagery around him: the houses, the hills, the sense of community. That was perhaps the most important thing for his people, their oneness.

Years passed as he grew into that community. He learned to hunt and to shoot. Community helped him to understand his people's wisdom, the way they managed their world. He lived through the years of hard snow, when nearly everyone starved through the winter. He lived through the death of his father, and his elevation to his father's position in the little community by the Downfall. His mating and his widowing, terrible as that was, both of those he lived again. Then came his part in the meeting with the Others, that awful time when the people discovered that they were not alone, and that the universe beyond their world was intrinsically evil, a place of pain and terror, and of singleness, loneliness, community not only unknown but hated. He relived his assumption with many others of the role of guardian, secret and covert as that had to be, lest the Others discover the treachery. Then came something worse still, the invasion the Others had warned of—first rumors of strange beings passing by the world, and then the actuality of it and their awful shapes, reminding everyone who saw them of the Others, whom so many had tried to forget.

It all came in scraps of memory. To part of him they were familiar. To the one suddenly in community with him, they were terror—content without context, strange faces, an eternity trapped in a body of the wrong shape, thinking thoughts shaped by the strangeness of that body and brain. No individuality, no privacy, but a low underlying undercurrent of others sharing your thoughts and never letting you alone. But there was something fascinating about this, a fulfillment of an old dream, not to be alone any more. There was something else going on here, something hidden, something lost—*what is that? No, what are you doing?*—something important, buried too securely for even those holding the secret to know, buried for their own good. Messengers carrying a secret even the messenger did not know. But it could not stay hidden for long, it was part of the fire, it would burst out—

No!

Don't be afraid—

No!

All right. All right, let it be.

A measure of calm, then, a sense of community restoring itself. Strange, to look at the world through such awful isolation, but it was better than being trapped in the darkness again alone. The core of light shone between them—*the Messenger!*—dimmed out—

* * * * *

—and Gabriel sat there gasping, staring into the shocked and panting face of the scout.

"What *happened?*" Gabriel said when he got his breath back.

Somehow it didn't surprise him when the scout said, in a soft growl, *"Nendhwe rraim nte'ithsaournte—!"* and what Gabriel heard at the same time was, "Not just *ourselves* in my mind—!"

Then the scout gasped and dropped the glowing luckstone on the floor between them.

Gabriel swallowed. There had been no way to understand this about the edanweir, no way to tell just by looking at them. They were a people psionic in small groups, their "community" operating best that way. They did not live in cities because they could not bear to. Increased numbers diluted the essence of their community. They were wise enough to have elected not to go down that road. They were most psionic in pairs—as Gabriel now knew.

He still didn't know the other's name, but then *how often do I think about my own name? I don't need to. I know who I am.*

Or I thought I did . . .

He touched his chest and said, "Gabriel. That's my name."

"Tlelai," said the scout. It was a soft half-growl, but Gabriel also heard it as a word in a strange language, and at the same time as a word in Standard, the Standard word much clearer to him. "My calling."

They looked at each other, both still breathing hard.

"Did you do that?" Gabriel said. "Did you make that happen?"

Tlelai's tail thrashed furiously. "Thought *you* did."

"Not me."

"You can hear me . . ."

"I hear strange noises," Tlelai said, "and proper words. Both together, but the words are louder."

They both looked at the stone.

"What *is* that?" Gabriel asked Tlelai.

Tlelai's tail thrashed again. "It might be from the mountains. Things like that come from there, they say."

Gabriel picked the stone. It glowed softly. "Did it hurt you?"

"It did not hurt my hand," said Tlelai, his tail becoming still. He looked at Gabriel, and suddenly the expression was completely readable. Fear and wonder, well mixed . . . but the fear predominated.

"You are alone," Tlelai said, in the same tone of voice in which a person might say to someone, *You are dying.*

"It's not a problem," Gabriel said.

Tlelai looked at him incredulously. "Look, never mind, just *listen* to me first," Gabriel said, afraid that this rapport would vanish as suddenly as it had come. "We did *not* come here to do you any harm. We didn't even know you were here. We are explorers."

The brown eyes flashed. "You come from out of the world," Tlelai said.

"That's right."

"So have others," said Tlelai, and the fear was profound.

Gabriel rubbed his face with his hands, hardly knowing where to begin. "I saw something about that. Will you tell me more? I need to understand."

"I'll tell," Tlelai said, "or others will. If you tell me why you came."

Oh, God . . . for there was another explanation that could be started in any number of places. "We heard there was a planet here. We came to see if that was true."

Tlelai hissed, and Gabriel clearly heard laughter, the sound of merriment in a heart. "Well, where else would the world be? Though . . . forgive me. Yours is elsewhere."

"A long way off." Gabriel looked at the stone, and back to Tlelai. "Do your people talk like this?"

Tlelai looked at him in confusion. "With stones? No."

"I mean, I couldn't understand you before. Now I can, and I see some things—that you see, or saw—"

Real confusion now. "Where else is understanding, if not shared? How else do people see, if not by comparison?"

Gabriel was on the brink of understanding, but too much was happening at once. "Let's talk about this later. I'm confused. For now, won't you let Enda out of there?"

"Enda?"

"My friend."

Tlelai's eyes went wide, but it was a gesture of anger. "She made *mewesh*. That's not permitted!"

"What's *mewesh?*"

Now Tlelai looked perplexed. "I cannot explain it. Others will have to do that, the advisers. We've sent for them."

"Makes sense," Gabriel said. "I could use some advice myself. What about Enda?"

"She must stay here."

"Then so will I," Gabriel said. He leaned wearily against the larder door.

Tlelai was silent a moment. "Why did she do that?" he said, very softly.

"Mindwalk? To try to talk to you, only that. She would never have willingly hurt you."

Tlelai's tail lashed, and now Gabriel knew that this particular gesture meant "no." "We know otherwise. Others . . . have done differently."

"She's not Others," said Gabriel. "The ones you've sent for— they're more edanweir?"

"Yes. They'll come in the morning."

"Advisers—"

"They specialize in history," said Tlelai, "and the implementation of history."

Gabriel grinned mirthlessly. There were a lot of ways that last statement could be taken. The local edanweir might have sent for someone from their government, the police possibly . . . or the executioners.

"I will gladly answer your people's questions about us," said Gabriel. "We both will, but I have questions to ask you too. Once that's done, we'll go away and never bother you again, if that's what you want."

"You really mean that," said Tlelai. He looked astonished.

"I wouldn't lie to you." Gabriel looked at the luckstone, and added, "I think maybe I *can't* lie to you. I seem to have been dragged into 'community,' with you anyway. Tell me something. Have you been dreaming strange dreams?"

Tlelai held very still. "For a while now. Yes."

"When did it start?"

"Months ago. Five, perhaps six."

"Darkness," Gabriel said, "and light."

"Light that burns," said Tlelai. "Great fear, but also excite-ment, again and again, and a little more each time."

"Yes," Gabriel said. "I thought I was the only one."

"I don't understand it," Tlelai said. "I don't understand how you can come from elsewhere and be like us. The Others were not." He was shaking now, and the fur stood out on him as if he was cold. "Everything is changing. Nothing is the way it used to be."

"Tell me about it, brother," Gabriel said softly. "Listen. Go get some sleep. I will too. When the advisers come in the morning, we'll talk again, assuming we still can."

"Once you are in community," said Tlelai, "there is no coming out again until you die."

"A good reason not to overdo it," said Gabriel, and shivered. He had had enough strangeness for one day.

Tlelai got up and rubbed his face, a gesture so familiar that Gabriel could have laughed, except it might have come out as a sob. Then Tlelai did something that Gabriel had seen other edan-weir do to each other on meeting and parting. He gave a small bow, with one arm reaching toward the ground and the other hand held in front of his face, covering his mouth.

Gabriel did not get up, but he recognized the gesture—to keep your breath from your brother's face, because you shared enough with him already, and to show him what your tail was doing, if he didn't know. Gabriel, sitting there against the larder door, covered his own mouth, bowed a little, and then grinned, leaned back, and put his arm up behind his shoulder, crooking the hand over his shoulder and wiggling the fingers, mimicking the tail he didn't have.

Hissing, Tlelai went down the hall. To the guard he said, "Don't trouble them tonight. They'll do no harm." He walked away into the faint light of the longhall, leaving Gabriel wonder-ing whether, despite the apparent improvement of relations, he and Enda were going to get out of this alive.

Chapter Fifteen

HIS SLEEP THAT night was mercifully dreamless. Gabriel did not sleep long, though, because the events of the previous evening had left him too strained and excited for his sleep to last long. He was also worried about Enda and wanted to talk to her.

She woke a short time after he did, when first light started to come in through the high-screened windows. Gabriel spent nearly an hour trying to express to her, with uncertain success, what a second or three of community with Tlelai had told him. The experience was rather like a dream, and some of the imagery had already faded.

"Someone's been here, though."

"Yes," said Enda. "Angela."

"Believe me, whoever they saw, it wasn't Angela. It wasn't anyone human, or any other species we know . . . I don't *think*."

"Who was it?"

"The harder I try," Gabriel said, "the less the memory responds. I'm going to have some questions for their 'advisers' this morning."

"Are these judges," Enda asked, "or religious leaders?"

"I'm not too sure about that," Gabriel said. "This 'community' thing is easier to understand and discuss while it's actually happening. This much I can tell you: I couldn't understand the guard this morning. I think maybe I won't be able to understand anyone without Tlelai around. These people are definitely psionic, though whether it's like the kind of psi we're familiar with, I don't have the experience to say."

"It sounds like you soon may," Enda said, looking thoughtfully at Gabriel through the metal mesh of the window in the door.

"I hope so," Gabriel muttered, "because I may need something like that to get you out. These people are furious with you. I don't know for sure that they're going to try to kill you, but I don't know that they *aren't* going to either. I wasn't able to get any clarification on why what Tlelai and I did was different from what you tried."

Enda bowed her head. "We may find out soon enough." She looked up again. "Do you hear that?"

Gabriel paused and listened. A low soft buzz was approaching. "Now what in the world makes *that* kind of sound?"

Enda blinked. " 'While it is dangerous to generalize . . .' "

Gabriel's grin was painful. "Please. Enda, I hate to leave you by yourself— "

"They will not kill me without warning; that at least seems plain. Go do what needs to be done."

Gabriel hurried out of the longhouse. Outside quite a few edanweir stood around in the common area around the houses— more, in fact, than he had seen in the whole settlement at any one time since he came. They all looked up into the sky, toward the source of the buzzing noise. Gabriel followed their gaze . . . and saw the airship coming in to land.

Gabriel stood there with his mouth open in astonishment and didn't care who might see it or misinterpret the gesture. The twenty-meter cylindrical exterior tapered down to points at the ends, and seemed to be made of tanned hides sewn together, but Gabriel suspected there was either an inner liner or some substance painted over the inside to make everything airtight. The buzz came from a pair of motors on each side that drove two propellers each. There were ailerons on the sides, a large rudder on the back, and another on the tail. A fairly roomy gondola hung on the bottom, one which Gabriel reckoned might hold eight edanweir. The craft was a beautiful bronzy color in the morning sun, possibly because of the lacquer the edanweir had used on the exterior.

Gas extraction technology, Gabriel thought, probably electrolysis— and by derivation from that, electroplating. Maybe metal brazing as well. He wondered what ran the engines that drove the propellers.

Depending what gas was inside the buoyancy capsule, he would have been chary of electricity or a chemical propellant, but there was no way to tell what these people might have come up with. They were ingenious.

Some of the edanweir ran forward to help tie the airship down. Suddenly Gabriel understood the rough circle of large rocks he had seen off to one side of the settlement the other day. Catches came loose, probably in response to a single control released from inside the gondola, and ropes dropped from the sides of the airship. The edanweir grabbed them and made them fast to the rocks, pulling the gondola almost down to ground level.

A hatch opened in the side of the gondola, and a party of five edanweir came out. Tlelai and some of his people went to greet them, and after a moment's conversation they turned and made their way toward the longhouse where Gabriel was standing.

Gabriel made the bow that Tlelai had shown him, not just for courtesy's sake, either, but from the feeling that this group, especially the one who led it, deserved it. Looking at the edanwe, whose fur was darkening round the muzzle and whose eyes were filmed, Gabriel got the same kind of sense that he used to get from the ambassador—a sense of patience, thoughtfulness, thoroughness, and authority. These were not people with whom you would trifle, whether or not they could have your partner killed.

The eldest one, the edanwe with the dark muzzle, looked closely at Gabriel. He was perhaps the most plainly dressed edanwe Gabriel had seen so far. Most of them seemed to favor complex weaves and bright colors in the vests they wore. This one wore a plain red-brown vest of supple leather that matched his fur.

"Things have changed since you and I last spoke," said Tlelai to the eldest edanwe. "We and our guests still do not understand each other completely, but there have been some improvements."

Gabriel was filled with relief that he could still understand Tlelai. To the eldest edanwe, he said, "Honorable one, I greet you. My friend and I apologize for troubling your people through ignorance. We have much to say to you, many questions to ask, and many to answer, if what Tlelai tells me is true."

"Stranger-in-community," said the eldest edanwe, "we greet you also. You seem very unlike other visitors we have had from out of the world. We will see exactly how deep that unlikeness goes."

He walked toward the longhouse. The other edanweir followed him, and Gabriel and Tlelai brought up the rear.

* * * * *

The next three or four hours were a nightmare, if an interesting one. Gabriel had hoped to start asking the edanweir questions about themselves right away, but this did not happen. The first half hour or so was spent getting the group seated on the cushions near the fire, serving them water, and distributing small plates of dried meat slices for them. All the initial conversation had to do with "community" matters. Gabriel discovered that this village was a temporary settlement, strictly seasonal. Come the winter, these people would be moving either to the very center of the equatorial area or underground.

When conversation turned to Gabriel, he was rather caught off guard. "Where is your own community?" said the eldest edanwe, who had not been formally named when they sat down, though all the others had. "Not your companion with whom you travel, but your bloodkin?"

This required an explanation about the planet Bluefall, which then was skillfully diverted into a discussion of human family structure and relationships. This led into a rather difficult explanation as to why Gabriel had not taken his father into the marines with him, who the marines were, where they lived, what they did . . .

Gabriel realized that he was being expertly pumped. He briefly considered trying to stonewall, then thought, there's no point. The only thing that's going to do any of us any good is the truth.

He answered every question they asked him, biding his time until he would be able to ask them questions of his own.

Gabriel kept his hand on the luckstone because there were times when the fringes of the discussion started to dissolve into growling or more structured edanweir speech without "translation," and the contact seemed to prevent this problem. The other problem Gabriel kept stumbling over was that there were words that even his "community" with Tlelai did not help him translate. He would sit puzzling at their meanings for long periods, until some other question jarred him out of his reflection.

After about an hour and a half of incessant questioning, silence fell. The eldest looked at Gabriel with amusement. "Whatever they teach you in your worlds, patience is part of it. Ask us what you like, and let us learn from you that way as well."

Gabriel smiled. "How long have your people been on this planet?"

"Since we have been a people," said the eldest. "Some thousands of years, certainly. This has always been our home."

"Who else has this world been home to?" Gabriel said.

The eldest threw him a sharp look. "There have been some who sought to claim it. We do not speak of them."

"If you mean the Others," said Gabriel, "they are not the ones I mean. There are buildings here that do not look like yours."

A profound silence fell among the edanweir. Some looked at the eldest.

His tail was twitching, a reflective gesture. "They are very old. We do not know who made them."

"Have you tried to discover that?"

The eldest edanwe's tail swung in the broad arc they used for "no," and he said, "Some have gone that way. They did not come back."

Gabriel nodded and said, "Are your people scattered so widely in this world strictly because of the weather? Because it is hard for many to live together when resources are strained?"

The eldest looked perplexed. "We live as we do because community does not survive if it is not separated."

Gabriel tried to work that one out.

"In the ancient days, our people tried living together," said the eldest, "in great groups of houses, but community faded, and only language was left. It was not enough. We grew to hate one another." He shuddered. "That was a terrible time. Many died. When it was over, we went back to living scattered, each group alone . . . with each group rejoicing in the presence of another when their paths chanced to cross. Each meeting is intended rather than accidental. Each shared joy is real rather than forced. We cannot live any other way."

This was hard for Gabriel to understand, coming as he did from a culture in which the word for the "right kind of living" came to mean "someone who lives in a city." Still, he wondered if perhaps his own kind had missed something somewhere along the line.

"So others are not a matter of fear for you," Gabriel said. "You do not fear the stranger, but Others, *the* Others—"

The tension in the little circle became thick. "You have been plain with us," said the eldest. "We must do the same with you."

He stopped, as if looking for where to begin. "Death is no stranger to our people. We are not immortal. Only once, in that terrible time when we tried to live together in crowds, did we ever experience murder. For thousands of years after that time was over, we did not know it again . . . until the Others came."

The eldest clenched his hands together. "Our lives until then had not been without trouble. Bad winters, death from wild beasts or from accidents in making and building, we had all those. Still, our world was good. We learned about the sky above us, the worlds around. We came to know that this world, this planet, was not everything, that we went around our star. That was a wonder. Some among us said that our sun was just one more like the many stars. That was a wonder too, but then, from those other stars, *they* came."

He trailed off, like someone very unwilling to speak a word, lest the reality behind it manifest itself. "They were death," the eldest said. "We did not recognize them as such, as first. The creatures who came seemed strange, but don't we at first seem strange to one another when we meet? When these strangers came, with shapes that were strange as well as personalities that differed, we were frightened. We thought we should work to over-come those fears."

He breathed out a few times, looking into the fire. "They spoke fair at first," he said. "They said they had knowledge to bring and gifts to give, and we should share in those gifts. Well, how would it be otherwise? We would treat them the same way ourselves. Many of us said that though these creatures looked strange, they were the working of the Powers among us, and they should be made welcome. They did give us some gifts. Wireless transmission, they gave us that technology, the heatstones, other things, but slowly some began to wonder at the behavior of the new people. From the New Ones came stories of how there were other forces out among the stars from which they came, forces that were not 'friendly.' " Gabriel heard the hesitation. There had been no word in this language for "unfriendly" until recently.

"They warned us of what those creatures would do if they came here," said the Eldest. "Take our homes, drive us out of them, make us 'slaves.' We did not know what those were at first. After a time we found out."

"Did they make *you* slaves?" Gabriel whispered.

His tail twitched. "They showed us slaves they had made earlier," he said. "These had been other kinds of creatures once. Like you, like her, but they were dead. They said, these were creatures from the stars who had fought with them. Their breath had been taken. Though dead, they lived and would serve these creatures forever. If any of us saw these other creatures from the stars or had dealings with them, we too would be made like those slaves. 'Harvested.' Taken away to serve them forever, in hatred and pain and eternal death."

Gabriel gulped. "That kind of creature," he said, "I *have* seen."

"Then it is true what they said, that you make them." The growl started.

"No!" Gabriel shouted. Heads turned all around.

"No," Gabriel said more gently. "We do not make them. I hate them more than anything." He turned his face away, trying to get a little control of himself.

There was silence for a while.

Gabriel clutched the luckstone, feeling for the connection.

After a while it came again, that thin thread of communication between two kinds of mind stretched taut by the strain of what they discussed.

"These things have been seen among our worlds too," Gabriel said, when he was sure they could understand him again. "None of our people know who makes them. They come to kill. They attack worlds that have no defense. Enda and I have fought them."

"*She* has fought them?" Tlelai said, incredulous.

Gabriel was starting to find this annoying. "I don't know everything these creatures have told you," Gabriel said, "but fraal aren't evil, or no more than the normal run of people. Her kind and mine have roamed the stars together for centuries. They knew us for a long time and did us no harm. Now we work together. Enda is my friend and would hurt no one."

"But she made *mewesh*," one of the other edanwe growled.

Gabriel could have sworn with frustration. The luckstone was a marvel, but there were still terms it seemed powerless to translate.

"You do not know what it means," said the Eldest. "Let me tell you in what other way they explained slavery. They came into the community of our minds *without being invited*. The heart of community is invitation. There is no other way in which it is established. The Powers invited the elements of the world into community with them at the beginning of things. That is how life came to be. *Consent.* The Others walked into our minds and dwelt there without consent and could not be removed. They learned our secrets, our loves and our lives. They made *mewesh* in our minds, the defilement. They forced our people to see the world the way they saw it, to desire what *they* desired. What they desired was horror, death. Those who could do that, the Others took away with them. Those who could not bear the *mewesh*, the unwanted presence of the Others in their minds, died horribly, in madness, in pain. All those who were in community with those who died, they died too. The Others made community itself, the quality that makes us people—they made that *fatal*, a vile thing. We could not stop them. They had weapons of which we had never dreamed. They went where they pleased and took what they pleased."

"Until they left," Gabriel said.

"They left because they found us useless," said the Eldest. "Oh, they threatened us first. They told us that if any others came to this world, we must tell them nothing of the ones who had been here before. They said that they would watch us to make sure we did not betray the secret, and then they went away, but the fear did not."

Gabriel knew plenty about the little spherical craft and their inhabitants, but this was the first time he had ever heard any breath of an explanation of where they came from. It frightened him. The possibility occurred to him that those who had heard explanations, of whatever kind, probably tended to die of them.

"You are courageous to tell us this," Gabriel said.

"We tell you this freely because it may not matter."

Because they are thinking of killing us anyway, Gabriel thought.

"When you and your companion came," said the Eldest, "we were frightened, but some among us said that you might not be like the Others. If you were . . . how could we stop you? So we watched. You came forth from your ship and seemed harmless enough."

"Except for the infernal machine," said Tlelai.

Gabriel covered his face with his hands. "Oh, please. I will smash the machine myself at the first opportunity. We did not realize that it was malfunctioning. It was supposed to help us learn to speak your language, and you ours."

There was some subdued hissing at that. "Well enough," said the Eldest. "So we did not trust you at first. Your companion looked somewhat like one of the Others. Some thought she was a messenger sent to spy on us. She showed no signs of this, and we began to think perhaps you were people, if strange ones."

The Eldest growled softly. "But then she made *mewesh*, and this we will not allow."

"She meant no harm!" Gabriel said.

"What *else* could she have meant but harm?" the Eldest said harshly. "There is no good use of those abilities. They are all about power, force, and slavery, no other use."

"You're wrong," Gabriel said. "In the worlds outside, there are many good uses for mindwalking. Don't ask me for details; I'm not expert in it."

The Eldest started to open his mouth, and Gabriel was sure he could hear what was coming. He was not up for it. "Now you listen to me," he said. "I am not leaving here without Enda, no matter what you think. She's my friend. If you try to stop us when we leave, I'll fight you, and very many of you will not get up afterwards. That will make me sad, but it's what will happen."

There was silence for a while after that. "You are a fighter," the Eldest said. He meant 'soldier,' but their language had no word for it, and even the concept was no more than a hint.

"Yes. That was my job."

"Why did you fight?"

Suddenly in memory it was dark around Gabriel, and only one distant light burned in that darkness. *To protect the Concord and the peace of her peoples against all threats overt and covert, public and private—*

"To defend those who could not," Gabriel said. "The children, the old ones, the people who only wanted to live and be let alone. To stop those who would take their homes and their lives from them."

"You would do that for *her?*"

"She saved me," Gabriel said. "I could have died. I would have been alone and friendless, without community." He looked very hard at the Eldest. "We have been a little community together. With some others, but mostly, she and I. So I am not going to let anything happen to her."

Silence fell.

"I just wish I had tried this before Enda did what she did," Gabriel said, turning the luckstone over morosely in his hands. "We might have avoided all this. We only wanted to talk to you, and none of the things we knew how to do were working. It was my idea." He looked at the Eldest again. "You should be blaming me, because I talked her into it."

One of the edanwe sitting with them now looked at the luck-stone and said, "The Others from the stars . . . when they came, they questioned us as to whether we knew of such things in our world. Strange things, old things, that behaved oddly."

Gabriel raised his eyebrows. "What did you tell them?"

The Eldest wrinkled his lips back, showing the fangs. "Nothing. We may live in community and be a trusting and innocent people, but we are hardly stupid."

Gabriel looked up sharply.

"They were seeking everywhere for things of power," the Eldest said. "Mighty objects that could move great weights, work wonders that we could not understand . . . or so they told us." He looked amused. "When they went away, they promised us great rewards if we could find such things for them when they came again. As if we would do anything for them, after what they did to us! As if we cared to seek out such things, which can have no good use if *they* desire them."

"Are you sure? What about *this?*" Gabriel held out the luck-stone. "Because of this, your kind and mine can speak together. Isn't that a good use?"

They looked at the stone.

"Only the simplest things have only a single use," Gabriel said, "and more than one use can make for problems. I hear people dream, now!" The sound of Gabriel's anger took his hosts by surprise. They shrank back a little, as if he were armed, not they. "I hear *him* dream!" Tlelai bowed his head.

"And I don't know how to stop," Gabriel said, more sadly. "The stone's use is a good one, but I don't know what I am any more."

"*Laidanhu,*" said one of the edanweir softly. The others stirred a little, looked at Gabriel.

Just what I need—another word that won't translate. "I don't mind hearing and understanding you, or being in community, a little, but I didn't need your dreams," Gabriel said softly. "I have enough trouble with my own. Here's another part of my life I can't go back to . . . the normal part, where I could sleep without fear."

"Lose that then," said one of them, pointing to the stone.

"I can't," said Gabriel, "not without understanding it better. Not without knowing what it's doing to me."

He paused. "You know something about that, I think," Gabriel said. "Fine. Maybe you're shy of telling me. It can wait, but meantime, I think my people can help you."

"We do not want more aliens here!" said the Eldest. "If the Others send the spies they promised, they will believe we have betrayed them. They will start taking our people and killing them. That would be bad enough, but they will not stay dead afterwards. If killing *you* is the price we must pay to keep them from doing that to us . . ."

Gabriel swallowed. Here came the gamble.

"It is possible," he said, "that it's already too late."

The edanweir stared.

"We may have been followed here," Gabriel said. "There is the possibility that some of those who follow"—he was shocked as he said it, for this particular possibility had not occurred to him until now—"may have told the Others where we've gone. If that's true, they may already be on their way here."

The growling that went up from the group around him now was truly furious. Gabriel held himself still. All his training was screaming that this would be a very good time to shoot his way out of there, get Enda, run for *Sunshine*, and leave the planet.

Yet Gabriel didn't move, though it was maybe the hardest thing he had ever done. He might have damaged this world irretrievably by the simple act of landing here. Angela Valiz, for all her fecklessness, would have done no such damage. No one was following *her*, but Gabriel had at least two intelligence services following him around. If the power behind those little spherical ships with their undead crews had been following him too . . . then he had a responsibility to help these people.

Assuming they didn't kill him first. The growls were getting louder.

Two edanweir were not growling. One was Tlelai, and the other was the eldest. He looked at Gabriel with some sorrow.

"What will you do then," said the eldest, "if they are coming?"

"I will stay here and help you fight," Gabriel said.

"Fight how?" Tlelai said. "Their weapons are greatly superior to ours."

"You have other weapons," Gabriel said, and held out the luck-stone, "don't you?"

Tlelai looked perplexed, but the Eldest looked at Gabriel with a slow and thoughtful expression, and his tail twitched.

"You are not the only one whose dreams have been strange of late," he said. "Does the locked room even realize that it is locked, until someone brings the key?"

He stood up. The others stood too. "I must send for another," the Eldest said. "It will take a day for her to arrive. When she comes, we'll speak again."

"What about my friend?" Gabriel said.

For a long time the Eldest looked at him. "Tomorrow."

He stood up, slowly, and the others stood with him. So did Gabriel.

"I will say this for you," said the Eldest. "Not one of the Others ever gave so much as a glance to the Downfall."

Gabriel's eyes widened. "So your people were watching us from our very first landing, that morning."

"The noise you made going over," said Tlelai, "how should we not? A whole raging herd of *mhwada* would have made less noise, but we were not going to move until we saw what you did."

Gabriel had to laugh. "I am glad to have seen those falls before I die, and I expect my dying to be a long time from now." He looked the Eldest in the eye. "So we'll talk again tomorrow."

He made the bow he had been taught. The Eldest returned it, and the group surrounded him and made their way to the door.

Gabriel brought up the rear with Tlelai. Just as they were coming out of the doors, an edanwe whom Gabriel had not seen before came running over the long ridge toward them at great speed. He came plunging down and barreled right into the crowd of other edanweir who were still outside admiring the airship. Some of them caught him and stopped him from falling over.

He staggered to his feet and hurried over to the Eldest. "There is another ship from the stars!" he cried.

"Where?" said Gabriel.

"Near yours," said the edanwe. "We have not gone near it. You should come."

Gabriel looked at Tlelai, and together they took off after the edanwe at a run.

Chapter Sixteen

ALL THE WAY, Gabriel was cursing. Once he had been willing enough to be followed into the middle of nowhere to bring matters with his shadows to some kind of conclusion, but now this "nowhere" had become *somewhere,* with people living in it whom he liked. He had brought his troubles down on them.

Worse still was the idea that some unknown species, or coalition of species, had been preying on Verge worlds. Possibly in a coordinated way, though there was no way to be sure of that at the moment, but the history of the lost colony at Silver Bell was no longer inexplicable or unique.

Had the people there been given the same kind of warning that the edanweir had? *Submit. Do our bidding. Serve us alive . . . or serve us dead.* Had there *been* any warning? What the Silver Bell colonists had done, how they responded except by that last cry for help, no one knew. They were gone without trace, except for the one creature, human no longer, alive no longer, that had attacked *Sunshine.* Gabriel and Enda had destroyed the ship but had saved the body, sheathed in strange armor oozing chemical slime. They had delivered it to Delde Sota on Iphus for autopsy, which revealed a medical chip buried in the changed and deteriorated human tissue. That chip had been implanted into a Silver Bell colonist years before. . . .

There were other odd disappearances in the Verge that could possibly be fitted into the same pattern. On Bluefall, Gabriel's own world, there had been a terrible day back in July of 2452 on which human activity there had simply ceased, and the inhabitants simply vanished. Doors were left open, meals half eaten, and when scheduled traders arrived in the system over the next days, everyone in a whole world's small but flourishing cities was simply *gone*. Now Gabriel wondered, did visitors arrive that day and take a whole world's worth of people away?

Kharls has to find out about this, Gabriel thought, as he and the edanweir ran up yet another hill. I think. I have to be really careful how I send the news back, since anyone carrying it is likely to suddenly become dead or worse.

They were only a couple of hills away, and the three edanweir showing him and Tlelai the way had slowed and were exploiting what cover they could find. They had begun fading further southward than the usual path that Gabriel and Enda used on their way to *Sunshine*, making their way behind one of the hill crests, in the direction of the Downfall. Gabriel was delighted to see that the cover was a lot better here than it had been, more scrubby.

"Up there," Tlelai said to him.

Gabriel, glancing at him, saw that he was hardly making any sound at all. Where were the words coming from? There was sense being expressed through Tlelai's particular form of psionics, but was he *speaking* any edanwe words, in the sense that Gabriel understood? Was the idea of an edanwe language itself an illusion promoted by telepathy?

He wished he could talk to Enda about it, but that would have to wait. Gabriel turned his attention to the way Tlelai was showing him—along the rear of this hill crest, then up to another long ridge reaching up toward the cliffs near the waterfall.

"Up there," Gabriel said, "okay, then what?"

There was a flicker in the back of his mind. In a flash he saw the way Tlelai meant to go, a way he had used to watch Gabriel and Enda a few days back. In his mind, Gabriel suddenly saw himself and Enda standing in the mist of the waterfall, looking up and away from the silent watchers. Gabriel gulped. It was strange to see yourself, not in a video image or or hologram, but in life through someone else's vision, peculiar but clear. That image was tinged with both fear and fascination: *strangers/aliens/harm/wonder . . .*

"Got it," Gabriel said, and gulped again as the image flashed away and he found himself looking only at the common day around him. The other edanweir were moving away cautiously, creeping toward the path that would take them up to the next ridge. Tlelai went after them, and Gabriel followed.

A few minutes spent crawling along with the others restored Gabriel's equanimity as he started to consider what they might find. Meanwhile, he didn't mind the communication with Tlelai and the others. It was certainly making his life easier. The rest, though—the flashes of insight that weren't his, of content for which the context came along belatedly if at all—they felt desperately strange.

He thought of his marine weapons instructor, not on the exercise floor for a change, but one night in the mess after dinner. *The wise man—I know there's no point in hoping any of you will ever be wise—but the wise man knows there's no situation in which he is unarmed. The situation itself is a weapon, if you have the sense to pick it up, turn it over in your mind, and look at it that way. The assertive mindset can find the 'pointy end' of anything—a rock, a dropped word, a passing reference . . .*

Gabriel pushed himself down flatter, following the others' example as they approached the hillcrest and prepared to make their way across slightly exposed ground. This ability, this situation, could be a weapon, as well. He disliked the thought of it. Gabriel preferred fighting with guns, knives—things he could touch. Wasn't it an irrational prejudice, preferring the physical to the nonphysical just because it was what he was used to?

The first scout was across and had hidden himself away in a patch of blue-green scrub deep enough for all of them easily to lie concealed. The second squirmed up to join him, and Gabriel looked to see how he could best manage this himself without being spotted. They had the advantage of being smaller than he was and able to flatten down harder. *Just keep your butt down,* their drill instructor had always said, *and you'll be all right.*

Gabriel crawled across, going as silently as he could even in the neighborhood of that gigantic and growing roar . . . and he kept his butt down. A few moments later, he was in the shrubbery with the first two edanweir. They were making their way among the shrubs off to Gabriel's left.

He followed them, amused to find a path leading between two or three layers of shrubs that clambered against the bank at the bottom of the rising cliffs. He crouched down low, being very careful not to show his head above the level of their cover.

Gabriel looked where the two edanweir were looking. One backed away from an open spot in the shrubbery, and Gabriel carefully peered through.

He was looking almost directly down at *Sunshine* from a point about a hundred meters in front of her. He swore appreciatively, for this hiding place had been completely hidden from his view when they came out. In fact he had looked directly at it and had seen nothing. The shape of the cliff made the vantage point look inaccessible.

This was good, because down beside *Sunshine* was the long, lean, well-armed ship that had killed Rae Alwhirn and had almost blown *Sunshine* to Kingdom Come. It was unoccupied at the moment, Gabriel thought, because *Sunshine*'s lift column was showing the light that indicated her lift had been accessed and was on the passenger level. This could only mean that the inner door was unlocked as well.

The other two edanweir looked at Gabriel, waiting to see what he would do. Tlelai came up behind him. "Who is this other?"

After that long conversation with the Eldest, Gabriel heard the possible implication in the words. "I don't know her personally, but she's already tried to kill me once. I think I may know who she works for, though."

"What should be done with her?"

Gabriel had a few ideas, all amusing, but none productive. "I don't want her running loose around the countryside, that's for sure. Let's catch her and bring her back for the Eldest. I have questions I want to ask her." He thought a moment, then said to Tlelai, "You *do* have another larder to stick her in?"

Tlelai grinned.

Gabriel undid one of his secret pockets, the seal of which was faired into the stitching of the normal pocket. From this he fished out the smallest pistol from *Sunshine*'s arms cabinet, the one which Helm had once described as a toy, only good for picking someone's nose with.

"Here," Gabriel said, handing the Nosepicker to Tlelai. "If she thinks all you people have are rifles, this may surprise her."

Tlelai took the pistol carefully.

"Here's the safety," Gabriel said, touched it off, then touched it on again. "This doesn't fire bullets. It's an energy weapon. It throws fire."

"That," Tlelai said with another grin, "you and I have done, haven't we?"

"You know," Gabriel said, "I believe we have." He looked down at the two ships again, considering.

We must not have damaged her all that badly. Interchangeable cargo hold, I guess, and the stardrive nowhere near it, a standard enough design. He frowned more deeply. *With this timing either she came in on her own from somewhere else, or she might actually have been riding on* Lighthouse *with us, a nasty possibility.*

Either way, she had to be taken out of circulation quickly. The Eldest was annoyed enough at Gabriel's presence and very annoyed at Enda's. Another offworlder would only strain matters further.

"All right," Gabriel said. "I'll go down. Keep an eye on things."

He could see the faint traces of a pathway down through the shrubs and scrubby cover toward the base of the smallest of the cliffs. As he went, he blessed the thunder of the waterfall. No one would hear any chance sounds with that roar behind him.

He sighed and reached into the secret pocket one more time to remove that second holdout, Helm's other gift, the two-"bladed" knife. He would not open it just now, but Gabriel set the second blade—the cellular microfilament that could cut through durasteel—on "ready." It would spring out of the handle when he grabbed it. Also down in the pocket was the luckstone, which he changed over to the pocket on the other side, to avoid possible accidents.

Gabriel slipped out of the scrub, brushed himself off, and went toward that second ship as warily as a man might who had suddenly found someone else sharing his parking place. He heard the faint click of relays from inside *Sunshine*. He didn't hurry, but went around the far side of the other ship and had a look. He started back, taking care to be well within sight of the cliff.

He was not surprised in the slightest to suddenly find standing in front of him a petite woman with big brown eyes, shining brown hair, and one of the biggest, blockiest two-handed weapons he had ever seen. The barrel of the weapon, a very impressive mass rifle, was trained squarely on his head. She was still dressed in the Aegis style, the kind of comfortable baggy pants and tunic that Gabriel had given up when he went into the marines. She had discarded the headscarf, and little bright tendrils of her hair lifted and glinted in the breeze.

"*You*," Gabriel said.

"Whatever that may mean to you," she said, "and I doubt it's very much—yes."

"How did you find us here?" Gabriel said, looking up at *Sunshine* as if expecting someone else to appear.

"She's not here," said the woman, "so don't bother. I'll chase her down after I've dealt with you. Do you mean, how did I find you on this planet? You should be able to guess that. Or on this spot?" She shrugged and smiled. "Plenty of heat sources down here, but only one that's ship-shaped. It had to be you. I was surprised you weren't a little more careful, but that fits the profile."

Gabriel frowned. "How did you get into my ship?"

"It wasn't difficult," the woman said, "but then your ship doesn't have all that many secrets from my firm. There was a lot of work done on it on Grith that you weren't clever enough to keep from happening . . . .you and your over-gunned friend." She looked around, smiling more broadly now. "You shouldn't have sent him away. That just made my job easier."

"Who *do* you work for, then?" Gabriel asked. "Not VoidCorp, I think. They're usually better at covering their tracks. No, I would say you're Concord Intel, dedicated, if slow."

He smiled at her as kindly as he could. Her face went hard—

he had hit correctly on that one—and Gabriel's smile broadened.

"What brings you here?" Gabriel said. "Not the touristic possibilities, though I think you'll agree they're considerable."

"Shut up, Connor," she said. "Don't push your luck. No one
would bother to come looking if you had an accident here."

"At least *one* person in the Concord would," Gabriel said.

Her face twitched, then set cold, and he saw her finger tight-
ening on the trigger. Just a little—but he had seen that gesture
before, in people who were having profound internal arguments
about whether or not to just go ahead and kill someone.

He knew he had no chance of getting that thing away from her.
At this distance, she would pound him like last Sunday's roast
fish before he could tuck and roll. There was always the knife, but
he hadn't rated it for throwing yet. He had no other holdouts
ready . . . except for the new weapon he didn't care for, the one
that wasn't solid and couldn't be held in the hands.

The idea came quick and clear, but Gabriel didn't know if he
could pull it off without touching the luckstone.

"Now, let's not be hasty," Gabriel said, working to sound
shaky. It wasn't hard. Meanwhile he tried to summon up that in-
mind flicker he had felt a while ago, catching the image of their
route here from Tlelai.

Nothing.

Oh, no, come on—

Nothing happened. Her finger twitched again. The sweat
popped out all over Gabriel. His vision skewed, as if someone
else was looking through his eyes. Gabriel stood there desperately hoping this didn't show somehow in his own face. *Tlelai,* he
thought, looking carefully at the woman and what she held, and
glancing over her head. *Now would be a very, very good time—*

His vision unskewed. Did he get that, Gabriel thought, feeling
briefly dizzy, or have I just wasted my time?

"Don't pass out on me, now," the woman said.

"Uh, believe me, I won't."

"Good, because there are all kinds of things we need to talk
about, like how you did what you did to my ship at Terivine."

"It wasn't half as final as I wanted," said Gabriel, "but it fulfilled the needs of the moment."

"Cute. You can tell me all about it once I've got you safe inside. Get moving," she said, and gestured with the gun.

"No," Gabriel said. "No, I don't think so."

Her smile went rather grim. "Always the marine. All the more reason for you to recognize this. Even set very low, it's going to cause you considerable damage . . . and there's nowhere around here to treat that kind of thing."

She is a complete idiot. At this range it wouldn't leave anything of me but smashed up bones and puréed tissue in a big torn bag of skin.

"We have a very nice phymech aboard *Sunshine*," Gabriel said. "Besides that, I wouldn't advise you to fire anything at the moment. They wouldn't like it."

" 'They'?"

He glanced over her shoulder.

She laughed. "Connor, that one's so old it appears in cave paintings. Now get—"

She broke off as the *crack* of the first gunshot went off behind her, almost instantly followed by the emphatic *thump* as it dug into the ground a half-meter behind her foot.

She whirled toward the sound of the gunfire, lifting her rifle to aim. Gabriel didn't waste the moment. Three strides and a jump, and she was turning again, but too late. He kicked the gun out of her hand. Gabriel came down half on top of her and grabbed her. They rolled on the ground, and he twisted his head aside as her fingers went for his eyes. A thumb hooked into his cheek, started to rip sideways. Nasty, Gabriel thought, but certainly a recommended move. He rolled over hard, wound up on top of her, leaned on his forearm over her throat, pushing down hard—

The painful pulling at his face stopped, and the hand dropped away. Gabriel opened his eyes again to see that someone's gun barrel, beautifully engraved with abstract half-spiral patterns, was resting right against her head. Another rifle, equally beautiful, rested against her neck.

Gabriel disentangled himself, pushed back and stood up, becoming part of the group of edanweir holding weapons on her. While one of them went off to fetch her weapon, Tlelai said, "Are all your kind this friendly?"

"Some are a lot more so," Gabriel said.

The edanweir were growling. The woman watched them, trying to keep her face from showing what was going on behind it . . . and not being too successful. The edanwe who had picked up her gun now brought it back and handed it to Gabriel. He turned it over admiringly in his hands. It was an AAMG-12 mass rifle—expensive, high-powered, one of the very best of its kind . . . as Gabriel knew well, for it was a weapon of choice for the Concord Marines. This one bore the proof marks of a Concord armory: a datestamp so recent there was no chance for it to have been stolen and resold.

"Been too long since I had one of these," Gabriel said to Tlelai. "I'll hang onto it, unless you want it."

Tlelai switched his tail a very emphatic "no" and asked, "Where did she come from?"

"She doesn't seem very eager to tell us that. Sounded like she thought she was going to be asking all the questions, a typical misapprehension."

"Would it not be simpler," said one of the other edanweir, "if we . . ." He held out his trigger finger and made an exaggerated firing gesture.

"No," Gabriel said. "I wouldn't kill her right now, anyway. She and I have things to discuss. If she doesn't cooperate, you can make a rug out of her later."

Gabriel saw that she was no longer having any success at all at keeping the fear out of her eyes.

"How are you talking to them?" she said. "What are you going to do to me?"

"Almost certainly something less lethal than you were going to do to me. If they let me, that is."

There. Let her wonder for a while, but what *would* the edanweir do to her? A third alien, with who knew what agenda . . .

"I may be able to keep them from killing you," Gabriel said, "but you're going to have to answer a lot of questions. If they, or I, get a sense you're lying . . ." He made what was intended to be an expressive *skkkt* sound, and a gesture of cutting his throat.

The two edanweir who had come with Gabriel and Tlelai looked at Gabriel with amusement, then repeated the gesture, being careful to do it where the woman could see it. Gabriel had all he could do to keep from laughing.

"Should we bind her before we bring her back?" said one of the edanweir.

Gabriel sighed. "Probably. She's won't understand what's going on, and it'll keep her from doing something stupid enough that we'll have to shoot her right away."

One of the edanweir produced some thin rope, with which they tied her wrists and hobbled her loosely enough to walk. The second one put a slipnoose of the same kind of cord around her neck. When they were done, Tlelai gestured at the woman, indicating that she should get up.

"If I were you," Gabriel said, "I wouldn't try these people's patience. They're strong for their size, and they hunt much bigger quarry than you or me. Check out their living room when they walk you through."

The woman got up, glared at Gabriel, brushed herself off as well as she could, and walked off amid her escort with something meant to resemble angry dignity.

Gabriel, standing by Tlelai, said, "That was a bad moment. Thanks, cousin."

Tlelai looked at him with some bemusement. Gabriel's heart pounded suddenly. Oh, God, I've done something wrong . . .

"Is it not proper to call you 'cousin'?" he said.

"I would have thought 'brother,' " said Tlelai.

Gabriel smiled. "Brother let it be. I want to check my ship and lock it up again . . . and I want a quick look at the outside of hers. Let's go see what needs to be done."

Chapter Seventeen

THEY MADE THEIR way back to the settlement without incident. Gabriel had been wondering what their prisoner would make of the airship when their little hunting party came over that last long ridge, but when they arrived, the airship was gone. Gabriel was relieved, though he couldn't have said why.

He half expected to find the Eldest and the others gone when he and Tlelai came into the longhall, but they were still there. Gabriel was very pleased to see that Enda had been removed from the larder and was sitting off on one side in a little nest of cushions by herself. She was still being guarded by two nervous-looking edanweir, but Gabriel found this much preferable to Enda being stuck in the meat locker.

For the moment he only smiled at her and went to see the Eldest, now standing off with his group to one side and watching the new alien being brought in. Gabriel was becoming better at reading expressions and was not surprised by the dismay he saw.

The Eldest lifted sorrowful eyes to him and said, "Why has this one come? Is she also an explorer?"

"No, sir," Gabriel said. "It's as I warned you. She's come looking for me."

"What will you do with her?"

"Until I find out more about exactly why she came, I can't tell you that. As soon as I know, I'll tell you what I discover."

Tlelai was looking at the Eldest from across the room, where he was helping the others make the woman secure.

"Discoveries are many today," said the Eldest. "It seems you had weapons we did not find at first."

"Yes," Gabriel said.

"And you did not use them."

"Why should I have? Besides, sir, I believe you knew I had at least one. I think it suited you to see what I'd do with it. I doubt I'd have had a chance to use it twice. Maybe not even once."

The Eldest waved his tail slowly. The gesture was partly one of reflection, partly of humor. "You are very unlike us. You have brought us into danger, yet you don't seek to escape that danger yourself."

"I couldn't do that," said Gabriel. "I wish none of this trouble was happening, but . . ." He nodded his head at the woman. "I've got to talk to her. After I'm finished, I think perhaps she should be kept where my friend was kept. I don't trust her."

"Nor do we," said the Eldest, "and only a little less than we would trust you, but that does not trouble you either, does it?"

"I wouldn't go so far as to say that," Gabriel said, "but I do understand."

He gave the Eldest the bow of courtesy and went to sit with Enda for a moment. "A moment of politics," he said.

She smiled and said, "Of all the creatures wandering about through space these days, humans and fraal are probably the most political animals. I understand, but I also overheard enough to appreciate what was going on. Nobility is all too rare."

"Don't tell me I've got something I don't have," Gabriel growled. "I brought us here. The situation being what it is, I may have screwed these people. Helping to clean up the mess isn't nobility." He smiled grimly. "It's just the marine tendency to enjoy giving his surroundings a good scrub."

Enda's ironic smile suggested that she did not believe Gabriel in the slightest. She raised her eyebrows, gazing over toward the other side of the room. "So this is our brown-eyed friend?"

"Not very friendly." Gabriel started to chuck the mass rifle he had taken from her among the cushions, then had another thought and held it out first to one, then the other of the two edanweir who were guarding Enda. They shrank back and emphatically wagged their tails "no."

"Right," Gabriel said, leaving the gun among the cushions for the moment. "I wouldn't make any fast moves toward that, if I were you."

"Such would not have been among my plans, I assure you."

Gabriel sighed. "Do you have *any* idea why these people are so upset about you? It's so bizarre . . ."

"Gabriel, despite our 'delicate and ethereal' looks, I assure you that not all my kind are angels," Enda said. "Fraal have at least as wide a range of behaviors as humans, and there have been killers and rogue mindwalkers among us before now . . . though not many. I would dislike the thought that someone of that sort had been out this way, terrorizing these people. I would *very* much dislike the thought that fraal are working with these 'Other' creatures, whatever they may be. You said you were not getting much in the way of imagery . . ."

Gabriel shook his head. "Either I'm not very good at exploiting 'community,' or the Eldest is very good at controlling what he broadcasts. Nearly all of that talk we had came out for me as abstracts only, no images. It's not like it is with Tlelai."

"There is some other connection between you two," Enda said, "the dreams."

"There's that, yes." Gabriel glanced up. "Tell me, though. When we got here, you said to me, 'I do not think they would necessarily believe us' about our coming in peace. How were you so sure?"

She was silent for a few moments. "Gabriel, I caught some images after our arrival that were less than reassuring. All I could do was suggest that we might have some trouble. I had no wish to create a self-fulfilling prophecy concerning something about which I might have been completely wrong. I was uneasy, and it seemed dishonest to keep it from you."

Gabriel nodded and looked back toward the Eldest. "They may still kill both of us. Community or not, they have too much to lose if we're not who and what we say we are, and *her* arrival hasn't helped."

"Yes," Enda said. "What will you do with her?"

"I can tell you what I'd like to do," Gabriel said, feeling his face. It was starting to get sore. "Though it might surprise our hosts. I think the guns are almost entirely for hunting. I doubt very much whether they ever use them on each other."

Enda sighed and looked around her. "A veritable paradise."

"Until the cold sets in, yeah," Gabriel said. "Apparently winter here is fairly amazing. Otherwise, I'd like to get us all out of here before we completely ruin their impression of what beings from our side of things are like."

He looked over at the woman who sat amid her cushions with very bad grace, hunched and scowling at the edanweir guarding her. It had occurred to Gabriel that space was genuinely a lot bigger than people thought. Isolated colonies were just that, quite hard to find even when you knew where they were. It was also occurring to him that the Others, whoever they were, might have spies in human space, that they had been told, for example, where Silver Bell was. By other humans?

Gabriel shuddered at the thought of the treachery, but there were some humans who would do anything for money, advantage, or power. Gabriel tried to push that thought away.

It wouldn't go. He looked over at this nameless woman and thought of how mole-ridden intelligence organizations could become, how they watched and infiltrated each other. If they could spy on each other, why couldn't these Others do the same thing? Where better to find out exactly what your enemies knew about you, and to help misdirect them?

It was a nasty thought, and seemed all too likely. Gabriel breathed out a long sad sigh, feeling briefly heartsick for the time when life had been simple, when he had not distrusted everyone he saw, or felt the need to look twice at everything to see if it really meant what it seemed to at first glance. The age of innocence, Gabriel thought, gone forever now.

He looked over at the woman who seemed to be from Concord Intelligence. He was determined to tell her nothing of any importance, no matter what she seemed to know. All the same, he had to get some useful information out of her, and wasn't sure how to go about it.

Still, he was fairly comfortable in this situation, and she wasn't. She had no idea what he might do, which was something Gabriel could use to his advantage.

Gabriel picked up the mass rifle again. "I would ask you to sit in on this," he said to Enda, standing, "but I think it might make our hosts nervous."

Enda shook her head. "I am quite content to sit here and watch you work whatever miracle you have in mind."

Gabriel checked the mass rifle again to make sure its safety was on, then went to where the woman was sitting. He sat down across from her, well out of reach, and put the mass rifle behind him, where he knew he could get at it quickly.

"All right," he said, "let's get *you* sorted out now. What's your name?"

She glared at him.

"You know, your face is going to get stuck that way if you keep doing that," Gabriel said. "A shame to ruin such good looks. At least give me a *fake* name, lady. I don't want to have to kill someone whose name I don't know."

The glare did not go away, but another emotion started to show around its edges. Fear.

"Aleen Delonghi," she said.

"Concord Intel?"

"Yes," she said reluctantly.

"I'd like some ID."

She looked at him as if he were out of his mind. "You think I have it in my pocket or something?"

"Not in your pocket," Gabriel said. "I know where they put the chip, in a general way. I don't have a reader with me at the moment, but I suppose I could dig it out of you." He reached into his pocket and came up with his knife. He flipped its safety off and shook out the "soft" blade, the microfilament nearly invisible in this light.

She blanched. "There's more overt ID in my ship," she said. "The combination for the side lock is 99664568."

"You think I'm going in there?" Gabriel said. "It's almost certainly boobytrapped. No, I'll wait until I have leisure to undo your security and have a nice long rummage. There are two things most on my mind at the moment. Why have you been following me, and why did you blow up Rae Alwhirn's ship?"

"I'm not willing to discuss either topic in such an insecure situation," she said scornfully.

"You'd better get it through your head that your own position is not very secure," Gabriel said. "I've no particular desire to kill you, but it might be safer than turning you loose to take your chances with the edanweir. They are not in a happy mood, and they are not a force to be discounted, even if they do look kind of cute and cuddly. They may not shoot each other with those guns, but *we* are most emphatically not 'they.' I'm amazed *I'm* not dead at the moment, and the minute I lose interest in you, *you* have problems, so you'd better start talking."

She looked down at the cushions.

"There's also the matter of your friend," Gabriel said. "The shadow at the back of our little fight above Rivendale."

"You're not making much sense."

"The other participant in this continuing hide-and-seek game," Gabriel said. "Miss Blue Eyes. Is she a friend of yours?"

"I don't know who you mean. She's certainly not part of my organization."

"I think she might be VoidCorp," said Gabriel. "They're the ones who would have the biggest axe to grind with me at the moment. The question is which of you started following me first? Or were you perhaps following *her* because she was following me, and then you lucked onto me as a result?"

DeLonghi just looked at him.

"There's always that possibility," Gabriel said. "Though if you really *are* working for Lorand Kharls, you should know that he has ways of knowing where I am." Gabriel thought about that. "That's a possibility too . . . that you're not as much in his confidence as you think you are, that he didn't give you access to his own particular method of finding me."

DeLonghi shook her head. "You're just fishing. You won't get anything that way."

"No, I suppose not," Gabriel said. For the moment, he folded the knife away and slipped it back in his pocket where the luckstone was. "It's a relief to know I'm not dealing with anyone very senior." She flushed. Right again, Gabriel thought. "If you were, you either wouldn't be here at all, or I would never have seen you before this afternoon, but Alwhirn," Gabriel said, *"why?* Why did you kill him? He was just a nutcase, an annoying one . . . but not really dangerous."

"He was about to fire on you," DeLonghi said.

Gabriel shot a glance over at Enda, remembering their earlier conversation. At the same time, he was stabbed through with the sudden certainty of a lie. Not "thinking the other person wasn't telling the truth," not an intimation that a lie was happening, but the *certainty* of it, as if Gabriel was doing it himself. Just behind the image of the lie was the shadow of truth. His hand was still on the luckstone.

"Lady," he said, taking it out of his pocket and rolling it absently between his hands, "there's really no point in you trying to hide the truth from me. One or two of these people and I have something in common, and our partnership, brief though it's been, seems to promote communication. Let's see how good it is at promoting some with you."

She didn't react. "Now I'm new at this," he said, "and it's entirely possible that I'll mess up somehow and burn your brains out, but since you won't cooperate otherwise, I think that's going to be on your own head. What's left of it."

In a sudden surge of motion DeLonghi lurched to her feet and tried to run. One of the edanweir standing nearby simply stuck out a foot, almost absently, and tripped her. Down she went.

"Just because people are small," Gabriel said, as they helped her back to her place on the cushions and put her ungently down again, "and you can't understand them, don't think they're weak or dumb." He glanced over at Tlelai, who stood nearby, keeping an eye on things. Gabriel composed himself and closed his eyes.

Tlelai he could feel nearby, like a heat source, but he was not Gabriel's chief interest at the moment. There was different kind of energy source nearby, less familiar. Spiky, resistant, strong in many ways, but also nervous. *There*, Gabriel thought, and bore in and down.

The shriek scared him. Gabriel had to blink and take a moment to compose himself, for three sets of imagery were suddenly fighting it out in his head. One was the real world, day, the edanweir and himself, seen from a meter or so away—again Gabriel's gut twisted at the oddness of seeing himself "live" through eyes that were not his. The second set of images was of the fight over Rivendale, a set of controls in front of him, and burning hot in his brain—four or five thoughts struggling for primacy.

Here's my chance. This guy could kill him—but she was not sure—*I can't let him just fall out of here, I need some leverage. Wouldn't it be simpler to kill him now?* "Shot while trying to escape." *No one would know. He's just a traitor, I don't see why they*—

The thoughts were muddled together in a mind in turmoil. Gabriel gulped, for his mouth was suddenly starting to water and his stomach was giving him difficulty, but there was yet another set of images. A huge ship, armed and armored *in extremis*, seen from a smaller vessel, going by very close—and a small man, saturnine, seemingly speaking quietly with Gabriel, though it was DeLonghi's point of view that was the source of the image. Gabriel smiled grimly at the sight of Lorand Kharls.

"I see," Gabriel said, looking up at Delonghi, who was pale and shaking. "Sorry that hurt. I would rather not hurt you, but there's a whole lot more, isn't there?" He closed his eyes again.

"No!" she screamed.

Gabriel opened one eye. "You're sure?"

She was white with fury and fear. "I thought he might have fired," she said. "That was a chance I couldn't take. You were too valuable for other things."

"What things?"

"I have no idea."

A lie, but he was reluctant to do anything further until his stomach calmed.

"You *do* have ideas," Gabriel said, "but you don't agree with them, do you? Kharls gave you orders, but you have problems with them. That's the heart of all this, isn't it? Loyalty." Gabriel grinned ferally. "Now you're thinking, 'What right has he to even mention the word, considering what he did?' What you *think* I did. That's the difference between us. I *know* I'm innocent, and I also know what *you* know . . . a little. Now I'll find out a little more."

He closed his eyes.

"We were letting you run!" Delonghi said. "To see where you would go."

"Kharls was letting me run, you mean," Gabriel said. Sick as he felt, he laughed. "Do you really think I didn't know it?"

She looked amazed.

"I may be a cashiered marine," said Gabriel, "but it's my uniform and my pension they took away, not my brains. What isn't plain is why *you* aren't interesting in letting me run. Who are you *really* working for?"

He had the satisfaction of seeing a terror more stark than any previous one erupt in her eyes. It was hastily sealed over again, but it gave him the wedge he wanted at the moment.

"Quite," Gabriel said, "but he sent you anyway. Two possibilities, then. He was waiting for you to come around to his way of thinking *en route* . . . or when you caught up with me and came to understand the situation. If so, you had a narrow escape. He would have been *very* annoyed if you'd killed me." Sweat broke out on her face. "Or he was waiting for you to reveal your real intentions. If you did, it was careless of you to leave living witnesses at Rivendale." One bead of sweat began to trickle down her face. Gabriel raised an eyebrow, watching it with interest. "There's a third possibility, isn't there?"

He gave her a small grim smile. "He sent you out here for *us* to get rid of, a tainted asset. No one would be surprised to hear that Gabriel Connor shot you up. Your service comes away untarnished, and I wind up with another black spot—something else for Kharls to hold over my head while I run around scaring things out of the bushes for him."

At that she looked completely blank. Gabriel filed that away for future reference.

"I suppose I'm going to have to talk to him about all this some day," Gabriel said. "If that last possibility turns out to be true, then I am going to have a bone to pick with him. He's judge, jury, and executioner already by right of his position as Concord Administrator. He doesn't need me doing his clean-up jobs for him. Let him find a marine still in uniform. In the meantime, I want to know *why* he's having me followed, and *why* Concord Intel and VoidCorp Intel are playing tag-team chase-the-Connor with each other. One cashiered traitor isn't reason enough to come all the way out to the edge of the Verge. The stakes are higher. *What's the reason?*"

She glared at him again. I'm not going to get anything further right this minute, Gabriel thought, not with my guts acting like this. He was having to concentrate on breathing slowly and deeply, and he wasn't sure how long his composure was going to last.

"We'll talk later," Gabriel said, "and that's going to be the last time we talk, Aleen Delonghi. If you don't tell me then what I want to know, you'd better make a note somewhere of what you want put on your gravestone, because if I don't kill you accidentally in getting the information out, I *will* kill you on purpose after we're done. Not to do Lorand Kharls a favor either, just consider it natural selection. I'll be helping the universe make sure that the next Intel officer to come along is smarter."

Gabriel turned toward Tlelai. "Would you stick her in the larder, brother?" he said. "I'll talk to her again in a couple of hours."

"Shall we feed her?"

Gabriel thought about that. He hadn't yet checked any of the edanweir food for compatibility, and he didn't want to kill Delonghi by accident. Then his stomach twisted inside him at just the *thought* of food.

"No, let it wait for the moment," Gabriel said. He jumped up, grabbed the mass rifle, and hurried outside.

Chapter Eighteen

ABOUT TWENTY MINUTES later he came back in and went to sit with Enda. Her expression was rather curious.

"I threw up," Gabriel said.

Enda looked at him with some compunction. "It is not easy work," she said, "mindwalking."

"That's not what I was doing. Otherwise the edanweir would have been all over me. This was something else, wasn't it?"

"That would be hard for me to say."

Gabriel sat and rubbed his eyes wearily while considering that phrasing. Enda could be very precise in her use of language sometimes.

"Minds have barriers for good reasons," Enda said. "Violating them exacts its own price. Additionally, it takes considerable strength to keep one's own thoughts discrete from another's when those barriers are removed. There is always a danger of everything suddenly running together in uncontrolled fusion. Even between members of the same species, such fusions can cause madness. Between *species* . . ." Enda shook her head. "Be very careful, Gabriel. You are walking on uncertain ground."

"I've been doing that ever since they cut me loose in that courtroom on Phorcys," Gabriel said. "Nothing new there." He looked uneasily out toward the door. "Meanwhile, I want to get *Sunshine* under cover somewhere, and I want to push this Delonghi woman's ship off that cliff."

"Surely not before going through it," Enda said, "to see what might be found."

"Oh, you're right," Gabriel said, morose. "Probably my

electrolytes are just in an uproar after my guts turning themselves inside out."

That made Gabriel think of a chance remark of Doctor Delde Sota's about his electrolytes not so long ago. She had insisted that she give him a checkup. The way his hair was going silver . . .

Do you need to be in its neighborhood for a certain length of time? he wondered. Is there something that needs to happen to activate this thing? He had no answers, and heaven only knew what other changes were happening.

Gabriel took out the luckstone and looked at it. With no warning, there came over him a peculiar moment of vertigo, in which the stone was still—in which it was the *only* thing still. All around it, things were being caused to move until it was in the right position for something to happen.

Something . . .

He shook his head, and the illusion faded. "In any case," Gabriel said, "I may be able to get some results from her later. If I don't, she may be less trouble dead."

Enda said nothing to that. "It is a shame Delde Sota is not here," she said. "She could quickly tell us everything worth knowing about that ship without having to so much as open its door."

"No question of that, but the one thing we *don't* need here right now is any more aliens. The Eldest has been keeping his ammo very dry, but I think much more pressure on him and he's going to act in what he sees as his people's best interest."

"At which point we would have to employ force to leave."

Gabriel stared at the mass rifle. "We'd have to be quick about it. They're not stupid people, and I'd hate to do it. It would ruin something special . . . and maybe make further good relations with them impossible."

Enda sighed. "Well, at least I begin to understand now why these people were making no headway with the translation modules. I have been watching you talk with them, and the conversations you report have much more content than could possibly be packed into the very few sounds they made. They do not really have a language as such, do they? Or one with very few words. Their communal psionic contact does most of the work."

"I think so," Gabriel said. "New concepts are traded around by small groups meeting directly . . . and apparently that happens a lot. I got the impression from Tlelai that they have a lot of these airships, and when people can't walk from settlement to settlement, they fly where they're going."

He found himself wondering as he spoke whether the "island" he had seen against the water of one of the inland lakes was in fact an airship on its way somewhere. "It's civilization without cities," Gabriel said. "I wouldn't have thought it was possible, but they seem to have found a way to manage it." He frowned. "If we don't do something, all this is going to be destroyed before anyone has a chance to understand it."

* * * * *

Gabriel spoke briefly to the Eldest about finding somewhere to hide *Sunshine.* The Eldest said he would look into it, and Gabriel went for a long walk to the ship and back, wanting to stretch his legs and get away from the image of Delonghi's white face, furious, impotent, and terrified. He was going to have to see it again at least once, and then, if she didn't cooperate, he was going to have to decide what to do with her. Locking her up in *Sunshine* was possible, but he resisted the idea. If she got loose, there would be trouble.

When he got there, Gabriel almost didn't go into the ship for fear of boobytrapping, but he didn't think Delonghi had had time, and even if she had, she struck him as too arrogant to have bothered. He went in without trouble and fetched some more prepackaged food and snacks for himself and Enda, along with one of the ship's analysis packs for alien foodstuffs—the amount of meat the edanweir kept around the place had been making him hungry.

Having taken care to change the combination on *Sunshine*'s outer access, Gabriel took his time on the walk back, as the day's afternoon began shading into dusk. The lights were being turned up in the longhouse when he got back and dropped off a ration pack for Enda, and another one for Aleen Delonghi, though this Gabriel gave to the guard outside the larder. He didn't yet want Delonghi to see him. Hungry but unwilling to settle in for the evening, he went out again and stood in the common space outside the settlement's houses.

Up on one of the hillsides to the west, silhouetted, he saw someone he thought he knew. There was no visible path, but the one up there knew the way, and Gabriel followed his thought. About twenty minutes' worth of hard climbing later, he was up on the westward ridge, sitting on a stone near its crest with Tlelai, and looking toward the sunset. One of the planet's two moons rode the sky in a sharp crescent.

"Your stranger," said Tlelai, "did she help you?"

"Not much," Gabriel said. "I want to get her out of here as quickly as I can. I'm just not sure that she'll cooperate."

"What if she does not?"

"Hard choices, brother," Gabriel said, and tucked himself up on the rock, arms wrapped around his knees, the mass rifle leaning against the stone.

"There have been nothing but such for us, lately," Tlelai said. His voice was sad. "Why *us?*"

"That's the question of the month," Gabriel said.

"What's happening now," Tlelai said, "would not have been my choice. I had no desire toward the higher learnings, toward science and art. I was a hunter. I was good at it. Life was untroubled, if lonely. I lost my mate—you saw that, I think." The image did not recur, for which Gabriel was briefly thankful. "It was a painful time, but I have been passing through it, and the pain had been growing less. Life looked like it might be good again. Then *this* happened." Tlelai gazed away across the mountainous terrain northward, away from the waterfall. "The sound of strange weapons in the middle of the night, and strange creatures killing each other."

"You were 'hearing' me the way I heard you?"

Tlelai flicked his ears forward for "yes" and said, "Thoughts I could not understand. Images that made no sense—though they did not frighten me, because they were not unfamiliar to *you*, but everything was desperately strange. When I first saw you, I was scared but also eager, for finally someone had come who could explain the things I was seeing."

"It'd take a year's worth of evenings," Gabriel said. "I don't think we have them. One way or another, soon now, Enda and I have got to leave. This Delonghi person is only the first to come after us; others will follow. I'm sorry it's turning out this way. It never occurred to me that there would be people here."

"Yet you came, and not just to this world," Tlelai said. *"Here."*

Gabriel nodded. That mystery was still much on his mind. He had thought their coming to this part of the planet was mere chance, Enda's finger picking a spot on the sitting room display for its potential scenic qualities. Now he was not so sure. That image came back to him of everything moving, *being* moved, places and events shifting configurations, while the luckstone stood still at the middle of it all. What was actually *doing* the moving?

"Well," Gabriel said, "it's made things easier for us two, anyway. I was going to ask you, though. Who is this person that the Eldest sent for?"

"I know of her," said Tlelai, "but I have never met her. She is *mahlahnwe'ir yahein*."

"I didn't get that," Gabriel said.

Tlelai waved his tail in slight exasperation. "I am not sure how to explain it any more simply than that."

"You said the Eldest was in charge of implementation of history," Gabriel said. "Is this lady like that?"

"Yes," Tlelai said, "I think so, but history backwards, not history forwards."

Gabriel clutched his head in mock exasperation. Tlelai hissed with laughter.

"Somehow the concept of backwards and forwards history were slighted in my education," Gabriel muttered. "Perhaps the noble hunter Tlelai would stop his noise for half a second and enlighten me."

Tlelai stopped, looking off westward again. "Thank you so much," Gabriel said. "Now what the hell kind of—"

"Be quiet," Tlelai said. His ears angled forward, then sideways again. "Do you hear that?"

It was a high whine, a long way up. *Now* what? Gabriel thought. It's just not fair! There was no mistaking the sound of system drives coming in, and the sound was no drive that Gabriel recognized. A couple of the sounds, at least, spoke of engines bigger than anyone *he* knew owned.

Gabriel sprang to his feet, his heart beginning to race. "Ships," he said. "Three, I think. I swear to space, as soon as we deal with whoever this is, I'm going to dig *Sunshine* the deepest hole you ever saw and dump her in it, and then I'm going to find a way to chuck Delonghi's damned ship over the edge of that waterfall! The things are a menace just parked out in the open like that." He picked up the mass rifle. "Tlelai, in the name of what little community we've got, for your people's sakes and mine, get back down there right now and tell the Eldest to let Enda go, let her get back to *Sunshine!* At worst she can get away and not trouble you any more. At best she can get up there and help a little when the shooting starts!"

"Shooting—"

"Brother, don't even think about it, you wouldn't last a second against a ship with only those," Gabriel said, glancing at Tlelai's beautiful rifle. "Though I really do want to try one later—if we live. Go, run, hurry!"

Tlelai took off toward the settlement. Gabriel stood, waiting for the first sight of something bearing down through the evening's high cloud. He started to run, too, the other way, down the far side of the hill, away from the waterfall, away from the settlement, into country he hadn't seen before.

It was complete madness, but there was nothing else Gabriel could do. Almost certainly, they had spotted *Sunshine* and Delonghi's miserable ship. Gabriel was betting that they would find a moving target more interesting than a sitting one, especially if it was human, male, alone, and seemed overtly to match the description of the man they were looking for.

Gabriel ran hard over the hill, down it and up the slope of the next one, checking the mass rifle's charge as he went. Full up. *I would have been nothing but a bag of blood and broken bones if she'd fired this!*

High above him, the drive notes of the ships changed, scaling down. *Definitely three of them,* he thought, *one smaller, two bigger, if I'm any judge.*

The sound dropped closer. One ship bloomed out of the cloud; it was the other one that had been parked at Rivendale. Then another, bigger ship followed with its partner. Both were long, sleek, nasty vessels with too many guns . . . and both sported the black, gray, and red VoidCorp logos on their tails.

One turned toward him. Gabriel came to the top of a hill, shoulder-rolled down the other side, scrambled to his feet just before hitting a big rock, and kept on going.

Plasma bolts hammered down on either side of him as the first of the ships went over low. The stink of burning vegetation and scorched earth filled the air as Gabriel flung himself down. His only advantage was that these weapons weren't suited for use against people on terrain.

The first ship was coming about. The second and third seemed to be heading toward the settlement. Gabriel shivered at the thought. As the first ship finished its circle, he prepared himself, crouching in what little cover he could find and feeling the adrenaline flush as he had felt it before in combat. What he really wanted right now was a mass cannon and an armored vehicle, but a mass rifle was terrific against armor . . . as long as you had the range right and fired at the right place. You just had to wait until the ship was right on top of you and pick a spot where the armor was weakest. There was no chance of bringing a ship down, but you could make one very unhappy. All Gabriel could do was hope that these people had no idea he had this weapon. It was a chance he would have to take. The ship came around again, dived toward him, then came shallow as if tryng to hover over him and fire.

Oh, they wouldn't, Gabriel thought. Would they? Yes!

He didn't bother firing at the belly, which would be too well armored. Instead, he took aim at one side pod, almost certainly an external coolant tank.

Don't wait for a better target, do it now!

He fired. A moment later, he saw what he wanted to see, a white-silver spiff of vapor bursting out of the side of the pod. The ship lurched, and Gabriel saw the other pod come around. He fired and hit that one too.

The pod disintegrated in a deafening but surprisingly flame-free explosion. The ship began to lift away from the ground, spiraling slightly, breaking off the attack.

The second big ship came. Gabriel looked up into the gun ports that were trained on him scarcely half a kilometer away. He lowered his rifle and said goodbye to life.

And that ship blew up. The blast hammered him to the ground. Gabriel had not registered the third scream of drive engines. The ship producing them had outrun its sound. With a huge clap of thunder, a narrow silvery shape came arrowing down out from the evening sky and arced away just above the expanding cloud of falling junk that had been the VoidCorp ship. Gabriel looked up at that shape and swallowed.

Longshot!

She shot away, bolts from her plasma cannons hammering at the ship that Gabriel had pinked with his mass rifle. Two big explosions shattered the back of the ship. It came spiraling down again, harder than any pilot would have dared. With a squeal and shout of bent and tortured metal—though not with the characteristic *crump* sound Gabriel had been hoping for—the VoidCorp ship slammed into the ground, spreading debris as it tore a trench in the earth.

Gabriel huddled down behind a slight rise in the turf. He was in his element, though he desperately wished he had some armor less permeable than his coverall. That third ship was still up there somewhere, but he couldn't think about that now—possibly didn't need to, for Helm was here. Gabriel concentrated on the wrecked ship in front of him.

Come on out. Ship's weapons won't do any good now, even if they're working.

Another sound—from behind him, a rush and scuttle of feet—and suddenly there were five or six edanweir riflers throwing themselves down onto the blue-green bracken around him. Gabriel was terrified for them, would have warned them off, but there was no time.

A groan and scream of metal sounded as a lock was forced open, and the VoidCorp ship's little complement slowly came out firing heavy charge rifles. Every one of them was armored and had heat-sensitive sights.

On one side of him and the other, edanweir went down, but the VoidCorp troops started doing the same. Their armor was good enough, but it could not stop all the edanweir bullets, aimed with the expertise of hunters who had to routinely hit a spot no bigger than a few centimeters on an animal big enough to trample them. The VoidCrop armor, like any other kind, had cracks and joints that could be exploited.

While the edanweir continued to fire mercilessly, Gabriel carefully picked his targets and let the mass rifle do the rest. As far as it was concerned, ship's armor was fair game, and personal armor was so much tissue paper.

Shortly, nothing but smoke was moving in or around the wrecked ship. Gabriel almost stood up, then heard engine noise again and went flat on his face.

Two more ships. The sound combined with the low cloud had fooled him. This one came in low, over the crashed ship. Too low, too slow! Gabriel grinned, lifted the mass rifle, and picked his spot. The third ship was a small ship, one he'd seen before . . . Miss Blue Eyes' ship. She couldn't believe what had happened to the other vessel and was coming in for a fast look. Gabriel fired, picking the best spot on the nose, right under the pilot's cabin.

The ship went by fifty meters above the ground, firing. Only half-seen, mass beams stitched the ground, ripping and tossing turf into the air, then stopped. A missile shot out from the clouds. The ship turned and sped upward, trying to evade—but too late.

The missile struck with a blinding flash of light, and the ship fell
out of the air, still keeping some forward momentum. The craft
went down just as the thunder from the explosion reached Gabriel
and the edanweir. To Gabriel's intense disappointment, the ship
did not burst into flames as it plowed into the ground.

Then came the other ship, firing as it headed straight down for
him. Gabriel cursed his luck for running out after such a nice run
and said goodbye to his life again.

Just as the plasma bolts began to come close enough to throw
burning turf and soil over Gabriel, *Longshot* swept down, firing.
Ignoring Gabriel and the edanweir, the ship broke away,
increased speed, and accelerated away. Helm chased the third
ship over in the general direction of the waterfall, then launched
something at it that Gabriel didn't see, only heard. It screamed
past the settlement, and for a moment drowned out even the
sound of the falls.

The ship arced upward, trying to escape. The sound arced up
after it, and the resulting explosion was spectacular, a great blinding bloom of yellow-red light. Super-heated vapor boiled up and
fire rained down into the veiling mist of the Downfall. Little
chunks and pieces tinkled down among the stones and were lost
in the roar and thunder of the water crashing into the gorge.

Something moved beside Gabriel. It was Tlelai, crawling to lie
shoulder to shoulder with him. For the moment Gabriel could
only spare him a glance as the last ship saw what had happened
to the other, spun itself rather clumsily on its yaw axis, and
headed straight up. Gabriel was confused to see Helm arrow past
over the gorge, ignoring it . . . and then he heard something that
confused him even more thoroughly.

Another ship! Not decelerating, either. The scream of wind
over airfoil surfaces up high told Gabriel that someone was
coming in hard and fast. A shape blossomed through cloud,
silver-orange in the early sunset, and laser beams lanced from it
in blinding lines at the VoidCorp ship.

Heading upwards still, that ship blew up. The accelerating,
burning fragments ascended gracefully for another hundred

meters or so before pausing in midair and then snowing back down to the ground in sparkling shards and splinters that burnt briefly before they tumbled and went out.

The attacking ship pulled out of the dive handsomely, ran off low across the gorge, and then made a big broad turn and came back to settle where Helm was already landing out of sight, most likely by *Sunshine*. As the last ship turned and Gabriel got a better view of the ship's configuration, his mouth dropped open.

"Good God," he said. "It's *Lalique*."

"What?" Tlelai said. "I didn't understand."

"Someone I know," Gabriel said.

"I thought you said you knew all these people."

"Not all personally," Gabriel said, "but one of these, one of the friends who came to help us, I didn't know she was coming."

"The Eldest," said Tlelai, "is not going to be pleased."

"He's not the only one," Gabriel muttered as *Lalique* settled out of sight. "Come on, brother, we've got one more person to deal with here."

They began to elbow their way toward the downed ship, though quite shortly they would run out of cover.

The shape that they saw hiding behind the ship's half-crushed skids didn't wait for them to come into full view. It started shooting at them both, and the beams scorched past them with truly unnerving accuracy. Though there was no seeing the shape's eyes in the last of the dusk's light, the flashes from the lasers made it plain that the silhouette shooting at them was that of the blue-eyed woman.

Damn it, Gabriel thought, aggrieved. Why are all these women trying to kill me? This isn't fair. Marines are supposed to have all the girls after them, sure, but not like this!

He was becoming very annoyed, for he and Tlelai were pinned down, and he couldn't use the mass rifle on her. He wanted to talk to her, but one shot from the mass rifle would have ended any chance of future conversation. Gabriel kept his head down and swore, trying to work out what to do next.

"Brother," Tlelai said, "does she need to be dead?"

"Am I tempted!" Gabriel said. "But no."

"All right," Tlelai replied. He waited a second, then rose out from behind their cover and took aim with one swift motion. An instant later, he fired.

Miss Blue Eyes shrieked and went down.

Tlelai looked regretful. "As you said, 'they' are not 'us,' " he said. "All the same, it is a shame."

They watched her for a moment, then Tlelai handed Gabriel the little pistol Gabriel had given him, and together they cautiously advanced. Gabriel was not sure what condition Blue Eyes might be in, but when they got close enough to see what Tlelai had done to her, Gabriel relaxed. She lay among several dead soldiers, her shin shattered by Tlelai's bullet. She had obviously fainted from the pain and was losing a lot of blood.

It took a while to get the bleeding stopped and the wound bound. Halfway through the process, Blue Eyes became conscious and began cursing in a dry, furious shriek of pain and rage.

"I can't believe this!" she yelled as Gabriel dragged her to her feet. "I've been shot by a damned teddybear!"

"I should mention that they eat meat," Gabriel said, "and they are very universal in their tastes. They've had someone from Concord Intelligence in their larder for a couple of days now."

She went white.

"We'll see how *you* like it in there," Gabriel said. "Come on, Tlelai. Let's take her back and add her to the collection."

Chapter Nineteen

AFTER GABRIEL AND Tlelai got back to the longhouse, the interrogation went quickly. For one, Gabriel wanted to get over to where the ships were to see Helm and Delde Sota as quickly as possible, and also because he refused to let Miss Blue Eyes anywhere near *Sunshine*'s phymech until she answered his questions.

"RS881 34PRM," was all she would give of her name, and Gabriel had to make do with that. "We came to *rescue* you," RS881 34PRM said, trying to sound hurt. "Your partner has been held in durance by these creatures—"

"Oh, come on!" Gabriel said. "Do you think I'm as dumb as you are? You've been traipsing around after me since Terivine, and I'm getting tired of it. As for being 'rescued,' I like these people a lot better than I like *you*. *They're* not going to like you at all, but you'll find that out soon enough."

"It hardly matters," RS881 34RPM muttered. "When the reinforcements get here, the local population is not going to be a big problem, not for long."

The pain was certainly useful in this regard: it had pushed her past caution. "So how long have you been up there?" Gabriel said. "Orbiting the planet, spying everything out? Well, there's this consolation at least: you won't have had time to send word back of what you've found—"

RS881 34PRM laughed at him and said, "Word's already gone back. Not of what's here. *That* can wait, but two cruisers will be here in short order. Word went out five days ago that there was a planet here, and you were headed for it. That was more than enough," she smiled sweetly, "and the reinforcements will be here any minute now."

Five days ago. It was not exactly the news Gabriel wanted, but it certainty was better than not knowing. "Why me exactly?" Gabriel asked.

RS881 34PRM laughed. "After what you've been up to on Grith, after what you pulled in the Thalaassa system, what makes you think you were going to enjoy an untroubled life? Some people decided the universe would be better off without you. I agree with them wholeheartedly. When you're dead, gazump goes your exploration contract, all perfectly legal, under salvage law."

"I'm not dead yet," Gabriel said.

She smiled.

"Still, it's nice to see someone who has her mind made up, after some of the people we've had through here lately. Never mind." He got up, looking for the Eldest, and finally saw him coming in the main doors, looking very grave.

Gabriel went to meet him, passing Enda over on the side. "Helm is here," he said to her, and then said to the Eldest, "Sir, the two remaining space vessels belong to friends of mine. They came to help me, though I didn't know they were going to."

"We cannot have any more of this!" the Eldest said. "There are too many aliens here as it is."

"Sir, I know," Gabriel said. "They will not trouble you long, I promise you. May I bring my friends to meet you, briefly, tomorrow morning?"

"Yes," said the Eldest, "but brief it must be. There is other business at hand."

Gabriel glanced toward Enda. "Sir, I had hoped you might let her go when this emergency began."

"If matters had gone on," said the Eldest, "I might have done so. In the meantime, however—"

Gabriel saw that matters were going to stay as they were, and that Enda was not yet in the clear. *What am I going to have to do to get her out of this?*

"We are waiting for one more opinion, as you know," said the Eldest. "Ask me tomorrow."

Gabriel bowed, and the Eldest passed inside, looking thoughtfully at Miss Blue Eyes as he passed.

Gabriel sighed and turned to Tlelai, who had come down to stand with him. "Tlelai," he said, "I can't waste any more time with her. Would you have our cousins fetch the other one out? As for this one . . ." He grinned. "Larder."

"My pleasure, brother," Tlelai said, and several edanweir took hold of RS881 34PRM and pushed her down the hall. She screamed all the way down, a sound abruptly dampened by the larder door closing.

Shortly, other edanweir came up bringing Aleen Delonghi. "Take her and welcome, cousin," one of them said to Gabriel. "She whines all day; it's a weariness to listen to her."

Delonghi's face changed significantly when she saw the look on Gabriel's face, and the scorched and muddied state he was in. "We're going back to my ship for the moment," Gabriel said, "and we're going to have that talk I promised you. It won't take long, then we're going to decide what to do about *your* ship, which has become an attractive nuisance—as you are to a much lesser degree—and whether or not you will actually be inside the ship when we do it. Come on."

He led the way, and the edanweir and Delonghi followed.

*   *   *   *   *

Gabriel came over that last hill to see Helm standing outside *Longshot* and looking up in wonder at what could be seen of the waterfall from the ships' parking place, while Delde Sota came out of the back lock and headed in his direction.

"Hold her here for a moment, would you, cousins?" he said, and trotted down the hill toward him.

Helm turned as he came—and was perhaps unprepared when Gabriel threw his arms around him and tried very hard to pick him up. "Helm," Gabriel muttered, "I don't think I've ever been so glad to see a ship in a crashdive in all my life."

Helm grinned. "Gonna give yourself a strain like that," he said. "You need to work on your leverage." He pushed Gabriel away, but his look was warm. "Any time."

Delde Sota joined them. "Conjecture: still breathing," she said, as Gabriel took her hand. "Grayer, though."

"We'll talk about that later," Gabriel said. "Right now we have a problem. These people are very grateful to you, but they don't like offworlders, and the less time we all spend here, the better. They've had a disagreement with Enda though, and I can't leave yet."

"Complexities," Delde Sota said. "Manageable."

Helm looked up at the edanweir waiting on the ridge. "I had a toy like one of those once," he said.

Gabriel winced. "The resemblance would have been purely coincidental, believe me. I'll tell you, I'd buy a hundred of any toy that could shoot like these people do. Delde Sota, one thing very quickly. Would you go have a talk with that woman's ship and see if it's set to blow up or do anything else antisocial? If it is, I want to get rid of it, and I'll blow it away right where it stands with *Sunshine,* if I have to."

"Opinion," said Delde Sota: "wise for your age, Gabriel Connor. Concord Intel vessel, boobytrapped, multiple mode. Time elapsed explosion for failed return, tamper trap, lift trap, other methods. Opinion: Aleen Delonghi (conjecture of proper name, many aliases in computer) not a very trusting person."

Gabriel wiped away sudden sweat from his forehead. "When would it have gone off?"

"Estimated time: seventy minutes past."

"Past what?"

"Terminology confusion. Plus seventy minutes."

"Seventy minutes *ago?*"

"Correct."

Gabriel stared. "How in the worlds did you—"

"Time check: *Longshot* has been in-system for six hours."

"Didn't just want to rush in," Helm said. "Probably just as well that we didn't. We saw our little friends arrive and were able to keep out of their sensors by staying around the far side of the planet. Can't imagine why they didn't break up their group and map separately. They would have found us."

"Arrogance," Gabriel said.

"Conjecture: possible, but convenient," Delde Sota said. "Had ample time to reconnoiter/scan/analyze her ship before action. Same avenues of attack available as at Rivendale." She glanced up at the hillside. "Option choice: explain so that Delonghi understands what has happened? Or allow her to draw wildly incorrect conclusions, such as system malfunction? Suggestion: two."

Gabriel's appreciation of Grid pilotry as practiced by the more expert mechalus was growing by the moment. "Definitely two. Let her think it's some kind of accident. It'll drive her crazy."

"Good technology is magic," Delde Sota said, with a sly smile. "Would have delayed arrival to watch discovery of failure of systems, but new visitors forced hand."

"Believe me, I preferred you two right where you were," Gabriel said. "No wonder she was so twitchy all the way back! She thought we were taking her straight back into an explosion . . . or one that had malfunctioned and might go off at any minute." He raised his eyebrows. "She never said a word."

"Suspicion: selfless desire to destroy traitor/accomplice overcame fear?" Delde Sota said.

"With that one? I think it was probably more like spite, or a sudden desire to commit suicide after messing up. Never mind. Did you find out anything else about that ship that we need to know?"

Delde Sota shrugged. "Expensive," she said. "Have decanted all data files into *Longshot*'s computers for convenience. Decryption ensuing. Estimate: six/eight hours."

"I didn't think anyone could break the Concord Intel encryption—"

"Useful myth," Delde Sota said. "Keeps people from trying. System changed frequently. Structure of system means that infrastructure and hardware remains the same. Without extensive hardware changes, extensive software changes are limited." She shrugged again. "Makes my job easier. Addendum: scanned *Sunshine*'s systems, computers, found nothing amiss. No connections to physical tampering, though you should check for that."

"Delde Sota," Gabriel said, "you are the most desirable of accessories."

The doctor smiled at him. "Query: after the fact? Query: brief errand, then entry?"

"By all means."

She went off for a moment, and Gabriel waved for the edanweir to bring Delonghi down. They handed her to Gabriel with some relief.

"Cousins," he said to them, "when you get back, please tell the Eldest I need to talk to him later. There are things he needs to know."

They agreed and left. Gabriel and Helm took Delonghi inside *Sunshine,* and settled themselves into the sitting room. Gabriel brought out some hot drinks and ration bars for Delonghi, who accepted them and tried hard not to show how hungry she was. Gabriel for his own part sipped his chai and tried to control the reaction to being shot at, the inevitable shaking, which was starting already. Helm simply sat there looking absolutely unrufflable, a human rock. Gabriel watched Delonghi's eyes stealing toward the mutant and then away again. It was fear or distaste or both.

Finally, about halfway through the second ration bar, Delonghi said, rather diffidently, "What happened out there?"

"VoidCorp," Gabriel said. "As I predicted."

"What brought *them* here?"

"The same thing that brought you here, apparently," Gabriel said. "Me, at least on the surface, but Miss Blue Eyes, that's the VC operative—I can't remember all those numbers at the moment—claims that word went out that this planet was 'live' as a destination went out five days ago. There's a leak somewhere. Just who did you report your departure to? Because, if what our Miss Blue Eyes says is true, and I think it is, the word for the cruisers to follow her in came right after that."

Delonghi looked horrified.

"You people have a serious hole in your security somewhere," Gabriel said. "There's the fourth possibility for you being sent out this way . . . to reveal, or make plain, the source of the leak. Someone back at headquarters who would have had to be told, perhaps? Lo and behold, you turn up here, and your VC shadow turns up hard on your heels. She didn't hurry. She gave you a day or so down here on your own to play around."

He put his chai aside. "Now it's time to get serious. I told you I knew you didn't come out here because of anything to do with my trial or my supposed treason. You had another agenda, or at least an additional one." He took his hand out of his pocket and folded his other hand over it, so as not to show the luckstone. It pulsed warm.

The flash of fear he caught from Delonghi made the hair stand up all over him. Gabriel tightened every muscle to keep from shuddering.

"I really don't want to do it," Gabriel said. "Don't make me. Don't withhold information, and for all sakes don't lie. Why did Lorand Kharls send you here? Don't say it was only to follow me. I was only an excuse."

She looked at Gabriel most reluctantly. Right then he heard a flash of the fight going on in her mind, all muddled together: *don't trust/told me to tell him/can't be trusted/terror/enemy . . .*

He swallowed hard, intent on hanging onto his composure.

"All right," she said. "There have been some, well, odd reports from travelers out this way. Independent shippers, explorers, others. Little ships have been seen, little spherical vessels, attacking isolated worlds or colonies and disappearing again."

She paused as Delde Sota came in and sat down in a spare fold-down seat.

"She's with us, as if you don't know," Gabriel said. "Go on."

Delonghi let out a breath. "These vessels have started to be associated with a new life form, or rather, an exploitation of old life forms . . . ones we know, sesheyans, humans, others. They are dead . . . but they still function somehow. They are encased in armor filled with some kind of chemical-laden acid slime or mucus that apparently helps to keep them alive, but eventually destroys the contents of the armor if it's breached." She frowned, that look of distaste again. "Reports of these creatures have been more frequent lately. Five months ago, a battalion of Concord Marines on Arist uncovered several such creatures in the aftermath of a battle with the klicks. The CO had reason to believe that the two species may have been working in tandem."

"These things are working with *klicks?*" Gabriel said, wide-eyed. As a former marine, Gabriel had heard little more than rumors about the arachnid-like species that had been dubbed "klicks," but even those rumors chilled his blood. "Son of a bitch. That's all we need."

"The reports haven't made much sense," Delonghi continued, "but they've been consistent, which in itself is troubling."

Gabriel shook his head at her news, uncertain what to make of it. "A couple of those reports are Enda's and mine," Gabriel said. "Corrivale system, and also Thalaassa. Ask Delde Sota over there. She did the autopsy on our first one."

The woman did a double-take. "Excuse me," she said. *"The* Delde Sota? As in—"

"Conjecture: positive identification, details better saved for another time," said Delde Sota. "Preference: to hear your explanation. Might increase your life span."

"You actually recovered a body?"

"Later," said Gabriel. "Tell us. Time's short."

Delonghi swallowed, obviously uneasy about what she was about to say. "The authorities who know about these creatures have tagged them with the name 'kroath.' "

"Why 'kroath'?"

"It's actually a bastardization of some Hatire word," she said. "One of the first reports of these creatures back in 2494 was from a Hatire supply ship destined for Diamond Point. The vessel, decimated beyond recovery, was found drifting out by Lecterion. The ship's distress signal claimed that they were being attacked by *ch'róth.*"

"Ch'róth?" Gabriel struggled with the word.

Delde Sota broke in. "Statement: *ch'róth,* Hatire term meaning 'not being, not living, not existing.' Addendum: can be translated as 'undead.' "

Delonghi nodded. "Naturally there is great concern about them."

"But not public," Helm said, "otherwise there'd be screaming from here to the Stellar Ring."

"No one wants to cause a panic," Delonghi said.

"Conjecture: no one wants enemy to know that knowledge about them is current," Delde Sota said. "Conjecture: may give time for surveillance/investigation/intelligence-gathering."

"That's right," Delonghi said. "The Concord wants to find out what species is behind these creatures—their making, as it were—and what their purpose is."

Species singular or plural? Gabriel wondered. He had gotten a definite impression from the Eldest that it was plural, but this was certainly not information he was going to give to Delonghi. He was also thinking, not of the small ships that had attacked them several times, but of the very large one that had slipped out of drivespace in the depths of the Thalaassa system. It had taken a long look at them and had immediately slipped away again— impossible for a ship to do without first recharging its stardrive, or so one would have thought.

"Any conjectures as to that purpose?" Gabriel said.

She breathed out. "Conquest," Delonghi said. "Plainly not a kind we would like, but there may be other motivations."

Gabriel found himself agreeing. For the meantime, he had to tell Delonghi something in return for coming this far. Gabriel took a long breath.

"They've been here," he said. "Tell Lorand Kharls that."

"They have? When?"

"The recent past." Gabriel was none too sure about the exact dating himself. The edanweir did not keep watch over time by calendar and clock as other species did.

"What did they do? How are there—"

"Survivors?" said Gabriel, rather bitterly, for normally there were none after such an encounter . . . or none in the normal sense. "They had nothing the visitors wanted."

"But this world, it's viable—"

Gabriel shook his head. "It would make you think that worlds aren't what they're after," he said. "Unfortunately, too many others are. I've got to start thinking about *them,* now, dammit."

"Yes, well," Delonghi said, for all the world as if she wasn't terribly concerned about the prospect of a couple of VoidCorp cruisers arriving. "So that's settled. Any further cooperation you can give me in this matter will be appreciated. If you'll just let me go back to my ship, I'll—"

"Your ship?" Gabriel laughed. "It blew up."

Delonghi stared at him.

"Or it should have," Gabriel said. "You think I didn't know? *Really.*" He smiled, just slightly. "You want to be careful what you assume. No, I think you'll find in the morning that you've lost that ship, a lot more quietly, though, than blowing it up along with my ship, me, and whoever else happened to be nearby. When you get back and you file your expense accounts with Lorand Kharls's office, you can explain everything to him. Probably he won't dock your pay for it. He's a reasonable man."

The look of fury in her eyes was nearly enough to pay Gabriel back for the annoyance she'd caused him so far.

"Helm, when we're finished here, we have a data drop to do," Gabriel said, "and I don't know if it's going to be convenient for us to drop her off on the way. Would you take Delonghi here back to, say, Aegis, if you're going that way? She can hitch a ride home on a Star Force vessel from there."

"No problem," Helm said. "We'll take care of her security in the meantime."

"Security?" Delonghi said. "What do you mean? I've established my bona fides, I have a right to move freely around the—"

"Not on the edanwe planet, you don't," Gabriel said. "Helm, remind me to ask Tlelai or the Eldest what their name for the planet is. I can't believe I missed that. Sorry, Delonghi. They don't want you here. They don't want any of us here, even me, and I'm in community, so you're just going to have to deal with being kept out of trouble, and frankly," Gabriel added, "considering my doubts about your bona fides, you're getting off lucky. Who *else* are you working for besides Lorand Kharls?"

She said nothing. Gabriel was flooded with a storm of images and emotions, mostly anger and fear. He closed his eyes for a moment, trying to sort through everything he was seeing . . . then realized that it was going to take him a while.

"Right," Gabriel said, and opened his eyes again. What was showing in Delonghi's face now was mostly fear. "That's more or less what I thought. Helm . . ."

Helm stood up and took Delonghi by the arm. She rose too, rather stiffly.

"Thank you," Gabriel said, "for not making it necessary for me to kill you."

Helm took her away. When the lift door had closed, Gabriel looked over at Delde Sota and said, "Was I too mean to her?"

"Opinion: kinder than required," Delde Sota said. Her braid slipped up over the edge of the table and wrapped around his wrist. "Have had this in mind for a while," she said. "Begins: physical evaluation. Stop twitching."

"That's not me," Gabriel said, "it's just that I was in a fight. Oh, don't look at me that way, *you* know what I mean!"

"Statement: always a challenge to know that," Delde Sota said, and smiled.

Gabriel sat there, let the luckstone drop out of his hand, and reached for his cup of chai.

"Negative," said Delde Sota suddenly. "Please pick up again."

He did, with a shrug, and drank the rest of his chai. Just then, Helm came back. "Thanks for taking her off my hands," Gabriel said. "I've been half afraid of what I might do to her."

"Been that long, has it?"

"*Helm . . .*" Gabriel said warningly, then he sighed. "Come to think of it, it *has* been that long. Every woman I've seen recently has tried to kill me. All the rest just want to sit and hold my hand."

He gave Delde Sota a look.

Helm chuckled loudly. "Well, I scanned Delonghi for you," he said. "She's clean. Either she didn't have time to equip herself with holdouts before you caught her, or she didn't think she needed to. Careless."

"The second, I think."

"Well, I locked her up in the secure small-cargo hold," Helm said. "She can bang around in there all she likes—it's built stowaway-proof to start with. What now?"

Gabriel rubbed his face and tried to think. "She's out of the way, at least. Now all I have to worry about is this other one. Miss Blue Eyes. I'd give her to you too, if I could. The edanweir are not precisely unfriendly, but they do *not* think the way we do, and too many aliens could definitely spoil the soup at this point, especially for Enda."

Helm looked at him oddly. "Who puts aliens in soup?"

"Just something my mother used to say."

"Now I see why you went into the marines," Helm said. "Even *their* cooking had to be better than hers."

Gabriel punched Helm completely ineffectively in the shoulder. "Anyway . . ."

"Why not just break Enda out?"

"It would be a mistake," Gabriel said. "Don't ask me for specifics. I can't give them to you. We have the weaponry to do it, but I don't have the will. Let's let this come to a head in its own time. If we have to . . ." He desperately hoped they did not.

"All right," Helm said. "One more day won't matter . . . will it?"

"Depends on tomorrow," Gabriel said, "but, oh, am I glad you two turned up when you did." He glanced out *Sunshine*'s view-shield. "Now, as for her . . ."

"They left for the night," Helm said. "Delde Sota gave Angela a hint. They'll come back in the morning."

"Oh joy," Gabriel said. "Well, thanks, Doctor . . . you were right on the money."

"Now what I want to know," Helm said, "before we all expire

of exhaustion and excitement here, is what the hell the delay was at the *Lighthouse*."

Gabriel looked at him. "What delay?"

"You know. You not making up your mind until the last minute. We hardly had time to get on one of the extra ships and say 'goodbye.' "

Gabriel shook his head. "What are you talking about?"

"You didn't book until barely half an hour before the thing left—"

"You're off your head. We booked ten hours before it left! Check the logs, or ask Enda tomorrow, if you don't believe me."

Helm sat there looking skeptical. "Well, *somebody* took their time about releasing the news into *Lighthouse*'s Grid," he said. "We checked about every five minutes for the better part of eight hours! I wasn't going to get on that bloody thing until I knew for sure that you were going. When I did know, it turned out the spars were full, and there was no room in internal docking! *Longshot* and *Lalique* wound up having to hitch on one of those Star Force ships that run escort for the *Lighthouse*." He frowned. "No access to the interior, and one of those exterior gun ports was trained on *Longshot* all the time. I didn't think much of it."

"Opinion: could have spent whole time drinking and shopping," Delde Sota said mildly. "Terrible waste of five days."

Gabriel had no idea what to make of this. *Was someone on Lighthouse trying to protect us somehow?* he thought. *And who? And why? Though it would explain a few things. For one, ID cards that got me into places not even Delde Sota should have been able to manage.*

"Helm, why didn't you let us know you were coming along?"

"Thought it might be better for you if you didn't know you were being followed," Helm said. "Anyone listening, or dealing with you, would have had the same idea, then—especially anyone listening to what you would otherwise have thought were private communications."

"Helm," Gabriel said, "you mean you . . ." He was in a turmoil, not knowing whether he liked or disliked the idea that his friends were so concerned for him that they would lie to him to help keep him safe. "Can't I trust *anybody?*"

"If you mean, can you trust me to let you go off into the middle of nowhere and get yourself shot up," Helm said with a smile, "then I suppose the answer is no, so just cope with it."

Delde Sota stood up, unwrapped her braid from Gabriel's arm and stretched. "Intention: intermission/analysis period," she said, and slipped out of the cabin.

Gabriel looked after her, then back at Helm.

Gabriel nodded. "Look, I didn't mean to give you trouble. Forget it."

"Besides," Helm said, "a little extra help out here might not hurt."

"You're right there," Gabriel said. He got up

"You going back there tonight?"

"Yeah," Gabriel said. "I don't like to leave Enda alone there. Not that I'm afraid for her, but . . . you know, moral support."

"I do know," Helm said.

"Yes," Gabriel said, "you do."

He punched Helm in the shoulder again, not quite as hard as the last time, and went out.

* * * * *

It was a terrible night. Gabriel lounged by the fire in the long-hall, stretched out with his feet up on one of the benches under the overhang of the fireplace. He tried desperately to sleep but couldn't. The thought of big ships, much too big for anything he and Helm could cope with, was shivering up and down his spine.

The cruisers, VoidCorp cruisers, would be on their way right now. They would have big stardrives, easily big enough to make one long thirty light-year starfall to Eldala, not the two or three smaller ones that might have given Gabriel time to come up with something.

Like what? he thought. Escape is no option. You get away fine, but the edanweir are still here, sitting ducks. VoidCorp will come in here and completely trash this beautiful place. It'll be one big corporate enterprise mine in a year. This people's culture, all the slow lovely things they do, the guns they don't use on each other, the airships they never thought of arming, the community . . . it'll be gone too, a precious thing changed forever. In a year, the edanweir would be little more than slaves.

No. There was nothing to do but stand and fight. With what? Two ships, maybe three, and a mass rifle.

Gabriel laughed, soft and bitter. Guiltily then, he looked up and around to see if he had awakened anyone. He saw no signs of movement. The edanweir and Enda were sound sleepers, and from here and there around the room he caught the sound of snores. The things the edanweir did, they did wholeheartedly. When they slept, they got on with it, even if they might all be dead the next morning.

He turned and was suddenly surprised to see the Eldest sitting on the opposite bench. Gabriel breathed out, unhappy. "Did I wake you up, sir?"

"I was not sleeping," said the Eldest and turned to the fire. The flames' golden light shone in his bronze-red fur, and his long striped tail shimmered in the firelight as it twitched.

"Because of what will happen?"

"If I knew what *would* happen," said the Eldest, "I would be a happy edanwe, but I have not that power. A relief to me, it is. I doubt I would care much for it. And you?"

"It would be good to know about it," Gabriel said, "only if it could then be changed."

"It would not be what *would* happen then," said the Eldest. "and knowing it might not have served the same purpose."

Gabriel smiled, if wearily. "I should go down and see what the VoidCorp agent is doing."

"She sleeps," said the Eldest, "but this is a strange thing, that we keep having to put your folk in with the meat. Some have been joking, claiming this may taint it."

Gabriel laughed and said, "I'd be tempted to agree with you . . . tonight, anyway. I am not terribly proud of my people at the moment. There are many good ones, many thousands of millions of them, but those don't seem to be the ones who're chasing me the hardest right now."

"We will then, I assume, need a bigger larder?" the Eldest said.

Gabriel shook his head. "Sir, if you would take my advice, you should take all your people and go far away from here, as soon as light comes again. I would take my ship away, off the planet. The one belonging to the first woman who came after me, that one I'd destroy. At the bottom of the Downfall, it would take a lot of finding."

"With her," said the Eldest, "you would do what, exactly?"

Gabriel rubbed his face. "My friend will take her off planet and send her back where she came from. As for the one in the larder at the moment, I haven't decided what to do with her."

The Eldest folded his arms and stared into the fire. "My problem," he said, "is similar." It was the first time Gabriel could recall him speaking other than in the plural. "And that one's ship?"

"I would get rid of it too, if hiding alone were enough," Gabriel said, "but it's not going to matter shortly. Those coming to see what happened to her in her hunt for me will be many times more powerful than anything you have seen . . . more like the Others. They are of intent just as evil, and you should not stay here to meet them."

"The first *hwoman*," said the Eldest, "no one will come after her?"

"Not with such speed. Her people are the more benevolent of the two powers hunting me and would prefer not to interfere on a settled world. She would doubtless be back among them long before they sent to look for her. The second group, VoidCorp, works in a very different way. They wouldn't care about interfering one way or the other."

"A peculiar benevolence," said the Eldest, "that sends this *hwoman* to kill you."

"I don't believe they sent her to do that. She's confused with concerns of her own, and though she claims to act for them, her action is not wholehearted."

"So you still would not harm her if you did not have to?"

"I know how it is to be confused." Gabriel leaned back against the chair. "Some people might kill you for it, but I won't. It seems like overreaction."

They sat there in quiet for a few minutes.

"*Laidanwe*," the Eldest said finally, as if trying out the sound of a word.

Gabriel shook his head and took the luckstone out of his pocket. He had been playing absently with it for a while. "It still doesn't make sense," he said. "There seem to be some concepts that just refuse to cooperate with my mindset—something that won't fit into the human head."

He noticed the Eldest looking at the luckstone. Gabriel held it out. "Want to look at it?"

The Eldest reached out his hand. For a moment as the stone passed they were in contact, the pale five-fingered hand and the dark six-fingered one, but the flash of enforced community that Gabriel feared did not come. The Eldest looked at the stone in his palm, then picked it up between the thumbs of the other hand, peering at it. It glowed dully under the ashy outer coat, the faint radiance almost lost in the firelight.

"Do you know how it does this?" Gabriel said. "How it makes me able to hear Tlelai, and the rest of you?"

The Eldest swung his tail "no" and said, "These things are thought to be very old. Perhaps older on our world than we are, though we have no way to be sure. We have never fully understood what they were, where they came from, or even what they do. If they do anything but glow . . ." He handed it back. "How did you come by it?"

"A friend gave it to me. Not even a friend really, someone I hardly knew. There are worlds, back in the part of space where I come from, where these lie all along the beaches, millions of them, like ordinary stones . . . or anyway, there are millions of stones that look like this, but none of them *act* like this."

"These are on your homeworld that you mentioned, this 'Bluefall'?"

"Huh? Oh, no," Gabriel said, "but beaches we have, though. They're about all we have." He laughed. "Eldest, nearly our whole world is water. Just here and there the land sticks up, and not much of it. There are chains of islands, big and small, and beaches strung all along them: white sand, or pink, or brown, or sometimes black where the land was volcanic." He leaned back and sighed. "It can be a nice life there. The climate's good. People are friendly on those little islands. Neighbors help each other. You have to, when the big storms come through. Sometimes things get hard when fresh water gets scarce in the summer, but you help each other through." He looked up again. "Like here, when the big snows come along."

"Not just our little lakes," the Eldest said, "but a world of waters . . ."

" 'Ocean' is the word we use."

The Eldest shook his head. "It makes no sense; I cannot hear it."

"You might have to see it," Gabriel said, then he grew quiet, because that seemed unlikely. It seemed unlikely that Gabriel would ever see it again, either.

"I wish I might," said the Eldest, "though I cannot tell how that might ever happen. Certainly that must be a great wonder, a world all covered with water."

"It shines from space," Gabriel said. "How it shines . . ."

He fell silent. When he looked up again, the Eldest was gone . . . and Gabriel wondered whether he had been dreaming.

Chapter Twenty

VERY EARLY THE next morning, before the sun was up, Gabriel went down to *Sunshine*, hoping for some quiet breakfast before the great wise one who was expected turned up. He was not surprised to see *Lalique* sitting next to *Longshot*. Gabriel sighed, wishing that this particular interview could be avoided, and went on down to the ships.

There was no sign of life aboard *Lalique* as yet. Gabriel stood for a moment listening to the roar of water in the predawn dusk, and then on a whim wandered down toward the place where he had viewed the Downfall with Enda before.

There were two figures down there, indistinct in the morning twilight and the mist, looking up into the torrent. Gabriel slowly made his way down toward them. Grawl heard him coming first. She turned and saluted him.

"Poetess," Gabriel said. "Angela."

"This is a great sight," said Grawl. "No greater there is in the worlds, perhaps."

"It's cold, though," Angela said.

Gabriel had to grin a little at that. "You should see it here when the winter closes in," he said. "This tries to freeze, they tell me. Once in a hundred years, it manages it. You don't want to know what the spring thaw sounds like."

"Might be worth hearing," Angela said.

"I'd bring a jacket," Gabriel said, "but I don't understand what you're doing here."

Angela gave him a look and said, "Helm talked us into it, not that it took much doing. We got to talking after we went to Aegis for repairs, and he said we owed you a favor. He had a point. You didn't have to stop for us."

"It's the law to stop when someone's disabled," Gabriel said.

"Yes, well, there are lots of laws," Angela said, "and who obeys them all? Or even some of them? *You* did, though."

"Thank you," Gabriel said. "I will duly note myself down as an angel of mercy."

"You're so cynical," Angela said. "Never mind. You can consider the favor paid. I won't say it wasn't a pleasure! When the doctor told us whose ships those were, we just settled in and had ourselves a little party."

"I saw that," Gabriel said. "It was nice shooting. You should be warned, though . . . there may be more. If favors are paid, this might be a good time to get out while things are quiet."

"You trying to get rid of us?" Angela said.

Grawl looked at Gabriel disapprovingly and said, "There is a battle toward, and it would be ill for my honor to forsake friends at such time."

"Yeah, well," Gabriel said, "Miss Blue Eyes and her crowd were one thing, but I think reinforcements may arrive shortly, because they'll have sent word back as to what they were going to do."

"Who's 'Miss Blue Eyes'?" Angela asked.

Gabriel laughed at the sudden sound of interest. "Oh, the Void-Corp agent," he said. "She was here 'to rescue me.'"

"I bet," Angela said. "People are turning up here with all kinds of excuses."

"Tell me," Gabriel said sourly. "Shortly half the Star Force is probably going to turn up, and Customs and Excise, and any other Intelligence organizations that have been slow getting the news. In the one place around here that really just needs to be left alone, but the worst of it is that there are a couple of VoidCorp cruisers coming, and there's not a damned thing in the world that can be done about that." He glanced up. "If I were you, honor or no honor, I'd be out of here before then."

Angela shrugged. "We'll see."

The flatness of it took Gabriel by surprise. "Look," he said, "Thanks. Thank you very much."

"You're welcome," Angela said.

Hurriedly, Gabriel turned and left.

*   *   *   *   *

He had no stomach for breakfast after all, but just went straight back to the longhouse where Enda, ignoring her guards with good grace, was combing her hair and putting herself in order for the day.

"Was there a problem?" she asked as he came in.

"Huh? No. Angela," said Gabriel. He sat down and watched Enda braid her hair. "If I didn't know better, I'd think Helm was trying to arrange something between us."

"Us?"

"Between Angela and me."

"Gabriel! Surely not," Enda said.

"Well, he'll be wasting his time if he is," Gabriel said. "She's not my type."

Enda gave him a look. "What is your type?"

Gabriel opened his mouth, then closed it again. Completely against his will, his thoughts went back to Elinke Dareyev. "Whatever it is," he said, annoyed with both the memory and the prospect of Angela, "not that. She doesn't . . ." He shook his head. "She doesn't think ahead."

"Ah, well," Enda said, looking sideways at Gabriel with her knowing smile, "that *is* a fault, I suppose." She finished putting her hair to rights and looked up at him. "By the way," she said, "I used the food tester kit that you brought along, and so far I have found nothing which either of our physiologies could not handle. The meat is *very* good; they brought me an excellent stew last night."

Gabriel smiled slightly. "Going to teach them to cook?"

"Oh, they have an excellent regional cuisine of their own," Enda said. "I might learn a few things from them."

If they let you live, Gabriel thought.

He turned his head then, hearing a faint buzzing from outside. "The airship?" Enda asked.

"I think so. Wait here, I'll be back shortly."

He went out into the morning, sighing a little at the sight of the settlement contrasted with the way it had been just the day before. There were bits of torn and burnt metal everywhere, scorch marks on the ground, a faint smell of burning hanging everywhere.

Typical, Gabriel thought. Humans arrive on a world and mess it up within hours.

Edanweir were already gathering near the landing area, and slowly, from the southwest, Gabriel saw the shape of the airship approaching, glinting bronzy-gold in the morning as it came in to land. The volunteer landing crew went out to catch the ropes with the ease of much practice.

The Eldest came up to stand by him, Tlelai following behind him. Gabriel nodded as the airship was made fast, and what turned out to be a total of about ten edanweir started getting out. When they had disembarked with various packages and other belongings, the airship took off again.

"It will cruise nearby until the *mahlahnwe'ir yahein* is done," Tlelai told him.

Gabriel nodded, watching the passengers disperse, wondering where the one was who would decide Enda's fate. He was distracted from this as, among the people coming in their general direction, he saw that one of the passengers was hardly into her second fur yet. Along with various others who stopped by the Eldest and bowed before moving on, this pair, a little one with mother or father—Gabriel still didn't know how to tell or whether the difference even mattered here—came over too. The older one made a respectful bow. The little one just looked up at him, big-eyed.

"This is only the second child I've seen here," Gabriel said softly to Tlelai. "Male? Female?"

"She," Tlelai said.

She was more like a little ball of red-and-cream-colored down than anything else, and Gabriel was completely charmed by her.

He thought of a picture of a fox cub he had seen once—little blunt
muzzle, little merry eyes, big sharp ears too big for the head. This
one was like that. She had a long way to go yet before she grew
into her ears. As he looked down at her, the little edanwe turned
and saw Gabriel. She went a few steps over to stand in front of
him, just staring.

He smiled.

"Hello there," Gabriel said, and got down on one knee so that
the two of them would be more at a level. He looked up at the
Eldest. "Sir, do you pick children up here?"

"Hold them, you mean? Of course."

"Would you like me to pick you up?" Gabriel said.

She put her little furry arms up to him immediately. Gabriel
lifted her up carefully. She was heavier than she looked, a fairly
substantial child. He jogged her a little in his arms and turned so
that she could look around her from a height.

"What a little bundle you are," Gabriel said, smiling more
broadly as she tried to grab some of his hair.

She didn't do too well; it was still too short. He wasn't entirely sure what this people's normal life span might be, but this little
creature was certainly nowhere near latency, the time that a
human would recognize as the threshold of adolescence. If she
were human, she might have been about five.

"What's your name?" he asked her.

She looked at him and said, *"Mahlahnwe'ir yahein."*

Gabriel's eyes widened. He turned to the Eldest.

Unaccountably, he had turned his back. Gabriel glanced at
Tlelai, then looked at the little armful again. The small edanwe
gazed at him with little clear eyes that were absolutely cheerful
and unconcerned. The world looked good to her; plainly, the
world *was* good to her. Her sense of community was untroubled.
Looking into those innocent eyes, Gabriel was suddenly heartsore
at the idea that she might not be able to live in a world like that
much longer, that her world was changing around her—

Things do change, but not that way.

The thought blazed into Gabriel's mind, irresistible, whiting everything out in a sheer blast of certainty. Not power. She had that, but she was not using it. Gabriel, staggered as he was, tried to find another word for what he felt in her—then stopped, realizing that humans are so unused to complete and untainted certainty that when they encounter it, they immediately try to describe it as something else. Arrogance, foolhardiness, folly. This was none of those. The little edanwe was hardly old enough to know what any of those meant. What she had, straight from the depths of time, was certainty of what to do, which way to go, what should next be done.

It was like looking into the sun. Gabriel could not bear it, and covering his eyes would not have helped, even if he could have moved a muscle. Something was looking through her at him: a knowledge that the edanweir possessed or were possessed by. In all the adults it was deeply buried, and Gabriel had only suspected its presence in a shadowy way. In this child it looked out through her like someone buried very deep, in a safe place, peering out into the world through a lens that, for the moment, was clear. It would not always be so, but this time, everything had begun to move together in the right way.

This was what the Others had come looking for and had failed to find. When their mindwalkers had gone abroad, part of the edanweir's horror and disgust for them came of the strangers not being in community, and from the Others' callous disregard for the sanctity and privacy of mind as they searched for whatever it was they hunted. The rest of it had to do with this buried knowledge, this ancient will, the presence of which the edanweir themselves had not suspected. Deep in their history, they had become, or had been made into, a hiding place for something . . . and that something, now threatened, was determined not to be found. A force that even the edanweir had not suspected, something long latent at the bottoms of their minds, rose up at the touch of the Others' mindwalkers and killed them. It killed the edanweir too— little consolation to them. The Others withdrew in confusion, probably thinking that this species presented unexpected problems and had nothing useful to offer them anyway, except as a sort of early warning system, giving the Others news about any other species that might come wandering through this so far unnoticed system.

Now the old will that had killed the Others' mindwalkers rose up to sit in judgment on Gabriel. There was no way he could have hidden anything from it. He stood frozen, blinded and helpless as he felt the power massing, but in his pocket, untroubled, something quietly began to glow.

It was as if the world under him rumbled, a roar like the Downfall, of recognition and resolve. This was the time. The slow, vast movement of configurations had moved into the correct shape. Now it could begin to happen.

As for the ones who would make it so—

Everything whited out again, so that Gabriel was lost. It took a while for him to recover his own feeling of self. He was still frozen, but now, trapped in the middle of this ancient power, he was suddenly aware that it was not just a time that it had been awaiting, but the coming of a particular object combining with a set of circumstances, a pattern into which all the pieces had finally fallen into place. He was part of it. He had been judged and found, not specifically wanting, but at least to be in the right place at the right time.

He started to get some feeling back in his body, and vision began to return. Suddenly Gabriel was not feeling quite so heartsore about changes to this world, now that he began to suspect what lay at the heart of it. He wondered if it was all of *them* he should be sorry for: VoidCorp, the Concord, all the other forces that were about to throw themselves against this old silent rock, not knowing what underlay it.

—and the knowledge that this was not even anything like the most major storehouse of this old power, another one, far greater, lay not too far away, not that far away at all.

His ears started to ring as hearing started to come back. *Where?*

She didn't know. The information had not been left all in one spot. That would have been most unwise and would have made it too easy for both sides, for those from whom it needed to be hidden; for those for whom it was intended, in their greatest need. They would find it . . . or else they wouldn't.

It's your problem now.

Gabriel blinked. He was standing, not outside in the air, but in the longhouse, by Enda's little nest of cushions. He was still holding the little edanwe, who was industriously pulling his beard. Enda's guards were gone, and Enda was lying unconscious among the cushions with a shocked expression on her face.

Gabriel reeled, but found his balance. "Enda—"

"She is all right," Tlelai said. "It's over, brother."

"You may go where you will," said the Eldest, who also stood there, "but we hope you will stay. There seems to be much to be done."

Gabriel swallowed and put the *Mahlahnwe'ir yahein* down. Yipping happily, she ran out into the sunshine again, and her parent went after her in a hurry.

Gabriel looked after her in astonishment, then turned back to the Eldest. "Does this mean you're not going to kill either of us now?"

"Yes," said the Eldest, "it does."

Gabriel noticed that there was no disclaimer attached to the statement, no "Oh, we would never have done that." The gaze of those old wise weary eyes rested in his and made it plain that, had they needed to be killed, the edanweir would have done it. With regret, yes . . . but without a moment's delay.

"I understand you, sir," Gabriel said. "I would have done the same in your position. Let us not waste any more concern on the matter."

"I was not going to," said the Eldest, and smiled very gently in the edanweir manner. "When your friend has recovered herself, let us eat and drink, and then quickly, to council. For they are coming . . ."

Chapter Twenty-One

THINGS STARTED HAPPENING fairly quickly. Suddenly there seemed to be more edanweir in the longhouse than Gabriel could remember, and there seemed to be an increase of purpose, of hurrying, which by itself surprised Gabriel. He had never before seen anyone there hurry.

He put all this to one side for a while and sat with Enda for a few minutes. She had begun to recover consciousness fairly quickly after Gabriel had come back to himself again, and now she was sitting up and had smoothed her clothes down and her hair back into place as if nothing had happened, but Gabriel knew better.

"What *happened* to you?" he asked.

Enda bowed her head. "I wish I could completely describe it," she said, "but that would imply a certainty I do not feel. I was judged, that I know."

"Favorably," Gabriel said.

"As you were," said Enda, "otherwise I think neither of us would now be breathing. If I was accepted, I think it was on your behalf."

"What makes you think that?"

"I would find it hard to say." Again that very precise phrasing, which was starting to make Gabriel wonder. "Gabriel, I do not know what the luckstone is, but plainly it is much more than we thought it was. Something here, or *someone* here—I would use the term loosely, if it is 'someone' they have been dead a long while—has been waiting for that stone to arrive, or one like it, at least. Until it, and you, and I, and everyone here, and this time and place and maybe this whole world could be examined, nothing could happen."

Gabriel looked at it, small and insignificant in his palm, not glowing now, just a little oval matte-black stone. "It's a Glassmaker relic, isn't it?"

"It could be," Enda said, "but it is possibly far older and has nothing to do with those people. We know little enough about the Glassmakers, whoever they were. In any case, something here recognizes *that* . . . and now much on this world will alter. Possibly much beyond it as well, but first there is the small matter of those VoidCorp ships. They are certainly interested in killing you; they will be delighted by this planet and its undefended people, and they will be here any time—"

"I know," Gabriel said. "Are you better? Can you get up? We should go have this out with the Eldest."

They went to him, off to one side where he was engaged in a hurried council with about six of his people, including Tlelai. As Gabriel and Enda came to them, the Eldest said, "We must go to the place I've been shown, and you must come with us . . . otherwise we will not be able to gain entry. Alarms have been broadcast on the radio to our people, the worldwide alarm we last used when the Others came. We have many underground places where we winter, and as many as can make their way there are doing so now, but we must make our way to the silent place with all haste. They are coming, and it may only be a matter of a very few hours before they arrive."

"I think it is less, if I heard the warning right," said Tlelai. "They are close—"

"Did *everyone* hear that?" Gabriel said, confused. "I thought it was just me."

"It may have started that way," said the Eldest, "but it changed, after you were proved. Much has changed . . ." He looked grave.

"I'll go fetch our friends," Gabriel said. "We'll bring the ships here, load them up, and leave right away. Any hole is a good hole to hide in when VoidCorp's coming."

Tlelai stared at him. "VoidCorp?" he said. "Is that your name for the Others?"

Gabriel stopped and stared. *"Excuse me?"*

"It is they who are coming," said Tlelai. "That is the message we were given. They have been alerted somehow. They are coming back to make good on their threats."

A great shiver went through Gabriel, but something else inside him said, *No they won't.*

"Right," Gabriel said. "The first thing to do is get under cover. After that . . . other plans, but first we run. Enda, sit tight, I'll be back shortly."

He took off for the "parking place" at a run.

* * * * *

Helm, Angela, Grawl, and Delde Sota were having breakfast together in *Longshot,* all very neighborly, when Gabriel burst in and ruined it for them. Angela in particular was confused by Delde Sota and Helm's alarm at what Gabriel had to tell them. They started to explain kroath to her, but she stopped them.

"We know about them," she said. "Grawl was involved with cleaning up after a skirmish at a colony-security job she worked once. This is amazing—no one else believed us when we mentioned the little round ships. We just gave it up after a while."

"Enemies of life," Grawl muttered, bristling. "I will battle them with joy."

"Them and VoidCorp both at once?" Angela said, sounding dubious. "Hiding in a hole sounds more realistic for the moment, partner, at least until some bigger guns turn up."

"We could watch them fight it out," Helm said.

"I'm more worried that they might get friendly," Gabriel said.

Helm stared at him. "You need that brain cleaned out, Gabe. It gets disgusting sometimes."

"Nasty thought, isn't it?" he said. "Never mind right now. We need all the ships we have handy. Delde Sota, can you fly Delonghi's ship?"

"Affirmative," the mechalus said. "Query: how many edanweir here?"

"Thirty at the moment."

"Let's go," Helm said.

Delde Sota caught Gabriel by the hand. "Intervention," she said. "Immediate. Advice: do not allow yourself to become separated from that stone until further analyses can be conducted."

"I don't intend to," Gabriel said, "believe me. Why?"

"Datum: considerable physiological changes in you over a very short time," Delde Sota said. "Difficult to analyze except broadly. Initial diagnosis: early symbiotic relationship, undifferentiated type. Implications: unknown. Suggestion: keep stone close. Don't rock the boat."

Gabriel nodded and said, "I'll keep that in mind. Come on, let's get these people out of here."

"Hey," Helm said. "What about you and Enda?"

Gabriel smiled, though it came hard at the moment. "We passed the test," he said. "Now we get to see if we'll live out the week."

* * * * *

They landed outside the settlement, and edanweir with small bags and bundles of belongings started streaming toward the ships and getting in. While Gabriel was helping Helm load edanweir into *Longshot*, one of the scouts came up to him and asked, "What about the screaming *hyuman?*"

"The screa—? Oh, Lord, Miss Blue Eyes," Gabriel said. "I completely forgot about her." He did not say how pleasant he found that, in retrospect. "We've got to get her out of the larder and stick her in the phymech . . ." Gabriel rubbed his eyes. "I wish I could just stick her in a hole and forget about her."

"That could be arranged," Helm growled.

"No, not like *that*. I'd dump her in your hold with Delonghi if I didn't think it would be bad for interstellar security."

"They might do each other in," said Helm, rather hopefully.

"It would be too much to ask," Gabriel said. "We'll take her, little though I like it."

"Sounds like you've got enough on your plate at the moment," Helm said. "We'll phymech her at our end. If Delde Sota can't mend her, she's busted too bad to keep."

"I'll leave that decision to you," Gabriel said.

They got back to loading edanweir. This took less time than Gabriel had feared—these people seemed short on possessions, although every one of them seemed to have a gun.

"This *is* a hunting camp," Tlelai said to Gabriel with some surprise, "didn't you know? Oh, we dislike large groups, yes, but we wouldn't *always* live so isolated."

Gabriel chuckled as he and Enda got into *Sunshine*. Tlelai and the Eldest came in behind them, joining the six or seven edanweir who were there already. They sealed the ship up, and Gabriel led the Eldest back to the sitting room and showed him the holographic map of—

Gabriel stopped then and turned to Tlelai. "Brother, it's late to be asking this, but what do call your planet?"

"The world, of course," Tlelai said, somewhat bemused. It came out. "Dhanwe'll."

"Danwell it is," Gabriel said. "You're going to have to forgive some of our people their accents." He turned back to the Eldest, and said, "Sir, where are we going?"

Gabriel reached into the display and turned it. The Eldest picked a spot about fifty kilometers away, one of those odd triangular structures they had seen. "Of those places which might serve your purpose," he said, "this one is closest."

"We're on our way," Gabriel said. He strapped himself into the right hand seat and brought up the fighting field. "You do not really think we might need that?" Enda said.

"The way my luck is running at the moment?" Gabriel said.

They lifted off and headed westward, closely followed by *Lalique, Longshot,* and Delonghi's ship. Fifty kilometers did not take long even in atmosphere, but Gabriel sat in the fighting field all the way and expected fire to start raining from the sky at any moment.

Five days ago . . . he thought, trying to work out where he had been and what messages might have been traveling in what direction at that point. The problem was that five days ago now felt like about a century. He had been through a lot, and he was sure that worse was to come, but that little splinter of certainty that had been driven into his brain would not let him be. *Something* was happening. It had been trying to happen for a long time, and a tremendous feeling of anticipation was beating at the back of his mind.

Other effects less comforting were occurring as well. The way the luckstone had begun to pulse in his pocket unnerved Gabriel. The pulses came, went, and came again, and as they approached that triangular structure, built on an otherwise inaccessible terrace halfway up a mountain, the pulsing became much stronger. Gabriel thought suddenly about the hole his luckstone had burned in *Sunshine*'s decking. It had nothing to do with anything in the local space, Gabriel thought. Angela was carrying stuff that came from here. A few stones, she said. Mine responded to something she was carrying. The way it's responding now . . .

The four ships landed on the mountain terrace and began unloading their passengers, including Miss Blue Eyes and Aleen Delonghi, both of whom said very little. The edanweir, excited and interested, piled out, chattering cheerfully to one another. Helm, though, looked rather sour as he got out.

"Nice and exposed here," he said. "Anybody could come along and blow all four ships away."

"We'll have bigger problems than that shortly," Gabriel said, turning to look at the great flat triangle of stone that simply lay there on the scrub and gravel of the terrace as if someone had dropped it there. He walked up to the slab. It was about a meter thick and about fifty meters on a side.

Gabriel looked over his shoulder. "Eldest?"

"We have never been able to enter these," said the Eldest. "We did not know they were anything to be entered. Perhaps if you step out on it—"

Gabriel swung himself up on the stone, took a few steps . . . stopped. Whatever the stuff was, it wasn't stone. It chimed softly, like a deep-voiced bell, with every step he took.

"Very strange . . ." Gabriel dropped to one knee on it, taking the luckstone out and placing it on the surface. Nothing happened.

"Well, now what?" he said. "If we can't?"

"Ahem," Enda said softly, and pointed.

In total silence, off to their left, the corner of the triangle had sunk straight down into the ground, revealing an opening about five meters wide, with a ramp reaching down into it.

Gabriel got down and walked with the others toward the ramp. They all went down into the dimness. The ramp spiraled off to one side and kept on spiraling down into a great silence and a huge space, to judge by the echoes. A faint golden light from below grew steadily stronger, or perhaps their eyes got more used to the dimness as they went.

Gabriel turned and noticed that Delde Sota was strolling past him with Miss Blue Eyes over her shoulder. Blue Eyes was unconscious.

"Pain?" Gabriel asked.

"Opinion: not to be trusted," said Delde Sota. "Opinion: affiliation suggests that some things are not good for her to see."

"What about Delonghi?"

"Your call," Delde Sota said.

Gabriel looked back at her. He had suspicions, but that was all they were at the moment, and he preferred to have something more concrete to go on.

"Let her stay conscious," Gabriel said, "but keep her secure."

"Noted."

Finally, they came out at what seemed to be the bottom level. Gabriel glanced up, seeing the opening to the ramp closed behind them. Light increased in the huge open space, which stretched back well into the mountain. The ceiling could not be perceived at all, though Gabriel knew in a general way where it had to be. The illusion that there *was* no ceiling, just an endless darkness like drivespace, was very strong.

They were in the middle of a vast smooth matte-dark floor, and standing about it, here and there, were shapes of the same dark stone, very simple, mostly geometrics: a pyramid or so, several erect slabs, a rectangular column, and a perfect sphere. Everything looked as if it was made of dark, smoky glass, but something told Gabriel that the material was far, far stronger than any human substance.

Gabriel had the luckstone in his hand and was in no doubt about the kinship. This was the same material, though it seemed a little rough and unfinished.

A key, he thought, to this . . . and what else?

"No dust," Angela said, dropping to a crouch and brushing her fingers across the surface. "Either someone here's a real demon housekeeper, or the place hasn't been opened since it was built."

"I'd buy that as a good guess," Gabriel said, walking in among the geometrical figures.

The sphere fascinated him. It was about two meters in diameter and balanced perfectly on a spot about ten centimeters across. Experimentally, he touched the luckstone to it, but nothing happened.

He walked on through that huge space, listening. There was a sense here of tremendous restrained power, but everything was perfectly silent. There was not even a hum in the walls or the floor to suggest what was happening here.

Enda came up with him. "It is a control center of some kind," Enda said, "though what it is controlling, I would not care to guess."

"The planet," Gabriel said. He walked on, listening. There was a faint, faint whispering at the edges of his brain. This was one of the places where the movement he had sensed from the luckstone was being propagated. The dreams had hinted at this, but only in veiled terms that Gabriel hadn't understood. Now that he walked in this place, it was beginning to find a way to speak to him and to the other—a way to tell them what was needed.

Gabriel looked around and saw Tlelai making his way toward him. His gun had been laid aside for the moment, and his eyes shone in the growing golden glow. Here and there, some of the constructs standing on the floor were awakening at their approach, beginning to pulse slightly. The luckstone was doing the same as everything slowly began to fit together, began to come into synch. The sourceless light, the light in the air, began to dim now. The only light was coming from the constructs.

Gabriel moved among them, waiting to see which way he was pulled. Tlelai came with him; Enda had gone off in another direction. This place, or others like it, would take it in turn to wake and manage things here, manipulating the forces of the world, manipulating not only the planet's weather, but even its magnetic field and all the other forces tangled around it. The planet itself had become a tool . . . or a weapon.

Suddenly Gabriel had no difficulty understanding why this world had been untouched for so long, why the first survey had failed, why Angela hadn't seen anything, and why the Others, powerful as they were, had finally gone away. The planet itself, or something based here, had made them do so, though perhaps more passively than in other cases. It had altered the way energy passed through space for hundreds of millions of kilometers around it. It had made the Concord survey ship suffer all kinds of mechanical difficulties. It had subtly affected everyone who had come here. Why is it allowing this access now?

Not because there was no choice, it could have killed all of them: him, Angela, Helm, all the others who had come there.

Why didn't it do that to the Others?

None of them had the key. None of them had a luckstone—a message . . . to tell something there that it was time, now. Gabriel was a messenger and had been carrying the message unwittingly. The message had been checked and found to be genuine. Matters had proceeded as they were proceeding now, for the Others had left silent methods of detection that called them back and had also called others. Now, while they were mired in their certainties, was the time to strike.

The darkening continued, and Gabriel looked up and could have sworn that he saw something moving in the darkness. He blinked. An illusion—

No illusion, Tlelai said, and Gabriel didn't hear him speak aloud at all this time. *I saw it too.*

Gabriel looked over at Enda. She stood there very still in the midst of all this, or not so still, Gabriel realized. She was trembling. It suddenly occurred to Gabriel that, for as long as they had known each other, Enda had never touched the luckstone, not once. It just seemed like one of her quirks, but now . . .

She went slowly over to one of the constructs. It was like a set of upright mirrors made from very thick glass, but they were all polished black. She touched one of them gingerly and jumped like someone getting a shock. The construct's surface came alive with strange characters and symbols that were completely unfamiliar to Gabriel.

"It is . . ." Enda gulped. "Whoever built this construct, it recognizes when a fraal touches it. It would appear to be a broadcast energy device, a sort of conduit. I do not know if it can be correctly described as a weapon. Perhaps originally it might have been used as a communications device, but it will serve our purpose."

"How can you be so sure?" Gabriel said.

She shivered and said, "It spoke to me. It remembers . . ." And Enda would not look at him again.

"We'd better do something," Gabriel said. "They're coming."

"I will do this," Enda said.

She went around the four mirrors, touching them one after another. Slowly they lit from within, as Gabriel's luckstone always did, with that faint golden interior glow. But it grew brighter.

Enda stopped, looked over at Gabriel, and said, "If I understand this correctly, it requires two or more to operate it, one to direct the energy, one to target. It describes the targeting routine as 'going into the darkness.' "

Gabriel smiled, though he was shaking all over. "I understand that," he said. "What do I need to do?"

"I believe simply touch one of these stones when I direct you to."

He moved toward them. So did Tlelai.

"This," said Tlelai, "is what we came for, eh, brother?"

"I'd say so," Gabriel replied.

Enda went into the center space between the stones. All of them were shining now, and the golden light lent an unusually warm cast to her features. Gabriel could not recall ever having seen such an expression of fear and resolve together on a fraal's

face, or for that matter, on a human's. Enda went in among the
stones like someone going to her death—

She stopped there, looked up and around, then slowly she
lifted her hands, put one flat against one of the stones, and one
flat against the other.

Gabriel saw the stones move, saw them gradually lean in
toward her as if they were holding her in place as much as she
was holding them.

His hand on the luckstone, Gabriel went up to one of the
stones, reached out to it . . . and hesitated. Now that he had finally come to it, the end of the normal part of his life, the part he
could not ever return to again, like being a marine—

No. He would not admit that, but at the same time, this change
was bidding fair to become permanent. He could try to refuse it,
but something told him that refusal might maim him. He could
accept it, but accepting it might kill him.

He could see it in his mind, that sudden bright threshold over
which his life, or something that had invaded his life, was now
daring him to step. He would have preferred any other challenge,
anything physical, anything with a gun at one end of it and an
enemy at the other, anything that needed a charge downhill or
single combat. Give me that and I'm your man, but not this . . .
not this last step into the darkness, into the fire. There was no
telling what lay on the other side of it. It would be nice if it were
something as simple as death.

There were no guarantees of that. Suddenly, he found himself
envying his comrades who had died on battlefields: in the ice cre-
vasses of Epsedra, in the desert on Hardcore, blown apart, burned
to cinders, but for all that, safely dead, buried, honored, their end
known, their work done. There was no telling what would happen
to him if he accepted this challenge and took the step into the
darkness and the fire.

Everyone was watching, waiting to see what he would do.
Tlelai, across at the other stone, was waiting for him. Gabriel
swallowed and touched the stone. The darkness fell around him,
and the fire . . .

* * * * *

He was not alone. Tlelai was there as well, and the two of them, in this empty place of darkness, were giants of fire, their shapes only vaguely reflecting their true forms, but still recognizably human and edanwe. They looked around, trying to get their bearings in the nothingness. Gabriel thought he heard a voice saying, *I remember. I remember too much.*

I will not let it destroy this life! Nor these lives—

Enda? he said. He could not see her anywhere.

Here, Gabriel. Wait. Look around you.

He and Tlelai did. The darkness around them was not total. In it, indistinct forms moved.

Something is coming, Tlelai said. *Are those ships?*

Gabriel peered through the darkness. Tlelai was right. Not so very far away from them were the shadows of three huge round vessels, seen dimly, as if through deep water. For the moment he and Tlelai could see into drivespace, as if with eyes and needing no detector.

I am learning what to do now, Enda said. *For your part, you must tell me where and when they will come out of drivespace. You must be* sure. *Once this is launched, it cannot be redirected.*

Trust Enda to find a weapon, Gabriel said. *She was always better at gunnery than I was.*

They peered through the darkness together. *There are more of them,* Tlelai said.

Gabriel looked in the direction he was indicating. Much more distant, there were other shapes coming: a pair of two and a group of three. Even through the dark, wavering medium, they were all identifiable as of stellar nations make, cruisers or better, and Gabriel was slightly less concerned about them at the moment. The ships in front of them, the ones plainly not from any known force in the galaxy, were their big problem right now.

You're right, Gabriel said, *but they're going to come out after this first bunch . . . a good while after. We'll have to take care of them some other way.*

He paused and concentrated on that eddying darkness in front of them. *Look,* Gabriel said. *You can see it if you look hard. There's a trace behind them, a wake. It seems to give an indication of where they're going to come out. It's hard to see real space and this space at the same time, but—*

I see this space, Tlelai said. *I see the real things of the world, riding on it, like a leaf on water, and underneath it, the way the other space bubbles up against it.*

They both peered into the darkness, each working to see in his own way. *Have you found the place?* Enda said. *Hurry, I cannot hold this long—*

Three forces coming out, Gabriel said. *Two big ships, one smaller one. About a hundred of the kroath ships, divided among the three.*

I need a time as well.

You don't want much, do you? Gabriel said. *Time. How are we supposed to judge that? There's no—*

There is, Tlelai said. *I can see it coming. I can count its coming by breaths, if that will help you.*

Close enough, Enda said. *Gabriel, how fast does an edanwe breathe?*

He realized that he didn't have the slightest idea. *It doesn't matter,* Tlelai said. *I can hear my heart beat. That may work better. One, two, three, four, five—*

Gabriel listened. *About a hundred ten per minute,* he said. *Tlelai! How many hundred and tens?*

Seven—

They are *close,* Gabriel thought. *Oh, God, what're we going to do?*

A hundred and ten million kilometers, Enda said. *It will have to do. Gabriel, Tlelai, show me the places.*

They indicated the three emergence spots. *All right,* Enda said. *I see what I must do. You must take the indicators I give you and hold them on those spots. You must not let them move, whatever happens, for those seven minutes. When I tell you, drop them immediately.*

Right, Gabriel said, and saw the three "indicators" Enda meant, three bright spots of light that appeared in the darkness before them.

He tried to reach out to one with his hands, and it moved as if trying to avoid him. By moving in its general direction and holding his hands out to control the energy flows, Gabriel guided it over to where it was needed, over one of the "bubbling" emergence points that he and Tlelai could see in the darkness. He held the indicator there with some difficulty; it seemed to want to travel.

Tlelai got control of the other one and held it in place as well. That left the third one. Gabriel tried to hold his one spot in place while "grabbing" for the other as well, but the first one started to slip.

No, let me, Tlelai said, and managed to hold it in place together. *There!*

It stayed.

Hold them there, Enda said. *I am setting up the energy transfer now.*

What will this do? Tlelai said.

I hope it will discommode them severely, said Enda. *Hold those indicators at all costs, do not let them slip.*

She paused. *Six minutes,* Enda said. *Starting . . . now.*

He could not remember ever having heard so passionless a voice from her. Enda's voice was usually so full of emotion: irony, humor, compassion, everything suitable to the moment and carefully phrased. Now all that was gone, replaced by a cool patience Gabriel was not sure he liked. Neither did he like the sense of the darkness around them, which shifted when Enda started her count. It pressed in. The ships continued to make their slow way toward the world, slow and intent, unhurried, like predators who know their prey cannot escape. Gabriel started to feel as if he was trapped in this darkness with them, that he could never get out.

He would stifle. He would die.

If I have to die, let me die in the light!

He had been in danger of death before, and he knew what to do about it. He hung on. Tlelai was there as well, and they hung on together, nothing but the feel and "sound" of each other's mind to keep them sane in the dark.

We'll last. We'll last, brother. We've been here before.

The fear built, but it was as much excitement now, that jittery rush of adrenaline that came just before the charge. The pressure built, but they could take it, they had been here, they had enough practice . . . just. What had not been in their experiences before was the terrible sense of some dark power trying to wrestle its way out of their hands, like a snake or some strangling thing. The indicator "spots" kept trying to jump out of place, and trying again, and the two of them had to keep pushing them back. It was hard, in the dark, and the fear was growing—

Five minutes.

Space began to seethe. Gabriel had not really thought of drive-space as something that might have any kind of physical motion associated with it, much less any kind of life. This version of drivespace had none of the featurelessness that mere visual exam-ination suggested as you passed through. There were currents in this, backwashes and eddies that had nothing to do with the ships passing through it. The fabric of drivespace itself seemed to be aware, somehow, of their presence, of their interference.

Or Something living in it did—

Four minutes.

It seemed to be pushing back at them, trying to make them lose their grip.

Could a dimension of space be sentient? Gabriel wondered. Could it possibly *know* what passed through? Was this just some natural expression of some kind of force, or reaction to force, that normally went uninterfered with in drivespace but was now per-ceptible because they were in this strange alien machine?

Three minutes.

Either way, it was getting much harder to keep the circles where they were supposed to be. They kept trying to slip.

Tlelai, Gabriel said, *are you all right?*

Holding . . . hard . . . brother . . .

Right. Hang on, and don't get your tail in a twist, it's just a few minutes more.

Sudden hissing came from that fiery shape over in the darkness. *Why would I twist my tail?*

Don't laugh. You're losing it!

I am not! More laughter. *Mind your own!*

They're fine.

They were. The pressure was increasing, the fear was increasing, drivespace writhed in their grip and tried to get away, the indicators tried to leap out of position but weren't allowed to. The ones Gabriel was handling started to burn him, but he hung on. He had been burned before. He had flung fire across this darkness in his dreams and been burned, and he had not died of it.

I'm not going to mess up the performance that all those experiences were rehearsals for. I've had guns burn me worse than this, oh, God, I have, but I had to keep firing then, and I will not let go now. I will not—

One minute!

Several long breaths went by . . . and then, above them, around them, as if they were in the midst of it, came starfall.

Strange and terrible it was to Gabriel to see it from both sides, from drivespace and real space, as if from underwater and above water at the same time. The huge round shapes rose slowly and inexorably out of drivespace, one starfall pure white, one deep blue, one black-red like sunset before a storm. Gabriel knew that third ship. If it was not the same ship that had risen out of drivespace to look at *Sunshine* and then sunk immediately away again, it was its sister. They were huge, dark green spherical vessels, shining and wound about with strange cordlike structures, almost organic-looking, like galled, puckered fruit. The "galls" started to shake themselves free of the parent growths as all the starfalls completed themselves, more and more of those deadly little spheres coming loose, tumbling away into a formation around the parent vessels.

Let go now! Enda said. *Hurry! Ten seconds.*

Gun ports started to glow faintly with coronal discharge as the ships readied their weapons. Gabriel burst out into a huge sweat, now that he had a body to sweat with again. But he was still seeing the view as if partially submerged in it, and the ships were there, huge, rolling now to bring their weapons to bear on the planet.

Five seconds.

No! Gabriel cried. *Not their world, no!*

The big ships started to move, the small kroath vessels flashed down toward the planet.

Now.

Everything abruptly blinked into blackness as the sun winked out.

From all around them a shriek of intolerable power went up, and everything else in the cavern went dark, all but Enda and the mirror-prism in which she was trapped like some creature anciently immured in amber. She burned like a carbon element in an old lamp, the air around her burned like plasma, the machine burned as if molten inside. Everything else was darkness.

Then the light came. It was a light that Gabriel and Tlelai had seen in their dreams, and which Gabriel had seen most recently when the past looked out at him of the little edanwe's mind: fire, the whole voracious fire of a sun concentrated for a fraction of a second into one beam, one ferocious pulse of energy that tore through the formation of ships.

It struck them and there was no formation left, gone, exploded in many small puffs of glitter and several large ones, totally vaporized, and then even the vapor was gone, nothing left but atoms stripped to ions and left glowing. Every ship was gone in a wink of the sun, which was now shining again as if nothing had happened. In the cavern, there was a shocked silence.

"Now *that*," Helm's voice said reverently out of the dark, "is a *weapon*. I *want* one."

That happened seven minutes ago, Enda said, *but you had to hold the aim. The beam runs down a conduit.*

Suddenly she sounded terribly tired. *I do not—* she said, and nothing more.

Light started to seep back again, and they all stood looking at each other. Gabriel went to Enda and helped her out of the machine. The structure itself was blackened—not the glossy matte-black it had been before, but scorched and burned. Blue-green electricity lanced across its surface with a crackling hiss, and smoke simmered from the stone, even though it was cool to the touch. Enda herself was slumped and looked worn and weary, as if a decade had come off her life all at once.

"I do not think this machine will work again," she said, very faintly, as Gabriel helped her away. "If it was designed to do what we used it for, then we did something wrong. Still, that may be for the better, I think."

"I'd say so," Gabriel said, feeling a little wobbly himself. "Let Helm find his own."

He could not rest just yet. Gabriel looked up into the image of the space above them, torn and roiling with a sudden ionization nebula from the destroyed ships. It was glorious, but there was a problem. Drivespace, unseen at the moment, still hid the vessels they had sensed behind the first ones.

"A whole lot of electronic messages must have gone out five days ago," Gabriel said softly. "It's going to take a month to sort *this* security breach out."

"She said two cruisers, did she not?" Tlelai said. "The screaming woman I shot."

"She did," Gabriel said, peering into the darkness, letting normal life fade away again as he put his hand into his pocket and gripped the luckstone. His perception of the great pool of drivespace came back, and in it the image of the two ships and the three coming after them.

"Maybe we can still do something," Gabriel said. "Come on, Tlelai, let's try it."

They went and took hold of the dark-mirror columns from which Enda had struck her blow. The stone seemed to pulse and hum discordantly at their touch.

Gabriel gulped. "Enda, you did say we can't use that again?"

"Even if we could, there is no time," she said. "The ships

would be unlikely to stay where they are for eight minutes."

"The ships?" the Eldest said.

"Our little ones? Not a chance," said Gabriel. "Eldest, we would all die trying. There are better ways."

He stared into the darkness. It eddied, it flowed . . . Water. The Downfall, and the irresistible thunder of it. The eddies in the pool at the bottom . . . the way they spun things around . . .

"Come on, Tlelai," Gabriel said. "Let's try it." He put his hands up against the stone and closed his eyes, shutting out the light.

On the other side of the stone, Tlelai did the same.

What are we doing? Tlelai asked.

See how those two are going to come out first, and those three are going to come out second, by maybe a couple of hours?

Yes.

What if we pushed the three in front of the two?

Tlelai shrugged his tail. *Why not? Let's try.*

Gabriel gripped the luckstone in his hand and pressed it hard against the slab he leaned against. *Come on,* he said to it. *I've danced to your tune all this while. Now you dance to mine. Just this once.*

He was fire again, a shape of fire, immense. So was Tlelai. It would not last, though. The strain was too great, the fabric of things was strained because of the imminent arrival of so many objects from drivespace. The two of them reached up into that dark liquid flow, splashed in it, moved it, changed one eddy, the one containing the three ships—swept it past the other, pushed it ahead. Nervous, they watched to see the pattern stabilize. There was some rocking and backflowing, but slowly the flow smoothed itself out, things rushed forward in the usual way . . . and the three were ahead of the two.

Gabriel was suddenly exhausted. He fell away from the stone, and Tlelai on his side did the same, staggering somewhat. "So now," he said, "we are safe for the moment."

"For the moment, brother," Gabriel said. "There are going to be a lot of uncomfortable ones after this, but none as bad as this has been . . . we'll hope."

He turned back to Enda, over whom Delde Sota was bending. The fraal was sitting on the floor, looking very weary. As Gabriel and Tlelai came back to her, she looked up and said, "A good day's work for all of us."

"Yes," Gabriel said, looking down at her and wondering, What has she remembered that she can't bear? Never mind her, am I even going to be human at the end of this process?

He went over to the Eldest, who was watching them with an expression that no one could read. "Sir," Gabriel said, "it might be well if your people stayed safe in here for a while, until matters in space resolve themselves. It may take a while. We'll go up to the ships, and come down to let you know."

The Eldest nodded. "This is the end of everything," he said, "is it not? The old world ends here."

"Yes," Gabriel said, "yes, but the new one will be very full of wonders, and when you tire of those, you have much to teach us. Do what you can."

Together with Enda, Tlelai and the rest of them, Gabriel headed for the ramp.

Chapter Twenty-Two

SYSTEM COMMS GOT very lively about an hour later when three Star Force vessels, all cruisers, burst out of drivespace and settled into orbit around Danwell. They were about to send out the standard all-channels hail to any explorers in the area, and were rather surprised when Gabriel hailed them first.

"Uh, interested to know how you knew we were in the area, *Sunshine*," said the comms officer for one of the vessels, a cruiser called *Buday*. "We weren't informed that you have drivespace detection."

"We don't," Gabriel said. "Listen, *Buday*, please be advised of two VoidCorp cruisers incoming to these coordinates. I expect them here in about two hours. They are probably here to pick up one of their operatives, who we would gladly turn over to you. They doubtless have other intents toward this planet, which is inhabited, repeat inhabited, by sentients."

"Uh, roger that *Sunshine*," said the comms officer, suddenly sounding much more interested. "We'll start the usual protection protocols."

There was a pause. Gabriel smiled gently, for this meant that, since the Concord vessels were on the scene first, they could implement cultural embargo immediately . . . and since they outnumbered the VoidCorp vessels, the Corpses wouldn't be able to do a thing about it.

"Another message for *Sunshine* from *Schmetterling* command," said the comms officer. "The Concord Administrator's compliments to Gabriel Connor, and he would be pleased to see him at Mr. Connor's earliest convenience."

Gabriel's smile went thin and amused. "My respects to the administrator," Gabriel said, "and if he would be so good as to send down a gig, I will be glad to see him immediately."

"Gig in twenty minutes, *Sunshine*," the voice replied.

Gabriel stood up, looked over at Enda, and said, "The sooner the better."

"What will you tell him?" Enda asked.

Gabriel chuckled. "As little as possible. I will also give Aleen Delonghi a ride back with me . . . and Miss Blue Eyes as well."

"Wouldn't Delonghi prefer to go back in her own ship?"

"I'm sure," Gabriel said, "but having the person she was supposed to be tailing drop her off in Kharls's lap like a lost package is a message he may remember. *She* certainly will." He grinned. "As for Blue Eyes, let Concord Intel pump her out and hang her up to dry. Maybe they'll find out something about that leak, though I'm not so sure." He stood up and stretched. "I'd better get changed and get this over with. Meanwhile, let's get the edanwe out of here and back to the settlement. I don't want to give our new arrivals any reason to start snooping around here."

* * * * *

Half an hour later Gabriel was standing outside a plain door in the corridor of the Star Force cruiser *Schmetterling*. The door slid open, and a slim young man he had seen before gestured Gabriel courteously in.

Gabriel entered the room, a plush carpeted place with artwork hanging from the wood-paneled walls. A huge window spanned one wall, giving a panoramic view of Danwell beneath the ship. There was a desk in the middle of the room, and standing beside it was something Gabriel had not seen before: a Concord Administrator in his state, wearing his dark robes of office and holding his tri-staff. Kharls bore little similarity to the small business-dressed man Gabriel had seen once before in a bare little room aboard this ship.

Ever so slightly, Gabriel bowed. "Sir," he said.

"There are a couple of matters I would like to discuss with you," Kharls said and gestured at a seat.

Gabriel took it. "I'm entirely at your disposal."

"I doubt that," Kharls said, sitting down himself. "First of all: the laws of science appear to be misbehaving in this area. You wouldn't know anything about that?"

"Sir," Gabriel said, "I know I'm a bad influence, but I don't think I'm *that* bad."

"Really," Kharls said. "We spent only a hundred and nineteen hours in this last starfall. As we both know, that is an impossibility."

"Someone counted wrong?" Gabriel said, his eyebrows up.

Kharls simply looked at him. "Second," he said. "There appears to have been some sort of space battle here in the very recent past."

Gabriel raised the eyebrows higher, a polite look.

"Weapons were used of such power that very little survived of what might be as many as three capital ships," Kharls said. "We are interested in this event."

"I may have missed it," Gabriel said. "We were busy with things down on the planet."

"There will be an aurora tonight that no one could miss," Kharls said, rather drily. "I recommend it to you."

He sat quiet for a moment, then said, "If such forces are moving out in the Verge, it would be in the best interests for everyone, Concord and otherwise, to know everything possible about them. Wouldn't you agree?"

"With respect, Administrator, no," Gabriel said. "There are forces and forces, and I am not convinced of the good intentions of even the best intentioned among them. For example, the Concord Intel agent to whom I gave a lift back . . . you had better watch out for her. I think she may be working for another organization besides yours or as well as yours."

"Any thoughts on who?"

Gabriel looked at him. "Why should I volunteer any?" he asked. "But no, no ideas that I trust. All the same, the feelings I got from her on this subject were not positive. Watch her."

Kharls bowed his head slightly. "Meanwhile you've found an inhabited planet . . . under rather unusual circumstances."

"I would agree with you on that." Gabriel folded his hands. "This is a very complex culture, not blocked, but slow-moving and deliberate. They have been selectively exploiting steam and electricity for hundreds of years. Their concept of progress is very different from our own—it has entirely to do with the mind, with philosophy and the understanding of science. Physical progress they see as something there's no rush about. Language is not a concept that they understand as we do. You will need to select psionic technicians to work with them, when the limited cultural contacts begin. In the meantime, though, they have had a bad week, and I would keep away from them a while, and keep others away from them."

"Yes," Kharls said. "About those others. It was our understanding that you didn't have stardrive detection equipment aboard. How did you know that the VoidCorp ships were incoming?"

Gabriel smiled. "Bad news travels fast?"

Kharls glanced at the tri-staff leaning against the desk. "Mr. Connor," he said, "wouldn't it be a lot easier if we leveled with each other?"

"Perhaps it would, Administrator," said Gabriel, "but your business has not been about making life easier for me. I hardly see why I should make yours easier for you." He sat back and said, "No, I think I might prefer to let matters rest as they are at the moment. As for the edanweir, they've had a very bad time of it . . . and creatures far worse than humans found them before we did. I believe you know who we mean. Delonghi mentioned them to me, though very reluctantly."

"We do not know their species names yet," said Kharls. "though there seems to be a growing tendency to call them 'kroath' after some Hatire word. They seem to be external, but that cannot be proven." He looked narrowly at Gabriel. "The name may blind us to something we very much need to know about them."

"That's as may be," Gabriel said. "My agenda is not yours— as you know very well, but I want these people protected. I would stay a while, but I think my presence there endangers them, so I will not be coming back any time soon. I want them properly taken care of, and mostly I want them left alone. They have a lot to teach us . . . if they survive, and if *we* do."

"Ah," said Kharls. "Well, that protection is one of the reasons I'm here. Naturally there would be tremendous interest from, well, certain sectors, in a planet so promising. It's important to see that no one gets carried away by the mere sight of it. If, as you say, these—edanweir?—have recently been attacked by forces we understand so little, it's important to have someone here who can defend them in the short term and establish a standing force—a discreet one—for the long term."

"I was going to ask what you were doing here at all," Gabriel said, "and in such force. I could almost think you started heading in this direction as soon you discovered I had bought an exploration contract."

Kharls smiled and said nothing.

"Probably just paranoia on my part," Gabriel said. "Meanwhile, you know what I want from you."

"A fair trial," Kharls said, "so you say. Where's the evidence you've been promising me?"

"I'm beginning to collect it," said Gabriel.

"There are ways in which matters could be sped up."

Gabriel simply sat and looked at Kharls, and shook his head, like someone who has expected a specific response and has not been disappointed.

"Not on your terms," said Gabriel. "*Nothing* on your terms. You've gotten enough out of me already . . . and will, I'm sure, find ways to get more. Meanwhile, I have my own business to attend to. Specifically," he said, and got up, "I have some mail to deliver to Coulomb. I wouldn't mind hitching a ride, if one of your ships are going that way. Otherwise . . ."

Kharls grinned at him in pure feral pleasure. It was a look that would have given Gabriel a shiver under more ordinary circumstances. He had the luckstone in his pocket, and he thought he could hear just a whisper of intent, of concept, the way he would have heard it from Tlelai: *Let him run.*

"Unfortunately I do not believe our schedule is likely to take us in that direction," said Kharls. He stood too. "A diversion would be noticed and commented on. I am sorry not to be able to help, this time. Perhaps some other. Your oaths, Connor, are they still in order?"

Once again, it was a question he had no business asking. The man was simply intolerable, yet Gabriel felt the faintest thread of admiration creeping through him. This was power, yes, habituated to itself and confident, but at the same time it was intelligent power—brutal, occasionally, but in a considered fashion. There was some part of Gabriel that could appreciate this, even when he was the target.

"Enough in order," said Gabriel, "not to have killed Delonghi for you."

There was that smile again, like that of one predator to another, if such could smile over a shared joke, or perhaps a shared meal. "Did she need it?"

"When we first met," said Gabriel, "almost certainly, but circumstance caused me to spare her. Afterwards, when we spoke on Danwell, she may still have needed it, but it didn't happen."

"Mercy?"

"Pragmatism," said Gabriel, "or just a very full schedule."

"Not fear?"

Now it was Gabriel's turn to grin, and he hoped the look was as feral. "Administrator," he said, "I hate to waste your time."

"Is there anything else you need to tell me?" said Kharls.

"Be sure I'll call you if there is," Gabriel said. He turned to the door, thinking of the luckstone, and of the whisper in his mind that told him of other hideaways, and one far, far greater than all the rest—and then he stopped.

"Oh," he said. "One thing."

Kharls watched him.

"I want to talk to you about a book called *Dodgson's Guide to First Contacts.*"

Kharls had the grace to look confused.

* * * * *

It was maybe another hour before Gabriel was on Danwell again, back at the settlement where the gig had dropped him at his request. The edanweir were settling themselves back into their usual routine, as much as they could after so bizarre a day. Gabriel was very glad to take himself back to *Sunshine* for a few quiet moments. There he found Enda in the sitting room, watering her bulb with some concern.

"It has been shockingly neglected," she said.

Gabriel sat down and felt a great weight roll off him, as if everything was right again, as if everything had gone back to normal. It was an illusion, but he enjoyed it, getting up and brewing himself a cup of chai.

"It won't die, will it?" Gabriel said.

"Oh, no," Enda said. "It is tougher than that." She gave him a thoughtful look. "Like some others I know."

Gabriel laughed very softly as he sat down with the chai. "Yes," he said, "there have been a lot of surprises this week. I was surprised, certainly, and as for you . . ."

He trailed off. Enda looked at him.

"You kept telling me you didn't have the training 'that some others had,' " Gabriel said. "Just what *have* you had?"

She did not look at him for some while. Finally, Enda met his eyes. "Gabriel," she said, "some time back, when we first met, I avoided asking you many questions which I might in the normal course of things have insisted on having answered. I do not recall you complaining about that."

Gabriel was quiet for a while. "No," he said.

"So now . . . it would be a matter of comfort to me if, for a while, you could avoid, in turn, pressing me for answers. I have not had an easy time of it of late. I would appreciate some time to recover my own grip on the world and the way things are going. I promise you answers to everything, but not right now."

He sighed. "You've done enough for me in letting me recover my grip," Gabriel said. "Though the gods know every time I think

I'm secure, I slip again. Just the way things are going, I suppose."
He looked at the luckstone in his hand. "I have a feeling they
won't go that way for long."

"No," Enda said. "When I first saw that, I thought the same."

He gave her a slightly surprised look. "Did you know what it
was?"

"Not at all clearly," Enda said. She bowed her head, not a gesture, just someone trying not to have to look at Gabriel. "When I
discovered that you had it . . . and then later when I started to
become suspicious of it . . . the thought crossed my mind that it
might somehow have been implicated in our meeting."

"How do you mean?"

She lifted her head again, looking abashed—not an expression
Gabriel was used to seeing from Enda. "There are forces moving
among the worlds that I would not pretend to understand," she
said. "I had suspected for some time that perhaps that little stone
was not as simple as the lightstones that people find on some
planets' beaches, but without evidence of what it might be
instead, why raise doubts or alarms? Why make you nervous
about it? It never did anything dangerous that either of us saw
until it burned a hole in the pilot cabin's deck."

She sighed. "Now we see that forces we cannot understand are
moving. People are being moved, singly and in great numbers.
Stellar nations are being moved, fleets, armies—but to what purpose?"

She looked at the luckstone. "We are fortunate," she said. "We
are standing in a place where we may someday be able to find
out, if our involvement with this great pattern of movement does
not kill us first. It may."

"I was wondering," Gabriel said, "whether the stone somehow
had something to do with what happened to me on *Falada*, the
deaths, Jacob Ricel, all the rest of it."

"You will have time now," Enda said, "a little time anyway, to
start to discover that. I would warn you, though, that I think we
are caught up in something big enough that it may grind down our
small personal concerns."

"It's going to have to be pretty good to do that," Gabriel said. "My concerns may be small, but they're *mine*. The universe comes second."

"Does it?" Enda said. "Your actions would make one think otherwise."

Gabriel wasn't sure what to say to that.

"Meanwhile," Enda said. "What about the contract?"

"I've already taken care of that," Gabriel said. "I've licensed the exploration rights for Danwell back to the CSS. They'll handle them for the Concord, and we'll get a continuing royalty, while the Concord will make sure that VoidCorp finds it permanently impossible to come along and try to get the locals to sign their rights away. How delighted the Concord are that matters have brought them to this area at such a sensitive time." Gabriel put his eyebrows up. "Have you considered what the odds on *that* would normally be?"

Enda smiled too. "We have been a useful excuse to some people," he said softly. "Probably we will be again. I am sure that the Concord Administrator will follow us, as he has until now, with great interest."

"Especially now that he knows I'm holding out on him," Gabriel said.

Enda gazed at him.

"Oh, he knows," Gabriel said. "I'm sure." He looked at the stone. "That . . . voice, that knowledge, said there were more such repositories of ancient things, that there is another one, a much greater one. 'And not too far away,' the little edanwe said to me. These things were put away out here in the Verge . . . maybe to keep them away from some enemy, maybe to save them for us? I don't know, but they have to be found. If this small armory is any indication of what's here, *we* have to find it. It may make the difference between us losing or winning this war, for it's a war we're in."

Enda tilted her head. "It may as well have been a museum as an armory," she said. "We must keep our minds open about that, but yes, it seems that both of us have become, in a strange way, keys to a very old storehouse. Now all we have to do is find it . . . find out what it is, where it is . . ."

"And keep the entire galaxy out of our hair while we try to do it," Gabriel said, "and try to work out who to give the secret to at last."

"Something of a challenge," Enda said. "We had better get started."

* * * * *

They would be leaving the next morning, all of them together, Gabriel and Enda in company with Helm, Delde Sota, Angela, and Grawl, all heading for Coulomb. Gabriel said his goodbyes to the Eldest and to Tlelai. They spent a good while sitting by the fire that night, discussing what might happen in the future, and what had happened to them both in the fire and the darkness. Finally, toward midnight, Gabriel got up. He and Tlelai went out into the darkness together, as Gabriel prepared to walk back to the ship's parking place.

"Take care of them all, hunter," Gabriel said, "and the little one, the wise one"—he thought of that blinding, innocent gaze— "tell her not to pull people's hair."

"I'll tell her that."

Gabriel dropped to one knee to equalize the height difference. They hugged each other hard. Gabriel stood up again, lifted a hand, headed away, and then stopped suddenly.

"The word you called me . . ." he said. "The one I couldn't hear."

"*Laidanwe*," Tlelai said, "the one who brings what must come."

Gabriel looked at him. "Harbinger," he said.

Tlelai switched his tail in the way that meant "yes" and said, "Come back when you can, brother."

"I will. Not soon, but I will."

* * * * *

It was a long quiet walk in the dark, but Gabriel knew the way extremely well by now. He came at last to the spot where *Sunshine, Longshot,* and *Lalique* were parked together, paused, and then went on past to the place where the waterfall roared its loudest.

There in the darkness he stood and simply listened to it, the huge noise, the drifting, pounding, shifting water, hammering down into the gorge, irresistible. He thought of the darkness in the ancient site under the mountain. He thought of the sense he had therein of time reaching back beyond sight. It had been falling for thousands of years. History, like the cataract, the vast moving majesty and weight of the past, would fall for thousands of years more. It would hammer down onto present history and the future, not to be stopped, not to be turned aside by one man any more than one drop of water, caught in the midst of that great fall, could turn the rest of it.

I am not a drop of water. I am a man. I know that I am in the fall, the torrent of history.

Is it possible that being a man is enough? That being sentient, being aware of the fall, is enough—not necessarily to turn the great flow —but to change what starts to happen to it afterwards? To have what I am, and what I do, be *about* something besides the senseless fall, besides surrendering to the gravity of the situation?

He stood there, watching the water come roaring down, wearing away the stones a drop at a time, and shouting down thought and reason and everything else. Finally, Gabriel smiled. Probably better to concentrate on being the drop and falling in the right place, he thought, and let history take care of itself.

Right now, there's Coulomb. After that . . . we'll see what the past has left for us to turn into the present.

He glanced at the luckstone in his hand, flipped it glowing in the air, pocketed it, and made his way back to *Sunshine.*

Glossary

Aegis - A G2 yellow star. The metropolitan center of the Verge.

AI - Artificial Intelligence. Sentient computer programming whose sophistication varies from model to model.

Aleerin - see mechalus

Altai Services - An investigative and research firm based in Tendril.

Alwhirn, Rae - An independent infotrader based in Sunbreak.

AU - Astronomical Unit. 150 million km

Austrin-Ontis Unlimited — A corporate stellar nation that is best known as the leading arms dealer in the Stellar Ring. Most Austrins view themselves as strong individualists with a deep sense of altruism.

Bluefall - Capital planet of the Aegis system. Ruled by the Regency government.

Builder - A section of fraal society that believes in integration with other species and cultures.

CCC - see Concord Communications Commission.

cerametal - An extremely strong alloy made from laminated ceramics and lightweight metals.

chai - tea

charge weapon - A firearm in which an electric firing pin ignites a chemical explosive into a white-hot plasma propellant, thus expelling a cerametallic slug at extremely high velocity.

CM armor - cerametal armor.

coldweek - The seven day "night" of Rivendale.

Concord - see Galactic Concord.

Concord Communications Commission - A commission that regulates all insterstellar communication in the Verge, the Concord Protectorates, and—theoretically—all of open space.

Concord Survey Service - A division of Star Force dedicated to scouting, surveying, and first contacts.

Conker - A derogatory term for citizens of the Galactic Concord.

Connor, Gabriel - A former Concord marine lieutenant.

Corrivale - An F2 yellow-white star. Also the name of the system.

Coulomb - A red dwarf near the edge of the Verge.

CSS - see Concord Survey Service.

Dareyev, Elinke - Captain of *Schmetterling*.

David, Lemke - A Star Force second lieutenant navigator.

Diamond Point - The capital city of Grith.

Dormant Inc. - An investigative and research firm in Old Space.

drivecore - The central engine core of a stardrive.

driveplan - A plan filed with a star system's traffic control stating a ship's planned destination, arrival time, and travel intentions.

driveship - Any spaceship that is equipped with a stardrive.

drivespace - The dimension into which starships enter through use of the stardrive. In this dimension, gravity works on a quantum level, thus enabling movement of a ship from one point in space to another in only 121 hours.

durasteel - Steel that has been strengthened at the molecular level.

edanwe (pl. edanweir) - A sentient species native to Danwell.

Eldala - An unexplored system rumored to be somewhere past Mantebron.

Enda - A fraal.

Epsedra - The site of a fierce battle involving Concord Marines.

Esephanne, Merielle - An inhabitant of Sunbreak.

eshk - A small aquatic bird native to Bluefall.

e-suit - An environment suit intended to keep the wearer safe from vacuum, extreme temperatures, and radiation.

external - A term used to describe anything that originates beyond known space.

Falada - A Concord Star Force Heavy Cruiser.

fraal - A non-Terran sentient species. Fraal are very slender, large-eyed humanoids.

Galactic Concord - The thirteenth stellar nation. Formed by the Treaty of Concord, Concord law and administration rule in the Verge, which is delegated Open Space.

galya - A vine native to Grith which produces scented flowers.

gig - A colloquial term for any ship-to-ground shuttle. Any small craft capable of transporting passengers or cargo from one place to another. Most have gravity induction engines and a fuel range of no more than 100 million kilometers.

gravity induction - A process whereby a cyclotron accelerates particles to near-light speeds, thereby creating gravitons between the particle and the surrounding mass. This process can be adjusted and redirected, thus allowing the force of gravity to be overcome. Most starships use a gravity induction engine for in-system travel.

Grawl - A weren poetess.

Grid - An interstellar computer network.

Grith - A moon of Hydrocus and the only habitable world in the Corrivale system.

Gyrofresia ondothalis fraalii - see "Ondothwait"

Hammer's Star - A yellow G5 star. The outermost Concord outpost in the Verge.

Hatire Community - A theocratic stellar nation founded on the principles of the generally anti-technology religion of the same name.

Hatire faith - A religion that preaches ascendence through union with the spirit of the Cosimir, a Precursor deity that the Hatire adopted as their own. Most Hatire tend to hold attitudes anatagonistic to technology and abhor all forms of man-machine integration.

hesai - A Fraal word meaning "wrong, incorrect, not true."

holocomm - holographic communication.

holodisplay - The display of a holocomm that can be viewed in either one, two, or three dimensions.

Humanity Reformation - A religion founded upon the belief that all human faiths—and humans in general—are flawed. Professing belief in a single deity, Reformers are expected to help themselves and better the society in which they find themselves.

imager - A camera that records holographic, three-dimensional images.

Inseer - A citizen of Insight.

Insight - A subsidiary of VoidCorp that broke away to form a separate stellar nation. Citizenry is dominated by freethinking Grid pilots who believe that humanity can reach its destiny only in Gridspace.

Iphus - A planet in the Corrivale system.

Iphus Collective - A mining facility run by StarMech Collective on Iphus.

JustWadeln - A software program developed by Insight that allows the user to learn space combat at ever-increasing levels of difficulty.

kalwine - An alcoholic beverage similar in flavor to grape-based wines, but made from kalgrain, a seed native to Sapphire.

Kharls, Lorand - A Concord Administrator.

klick - A hostile, arachnid-like external species of unknown origin. Few facts are known about the klicks, though they are the prime suspects for the destruction of the Silver Bell colony.

kroath - A hostile external species of unknown origin.

Lalique - Angela Valiz's starship.

lanth cell - The standard lanthanide battery used to power most small electronic equipment and firearms.

Lecterion - A gas giant of the Corrivale system.

Lighthouse - A huge space station capable of 50 light-year starfalls that roams the Verge.

Longshot - Helm Ragnarsson's weapon-laden starship.

Long Silence - That period of time when the Stellar Nations lost contact with the Verge because of the Second Galactic War.

Lucullus - A binary star system in the Verge.

Mantebron - One of the outermost star systems of the Verge.

Mask & Bauble Studios - An entertainment production studio on Bluefall.

mass weapon - A weapon that fires a ripple of intense gravity waves, striking its target like a massive physical blow.

mass reactor - The primary power source of a stardrive. The reactor collects, stores, and processes dark matter, thus producing massive amounts of energy.

mechalus - The most common term used for an Aleerin, a sentient humanoid symbiote species that has achieved a union between biological life and cybernetic enhancements.

Melanchthon RGF - An investigative and research firm in Old Space.

Melek, Rov - An inhabitant of Sunbreak.

mhwada - A large, herbiverous herding beast native to Danwell.

mindwalker - Any being proficient with psionic powers.

neurocircuitry - Cybernetic implants intended to fuse electronic or mechanical systems with a living biological entity.

neutralizer coat - A jacket designed to absorb light pulses from electric or energy weapons.

Ondothwait - A plant. Scientific name: Gyrofresia ondothalis fraalii.

Oraan - A fraal chef in Sunbreak.

Orion League - A heterogenous stellar nation founded on principles
of freedom and equal rights for all sentients.

Phorcys - A planet of the Thalaassa system.

phymech - An automated emergency medical system with a fairly
sophisticated AI system. Most phymechs come with fairly
specialized medical supplies—skinfilms, bandages,
antiseptics, painkillers and so on.

plasma weapon - A weapon that converts an electro-chemical
mixture into white-hot plasma and then utilizes a magnetic
accelerator to throw a blast of the plasma at the target. The
super-heated plasma explodes upon striking its target.

Quatsch - Rae Alwhirn's starship.

Ragnarsson, Helm - A human mutant.

rail cannon - An electromagnetic accelerator that fires projectiles at
extremely high velocities.

ramscoop - A hydrogen collector.

Rand - Lorand Kharls's assistant.

Regency Expansion Bureau - That segment of the Regency
government that oversees matters of infrastructure.

Rhynchus - The outermost planet of the Thalaassa system.

riglia - A sentient avian species native to Rivendale.

Rivendale - The only habitable world of the Terivine system.

rlin noch'i - The common garb of the mechalus. Consists of a multi-
pocketed smartsuit and soft boots.

RoanTech - One of the major manufacturers of stardrive engines.

sabot weapon - A firearm that uses electromagnetic pulses to
accelerate a discarding-rocket slug at hypersonic speeds.

Sapphire - Capital world of the Borealis Republic.

Schmetterling - A Concord Star Force Heavy Cruiser.

Sealed Knot, the - A mechalus symbol favored by medical
practitioners of that species.

seeker - The formal term given to initiates of the Orlamu faith.

sesheyan - A bipedal sentient species possessing long, bulbous
heads, large ears, and eight light-sensitive eyes. Most
sesheyans are about 1.7 meters tall and have two leathery
wings that span between 2.5 - 4 meters. Sheya, the sesheyan
homeworld, has been subjugated by VoidCorp. However, a
substantial population of "free sesheyans" live on Grith.

Se'tali - The chief port authority in Diamond Point.

Shei? - A Fraal interrogative meaning, "You call?"

Silence, the - see the Long Silence.

Silver Bell - A Borealin colony on Spes that was completely
  annihilated by unknown forces in 2489 but has since been
  partially rebuilt.

skinfilm - An artifical polymer membrance, usually only a few
  molecules thick, that is often used for sanitary protection or
  containment.

sniffer - A ramscoop detecting device.

Sota, Delde - A mechalus doctor and former Grid pilot.

spaceport - A planetary landing zone for driveships.

spee-g - short for specific gravity.

Spes – The innermost planet of the Hammer's Star system.

spidermist - A multicellular, bioelectric creature native to Rivendale.

stardrive - The standard starship engine that combines a gravity
  induction coil and a mass reactor to open a temporary
  singularity in space and thus allow a ship to enter drivespace.
  All jumps take 121 hours, no matter the distance.

starfall - The term used to describe a ship entering drivespace.

Star Force - The naval branch of the Concord military.

StarMech Collective - A high technology-oriented stellar nation.

starport - A zero-g, orbital docking zone for driveships.

starrise - The term used to describe a ship leaving drivespace.

stellar nations - The thirteeen sovereign governing the Stellar Ring,
  the center of which is Sol (Earth).

STG shuttle - Space-To-Ground shuttle.

Sunbreak - A city of Rivendale.

system drive - Any form of non-stardrive propulsion used for inner
  system traffic.

Tendril - An F1 blue star. Also the name of the system.

Terivine - A trinary Verge system consisting of two G-class stars and
  one K-class orange dwarf.

Thalaassa - An F2 yellow star. Also the name of the system.

Thuldan Empire - A militaristic, fiercely patriotic stellar nation that
  considers the unity of humanity under the Thuldan banner to
  be its manifest destiny. The largest of the stellar nations.

Tlelai - An edanwe hunter.

Treaty of Concord, the - The Treaty that ended the Second Galactic
  War and formed the Galactic Concord.

tri-staff - The traditional weapon carried by Concord Administrators.

Valiz, Angela - A human trader.

Verge, the - A frontier region of space originally colonized by the
    stellar nations that was cut off during the Second Galactic
    War.

verjuice - A beverage made from the berry of the verrillia plant in
    the Borealis Republic.

VoidCorp - A corporate stellar nation. Citizens are referred to as
    Employees and all have an assigned number.

Wanderer - 1.) Fraal: A term used to describe that segment of fraal
    culture that prefers life aboard their wandering city-ships
    rather than settling down to mingle with other species.
    2.) Sesheyan: Weyshe the Wanderer, a sesheyan deity.

warmweek - The seven day "day" of Rivendale.

Watertower District - A posh district of Regency Island where Mask
    & Bauble studios is located.

weren - A sentient species native to the planet Kurg. Most weren
    stand well over 2 meters tall, are covered in thick fur, and
    have sharp claws. Male weren have large tusks protruding
    from the bottom jaw.

STAR✴DRIVE™
NOVELS

ON THE VERGE
Roland J. Green

Danger and intrigue explode in the Verge as Arist, a frozen world on the borders of known space, erupts into a war between weren and human colonists. When Concord Marines charge in to prevent the conflict from escalating off-world, but they soon discover that even darker forces are at work on Arist.

STARFALL
Edited by Martin H. Greenberg

Contributors include Diane Duane, Kristine Katherine Rusch, Robert Silverberg and Karen Haber, Dean Wesley Smith, and Michael A. Stackpole. A collection of short stories detailing the adventure, the mystery, and the unending wonder in the Verge!

Available April 1999.

ZERO POINT
Richard Baker

Peter Sokolov, a bounty hunter and cybernetic killer for hire, is caught up in a deadly struggle for power and supremacy in the black abyss between the stars.

Available June 1999.

First in the past.
First in the future.